FAIR MARGARET

H. RIDER HAGGARD

1st WORLD
LIBRARY
Literary Society

Fair Margaret

H. Rider Haggard

© 1st World Library, 2006
PO Box 2211
Fairfield, IA 52556
www.1stworldlibrary.com
First Edition

LCCN: 2006936188

Softcover ISBN: 978-1-4218-3050-6
Hardcover ISBN: 978-1-4218-2950-0
eBook ISBN: 978-1-4218-3150-3

Purchase *"Fair Margaret"*
as a traditional bound book at:
www.1stWorldLibrary.com/purchase.asp?ISBN=978-1-4218-3050-6

1st World Library is a literary, educational organization
dedicated to:

- Creating a free internet library of downloadable ebooks

- Hosting writing competitions and offering book
publishing scholarships.

Interested in more 1st World Library books?
contact: literacy@1stworldlibrary.com
Check us out at: www.1stworldlibrary.com

1st World Library Literary Society

Giving Back to the World

"If you want to work on the core problem, it's early school literacy."

- James Barksdale, former CEO of Netscape

"No skill is more crucial to the future of a child, or to a democratic and prosperous society, than literacy."

- Los Angeles Times

Literacy... means far more than learning how to read and write... The aim is to transmit... knowledge and promote social participation."

- UNESCO

"Literacy is not a luxury, it is a right and a responsibility. If our world is to meet the challenges of the twenty-first century we must harness the energy and creativity of all our citizens."

- President Bill Clinton

"Parents should be encouraged to read to their children, and teachers should be equipped with all available techniques for teaching literacy, so the varying needs and capacities of individual kids can be taken into account."

- Hugh Mackay

CONTENTS

CHAPTER I

HOW PETER MET THE SPANIARD

It was a spring afternoon in the sixth year of the reign of King Henry VII. of England. There had been a great show in London, for that day his Grace opened the newly convened Parliament, and announced to his faithful people—who received the news with much cheering, since war is ever popular at first—his intention of invading France, and of leading the English armies in person. In Parliament itself, it is true, the general enthusiasm was somewhat dashed when allusion was made to the finding of the needful funds; but the crowds without, formed for the most part of persons who would not be called upon to pay the money, did not suffer that side of the question to trouble them. So when their gracious liege appeared, surrounded by his glittering escort of nobles and men-at-arms, they threw their caps into the air, and shouted themselves hoarse.

The king himself, although he was still young in years, already a weary-looking man with a fine, pinched face, smiled a little sarcastically at their clamour; but, remembering how glad he should be to hear it who still sat upon a somewhat doubtful throne, said a few soft words, and sending for two or three of the leaders of the people, gave them his royal hand, and suffered certain children to touch his robe that they might be cured of the Evil. Then, having paused a while to receive petitions from poor folk, which he handed to one of his officers to be read, amidst renewed shouting he passed on to the great feast that was made ready in his palace of Westminster.

Among those who rode near to him was the ambassador, de Ayala, accredited to the English Court by the Spanish sovereigns, Ferdinand and Isabella, and his following of splendidly attired lords and secretaries. That Spain was much in favour there was evident from his place in the procession. How could it be otherwise, indeed, seeing that already, four years or more before, at the age of twelve months, Prince Arthur, the eldest son of the king, had been formally affianced to the Infanta Catherine, daughter of Ferdinand and Isabella, aged one year and nine months? For in those days it was thought well that the affections of princes and princesses should be directed early into such paths as their royal parents and governors considered likely to prove most profitable to themselves.

At the ambassador's left hand, mounted on a fine black horse, and dressed richly, but simply, in black velvet, with a cap of the same material in which was fastened a single pearl, rode a tall cavalier. He was about five-and-thirty years of age, and very handsome, having piercing black eyes and a stern, clean-cut face.

In every man, it is said, there can be found a resemblance, often far off and fanciful enough, to some beast or bird or other creature, and certainly in this case it was not hard to discover. The man resembled an eagle, which, whether by chance or design, was the crest he bore upon his servants' livery, and the trappings of his horse. The unflinching eyes, the hooked nose, the air of pride and mastery, the thin, long hand, the quick grace of movement, all suggested that king of birds, suggested also, as his motto said, that what he sought he would find, and what he found he would keep. Just now he was watching the interview between the English king and the leaders of the crowd whom his Grace had been pleased to summon, with an air of mingled amusement and contempt.

H. Rider Haggard

"You find the scene strange, Marquis," said the ambassador, glancing at him shrewdly.

"Senor, here in England, if it pleases your Excellency," he answered gravely, "Senor d'Aguilar. The marquis you mentioned lives in Spain—an accredited envoy to the Moors of Granada; the Senor d'Aguilar, a humble servant of Holy Church," and he crossed himself, "travels abroad—upon the Church's business, and that of their Majesties'."

"And his own too, sometimes, I believe," answered the ambassador drily. "But to be frank, what I do not understand about you, Senor d'Aguilar, as I know that you have abandoned political ambitions, is why you do not enter my profession, and put on the black robe once and for all. What did I say—black? With your opportunities and connections it might be red by now, with a hat to match."

The Senor d'Aguilar smiled a little as he replied.

"You said, I think, that sometimes I travel on my own business. Well, there is your answer. You are right, I have abandoned worldly ambitions—most of them. They are troublesome, and for some people, if they be born too high and yet not altogether rightly, very dangerous. The acorn of ambition often grows into an oak from which men hang."

"Or into a log upon which men's heads can be cut off. Senor, I congratulate you. You have the wisdom that grasps the substance and lets the shadows flit. It is really very rare."

"You asked why I do not change the cut of my garments," went on d'Aguilar, without noticing the interruption. "Excellency, to be frank, because of my own business. I have failings like other men. For instance, wealth is that substance of which you spoke, rule is the shadow; he who has the wealth has the real rule. Again, bright eyes may draw me, or a hate may seek its slaking, and these things do not suit robes, black or red."

"Yet many such things have been done by those who wore them," replied the ambassador with meaning.

"Aye, Excellency, to the discredit of Holy Church, as you, a priest, know better than most men. Let the earth be evil as it must; but let the Church be like heaven above it, pure, unstained, the vault of prayer, the house of mercy and of righteous judgment, wherein walks no sinner such as I," and again he crossed himself.

There was a ring of earnestness in the speaker's voice that caused de Ayala, who knew something of his private reputation, to look at him curiously.

"A true fanatic, and therefore to us a useful man," he thought to himself, "though one who knows how to make the best of two worlds as well as most of them;" but aloud he said, "No wonder that our Church rejoices in such a son, and that her enemies tremble when he lifts her sword. But, Senor, you have not told me what you think of all this ceremony and people."

"The people I know well, Excellency, for I dwelt among them in past years and speak their language; and that is why I have left Granada to look after itself for a while, and am here to-day, to watch and make report—" He checked himself, then added, "As for the ceremony, were I a king I would have it otherwise. Why, in that house just now those vulgar Commons—for so they call them, do they not?—almost threatened their royal master when he humbly craved a tithe of the country's wealth to fight the country's war. Yes, and I saw him turn pale and tremble at the rough voices, as though their echoes shook his throne. I tell you, Excellency, that the time will come in this land when those Commons will be king. Look now at that fellow whom his Grace holds by the hand, calling him 'sir' and 'master,' and yet whom he knows to be, as I do, a heretic, a Jew in disguise, whose sins, if he had his rights, should be purged by fire. Why, to my knowledge last night, that Israelite said things against the Church—"

H. Rider Haggard

"Whereof the Church, or its servant, doubtless made notes to be used when the time comes," broke in de Ayala. "But the audience is done, and his Highness beckons us forward to the feast, where there will be no heretics to vex us, and, as it is Lent, not much to eat. Come, Senor! for we stop the way."

Three hours had gone by, and the sun sank redly, for even at that spring season it was cold upon the marshy lands of Westminster, and there was frost in the air. On the open space opposite to the banqueting-hall, in front of which were gathered squires and grooms with horses, stood and walked many citizens of London, who, their day's work done, came to see the king pass by in state. Among these were a man and a lady, the latter attended by a handsome young woman, who were all three sufficiently striking in appearance to attract some notice in the throng.

The man, a person of about thirty years of age, dressed in a merchant's robe of cloth, and wearing a knife in his girdle, seemed over six feet in height, while his companion, in her flowing, fur-trimmed cloak, was, for a woman, also of unusual stature. He was not, strictly speaking, a handsome man, being somewhat too high of forehead and prominent of feature; moreover, one of his clean-shaven cheeks, the right, was marred by the long, red scar of a sword-cut which stretched from the temple to the strong chin. His face, however, was open and manly, if rather stern, and the grey eyes were steady and frank. It was not the face of a merchant, but rather that of one of good degree, accustomed to camps and war. For the rest, his figure was well-built and active, and his voice when he spoke, which was seldom, clear and distinct to loudness, but cultivated and pleasant—again, not the voice of a merchant.

Of the lady's figure little could be seen because of the long cloak that hid it, but the face, which appeared within its hood when she turned and the dying sunlight filled her eyes, was lovely indeed, for from her birth to her death-day Margaret Castell—fair Margaret, as she was called—had this gift to a degree that is rarely granted to woman. Rounded and flower-like was that face, most delicately tinted also, with rich and curving lips and a broad, snow-white brow. But the wonder of it, what distinguished her above everything else from other beautiful women of her time, was to be found in her eyes, for these were not blue or grey, as might have been expected from her general colouring, but large, black, and lustrous; soft, too, as the eyes of a deer, and overhung by curling lashes of an ebon black. The effect of these eyes of hers shining above those tinted cheeks and beneath the brow of ivory whiteness was so strange as to be almost startling. They caught the beholder and held him, as might the sudden sight of a rose in snow, or the morning star hanging luminous among the mists of dawn. Also, although they were so gentle and modest, if that beholder chanced to be a man on the good side of fifty it was often long before he could forget them, especially if he were privileged to see how well they matched the hair of chestnut, shading into black, that waved above them and fell, tress upon tress, upon the shapely shoulders and down to the slender waist.

Peter Brome, for he was so named, looked a little anxiously about him at the crowd, then, turning, addressed Margaret in his strong, clear voice.

"There are rough folk around," he said; "do you think you should stop here? Your father might be angered, Cousin."

Here it may be explained that in reality their kinship was of the slightest, a mere dash of blood that came to her through her mother. Still they called each other thus, since it is a convenient title that may mean much or nothing.

"Oh! why not?" she answered in her rich, slow tones, that had in them some foreign quality, something soft and sweet as the caress of a southern wind at night. "With you, Cousin," and she glanced approvingly at his stalwart, soldier-like form, "I have nothing to fear from men, however rough, and I do greatly want to see the king close by, and so does Betty. Don't you, Betty?" and she turned to her companion.

H. Rider Haggard

Betty Dene, whom she addressed, was also a cousin of Margaret, though only a distant connection of Peter Brome. She was of very good blood, but her father, a wild and dissolute man, had broken her mother's heart, and, like that mother, died early, leaving Betty dependent upon Margaret's mother, in whose house she had been brought up. This Betty was in her way remarkable, both in body and mind. Fair, splendidly formed, strong, with wide, bold, blue eyes and ripe red lips, such was the fashion of her. In speech she was careless and vigorous. Fond of the society of men, and fonder still of their admiration, for she was romantic and vain, Betty at the age of five-and-twenty was yet an honest girl, and well able to take care of herself, as more than one of her admirers had discovered. Although her position was humble, at heart she was very proud of her lineage, ambitious also, her great desire being to raise herself by marriage back to the station from which her father's folly had cast her down—no easy business for one who passed as a waiting-woman and was without fortune.

For the rest, she loved and admired her cousin Margaret more than any one on earth, while Peter she liked and respected, none the less perhaps because, try as she would—and, being nettled, she did try hard enough—her beauty and other charms left him quite unmoved.

In answer to Margaret's question she laughed and answered:

"Of course. We are all too busy up in Holborn to get the chance of so many shows that I should wish to miss one. Still, Master Peter is very wise, and I am always counselled to obey him. Also, it will soon be dark."

"Well, well," said Margaret with a sigh and a little shrug of her shoulders, "as you are both against me, perhaps we had best be going. Next time I come out walking, cousin Peter, it shall be with some one who is more kind."

Then she turned and began to make her way as quickly as she

could through the thickening crowd. Finding this difficult, before Peter could stop her, for she was very swift in her movements, Margaret bore to the right, entering the space immediately in front of the banqueting-hall where the grooms with horses and soldiers were assembled awaiting their lords, for here there was more room to walk. For a few moments Peter and Betty were unable to escape from the mob which closed in behind her, and thus it came about that Margaret found herself alone among these people, in the midst, indeed, of the guard of the Spanish ambassador de Ayala, men who were notorious for their lawlessness, for they reckoned upon their master's privilege to protect them. Also, for the most part, they were just then more or less in liquor.

One of these fellows, a great, red-haired Scotchman, whom the priest-diplomatist had brought with him from that country, where he had also been ambassador, suddenly perceiving before him a woman who appeared to be young and pretty, determined to examine her more closely, and to this end made use of a rude stratagem. Pretending to stumble, he grasped at Margaret's cloak as though to save himself, and with a wrench tore it open, revealing her beautiful face and graceful figure.

"A dove, comrades!—a dove!" he shouted in a voice thick with drink, "who has flown here to give me a kiss." And, casting his long arms about her, he strove to draw her to him.

"Peter! Help me, Peter!" cried Margaret as she struggled fiercely in his grip.

"No, no, if you want a saint, my bonny lass," said the drunken Scotchman, "Andrew is as good as Peter," at which witticism those of the others who understood him laughed, for the man's name was Andrew.

Next instant they laughed again, and to the ruffian Andrew it seemed as though suddenly he had fallen into the power of a whirlwind. At least Margaret was wrenched away from him, while he spun round and round to fall violently upon his face.

"That's Peter!" exclaimed one of the soldiers in Spanish.

"Yes," answered another, "and a patron saint worth having"; while a third pulled the recumbent Andrew to his feet.

The man looked like a devil. His cap had gone, and his fiery red hair was smeared with mud. Moreover, his nose had been broken on a cobble stone, and blood from it poured all over him, while his little red eyes glared like a ferret's, and his face turned a dirty white with pain and rage. Howling out something in Scotch, of a sudden he drew his sword and rushed straight at his adversary, purposing to kill him.

Now, Peter had no sword, but only his short knife, which he found no time to draw. In his hand, however, he carried a stout holly staff shod with iron, and, while Margaret clasped her hands and Betty screamed, on this he caught the descending blow, and, furious as it was, parried and turned it. Then, before the man could strike again, that staff was up, and Peter had leapt upon him. It fell with fearful force, breaking the Scotchman's shoulder and sending him reeling back.

"Shrewdly struck, Peter! Well done, Peter!" shouted the spectators.

But Peter neither saw nor heard them, for he was mad with rage at the insult that had been offered to Margaret. Up flew the iron-tipped staff again, and down it came, this time full on Andrew's head, which it shattered like an egg-shell, so that the brute fell backwards, dead.

For a moment there was silence, for the joke had taken a tragic turn. Then one of the Spaniards said, glancing at the prostrate form:

"Name of God! our mate is done for. That merchant hits hard."

Instantly there arose a murmur among the dead man's

comrades, and one of them cried:

"Cut him down!"

Understanding that he was to be set on, Peter sprang forward and snatched the Scotchman's sword from the ground where it had fallen, at the same time dropping his staff and drawing his dagger with the left hand. Now he was well armed, and looked so fierce and soldier-like as he faced his foes, that, although four or five blades were out, they held back. Then Peter spoke for the first time, for he knew that against so many he had no chance.

"Englishmen," he cried in ringing tones, but without shifting his head or glance, "will you see me murdered by these Spanish dogs?"

There was a moment's pause, then a voice behind cried:

"By God! not I," and a brawny Kentish man-at-arms ranged up beside him, his cloak thrown over his left arm, and his sword in his right hand.

"Nor I," said another. "Peter Brome and I have fought together before."

"Nor I," shouted a third, "for we were born in the same Essex hundred."

And so it went on, until there were as many stout Englishmen at his side as there were Spaniards and Scotchmen before him.

"That will do," said Peter, "we want no more than man to man. Look to the women, comrades behind there. Now, you murderers, if you would see English sword-play, come on, or, if you are afraid, let us go in peace."

"Yes, come on, you foreign cowards," shouted the mob, who did not love these turbulent and privileged guards.

H. Rider Haggard

By now the Spanish blood was up, and the old race-hatred awake. In broken English the sergeant of the guard shouted out some filthy insult about Margaret, and called upon his followers to "cut the throats of the London swine." Swords shone red in the red sunset light, men shifted their feet and bent forward, and in another instant a great and bloody fray would have begun.

But it did not begin, for at that moment a tall senor, who had been standing in the shadow and watching all that passed, walked between the opposing lines, as he went striking up the swords with his arm.

"Have done," said d'Aguilar quietly, for it was he, speaking in Spanish. "You fools! do you want to see every Spaniard in London torn to pieces? As for that drunken brute," and he touched the corpse of Andrew with his foot, "he brought his death upon himself. Moreover, he was not a Spaniard, there is no blood quarrel. Come, obey me! or must I tell you who I am?"

"We know you, Marquis," said the leader in a cowed voice. "Sheath your swords, comrades; after all, it is no affair of ours."

The men obeyed somewhat unwillingly; but at this moment arrived the ambassador de Ayala, very angry, for he had heard of the death of his servant, demanding, in a loud voice, that the man who had killed him should be given up.

"We will not give him up to a Spanish priest," shouted the mob. "Come and take him if you want him," and once more the tumult grew, while Peter and his companions made ready to fight.

Fighting there would have been also, notwithstanding all that d'Aguilar could do to prevent it; but of a sudden the noise began to die away, and a hush fell upon the place. Then between the uplifted weapons walked a short, richly clad man, who turned suddenly and faced the mob. It was King

Henry himself.

"Who dare to draw swords in my streets, before my very palace doors?" he asked in a cold voice.

A dozen hands pointed at Peter.

"Speak," said the king to him.

"Margaret, come here," cried Peter; and the girl was thrust forward to him.

"Sire," he said, "that man," and he pointed to the corpse of Andrew, "tried to do wrong to this maiden, John Castell's child. I, her cousin, threw him down. He drew his sword and came at me, and I killed him with my staff. See, it lies there. Then the Spaniards—his comrades—would have cut me down, and I called for English help. Sire, that is all."

The king looked him up and down.

"A merchant by your dress," he said; "but a soldier by your mien. How are you named?"

"Peter Brome, Sire."

"Ah! There was a certain Sir Peter Brome who fell at Bosworth Field—not fighting for me," and he smiled. "Did you know him perchance?"

"He was my father, Sire, and I saw him slain—aye, and slew the slayer."

"Well can I believe it," answered Henry, considering him. "But how comes it that Peter Brome's son, who wears that battle scar across his face, is clad in merchant's woollen?"

"Sire," said Peter coolly, "my father sold his lands, lent his all to the Crown, and I have never rendered the account.

Therefore I must live as I can."

The king laughed outright as he replied:

"I like you, Peter Brome, though doubtless you hate me."

"Not so, Sire. While Richard lived I fought for Richard. Richard is gone; and, if need be, I would fight for Henry, who am an Englishman, and serve England's king."

"Well said, and I may have need of you yet, nor do I bear you any grudge. But, I forgot, is it thus that you would fight for me, by causing riot in my streets, and bringing me into trouble with my good friends the Spaniards?"

"Sire, you know the story."

"I know your story, but who bears witness to it? Do you, maiden, Castell the merchant's daughter?"

"Aye, Sire. The man whom my cousin killed maltreated me, whose only wrong was that I waited to see your Grace pass by. Look on my torn cloak."

"Little wonder that he killed him for the sake of those eyes of yours, maiden. But this witness may be tainted." And again he smiled, adding, "Is there no other?"

Betty advanced to speak, but d'Aguilar, stepping forward, lifted his bonnet from his head, bowed and said in English:

"Your Grace, there is; I saw it all. This gallant gentleman had no blame. It was the servants of my countryman de Ayala who were to blame, at any rate at first, and afterwards came the trouble."

Now the ambassador de Ayala broke in, claiming satisfaction for the killing of his man, for he was still very angry, and saying that if it were not given, he would report the matter to their Majesties of Spain, and let them know how their servants were treated in London.

At these words Henry grew grave, who, above all things, wished to give no offence to Ferdinand and Isabella.

"You have done an ill day's work, Peter Brome," he said, "and one of which my attorney must consider. Meanwhile, you will be best in safe keeping," and he turned as though to order his arrest.

"Sire," exclaimed Peter, "I live at Master Castell's house in Holborn, nor shall I run away."

"Who will answer for that," asked the king, "or that you will not make more riots on your road thither?"

"I will answer, your Grace," said d'Aguilar quietly, "if this lady will permit that I escort her and her cousin home. Also," he added in a low voice, "it seems to me that to hale him to a prison would be more like to breed a riot than to let him go."

Henry glanced round him at the great crowd who were gathered watching this scene, and saw something in their faces which caused him to agree with d'Aguilar.

"So be it, Marquis," he said. "I have your word, and that of Peter Brome, that he will be forthcoming if called upon. Let that dead man be laid in the Abbey till to-morrow, when this matter shall be inquired of. Excellency, give me your arm; I have greater questions of which I wish to speak with you ere we sleep."

CHAPTER II

JOHN CASTELL

When the king was gone, Peter turned to those men who had stood by him and thanked them very heartily. Then he said to Margaret:

"Come, Cousin, that is over for this time, and you have had your wish and seen his Grace. Now, the sooner you are safe at home, the better I shall be pleased."

"Certainly," she replied. "I have seen more than I desire to see again. But before we go let us thank this Spanish senor—" and she paused.

"D'Aguilar, Lady, or at least that name will serve," said the Spaniard in his cultured voice, bowing low before her, his eyes fixed all the while upon her beautiful face.

"Senor d'Aguilar, I thank you, and so does my cousin, Peter Brome, whose life perhaps you saved—don't you, Peter? Oh! and so will my father."

"Yes," answered Peter somewhat sulkily, "I thank him very much; though as for my life, I trusted to my own arm and to those of my friends there. Good night, Sir."

"I fear, Senor," answered d'Aguilar with a smile, "that we cannot part just yet. You forget, I have become bond for you, and must therefore accompany you to where you live, that I may certify the place. Also, perhaps, it is safest, for these countrymen of mine are revengeful, and, were I not with you, might waylay you."

Now, seeing from his face that Peter was still bent upon declining this escort, Margaret interposed quickly.

"Yes, that is wisest, also my father would wish it. Senor, I will show you the way," and, accompanied by d'Aguilar, who gallantly offered her his arm, she stepped forward briskly, leaving Peter to follow with her cousin Betty.

Thus they walked in the twilight across the fields and through the narrow streets beyond that lay between Westminster and Holborn. In front tripped Margaret beside her stately cavalier, with whom she was soon talking fast enough in Spanish, a tongue which, for reasons that shall be explained, she knew well, while behind, the Scotchman's sword still in his hand, and the handsome Betty on his arm, came Peter Brome in the worst of humours.

John Castell lived in a large, rambling, many-gabled, house, just off the main thoroughfare of Holborn, that had at the back of it a garden surrounded by a high wall. Of this ancient place the front part served as a shop, a store for merchandise, and an office, for Castell was a very wealthy trader—how wealthy none quite knew—who exported woollen and other goods to Spain under the royal licence, bringing thence in his own ships fine, raw Spanish wool to be manufactured in England, and with it velvet, silks, and wine from Granada; also beautiful inlaid armour of Toledo steel. Sometimes, too, he dealt in silver and copper from the mountain mines, for Castell was a banker as well as a merchant, or rather what answered to that description in those days.

It was said that beneath his shop were dungeon-like store-vaults, built of thick cemented stone, with iron doors through which no thief could break, and filled with precious things.

However this might be, certainly in that great house, which in the time of the Plantagenets had been the fortified palace of a noble, existed chambers whereof he alone knew the secret, since no one else, not even his daughter or Peter, ever crossed their threshold. Also, there slept in it a number of men-servants, very stout fellows, who wore knives or swords beneath their cloaks, and watched at night to see that all was well. For the rest, the living-rooms of this house where Castell, Margaret his daughter, and Peter dwelt, were large and comfortable, being new panelled with oak after the Tudor fashion, and having deep windows that looked out upon the garden.

When Peter and Betty reached the door, not that which led into the shop, but another, it was to find that Margaret and d'Aguilar, who were walking very quickly, must have already passed it, since it was shut, and they had vanished. At his knock—a hard one—a serving-man opened, and Peter strode through the vestibule, or ante-chamber, into the hall, where for the most part they ate and sat, for thence he heard the sound of voices. It was a fine room, lit by hanging lamps of olive oil, and having a large, open hearth where a fire burned pleasantly, while the oaken table in front of it was set for supper. Margaret, who had thrown off her cloak, stood warming herself at the fire, and the Senor d'Aguilar, comfortably seated in a big chair, which he seemed to have known for years, leaned back, his bonnet in his hand, and watched her idly.

Facing them stood John Castell, a stout, dark-bearded man of between fifty and sixty years of age, with a clever, clean-cut face and piercing black eyes. Now, in the privacy of his home, he was very richly attired in a robe trimmed with the costliest fur, and fastened with a gold chain that had a jewel on its clasp. When Castell served in his shop or sat in his counting-house no merchant in London was more plainly dressed; but at night, loving magnificence at heart, it was his custom thus to indulge in it, even when there were none to see him. From the way in which he stood, and the look upon his face, Peter knew at once that he was much disturbed. Hearing his step, Castell wheeled round and addressed him at once in the clear, decided voice which was his characteristic.

"What is this I am told, Peter? A man killed by you before the palace gates? A broil! A public riot in which things went near to great bloodshed between the English, with you at the head of them, and the bodyguard of his Excellency, de Ayala. You arrested by the king, and bailed out by this senor. Is all this true?"

"Quite," answered Peter calmly.

"Then I am ruined; we are all ruined. Oh! it was an evil hour when I took one of your bloodthirsty trade into my house. What have you to say?"

"Only that I want my supper," said Peter. "Those who began the story can finish it, for I think their tongues are nimbler than my own," and he glanced wrathfully at Margaret, who laughed outright, while even the solemn d'Aguilar smiled.

"Father," broke in Margaret, "do not be angry with cousin Peter, whose only fault is that he hits too hard. It is I who am to blame, for I wished to stop to see the king against his will and Betty's, and then—then that brute," and her eyes filled with tears of shame and anger, "caught hold of me, and Peter threw him down, and afterwards, when he attacked him with a sword, Peter killed him with his staff, and—all the rest happened."

"It was beautifully done," said d'Aguilar in his soft voice and foreign accent. "I saw it all, and made sure that you were dead. The parry I understood, but the way you got your smashing blow in before he could thrust again—ah! that—"

"Well, well," said Castell, "let us eat first and talk afterwards. Senor d'Aguilar, you will honour my poor board, will you not, though it is hard to come from a king's feast to a merchant's fare?"

"It is I who am honoured," answered d'Aguilar; "and as for the feast, his Grace is sparing in this Lenten season. At least, I could get little to eat, and, therefore, like the senor Peter, I am starved."

Castell rang a silver bell which stood near by, whereon servants brought in the meal, which was excellent and plentiful. While they were setting it on the table, the merchant went to a cupboard in the wainscoting, and took thence two flasks, which he uncorked himself with care, saying that he would give the senor some wine of his own country. This done, he said a Latin grace and crossed himself, an example which d'Aguilar followed, remarking that he was glad to find that he was in the house of a good Christian.

"What else did you think that I should be?" asked Castell, glancing at him shrewdly.

"I did not think at all, Senor," he answered; "but alas! every one is not a Christian. In Spain, for instance, we have many Moors and—Jews."

"I know," said Castell, "for I trade with them both."

"Then you have never visited Spain?"

"No; I am an English merchant. But try that wine, Senor; it came from Granada, and they say that it is good."

D'Aguilar tasted it, then drank off his glass.

"It is good, indeed," he said; "I have not its equal in my own cellars there."

"Do you, then, live in Granada, Senor d'Aguilar?" asked Castell.

"Sometimes, when I am not travelling. I have a house there which my mother left me. She loved the town, and bought an old palace from the Moors. Would you not like to see Granada, Senora?" he asked, turning to Margaret as though to change the subject. "There is a wonderful building there called the Alhambra; it overlooks my house."

"My daughter is never likely to see it," broke in Castell; "I do not purpose that she should visit Spain."

"Ah! you do not purpose; but who knows? God and His saints alone," and again he crossed himself, then fell to describing the beauties of Granada.

He was a fine and ready talker, and his voice was very pleasant, so Margaret listened attentively enough, watching his face, and forgetting to eat, while her father and Peter watched them both. At length the meal came to an end, and when the serving-men had cleared away the dishes, and they were alone, Castell said:

"Now, kinsman Peter, tell me your story."

So Peter told him, in few words, yet omitting nothing.

"I find no blame in you," said the merchant when he had done, "nor do I see how you could have acted otherwise than you did. It is Margaret whom I blame, for I only gave her leave to walk with you and Betty by the river, and bade her beware of crowds."

"Yes, father, the fault is mine, and for it I pray your pardon," said Margaret, so meekly that her father could not find the heart to scold her as he had meant to do.

"You should ask Peter's pardon," he muttered, "seeing that he is like to be laid by the heels in a dungeon over this business, yes, and put upon his trial for causing the man's death. Remember, he was in the service of de Ayala, with whom our liege wishes to stand well, and de Ayala, it seems, is very angry."

Now Margaret grew frightened, for the thought that harm might come to Peter cut her heart. The colour left her cheek, and once again her eyes swam with tears.

"Oh! say not so," she exclaimed. "Peter, will you not fly at once?"

"By no means," he answered decidedly. "Did I not say it to the king, and is not this foreign lord bond for me?"

"What can be done?" she went on; then, as a thought struck her, turned to d'Aguilar, and, clasping her slender hands, looked pleadingly into his face and asked: "Senor, you who are so powerful, and the friend of great people, will you not help us?"

"Am I not here to do so, Senora? Although I think that a man who can call half London to his back, as I saw your cousin do, needs little help from me. But listen, my country has two ambassadors at this Court—de Ayala, whom he has offended, and Doctor de Puebla, the friend of the king; and, strangely enough, de Puebla does not love de Ayala. Yet he does love money, which perhaps will be forthcoming. Now, if a charge is to be laid over this brawl, it will probably be done, not by the churchman, de Ayala, but through de Puebla, who knows your laws and Court, and—do you understand me, Senor Castell?"

"Yes," answered the merchant; "but how am I to get at de Puebla? If I were to offer him money, he would only ask more."

"I see that you know his Excellency," remarked d'Aguilar drily. "You are right, no money should be offered; a present must be made after the pardon is delivered—not before. Oh! de Puebla knows that John Castell's word is as good in London as it is among the Jews and infidels of Granada and the merchants of

Seville, at both of which places I have heard it spoken."

At this speech Castell's eyes flickered, but he only answered:

"May be; but how shall I approach him, Senor?"

"If you will permit me, that is my task. Now, to what amount will you go to save our friend here from inconvenience? Fifty gold angels?"

"It is too much," said Castell; "a knave like that is not worth ten. Indeed, he was the assailant, and nothing should be paid at all."

"Ah! Senor, the merchant is coming out in you; also the dangerous man who thinks that right should rule the world, not kings—I mean might. The knave is worth nothing, but de Puebla's word in Henry's ear is worth much."

"Fifty angels be it then," said Castell, "and I thank you, Senor, for your good offices. Will you take the money now?"

"By no means; not till I bring the debt discharged. Senor, I will come again and let you know how matters stand. Farewell, fair maiden; may the saints intercede for that dead rogue who brought me into your company, and that of your father and your cousin of the quick eye and the stalwart arm! Till we meet again," and, still murmuring compliments, he bowed himself out of the room in charge of a manservant.

"Thomas," said Castell to this servant when he returned, "you are a discreet fellow; put on your cap and cloak, follow that Spaniard, see where he lodges, and find out all you can about him. Go now, swiftly."

The man bowed and went, and presently Castell, listening, heard a side door shut behind him. Then he turned and said to the other two:

H. Rider Haggard

"I do not like this business. I smell trouble in it, and I do not like the Spaniard either."

"He seems a very gallant gentleman, and high-born," said Margaret.

"Aye, very gallant—too gallant, and high-born—too high-born, unless I am mistaken. So gallant and so high-born—" And he checked himself, then added, "Daughter, in your wilfulness you have stirred a great rock. Go to your bed and pray God that it may not fall upon your house and crush it and us."

So Margaret crept away frightened, a little indignant also, for after all, what wrong had she done? And why should her father mistrust this splendid-looking Spanish cavalier?

When she was gone, Peter, who all this while had said little, looked up and asked straight out:

"What are you afraid of, Sir?"

"Many things, Peter. First, that use will be made of this matter to extort much money from me, who am known to be rich, which is a sin best absolved by angels. Secondly, that if I make trouble about paying, other questions will be set afoot."

"What questions?"

"Have you ever heard of the new Christians, Peter, whom the Spaniards call Maranos?"

He nodded.

"Then you know that a Marano is a converted Jew. Now, as it chances—I tell you who do not break secrets—my father was a Marano. His name does not matter—it is best forgotten; but he fled from Spain to England for reasons of his own, and took that of the country whence he came—Castile, or Castell. Also, as it is not lawful for Jews to live in England, he became converted to the Christian faith—seek not to know his motives, they are buried with him. Moreover, he converted me, his only child, who was but ten years old, and cared little whether I swore by 'Father Abraham' or by the 'Blessed Mary.' The paper of my baptism lies in my strong box still. Well, he was clever, and built up this business, and died unharmed five-and-twenty years ago, leaving me already rich. That same year I married an Englishwoman, your mother's second cousin, and loved her and lived happily with her, and gave her all her heart could wish. But after Margaret's birth, three-and-twenty years gone by, she never had her health, and eight years ago she died. You remember her, since she brought you here when you were a stout lad, and made me promise afterwards that I would always be your friend, for except your father, Sir Peter, none other of your well-born and ancient family were left. So when Sir Peter—against my counsel, staking his all upon that usurping rogue Richard, who had promised to advance him, and meanwhile took his money—was killed at Bosworth, leaving you landless, penniless, and out of favour, I offered you a home, and you, being a wise man, put off your mail and put on woollen and became a merchant's partner, though your share of profit was but small. Now, again you have changed staff for steel," and he glanced at the Scotchman's sword that still lay upon a side table, "and Margaret has loosed that rock of which I spoke to her."

"What is the rock, Sir?"

"That Spaniard whom she brought home and found so fine."

"What of the Spaniard?"

"Wait a while and I will tell you." And, taking a lamp, he left the room, returning presently with a letter which was written in cipher, and translated upon another sheet in John Castell's own hand.

"This," he said, "is from my partner and connection, Juan

Bernaldez, a Marano, who lives at Seville, where Ferdinand and Isabella have their court. Among other matters he writes this: 'I warn all brethren in England to be careful. I have it that a certain one whose name I will not mention even in cipher, a very powerful and high-born man, and, although he appears to be a pleasure-seeker only, and is certainly of a dissolute life, among the greatest bigots in all Spain, has been sent, or is shortly to be sent, from Granada, where he is stationed to watch the Moors, as an envoy to the Court of England to conclude a secret treaty with its king. Under this treaty the names of rich Maranos that are already well known here are to be recorded, so that when the time comes, and the active persecution of Jews and Maranos begins, they may be given up and brought to Spain for trial before the Inquisition. Also he is to arrange that no Jew or Marano may be allowed to take refuge in England. This is for your information, that you may warn any whom it concerns.'"

"You think that d'Aguilar is this man?" asked Peter, while Castell folded up the letter and hid it in the pocket of his robe.

"I do; indeed I have heard already that a fox was on the prowl, and that men should look to their hen-houses. Moreover, did you note how he crossed himself like a priest, and what he said about being among good Christians? Also, it is Lent and a fast-day, and by ill-fortune, although none of us ate of it, there was meat upon the table, for as you know," he added hurriedly, "I am not strict in such matters, who give little weight to forms and ceremonies. Well, he observed it, and touched fish only, although he drank enough of the sweet wine. Doubtless a report of that meat will go to Spain by the next courier."

"And if it does, what matter? We are in England, and Englishmen will not suffer their Spanish laws and ways. Perhaps the senor d'Aguilar learned as much as that to-night outside the banqueting-hall. There is something to be feared from this brawl at home; but while we are safe in London, no more from Spain."

"I am no coward, but I think there is much more to be feared, Peter. The arm of the Pope is long, and the arm of the crafty Ferdinand is longer, and both of them grope for the throats and moneybags of heretics."

"Well, Sir, we are not heretics."

"No, perhaps not heretics; but we are rich, and the father of one of us was a Jew, and there is something else in this house which even a true son of Holy Church might desire," and he looked at the door through which Margaret had passed to her chamber.

Peter understood, for his long arms moved uneasily, and his grey eyes flashed.

"I will go to bed," he said; "I wish to think."

"Nay, lad," answered Castell, "fill your glass and stay awhile. I have words to say to you, and there is no time like the present. Who knows what may happen to-morrow?"

CHAPTER III

PETER GATHERS VIOLETS

Peter obeyed, sat down in a big oak chair by the dying fire, and waited in his silent fashion.

"Listen," said Castell. "Fifteen months ago you told me something, did you not?"

Peter nodded.

"What was it, then?"

"That I loved my cousin Margaret, and asked your leave to tell her so."

"And what did I answer?"

"That you forbade me because you had not proved me enough, and she had not proved herself enough; because, moreover, she would be very wealthy, and with her beauty might look high in marriage, although but a merchant's daughter."

"Well, and then?"

"And then—nothing," and Peter sipped his wine deliberately and put it down upon the table.

"You are a very silent man, even where your courting is

concerned," said Castell, searching him with his sharp eyes.

"I am silent because there is no more to say. You bade me be silent, and I have remained so."

"What! Even when you saw those gay lords making their addresses to Margaret, and when she grew angry because you gave no sign, and was minded to yield to one or the other of them?"

"Yes, even then—it was hard, but even then. Do I not eat your bread? and shall I take advantage of you when you have forbid me?"

Castell looked at him again, and this time there were respect and affection in his glance.

"Silent and stern, but honest," he said as though to himself, then added, "A hard trial, but I saw it, and helped you in the best way by sending those suitors—who were worthless fellows—about their business. Now, say, are you still of the same mind towards Margaret?"

"I seldom change my mind, Sir, and on such a business, never."

"Good! Then I give you my leave to find out what her mind may be."

In the joy which he could not control, Peter's face flushed. Then, as though he were ashamed of showing emotion, even at such a moment, he took up his glass and drank a little of the wine before he answered.

"I thank you; it is more than I dared to hope. But it is right that I should say, Sir, that I am no match for my cousin Margaret. The lands which should have been mine are gone, and I have nothing save what you pay me for my poor help in this trade; whereas she has, or will have, much."

Castell's eyes twinkled; the answer amused him.

"At least you have an upright heart," he said, "for what other man in such a case would argue against himself? Also, you are of good blood, and not ill to look on, or so some maids might think; whilst as for wealth, what said the wise king of my people?—that ofttimes riches make themselves wings and fly away. Moreover, man, I have learned to love and honour you, and sooner would I leave my only child in your hands than in those of any lord in England."

"I know not what to say," broke in Peter.

"Then say nothing. It is your custom, and a good one—only listen. Just now you spoke of your Essex lands in the fair Vale of Dedham as gone. Well, they have come back, for last month I bought them all, and more, at a price larger than I wished to give because others sought them, and but this day I have paid in gold and taken delivery of the title. It is made out in your name, Peter Brome, and whether you marry my daughter, or whether you marry her not, yours they shall be when I am gone, since I promised my dead wife to befriend you, and as a child she lived there in your Hall."

Now moved out of his calm, the young man sprang from his seat, and, after the pious fashion of the time, addressed his patron saint, on whose feast-day he was born.

"Saint Peter, I thank thee—"

"I asked you to be silent," interrupted Castell, breaking him short. "Moreover, after God, it is one John who should be thanked, not St. Peter, who has no more to do with these lands than Father Abraham or the patient Job. Well, thanks or no thanks, those estates are yours, though I had not meant to tell you of them yet. But now I have something to propose to you. Say, first, does Margaret think aught of that wooden face and those shut lips of yours?"

"How can I know? I have never asked her; you forbade me."

"Pshaw! Living in one house as you do, at your age I would have known all there was to know on such a matter, and yet kept my word. But there, the blood is different, and you are somewhat over-honest for a lover. Was she frightened for you, now, when that knave made at you with the sword?"

Peter considered the question, then answered:

"I know not. I did not look to see; I looked at the Scotchman with his sword, for if I had not, I should have been dead, not he. But she was certainly frightened when the fellow caught hold of her, for then she called for me loud enough."

"And what is that? What woman in London would not call for such a one as Peter Brome in her trouble? Well, you must ask her, and that soon, if you can find the words. Take a lesson from that Spanish don, and scrape and bow and flatter and tell stories of the war and turn verses to her eyes and hair. Oh, Peter! are you a fool, that I at my age should have to teach you how to court a woman?"

"Mayhap, Sir. At least I can do none of these things, and poesy wearies me to read, much more to write. But I can ask a question and take an answer."

Castell shook his head impatiently.

"Ask the question, man, if you will, but never take the answer if it is against you. Wait rather, and ask it again—"

"And," went on Peter without noticing, his grey eyes lighting with a sudden fire, "if need be, I can break that fine Spaniard's bones as though he were a twig."

"Ah!" said Castell, "perhaps you will be called upon to make your words good before all is done. For my part, I think his bones will take some breaking. Well, ask in your own way—only ask and let me hear the answer before to-morrow night. Now it grows late, and I have still something to say. I am in danger here. My wealth is noised abroad, and many covet it, some in high places, I think. Peter, it is in my mind to have done with all this trading, and to withdraw me to spend my old age where none will take any notice of me, down at that Hall of yours in Dedham, if you will give me lodging. Indeed for a year and more, ever since you spoke to me on the subject of Margaret, I have been calling in my moneys from Spain and England, and placing them out at safe interest in small sums, or buying jewels with them, or lending them to other merchants whom I trust, and who will not rob me or mine. Peter, you have worked well for me, but you are no chapman; it is not in your blood. Therefore, since there is enough for all of us and more, I shall pass this business and its goodwill over to others, to be managed in their name, but on shares, and if it please God we will keep next Yule at Dedham."

As he spoke the door at the far end of the hall opened, and through it came that serving-man who had been bidden to follow the Spaniard.

"Well," said Castell, "what tidings?"

The man bowed and said:

"I followed the Don as you bade me to his lodging, which I reached without his seeing me, though from time to time he stopped to look about him. He rests near the palace of Westminster, in the same big house where dwells the ambassador de Ayala, and those who stood round lifted their bonnets to him.

"Watching I saw some of these go to a tavern, a low place that is open all night, and, following them there, called for a drink and listened to their talk, who know the Spanish tongue well, having worked for five years in your worship's house at Seville. They spoke of the fray to-night, and said that if they could catch that long-legged fellow, meaning Master Brome yonder, they would put a knife into him, since he had shamed them by killing the Scotch knave, who was their officer and the best swordsman in their company, with a staff, and then setting his British bulldogs on them. I fell into talk with them, saying that I was an English sailor from Spain, which they were too drunk to question, and asked who might be the tall don who had interfered in the fray before the king came. They told me he is a rich senor named d'Aguilar, but ill to serve in Lent because he is so strict a churchman, although not strict in other matters. I answered that to me he looked like a great noble, whereon one of them said that I was right, that there was no blood in Spain higher than his, but unfortunately, there was a bend in its stream, also an inkpot had been upset into it."

"What does that mean?" asked Peter.

"It is a Spanish saying," answered Castell, "which signifies that a man is born illegitimate, and has Moorish blood in his veins."

"Then I asked what he was doing here, and the man answered that I had best put that question to the Holy Father and to the Queen of Spain. Lastly, after I had given the soldier another cup, I asked where the don lived, and whether he had any other name. He replied that he lived at Granada for the most part, and that if I called on him there I should see some pretty ladies and other nice things. As for his name, it was the Marquis of Nichel. I said that meant Marquis of Nothing, whereon the soldier answered that I seemed very curious, and that was just what he meant to tell me—nothing. Also he called to his comrades that he believed I was a spy, so I thought it time to be going, as they were drunk enough to do me a mischief."

"Good," said Castell. "You are watchman tonight, Thomas, are you not? See that all doors are barred so that we may sleep without fear of Spanish thieves. Rest you well, Peter. Nay, I do not come yet; I have letters to send to Spain by the ship which sails to-morrow night."

When Peter had gone, John Castell extinguished all the lamps save one. This he took in his hand and passed from the hall into an apartment that in old days, when this was a noble's house, had been the private chapel. There was an altar in it, and over the altar a crucifix. For a few moments Castell knelt before the altar, for even now, at dead of night, how knew he what eyes might watch him? Then he rose and, lamp in hand, glided behind it, lifted some tapestry, and pressed a spring in the panelling beneath. It opened, revealing a small secret chamber built in the thickness of the wall and without windows; a mere cupboard that once perhaps had been a place where a priest might robe or keep the sacred vessels.

In this chamber was a plain oak table on which stood candles and an ark of wood, also some rolls of parchment. Before this table he knelt down, and put up earnest prayers to the God of Abraham, for, although his father had caused him to be baptized into the Christian Church as a child, John Castell remained a Jew. For this good reason, then, he was so much afraid, knowing that, although his daughter and Peter knew nothing of his secret, there were others who did, and that were it revealed ruin and perhaps death would be his portion and that of his house, since in those days there was no greater crime than to adore God otherwise than Holy Church allowed. Yet for many years he had taken the risk, and worshipped on as his fathers did before him.

His prayer finished, he left the place, closing the spring-door behind him, and passed to his office, where he sat till the morning light, first writing a letter to his correspondent at Seville, and then painfully translating it into cipher by aid of a secret key. His task done, and the cipher letter sealed and directed, he burned the draft, extinguished his lamp, and, going to the window, watched the rising of the sun. In the garden beneath blackbirds sang, and the pale primroses were abloom.

"I wonder," he said aloud, "whether when those flowers come again I shall live to see them. Almost I feel as though the rope were tightening about my throat at last; it came upon me while that accursed Spaniard crossed himself at my table. Well, so be it; I will hide the truth while I can, but if they catch me I'll not deny it. The money is safe, most of it; my wealth they shall never get, and now I will make my daughter safe also, as with Peter she must be. I would I had not put it off so long; but I hankered after a great marriage for her, which, being a Christian, she well might make. I'll mend that fault; before to-morrow's morn she shall be plighted to him, and before May-day his wife. God of my fathers, give us one month more of peace and safety, and then, because I have denied Thee openly, take my life in payment if Thou wilt."

Before John Castell went to bed Peter was already awake—indeed, he had slept but little that night. How could he sleep whose fortunes had changed thus wondrously between sun set and rise? Yesterday he was but a merchant's assistant—a poor trade for one who had been trained to arms, and borne them bravely. To-day he was a gentleman again, owner of the broad lands where he was bred, and that had been his forefathers' for many a generation. Yesterday he was a lover without hope, for in himself he had never believed that the rich John Castell would suffer him, a landless man, to pay court to his daughter, one of the loveliest and wealthiest maids in London. He had asked his leave in past days, and been refused, as he had expected that he would be refused, and thenceforward, being on his honour as it were, he had said no tender word to Margaret, nor pressed her hand, nor even looked into her eyes and sighed. Yet at times it had seemed to him that she would not have been ill-pleased if he had done one of these things, or all; that she wondered, indeed, that he did not, and thought none the better of him for his abstinence. Moreover, now he learned that her father wondered also, and this was a strange reward of virtue.

For Peter loved Margaret with heart and soul and body. Since he, a lad, had played with her, a child, he loved her, and no

H. Rider Haggard

other woman. She was his thought by day and his dream by night, his hope, his eternal star. Heaven he pictured as a place where for ever he would be with Margaret, earth without her could be nothing but a hell. That was why he had stayed on in Castell's shop, bending his proud neck to this tradesman's yoke, doing the bidding and taking the rough words of chapmen and of lordly customers, filling in bills of exchange, and cheapening bargains, all without a sign or murmur, though oftentimes he felt as though his gorge would burst with loathing of the life. Indeed, that was why he had come there at all, who otherwise would have been far away, hewing a road to fame and fortune, or digging out a grave with his broadsword. For here at least he could be near to Margaret, could touch her hand at morn and evening, could watch the light shine in her beauteous eyes, and sometimes, as she bent over him, feel her breath upon his hair. And now his purgatory was at an end, and of a sudden the gates of joy were open.

But what if Margaret should prove the angel with the flaming sword who forbade him entrance to his paradise? He trembled at the thought. Well, if so, so it must be; he was not the man to force her fancy, or call her father to his aid. He would do his best to win her, and if he failed, why then he would bless her, and let her go.

Peter could lie abed no longer, but rose and dressed himself, although the dawn was not fully come. By his open window he said his prayers, thanking God for mercies past, and praying that He would bless him in his great emprise. Presently the sun rose, and there came a great longing on him to be alone in the countryside, he who was country-born and hated towns, with only the sky and the birds and the trees for company.

But here in London was no country, wherever he went he would meet men; moreover, he remembered that it might be best that just now he should not wander through the streets unguarded, lest he should find Spaniards watching to take him unawares. Well, there was the garden; he would go thither, and walk a while. So he descended the broad oak stairs, and, unbolting a door, entered this garden, which, though not too well kept, was large for London, covering an acre of ground perhaps, surrounded by a high wall, and having walks, and at the end of it a group of ancient elms, beneath which was a seat hidden from the house. In summer this was Margaret's favourite bower, for she too loved Nature and the land, and all the things it bore. Indeed, this garden was her joy, and the flowers that grew there were for the most part of her own planting—primroses, snowdrops, violets, and, in the shadow of the trees, long hartstongue ferns.

For a while Peter walked up and down the central path, and, as it chanced, Margaret, who also had risen early and not slept too well, looking through her window curtains, saw him wandering there, and wondered what he did at this hour; also, why he was dressed in the clothes he wore on Sundays and holidays. Perhaps, she thought, his weekday garments had been torn or muddied in last night's fray. Then she fell to thinking how bravely he had borne him in that fray. She saw it all again; the great red-headed rascal tossed up and whirled to the earth by his strong arms; saw Peter face that gleaming steel with nothing but a staff; saw the straight blows fall, and the fellow go reeling to the earth, slain with a single stroke.

Ah! her cousin, Peter Brome, was a man indeed, though a strange one, and remembering certain things that did not please her, she shrugged her ivory shoulders, turned red, and pouted. Why, that Spaniard had said more civil words to her in an hour than had Peter in two years, and he was handsome and noble-looking also; but then the Spaniard was—a Spaniard, and other men were—other men, whereas Peter was—Peter, a creature apart, one who cared as little for women as he did for trade.

Why, then, if he cared for neither women nor trade, did he stop here? she wondered. To gather wealth? She did not think it; he seemed to have no leanings that way either. It was a mystery. Still, she could wish to get to the bottom of Peter's heart, just to see what was hid there, since no man has a right

H. Rider Haggard

to be a riddle to his loving cousin. Yes, and one day she would do it, cost what it might.

Meanwhile, she remembered that she had never thanked Peter for the brave part which he had played, and, indeed, had left him to walk home with Betty, a journey that, as she gathered from her sprightly cousin's talk while she undressed her, neither of them had much enjoyed. For Betty, be it said here, was angry with Peter, who, it seemed, once had told her that she was a handsome, silly fool, who thought too much of men and too little of her business. Well, since after the day's work had begun she would find no opportunity, she would go down and thank Peter now, and see if she could make him talk for once.

So Margaret threw her fur-trimmed cloak about her, drawing its hood over her head, for the April air was cold, and followed Peter into the garden. When she reached it, however, there was no Peter to be seen, whereon she reproached herself for having come to that damp place so early and meditated return. Then, thinking that it would look foolish if any had chanced to see her, she walked down the path pretending to seek for violets, and found none. Thus she came to the group of great elms at the end, and, glancing between their ancient boles, saw Peter standing there. Now, too, she understood why she could find no violets, for Peter had gathered them all, and was engaged, awkwardly enough, in trying to tie them and some leaves into a little posy by the help of a stem of grass. With his left hand he held the violets, with his right one end of the grass, and since he lacked fingers to clasp the other, this he attempted with his teeth. Now he drew it tight, and now the brittle grass stem broke, the violets were scattered, and Peter used words that he should not have uttered even when alone.

"I knew you would break it, but I never thought you could lose your temper over so small a thing, Peter," said Margaret; and he in the shadow looked up to see her standing there in the sunlight, fresh and lovely as the spring itself.

Solemnly, in severe reproof, she shook her head, from which the hood had fallen back, but there was a smile upon her lips, and laughter in her eyes. Oh! she was beautiful, and at the sight of her Peter's heart stood still. Then, remembering what he had just said, and certain other things that Master Castell had said, he blushed so deeply that her own cheeks went red in sympathy. It was foolish, but she could not help it, for about Peter this morning there was something strange, something that bred blushes.

"For whom are you gathering violets so early," she asked, "when you ought to be praying for that Scotchman's soul?"

"I care nothing for his soul," answered Peter testily. "If the brute had one, he can look after it himself; and I was gathering the violets—for you."

She stared. Peter was not in the habit of making her presents of flowers. No wonder he had looked strange.

"Then I will help you to tie them. Do you know why I am up so early? It is for your sake. I behaved badly to you last night, for I was cross because you wanted to thwart me about seeing the king. I never thanked you for all you did, you brave Peter, though I thanked you enough in my heart. Do you know that when you stood there with that sword, in the middle of those Englishmen, you looked quite noble? Come out into the sunlight, and I will thank you properly."

In his agitation Peter let the remainder of the flowers fall. Then an idea struck him, and he answered:

"Look! I can't; if you are really grateful for nothing at all, come in here and help me to pick up these violets—a pest on their short stalks!"

She hesitated a little, then by degrees drew nearer, and, bending down, began to find the flowers one by one. Peter had scattered them wide, so that at first the pair were some way apart, but when only a few remained, they drew close. Now there was but one violet left, and, both stretching for it, their hands met. Margaret held the violet, and Peter held Margaret's fingers. Thus linked they straightened themselves, and as they rose their faces were very near together and oh! most sweet were Margaret's wonderful eyes; while in the eyes of Peter there shone a flame. For a second they looked at each other, and then of a sudden he kissed her on the lips.

CHAPTER IV

LOVERS DEAR

"Peter!" gasped Margaret—"*Peter!*"

But Peter made no answer, only he who had been red of face went white, so that the mark of the sword-cut across his cheek showed like a scarlet line upon a cloth.

"Peter!" repeated Margaret, pulling at her hand which he still held, "do you know what you have done?"

"It seems that you do, so what need is there for me to tell you?" he muttered.

"Then it was not an accident; you really meant it, and you are not ashamed."

"If it was, I hope that I may meet with more such accidents."

"Peter, leave go of me. I am going to tell my father, at once."

His face brightened.

"Tell him by all means," he said; "he won't mind. He told me—"

"Peter, how dare you add falsehood to—to—you know what. Do you mean to say that my father told you to kiss me, and at

H. Rider Haggard

six o'clock in the morning, too?"

"He said nothing about kissing, but I suppose he meant it. He said that I might ask you to marry me."

"That," replied Margaret, "is a very different thing. If you had asked me to marry you, and, after thinking it over for a long while, I had answered Yes, which of course I should not have done, then, perhaps, before we were married you might have— Well, Peter, you have begun at the wrong end, which is very shameless and wicked of you, and I shall never speak to you again."

"I daresay," said Peter resignedly; "all the more reason why I should speak to you while I have the chance. No, you shan't go till you have heard me. Listen. I have been in love with you since you were twelve years old—"

"That must be another falsehood, Peter, or you have gone mad. If you had been in love with me for eleven years, you would have said so."

"I wanted to, always, but your father refused me leave. I asked him fifteen months ago, but he put me on my word to say nothing."

"To say nothing—yes, but he could not make you promise to show nothing."

"I thought that the one thing meant the other; I see now that I have been a fool, and, I suppose, have overstayed my market," and he looked so depressed that Margaret relented a little.

"Well," she said, "at any rate it was honest, and of course I am glad that you were honest."

"You said just now that I told falsehoods—twice; if I am honest, how can I tell falsehoods?"

"I don't know. Why do you ask me riddles? Let me go and try to forget all this."

"Not till you have answered me outright. Will you marry me, Margaret? If you won't, there will be no need for you to go, for I shall go and trouble you no more. You know what I am, and all about me, and I have nothing more to say except that, although you may find many finer husbands, you won't find one who would love and care for you better. I know that you are very beautiful and very rich, while I am neither one nor the other, and often I have wished to Heaven that you were not so beautiful, for sometimes that brings trouble on women who are honest and only have one heart to give, or so rich either. But thus things are, and I cannot change them, and, however poor my chance of hitting the dove, I determined to shoot my bolt and make way for the next archer. Is there any chance at all, Margaret? Tell me, and put me out of pain, for I am not good at so much talking."

Now Margaret began to grow disturbed; her wayward assurance departed from her.

"It is not fitting," she murmured, "and I do not wish—I will speak to my father; he shall give you your answer."

"No need to trouble him, Margaret. He has given it already. His great desire is that we should marry, for he seeks to leave this trade and to live with us in the Vale of Dedham, in Essex, where he has bought back my father's land."

"You are full of strange tidings this morning, Peter."

"Yes, Margaret, our wheel of life that went so slow turns fast enough to-day, for God above has laid His whip upon the horses of our Fate, and they begin to gallop, whither I know not. Must they run side by side, or separate? It is for you to say."

"Peter," she said, "will you not give me a little time?"

H. Rider Haggard

"Aye, Margaret, ten whole minutes by the clock, and then if it is nay, all your life, for I pack my chest and go. It will be said that I feared to be taken for that soldier's death."

"You are unkind to press me so."

"Nay, it is kindest to both of us. Do you then love some other man?"

"I must confess I do," she murmured, looking at him out of the corners of her eyes.

Now Peter, strong as he was, turned faint, and in his agitation let go her hand which she lifted, the violets still between her fingers, considering it as though it were a new thing to her.

"I have no right to ask you who he is," he muttered, striving to control himself.

"Nay, but, Peter, I will tell you. It is my father—what other man should I love?"

"Margaret!" he said in wrath, "you are fooling me."

"How so? What other man should I love—unless, indeed, it were yourself?"

"I can bear no more of this play," he said. "Mistress Margaret, I bid you farewell. God go with you!" And he brushed past her.

"Peter," she said when he had gone a few yards, "would you have these violets as a farewell gift?"

He turned and hesitated.

"Come, then, and take them."

So back he came, and with little trembling fingers she began to fasten the flowers to his doublet, bending ever nearer as she fastened, until her breath played upon his face, and her hair brushed his bonnet. Then, it matters not how, once more the violets fell to earth, and she sighed, and her hands fell also, and he put his strong arms round her and drew her to him and kissed her again and yet again on the hair and eyes and lips; nor did Margaret forbid him.

At length she thrust him from her and, taking him by the hand, led him to the seat beneath the elms, and bade him sit at one end of it, while she sat at the other.

"Peter," she whispered, "I wish to speak with you when I can get my breath. Peter, you think poorly of me, do you not? No—be silent; it is my turn to talk. You think that I am heartless, and have been playing with you. Well, I only did it to make sure that you really do love me, since, after that—accident of a while ago (when we were picking up the violets, I mean), you would have been in honour bound to say it, would you not? Well, now I am quite sure, so I will tell you something. I love you many times as well as you love me, and have done so for quite as long. Otherwise, should I not have married some other suitor, of whom there have been plenty? Aye, and I will tell you this to my sin and shame, that once I grew so angry with you because you would not speak or give some little sign, that I went near to it. But at the last I could not, and sent him about his business also. Peter, when I saw you last night facing that swordsman with but a staff, and thought that you must die, oh! then I knew all the truth, and my heart was nigh to bursting, as, had you died, it would have burst. But now it is all done with, and we know each other's secret, and nothing shall ever part us more till death comes to one or both."

Thus Margaret spoke, while he drank in her words as desert sands, parched by years of drought, drink in the rain—and watched her face, out of which all mischief and mockery had departed, leaving it that of a most beauteous and most earnest woman, to whom a sense of the weight of life, with its mingled joys and sorrows, had come home suddenly. When she had finished, this silent man, to whom even his great happiness brought few words, said only:

"God has been very good to us. Let us thank God."

So they did, then, even there, seated side by side upon the bench, because the grass was too wet for them to kneel on, praying in their simple, childlike faith that the Power which had brought them together, and taught them to love each other, would bless them in that love and protect them from all harms, enemies, and evils through many a long year of life.

Their prayer finished, they sat together on the seat, now talking, and now silent in their joy, while all too fast the time wore on. At length—it was after one of these spells of blissful silence—a change came over them, such a change as falls upon some peaceful scene when, unexpected and complete, a black stormcloud sweeps across the sun, and, in place of its warm light, pours down gloom full of the promise of tempest and of rain. Apprehension got a hold of them. They were both afraid of what they could not guess.

"Come," she said, "it is time to go in. My father will miss us."

So without more words or endearments they rose and walked side by side out of the shelter of the elms into the open garden. Their heads were bent, for they were lost in thought, and thus it came about that Margaret saw her feet pass suddenly into the shadow of a man, and, looking up, perceived standing in front of her, grave, alert, amused, none other than the Senor d'Aguilar. She uttered a little stifled scream, while Peter, with the impulse that causes a brave and startled hound to rush at that which frightens it, gave a leap forward towards the Spaniard.

"Mother of God! do you take me for a thief?" he asked in a laughing voice, as he stepped to one side to avoid him.

"Your pardon," said Peter, shaking himself together; "but you surprised us appearing so suddenly where we never thought to see you."

"Any more than I thought to see you here, for this seems a strange place to linger on so cold a morning," and he looked at them again with his curious, mocking eyes that appeared to read the secret of their souls, while they grew red as roses beneath his scrutiny. "Permit me to explain," he went on. "I came here thus early on your service, to warn you, Master Peter, not to go abroad to-day, since a writ is out for your arrest, and as yet I have had no time to quash it by friendly settlement. Well, as it chanced, I met that handsome lady who was with you yesterday, returning from her marketing—a friendly soul—she says she is your cousin. She brought me to the house, and having learned that your father, whom I wished to see, was at his prayers, good man, in the old chapel, led me to its door and left me to seek him. I entered, but could not find him, so, having waited a while, strayed into this garden through the open door, purposing to walk here till some one should appear, and, you see, I have been fortunate beyond my expectations or deserts."

"So!" said Peter shortly, for the man's manner and elaborated explanations filled him with disgust. "Let us seek Master Castell that he may hear the story."

"And we thank you much for coming to warn us," murmured Margaret. "I will go find my father," and she slipped past him towards the door.

D'Aguilar watched her enter it, then turned to Peter and said:

"You English are a hardy folk who take the spring air so early. Well, in such company I would do the same. Truly she is a beauteous maiden. I have some experience of the sex, but never do I remember one so fair."

"My cousin is well enough," answered Peter coldly, for this

Spaniard's very evident admiration of Margaret did not please him.

"Yes," answered d'Aguilar, taking no notice of his tone, "she is well enough to fill the place, not of a merchant's daughter, but of a great lady—a countess reigning over towns and lands, or a queen even; the royal robes and ornaments would become that carriage and that brow."

"My cousin seeks no such state who is happy in her quiet lot," answered Peter again; then added quickly, "See, here comes Master Castell seeking you."

D'Aguilar advanced and greeted the merchant courteously, noticing as he did so that, notwithstanding his efforts to appear unconcerned, Castell seemed ill at ease.

"I am an early visitor," he said, "but I knew that you business folk rise with the lark, and I wished to catch our friend here before he went out," and he repeated to him the reason of his coming.

"I thank you, Senor," answered Castell. "You are very good to me and mine. I am sorry that you have been kept waiting. They tell me that you looked for me in the chapel, but I was not there, who had already left it for my office."

"So I found. It is a quaint place, that old chapel of yours, and while I waited I went to the altar and told my beads there, which I had no time to do before I left my lodgings."

Castell started almost imperceptibly, and glanced at d'Aguilar with his quick eyes, then turned the subject and asked if he would not breakfast with them. He declined, however, saying that he must be about their business and his own, then promptly proposed that he should come to supper on the following night that was—Sunday—and make report how things had gone, a suggestion that Castell could not but accept.

So he bowed and smiled himself out of the house, and walked thoughtfully into Holborn, for it had pleased him to pay this visit on foot, and unattended. At the corner whom should he meet again but the tall, fair-haired Betty, returning from some errand which she had found it convenient to fulfil just then.

"What," he said, "you once more! The saints are very kind to me this morning. Come, Senora, walk a little way with me, for I would ask you a few questions."

Betty hesitated, then gave way. It was seldom that she found the chance of walking through Holborn with such a noble-looking cavalier.

"Never look at your working-dress," he said.

"With such a shape, what matters the robe that covers it?"—a compliment at which Betty blushed, for she was proud of her fine figure.

"Would you like a mantilla of real Spanish lace for your head and shoulders? Well, you shall have one that I brought from Spain with me, for I know no other lady in the land whom it would become better. But, Mistress Betty, you told me wrong about your master. I went to the chapel and he was not there."

"He was there, Senor," she answered, eager to set herself right with this most agreeable and discriminating foreigner, "for I saw him go in a moment before, and he did not come out again."

"Then, Senora, where could he have hidden himself? Has the place a crypt?"

"None that I have heard of; but," she added, "there is a kind of little room behind the altar."

"Indeed. How do you know that? I saw no room."

"Because one day I heard a voice behind the tapestry, Senor, and, lifting it, saw a sliding door left open, and Master Castell kneeling before a table and saying his prayers aloud."

"How strange! And what was there on the table?"

"Only a queer-shaped box of wood like a little house, and two candlesticks, and some rolls of parchment. But I forgot, Senor; I promised Master Castell to say nothing about that place, for he turned and saw me, and came at me like a watchdog out of its kennel. You won't say that I told you, will you, Senor?"

"Not I; your good master's private cupboard does not interest me. Now I want to know something more. Why is that beautiful cousin of yours not married? Has she no suitors?"

"Suitors, Senor? Yes, plenty of them, but she sends them all about their business, and seems to have no mind that way."

"Perhaps she is in love with her cousin, that long-legged, strong-armed, wooden-headed Master Brome."

"Oh! no, Senor, I don't think so; no lady could be in love with him—he is too stern and silent."

"I agree with you, Senora. Then perhaps he is in love with her."

Betty shook her head, and replied:

"Peter Brome doesn't think anything of women, Senor. At least he never speaks to or of them."

"Which shows that probably he thinks about them all the more. Well, well, it is no affair of ours, is it? Only I am glad to hear that there is nothing between them, since your mistress ought to marry high, and be a great lady, not a mere merchant's wife."

"Yes, Senor. Though Peter Brome is not a merchant, at least by birth, he is high-born, and should be Sir Peter Brome if his father had not fought on the wrong side and sold his land. He is a soldier, and a very brave one, they say, as all might see last night."

"No doubt, and perhaps would make a great captain, if he had the chance, with his stern face and silent tongue. But, Senora Betty, say, how comes it that, being so handsome," and he bowed, "you are not married either? I am sure it can be from no lack of suitors."

Again Betty, foolish girl, flushed with pleasure at the compliment.

"You are right, Senor," she answered. "I have plenty of them; but I am like my cousin—they do not please me. Although my father lost his fortune, I come of good blood, and I suppose that is why I do not care for these low-born men, and would rather remain as I am than marry one of them."

"You are quite right," said d'Aguilar in his sympathetic voice. "Do not stain your blood. Marry in your own class, or not at all, which, indeed, should not be difficult for one so beautiful and charming." And he looked into her large eyes with tender admiration.

This quality, indeed, soon began to demonstrate itself so actively, for they were now in the fields where few people wandered, that Betty, who although vain was proud and upright, thought it wise to recollect that she must be turning homewards. So, in spite of his protests, she left him and departed, walking upon air.

How splendid and handsome this foreign gentleman was, she thought to herself, really a great cavalier, and surely he admired her truly. Why should he not? Such things had often been. Many a rich lady whom she knew was not half so handsome or so well born as herself, and would make him a worse wife—that is, and the thought chilled her somewhat—if he were not already married.

From all of which it will be seen that d'Aguilar had quickly succeeded in the plan which only presented itself to him a few hours before. Betty was already half in love with him. Not that he had any desire to possess this beautiful but foolish woman's heart, who saw in her only a useful tool, a stepping-stone by means of which he might draw near to Margaret.

For with Margaret, it may be said at once, he was quite in love. At the sight of her sweet yet imperial beauty, as he saw her first, dishevelled, angry, frightened, in the crowd outside the king's banqueting-hall, his southern blood had taken sudden fire. Finished voluptuary though he was, the sensation he experienced then was quite new to him. He longed for this woman as he had never longed for any other, and, what is more, he desired to make her his wife. Why not? Although there was a flaw in it, his rank was high, and therefore she was beneath him; but for this her loveliness would atone, and she had wit and learning enough to fill any place that he could give her. Also, great as was his wealth, his wanton, spendthrift way of life had brought him many debts, and she was the only child of one of the richest merchants in England, whose dower, doubtless, would be a fortune that many a royal princess might envy. Why not again? He would turn Inez and those others adrift—at any rate, for a while—and make her mistress of his palace there in Granada. Instantly, as is often the fashion of those who have Eastern blood in their veins, d'Aguilar had made up his mind, yes, before he left her father's table on the previous night. He would marry Margaret and no other woman.

Yet at once he had seen many difficulties in his path. To begin with, he mistrusted him of Peter, that strong, quiet man who could kill a great armed knave with his stick, and at a word call half London to his side. Peter, he was sure, being human, must be in love with Margaret, and he was a rival to be feared. Well, if Margaret had no thoughts of Peter, this mattered nothing, and if she had—and what were they doing together in the garden that morning?—Peter must be got rid of, that was all. It was easy enough if he chose to adopt certain means; there were many of those Spanish fellows who would not mind sticking a knife into his back in the dark.

But sinful as he was, at such steps his conscience halted. Whatever d'Aguilar had done, he had never caused a man to be actually murdered, he who was a bigot, who atoned for his misdoings by periods of remorse and prayer, in which he placed his purse and talents at the service of the Church, as he was doing at this moment. No, murder must not be thought of; for how could any absolution wash him clean of that stain? But there were other ways. For instance, had not this Peter, in self-defence it is true, killed one of the servants of an ambassador of Spain? Perhaps, however, it would not be necessary to make use of them. It had seemed to him that the lady was not ill pleased with him, and, after all, he had much to offer. He would court her fairly, and if he were rejected by her, or by her father, then it would be time enough to act. Meanwhile, he would keep the sword hanging over the head of Peter, pretending that it was he alone who had prevented it from falling, and learn all that he could as to Castell and his history.

Here, indeed, Fortune, in the shape of the foolish Betty, had favoured him. Without a doubt, as he had heard in Spain, and been sure from the moment that he first saw him, Castell was still secretly a Jew. Mistress Betty's story of the room behind the altar, with the ark and the candles and the rolls of the Law, proved as much. At least here was evidence enough to send him to the fires of the Inquisition in Spain, and, perhaps, to drive him out of England. Now, if John Castell, the Spanish Jew, should not wish, for any reason, to give him his daughter in marriage, would not a hint and an extract from the Commissions of their Majesties of Spain and the Holy Father suffice to make him change his mind?

Thus pondering, d'Aguilar regained his lodgings, where his

first task was to enter in a book all that Betty had told him, and all that he had observed in the house of John Castell.

CHAPTER V

CASTELL'S SECRET

In John Castell's house it was the habit, as in most others in those days, for his dependents, clerks, and shopmen to eat their morning and mid-day meals with him in the hall, seated at two lower tables, all of them save Betty, his daughter's cousin and companion, who sat with them at the upper board. This morning Betty's place was empty, and presently Castell, lifting his eyes, for he was lost in thought, noted it, and asked where she might be—a question that neither Margaret nor Peter could answer.

One of the servants at the lower table, however—it was that man who had been sent to follow d'Aguilar on the previous night—said that as he came down Holborn a while before he had seen her walking with the Spanish don, a saying at which his master looked grave.

Just as they were finishing their meal, a very silent one, for none of them seemed to have anything to say, and after the servants had left the hall, Betty arrived, flushed as though with running.

"Where have you been that you are so late?" asked Castell.

"To seek the linen for the new sheets, but it was not ready," she answered glibly. "The mercer kept you waiting long," remarked Castell quietly. "Did you meet any one?"

"Only the folk in the street."

"I will ask you no more questions, lest I should cause you to lie and bring you into sin," said Castell sternly. "Girl, how far did you walk with the Senor d'Aguilar, and what was your business with him?"

Now Betty knew that she had been seen, and that it was useless to deny the truth.

"Only a little way," she answered, "and that because he prayed me to show him his path."

"Listen, Betty," went on Castell, taking no notice of her words. "You are old enough to guard yourself, therefore as to your walking abroad with gallants who can mean you no good I say nothing. But know this—no one who has knowledge of the matters of my house," and he looked at her keenly, "shall mix with any Spaniard. If you are found alone with this senor any more, that hour I have done with you, and you never pass my door again. Nay, no words. Take your food and eat it elsewhere."

So she departed half weeping, but very angry, for Betty was strong and obstinate by nature. When she had gone, Margaret, who was fond of her cousin, tried to say some words on her behalf; but her father stopped her.

"Pshaw!" he said, "I know the girl; she is vain as a peacock, and, remembering her gentle birth and good looks, seeks to marry above her station; while for some purpose of his own— an ill one, I'll warrant—that Spaniard plays upon her weakness, which, if it be not curbed, may bring trouble on us all. Now, enough of Betty Dene; I must to my work."

"Sir," said Peter, speaking for the first time, "we would have a private word with you."

"A private word," he said, looking up anxiously. "Well, speak on. No, this place is not private; I think its walls have ears. Follow me," and he led the way into the old chapel, whereof, when they had all passed it, he bolted the door. "Now," he said, "what is it?"

"Sir," answered Peter, standing before him, "having your leave at last, I asked your daughter in marriage this morning."

"At least you lose no time, friend Peter; unless you had called her from her bed and made your offer through the door you could not have done it quicker. Well, well, you ever were a man of deeds, not words, and what says my Margaret?"

"An hour ago she said she was content," answered Peter.

"A cautious man also," went on Castell with a twinkle in his eye, "who remembers that women have been known to change their minds within an hour. After such long thought, what say you now, Margaret?"

"That I am angry with Peter," she answered, stamping her small foot, "for if he does not trust me for an hour, how can he trust me for his life and mine?"

"Nay, Margaret, you do not understand me," said Peter. "I wished not to bind you, that is all, in case—"

"Now you are saying it again," she broke in vexed, and yet amused. "Do so a third time, and I will you at your word."

"It seems best that I should remain silent. Speak you," said Peter humbly.

"Aye, for truly you are a master of silence, as I should know, if any do," replied Margaret, bethinking her of the weary months and years of waiting. "Well, I will answer for you.—Father, Peter was right; I am content to marry him, though to do so will be to enter the Order of the Silent Brothers. Yes, I am content; not for himself, indeed, who has so many faults, but

H. Rider Haggard

for myself, who chance to love him," and she smiled sweetly enough.

"Do not jest on such matters, Margaret."

"Why not, father? Peter is solemn enough for both of us—look at him. Let us laugh while we may, for who knows when tears may come?"

"A good saying," answered Castell with a sigh. "So you two have plighted your troth, and, my children, I am glad of it, for who knows when those tears of which Margaret spoke may come, and then you can wipe away each other's? Take now her hand, Peter, and swear by the Rood, that symbol which you worship"—here Peter glanced at him, but he went on—"swear, both of you that come what may, together or separate, through good report or evil report, through poverty or wealth, through peace or persecutions, through temptation or through blood, through every good or ill that can befall you in this world of bittersweet, you will remain faithful to your troth until you be wed, and after you are wed, faithful to each other till death do part you."

These words he spoke to them in a voice that was earnest almost to passion, searching their faces the while with his quick eyes as though he would read their very hearts. His mood crept from him to them; once again they felt something of that fear which had fallen on them in the garden when they passed into the shadow of the Spaniard. Very solemnly then, and with little of true lovers' joy, did they take each other's hands and swear by the Cross and Him Who hung on it, that through these things, and all others they could not foretell, they would, if need were, be faithful to the death.

"And beyond it also," added Peter; while Margaret bowed her stately head in sweet assent.

"Children," said Castell, "you will be rich—few richer in this land—though mayhap it would be wise that you should not show all your wealth at once, or ape the place of a great house, lest envy should fall upon your heads and crush you. Be content to wait, and rank will find you in its season, or if not you, your children. Peter, I tell you now, lest I should forget it, that the list of all my moneys and other possessions in chattels or lands or ships or merchandise is buried beneath the floor of my office, just under where my chair stands. Lift the boards and dig away a foot of rubbish, and you will find a stone trap, and below an iron box with the deeds, inventories, and some very precious jewels. Also, if by any mischance that box should be lost, duplicates of nearly all these papers are in the hands of my good friend and partner in our inland British trade, Simon Levett, whom you know. Remember my words, both of you."

"Father," broke in Margaret in an anxious voice, "why do you speak of the future thus?—I mean, as though you had no share in it? Do you fear aught?"

"Yes, daughter, much, or rather I expect, I do not fear, who am prepared and desire to meet all things as they come. You have sworn that oath, have you not? And you will keep it, will you not?"

"Aye!" they answered with one breath.

"Then prepare you to feel the weight of the first of those trials whereof it speaks, for I will no longer hold back the truth from you. Children, I, whom for all these years you have thought of your own faith, am a Jew as my forefathers were before me, back to the days of Abraham."

The effect of this declaration upon its hearers was remarkable. Peter's jaw dropped, and for the second time that day his face went white; while Margaret sank down into a chair that stood near by, and stared at him helplessly. In those times it was a very terrible thing to be a Jew. Castell looked from one to the other, and, feeling the insult of their silence, grew angry.

"What!" he exclaimed in a bitter voice, "are you like all the others? Do you scorn me also because I am of a race more ancient and honourable than those of any of your mushroom lords and kings? You know my life: say, what have I done wrong? Have I caught Christian children and crucified them to death? Have I defrauded my neighbour or oppressed the poor? Have I mocked your symbol of the Host? Have I conspired against the rulers of this land? Have I been a false friend or a cruel father? You shake your heads; then why do you stare at me as though I were a thing accursed and unclean? Have I not a right to the faith of my fathers? May I not worship God in my own fashion?" And he looked at Peter, a challenge in his eyes. "Sir," answered Peter, "without a doubt you may, or so it seems to me. But then, why for all these years have you appeared to worship Him in ours?"

At this blunt question, so characteristic of the speaker, Castell seemed to shrink like a pin-pricked bladder, or some bold fighter who has suddenly received a sword-thrust in his vitals. All courage went out of the man, his fiery eyes grew tame, he appeared to become visibly smaller, and to put on something of the air of those mendicants of his own race, who whine out their woes and beg alms of the passer-by. When next he spoke, it was as a suppliant for merciful judgment at the hands of his own child and her lover.

"Judge me not harshly," he said. "Think what it is to be a Jew—an outcast, a thing that the lowest may spurn and spit at, one beyond the law, one who can be hunted from land to land like a mad wolf, and tortured to death, when caught, for the sport of gentle Christians, who first have stripped him of his gains and very garments. And then think what it means to escape all these woes and terrors, and, by the doffing of a bonnet, and the mumbling of certain prayers with the lips in public, to find sanctuary, peace, and protection within the walls of Mother Church, and thus fostered, to grow rich and great."

He paused as though for a reply, but as they did not speak, went on:

"Moreover, as a child, I was baptized into your Church; but my heart, like that of my father, remained with the Jews, and where the heart goes the feet follow."

"That makes it worse," said Peter, as though speaking to himself.

"My father taught me thus," Castell went on, as though pleading his case before a court of law.

"We must answer for our own sins," said Peter again.

Then at length Castell took fire.

"You young folk, who as yet know little of the terrors of the world, reproach me with cold looks and colder words," he said; "but I wonder, should you ever come to such a pass as mine, whether you will find the heart to meet it half as bravely? Why do you think that I have told you this secret, that I might have kept from you as I kept it from your mother, Margaret? I say because it is a part of my penance for the sin which I have sinned. Aye, I know well that my God is a jealous God, and that this sin will fall back on my head, and that I shall pay its price to the last groat, though when and how the blow will strike me I know not. Go you, Peter, or you, Margaret, and denounce me if you will. Your priests will speak well of you for the deed, and open to you a shorter road to Heaven, and I shall not blame you, nor lessen your wealth by a single golden noble."

"Do not speak so madly, Sir," said Peter; "these matters are between you and God. What have we to do with them, and who made us judges over you? We only pray that your fears may come to nothing, and that you may reach your grave in peace and honour."

"I thank you for your generous words, which are such as befit your nature," said Castell gently; "but what says Margaret?"

"I, father?" she answered, wildly. "Oh! I have nothing to say. He is right. It is between you and God; but it is hard that I must lose my love so soon." Peter looked up, and Castell answered:

"Lose him! Why, what did he swear but now?"

"I care not what he swore; but how can I ask him, who is of noble, Christian birth, to marry the daughter of a Jew who all his life has passed himself off as a worshipper of that Jesus Whom he denies?"

Now Peter held up his hand.

"Have done with such talk," he said. "Were your father Judas himself, what is that to you and me? You are mine and I am yours till death part us, nor shall the faith of another man stand between us for an hour. Sir, we thank you for your confidence, and of this be sure, that although it makes us sorrowful, we do not love or honour you the less because now we know the truth."

Margaret rose from her chair, looked a while at her father, then with a sob threw herself suddenly upon his breast.

"Forgive me if I spoke bitterly," she said, "who, not knowing that I was half a Jewess, have been taught to hate their race. What is it to me of what faith you are, who think of you only as my dearest father?"

"Why weep then?" asked Castell, stroking her hair tenderly.

"Because you are in danger, or so you say, and if anything happened to you—oh! what shall I do then?"

"Accept it as the will of God, and bear the blow bravely, as I hope to do, should it fall," he answered, and, kissing her, left the chapel.

"It seems that joy and trouble go hand in hand," said Margaret, looking up presently.

"Yes, Sweet, they were ever twins; but provided we have our share of the first, do not let us quarrel with the second. A pest on the priests and all their bigotry, say I! Christ sought to convert the Jews, not to kill them; and for my part I can honour the man who clings to his own faith, aye, and forgive him because they forced him to feign to belong to ours. Pray then that neither of us may live to commit a greater sin, and that we may soon be wed and dwell in peace away from London, where we can shelter him."

"I do—I do," she answered, drawing close to Peter, and soon they forgot their fears and doubts in each other's arms.

On the following morning, that of Sunday, Peter, Margaret, and Betty went together to Mass at St. Paul's church; but Castell said that he was ill, and did not come. Indeed, now that his conscience was stirred as to the double life he had led so long, he purposed, if he could avoid it, to worship in a Christian church no more. Therefore he said that he was sick; and they, knowing that this sickness was of the heart, answered nothing. But privately they wondered what he would do who could not always remain sick, since not to go to church and partake of its Sacraments was to be published as a heretic.

But if he did not accompany them himself, Castell, without their knowledge, sent two of his stoutest servants, bidding these keep near to them and see that they came home safe.

Now, when they left the church, Peter saw two Spaniards, whose faces he thought he knew, who seemed to be watching them, but, as he lost sight of them presently in the throng, said nothing. Their shortest way home ran across some fields and gardens where there were few houses. This lane, then, they followed, talking earnestly to each other, and noting nothing till Betty behind called out to them to beware. Then Peter looked up and saw the two Spaniards scrambling through a gap in the fence not six paces ahead of them, saw also that they laid their hands upon their sword-hilts.

"Let us pass them boldly," he muttered to Margaret; "I'll not turn my back on a brace of Spaniards," but he also laid his hand upon the hilt of the sword he wore beneath his cloak, and bade her get behind him.

Thus, then, they came face to face. Now, the Spaniards, who were evil-looking fellows, bowed courteously enough, and asked if he were not Master Peter Brome. They spoke in Spanish; but, like Margaret Peter knew this tongue, if not too well, having been taught it as a child, and practised it much since he came into the service of John Castell, who used it largely in his trade.

"Yes," he answered. "What is your business with me?"

"We have a message for you, Senor, from a certain comrade of ours, one Andrew, a Scotchman, whom you met a few nights ago," replied the spokesman of the pair. "He is dead, but still he sends his message, and it is that we should ask you to join him at once. Now, all of us brothers have sworn to deliver that message, and to see that you keep the tryst. If some of us should chance to fail, then others will meet you with the message until you keep that tryst."

"You mean that you wish to murder me," said Peter, setting his mouth and drawing the sword from beneath his cloak. "Well, come on, cowards, and we will see whom Andrew gets for company in hell to-day. Run back, Margaret and Betty— run." And he tore off his cloak and threw it over his left arm.

So for a moment they stood, for he looked fierce and ill to deal with. Then, just as they began to feint in front of him, there came a rush of feet, and on either side of Peter appeared the two stout serving-men, also sword in hand.

"I am glad of your company," he said, catching sight of them out of the corners of his eyes. "Now, Senors Cut-throats, do you still wish to deliver that message?"

The answer of the Spaniards, who saw themselves thus unexpectedly out-matched, was to turn and run, whereon one of the serving-men, picking up a big stone that lay in the path, hurled it after them with all his force. It struck the hindmost Spaniard full in the back, and so heavy was the blow that he fell on to his face in the mud, whence he rose and limped away, cursing them with strange, Spanish oaths, and vowing vengeance.

"Now," said Peter, "I think that we may go home in safety, for no more messengers will come from Andrew to-day."

"No," gasped Margaret, "not to-day, but to-morrow or the next day they will come, and oh! how will it end?"

"That God knows alone," answered Peter gravely as he sheathed his sword.

When the story of this attempt was told to Castell he seemed much disturbed.

"It is clear that they have a blood-feud against you on account of that Scotchman whom you killed in self-defence," he said anxiously. "Also these Spaniards are very revengeful, nor have they forgiven you for calling the English to your aid against them. Peter, I fear that if you go abroad they will murder you."

"Well, I cannot stay indoors always, like a rat in a drain," said Peter crossly, "so what is to be done? Appeal to the law?"

"No; for you have just broken the law by killing a man. I think you had best go away for a while till this storm blows over."

"Go away! Peter go away?" broke in Margaret, dismayed.

"Yes," answered her father. "Listen, daughter. You cannot be married at once. It is not seemly; moreover, notice must be given and arrangement made. A month hence will be soon enough, and that is not long for you to wait who only became affianced yesterday. Also, until you are wed, no word must be said to any one of this betrothal of yours, lest those Spaniards should lay their feud at your door also, and work you some mischief. Let none know of it, I charge you, and in company be distant to each other, as though there were nothing between you."

"As you will, Sir," replied Peter; "but for my part I do not like all these hidings of the truth, which ever lead to future trouble. I say, let me bide here and take my chance, and let us be wed as soon as may be."

"That your wife may be made a widow before the week is out, or the house burnt about our ears by these rascals and their following? No, no, Peter; walk softly that you may walk safely. We will hear the report of the Spaniard d'Aguilar, and afterwards take counsel."

CHAPTER VI

FAREWELL

D'Aguilar came to supper that night as he had promised, and this time not on foot and unattended, but with pomp and circumstance as befitted a great lord. First appeared two running footmen to clear the way; then followed D'Aguilar, mounted on a fine white horse, and splendidly apparelled in a velvet cloak and a hat with nodding ostrich plumes, while after him rode four men-at-arms in his livery.

"We asked one guest, or rather he asked himself, and we have got seven, to say nothing of their horses," grumbled Castell, watching their approach from an upper window. "Well, we must make the best of it. Peter, go, see that man and beast are fed, and fully, that they may not grumble at our hospitality. The guard can eat in the little hall with our own folk. Margaret, put on your richest robe and your jewels, those which you wore when I took you to that city feast last summer. We will show these fine, foreign birds that we London merchants have brave feathers also."

Peter hesitated, misdoubting him of the wisdom of this display, who, if he could have his will, would have sent the Spaniard's following to the tavern, and received him in sober garments to a simple meal.

But Castell, who seemed somewhat disturbed that night, who loved, moreover, to show his wealth at times after the fashion

H. Rider Haggard

of a Jew, began to fume and ask if he must go himself. So the end of it was that Peter went, shaking his head, while, urged to it by her father, Margaret departed also to array herself.

A few minutes later Castell, in his costliest feast-day robe, greeted d'Aguilar in the ante-hall, and, the two of them being alone, asked him how matters went as regarded de Ayala and the man who had been killed.

"Well and ill," answered d'Aguilar. "Doctor de Puebla, with whom I hoped to deal, has left London in a huff, for he says that there is not room for two Spanish ambassadors at Court, so I had to fall back upon de Ayala after all. Indeed, twice have I seen that exalted priest upon the subject of the well-deserved death of his villainous servant, and, after much difficulty, for having lost several men in such brawls, he thought his honour touched, he took the fifty gold angels—to be transmitted to the fellow's family, of course, or so he said—and gave a receipt. Here it is," and he handed a paper to Castell, who read it carefully.

It was to the effect that Peter Brome, having paid a sum of fifty angels to the relatives of Andrew Pherson, a servant of the Spanish ambassador, which Andrew the said Peter had killed in a brawl, the said ambassador undertook not to prosecute or otherwise molest the said Peter on account of the manslaughter which he had committed.

"But no money has been paid," said Castell.

"Indeed yes, I paid it. De Ayala gives no receipts against promises."

"I thank you for your courtesy, Senor. You shall have the gold before you leave this house. Few would have trusted a stranger thus far."

D'Aguilar waved his hand.

"Make no mention of such a trifle. I would ask you to accept it as a token of my regard for your family, only that would be to affront so wealthy a man. But listen, I have more to say. You are, or rather your kinsman Peter, is still in the wood. De Ayala has pardoned him; but there remains the King of England, whose law he has broken. Well, this day I have seen the King, who, by the way, talked of you as a worthy man, saying that he had always thought only a Jew could be so wealthy, and that he knew you were not, since you had been reported to him as a good son of the Church," and he paused, looking at Castell.

"I fear his Grace magnifies my wealth, which is but small," answered Castell coolly, leaving the rest of his speech unnoticed. "But what said his Grace?"

"I showed him de Ayala's receipt, and he answered that if his Excellency was satisfied, he was satisfied, and for his part would not order any process to issue; but he bade me tell you and Peter Brome that if he caused more tumult in his streets, whatever the provocation, and especially if that tumult were between English and Spaniards, he would hang him at once with trial or without it. All of which he said very angrily, for the last thing which his Highness desires just now is any noise between Spain and England."

"That is bad," answered Castell, "for this very morning there was near to being such a tumult," and he told the story of how the two Spaniards had waylaid Peter, and one of them been knocked down by the serving-man with a stone. At this news d'Aguilar shook his head.

"Then that is just where the trouble lies," he exclaimed. "I know it from my people, who keep me well informed, that all those servants of de Ayala, and there are more than twenty of them, have sworn an oath by the Virgin of Seville that before they leave this land they will have your kinsman's blood in payment for that of Andrew Pherson, who, although a Scotchman, was their officer, and a brave man whom they loved much. Now, if they attack him, as they will, there must be a brawl, for Peter fights well, and if there is a brawl, though Peter and the English get the best of it, as very likely they may, Peter will certainly be hanged, for so the King has promised."

"Before they leave the land? When do they leave it?"

"De Ayala sails within a month, and his folk with him, for his co-ambassador, the Doctor de Puebla, will bear with him no more, and has written from the country house where he is sulking that one of them must go."

"Then I think it is best, Senor, that Peter should travel for a month."

"Friend Castell, you are wise; I think so too, and, I counsel you, arrange it at once. Hush! here comes the lady, your daughter."

As he spoke, Margaret appeared descending the broad oak stairs which led into the ante-room. Holding a lamp in her hand, she was in full light, whereas the two men stood in the shadow. She wore a low-cut dress of crimson velvet, embroidered about the bodice with dead gold, which enhanced the dazzling whiteness of her shapely neck and bosom. Round her throat hung a string of great pearls, and on her head was a net of gold, studded with smaller pearls, from beneath which her glorious, chestnut-black hair flowed down in rippling waves almost to her knees. Having her father's bidding so to do, she had adorned herself thus that she might look her fairest, not in the eyes of their guest, but in those of her new-affianced husband. So fair was she seen thus that d'Aguilar, the artist, the adorer of loveliness, caught his breath and shivered at the sight of her.

"By the eleven thousand virgins!" he said, "your daughter is more beautiful than all of them put together. She should be crowned a queen, and bewitch the world."

"Nay, nay, Senor," answered Castell hurriedly; "let her remain humble and honest, and bewitch her husband."

"So I should say if I were the husband," he muttered, then stepped forward, bowing, to meet her.

Now the light of the silver lamp she held on high flowed over the two of them, d'Aguilar and Margaret, and certainly they seemed a well-matched pair. Both were tall and cast by Nature in a rich and splendid mould; both had that high air of breeding which comes with ancient blood—for what bloods are more ancient than those of the Jew and the Eastern?—both were slow and stately of movement, low-voiced, and dignified of speech. Castell noted it and was afraid, he knew not of what.

Peter, entering the room by another door, clad only in his grey clothes, for he would not put on gay garments for the Spaniard, noted it also, and with the quick instinct of love knew this magnificent foreigner for a rival and an enemy. But he was not afraid, only jealous and angry. Indeed, nothing would have pleased him better then than that the Spaniard should have struck him in the face, so that within five minutes it might be shown which of them was the better man. It must come to this, he felt, and very glad would he have been if it could come at the beginning and not at the end, so that one or the other of them might be saved much trouble. Then he remembered that he had promised to say or show nothing of how things stood between him and Margaret, and, coming forward, he greeted d'Aguilar quietly but coldly, telling him that his horses had been stabled, and his retinue accommodated.

The Spaniard thanked him very heartily, and they passed in to supper. It was a strange meal for all four of them, yet outwardly pleasant enough. Forgetting his cares, Castell drank gaily, and began to talk of the many changes which he had seen in his life, and of the rise and fall of kings. D'Aguilar talked also, of the Spanish wars and policy, for in the first he

H. Rider Haggard

had seen much service, and of the other he knew every turn. It was easy to see that he was one of those who mixed with courts, and had the ear of ministers and majesty. Margaret also, being keen-witted and anxious to learn of the great world that lay beyond Holborn and London town, asked questions, seeking to know, amongst other things, what were the true characters of Ferdinand, King of Aragon, and Isabella his wife, the famous queen.

"I will tell you in few words, Senora. Ferdinand is the most ambitious man in Europe, false also if it serves his purpose. He lives for self and gain—that money and power. These are his gods, for he has no true religion. He is not clever but, being very cunning, he will succeed and leave a famous name behind him."

"An ugly picture," said Margaret. "And what of his queen?"

"She," answered d'Aguilar, "is a great woman, who knows how to use the temper of her time and so attain her ends. To the world she shows a tender heart, but beneath it lies hid an iron resolution."

"What are those ends?" asked Margaret again.

"To bring all Spain under her rule; utterly to crush the Moors and take their territories; to make the Church of Christ triumphant upon earth; to stamp out heresy; to convert or destroy the Jews," he added slowly, and as he spoke the words, Peter, watching, saw his eyes open and glitter like a snake's— "to bring their bodies to the purifying flames, and their vast wealth into her treasury, and thus earn the praise of the faithful upon earth, and for herself a throne in heaven."

For a while there was silence after this speech, then Margaret said boldly:

"If heavenly thrones are built of human blood and tears, what stone and mortar do they use in hell, I wonder?" Then, without pausing for an answer, she rose, saying that she was weary, curtseyed to d'Aguilar, her father and Peter, each in turn, and left the hall.

When she had gone the talk flagged, and presently d'Aguilar asked for his men and horses and departed also, saying as he went:

"Friend Castell, you will repeat my news to your good kinsman here. I pray for all your sakes that he may bow his head to what cannot be helped, and thus keep it safe upon his shoulders."

"What meant the man?" asked Peter, when the sound of the horses' hoofs had died away.

Castell told him of what had passed between him and d'Aguilar before supper, and showed him de Ayala's receipt, adding in a vexed voice:

"I have forgotten to repay him the gold; it shall be sent tomorrow."

"Have no fear; he will come for it," answered Peter coldly. "Now, if I have my way, I will take the risk of these Spaniards' swords and King Henry's rope, and bide here."

"That you must not do," said Castell earnestly, "for my sake and Margaret's, if not for yours. Would you make her a widow before she is a wife? Listen: it is my wish that you travel down to Essex to take delivery of your father's land in the Vale of Dedham and see to the repairing of the mansion house, which, I am told, needs it much. Then, when these Spaniards are gone, you can return and at once be married, say one short month hence."

"Will not you and Margaret come with me to Dedham?"

Castell shook his head.

"It is not possible. I must wind up my affairs, and Margaret cannot go with you alone. Moreover, there is no place for her to lodge. I will keep her here till you return."

"Yes, Sir; but will you keep her safe? The cozening words of Spaniards are sometimes more deadly than their swords."

"I think that Margaret has a medicine against all such arts," answered her father with a little smile, and left him.

On the morrow when Castell told Margaret that her lover must leave her for a while that night—for this Peter would not do himself—she prayed him even with tears that he would not send him so far from her, or that they might all go together. But he reasoned with her kindly, showing her that the latter was impossible, and that if Peter did not go at once it was probable that Peter would soon be dead, whereas, if he went, there would be but one short month of waiting till the Spaniards had sailed, after which they might be married and live in peace and safety.

So she came to see that this was best and wisest, and gave way; but oh! heavy were those hours, and sore was their parting. Essex was no far journey, and to enter into lands which only two days before Peter believed he had lost for ever, no sad errand, while the promise that at the end of a single month he should return to claim his bride hung before them like a star. Yet they were sad-hearted, both of them, and that star seemed very far away.

Margaret was afraid lest Peter might be waylaid upon the road, but he laughed at her, saying that her father was sending six stout men with him as an escort, and thus companioned he feared no Spaniards. Peter, for his part, was afraid lest d'Aguilar might make love to her while he was away. But now she laughed at him, saying that all her heart was his, and that she had none to give to d'Aguilar or any other man. Moreover, that England was a free land in which women, who were no king's wards, could not be led whither they did not wish to go.

So it seemed that they had naught to fear, save the daily chance of life and death. And yet they were afraid.

"Dear love," said Margaret to him after she had thought a while, "our road looks straight and easy, and yet there may be pitfalls in it that we cannot guess. Therefore you must swear one thing to me: That whatever you shall hear or whatever may happen, you will never doubt me as I shall never doubt you. If, for instance, you should be told that I have discarded you, and given myself to some other husband; if even you should believe that you see it signed by my hand, or if you think that you hear it told to you by my voice—still, I say, believe it not."

"How could such a thing be?" asked Peter anxiously.

"I do not suppose that it could be; I only paint the worst that might happen as a lesson for us both. Heretofore my life has been calm as a summer's day; but who knows when winter storms may rise, and often I have thought that I was born to know wind and rain and lightning as well as peace and sunshine. Remember that my father is a Jew, and that to the Jews and their children terrible things chance at times. Why, all this wealth might vanish in an hour, and you might find me in a prison, or clad in rags begging my bread. Now do you swear?" and she held towards him the gold crucifix that hung upon her bosom.

"Aye," he said, "I swear it by this holy token and by your lips," and he kissed first the cross and then her mouth, adding, "Shall I ask the same oath of you?"

She laughed.

"If you will; but it is not needful. Peter, I think that I know you too well; I think that your heart will never stir even if I be dead and you married to another. And yet men are men, and women have wiles, so I will swear this: That should you slip, perchance, and I live to learn it, I will try not to judge you harshly." And again she laughed, she who was so certain of her empire over this man's heart and body.

"Thank you," said Peter; "but for my part I will try to stand straight upon my feet, so should any tales be brought to you of me, sift them well, I pray you."

Then, forgetting their doubts and dreads, they talked of their marriage, which they fixed for that day month, and of how they would dwell happily in Dedham Vale. Also Margaret, who well knew the house, named the Old Hall, where they should live, for she had stayed there as a child, gave him many commands as to the new arrangement of its chambers and its furnishing, which, as there was money and to spare, could be as costly as they willed, saying that she would send him down all things by wain so soon as he was ready for them.

Thus, then, the hours wore away, until at length night came and they took their last meal together, the three of them, for it was arranged that Peter should start at moonrise, when none were about to see him go. It was not a very happy meal, and, though they made a brave show of eating, but little food passed their lips. Now the horses were ready, and Margaret buckled on Peter's sword and threw his cloak about his shoulders, and he, having shaken Castell by the hand and bade him guard their jewel safely, without more words kissed her in farewell, and went.

Taking the silver lamp in her hand, she followed him to the ante-room. At the door he turned and saw her standing there gazing after him with wide eyes and a strained, white face. At the sight of her silent pain almost his heart failed him, almost he refused to go. Then he remembered, and went.

For a while Margaret still stood thus, until the sound of the horses' hoofs had died away indeed. Then she turned and said:

"Father, I know not how it is, but it seems to me that when Peter and I meet again it will be far off, yes, far off upon the stormy sea—but what sea I know not." And without waiting for an answer she climbed the stairs to her chamber, and there wept herself to sleep.

Castell watched her depart, then muttered to himself:

"Pray God she is not foresighted like so many of our race; and yet why is my own heart so heavy? Well, according to my judgment, I have done my best for him and her, and for myself I care nothing."

H. Rider Haggard

CHAPTER VII

NEWS FROM SPAIN

Peter Brome was a very quiet man, whose voice was not often heard about the place, and yet it was strange how dull and different the big, old house in Holborn seemed without him. Even the handsome Betty, with whom he was never on the best of terms, since there was much about her of which he disapproved, missed him, and said so to her cousin, who only answered with a sigh. For in the bottom of her heart Betty both feared and respected Peter. The fear was of his observant eyes and caustic words, which she knew were always words of truth, and the respect for the general uprightness of his character, especially where her own sex was concerned.

In fact, as has been hinted, some little time before, when Peter had first come to live with the Castells, Betty, thinking him a proper man of gentle birth, such a one indeed as she would wish to marry, had made advances to him, which, as he did not seem to notice them, became by degrees more and more marked. What happened at last they two knew alone, but it was something that caused Betty to become very angry, and to speak of Peter to her friends as a cold-blooded lout who thought only of work and gain. The episode was passing, and soon forgotten by the lady in the press of other affairs; but the respect remained. Moreover, on one or two occasions, when the love of admiration had led her into griefs, Peter had proved a good friend, and what was better, a friend who did not talk. Therefore she wished him back again, especially now, when something that was more than mere vanity and desire for excitement had taken hold of her, and Betty found herself being swept off her feet into very deep and doubtful waters.

The shopmen and the servants missed him also, for to him all disputes were brought for settlement, nor, provided it had not come about through lack of honesty, were any pains too great for him to take to help them in a trouble. Most of all Castell missed him, since until Peter had gone he did not know how much he had learned to rely upon him, both in his business and as a friend. As for Margaret, her life without him was one long, empty night.

Thus it chanced that in such a house any change was welcome, and, though she liked him little enough, Margaret was not even displeased when one morning Betty told her that the lord d'Aguilar was coming to call on her that day, and purposed to bring her a present.

"I do not seek his presents," said Margaret indifferently; then added, "But how do you know that, Betty?"

The young woman coloured, and tossed her head as she answered:

"I know it, Cousin, because, as I was going to visit my old aunt yesterday, who lives on the wharf at Westminster, I met him riding, and he called out to me, saying that he had a gift for you and one for me also."

"Be careful you do not meet him too often, Betty, when you chance to be visiting your aunt. These Spaniards are not always over-honest, as you may learn to your sorrow."

"I thank you for your good counsel," said Betty, shortly, "but I, who am older than you, know enough of men to be able to guard myself, and can keep them at a distance."

"I am glad of it, Betty, only sometimes I have thought that the distance was scarcely wide enough," answered Margaret, and left the subject, for she was thinking of other things.

That afternoon, when Margaret was walking in the garden, Betty, whose face seemed somewhat flushed, ran up to her and said that the lord d'Aguilar was waiting in the hall.

"Very good," answered Margaret, "I will come. Go, tell my father, that he may join us. But why are you so disturbed and hurried?" she added wonderingly.

"Oh!" answered Betty, "he has brought me a present, so fine a present—a mantle of the most wonderful lace that ever I saw, and a comb of mottled shell mounted in gold to keep it off the hair. He made me wait while he showed me how to put it on, and that was why I ran."

Margaret did not quite see the connection; but she answered slowly:

"Perhaps it would have been wiser if you had run first. I do not understand why this fine lord brings you presents."

"But he has brought one for you also, Cousin, although he would not say what it was."

"That I understand still less. Go, tell my father that the Senor d'Aguilar awaits him."

Then she went into the hall, and found d'Aguilar looking at an illuminated Book of Hours in which she had been reading, that was written in Spanish in one column and in Latin in that opposite. He greeted her in his usual graceful way, that, where Margaret was concerned, was easy and well-bred without being bold, and said at once:

"So you read Spanish, Senora?"

"A little. Not very well, I fear."

"And Latin also?"

"A little again. I have been taught that tongue. By studying them thus I try to improve myself in both."

"I perceive that you are learned as you are beautiful," and he bowed courteously.

"I thank you, Senor; but I lay claim to neither grace."

"What need is there to claim that which is evident?" replied d'Aguilar; then added, "But I forgot, I have brought you a present, if you will be pleased to accept it. Or, rather, I bring you what is your own, or at the least your father's. I bargained with his Excellency Don de Ayala, pointing out that fifty gold angels were too much to pay for that dead rogue of his; but he would give me nothing back in money, since with gold he never parts. Yet I won some change from him, and it stands without your door. It is a Spanish jennet of the true Moorish blood, which, hundreds of years ago, that people brought with them from the East. He needs it no longer, as he returns to Spain, and it is trained to bear a lady." Margaret did not know what to answer, but, fortunately, at that moment her father appeared, and to him d'Aguilar repeated his tale, adding that he had heard his daughter say that the horse she rode had fallen with her, so that she could use it no more.

Now, Castell did not wish to accept this gift, for such he felt it to be; but d'Aguilar assured him that if he did not he must sell it and return him the price in money, as it did not belong to him. So, there being no help for it, he thanked him in his daughter's name and his own, and they went into the stable-yard, whither it had been taken, to look at this horse.

The moment that Castell saw it he knew that it was a creature of great value, pure white in colour, with a long, low body, small head, gentle eyes, round hoofs, and flowing mane and tail, such a horse, indeed, as a queen might have ridden. Now again he was confused, being sure that this beast had never been given back as a luck-penny, since it would have fetched more than the fifty angels on the market; moreover, it was harnessed with a woman's saddle and bridle of the most beautifully worked red Cordova leather, to which were attached a silver bit and stirrup. But d'Aguilar smiled, and vowed that things were as he had told them, so there was nothing more to be said. Margaret, too, was so pleased with the mare, which she longed to ride, that she forgot her scruples, and tried to believe that this was so. Noting her delight, which she could not conceal as she patted the beautiful beast, d'Aguilar said:

"Now I will ask one thing in return for the bargain that I have made—that I may see you mount this horse for the first time. You told me that you and your father were wont to go out together in the morning. Have I your leave, Sir," and he turned to Castell, "to ride with you before breakfast, say, at seven of the clock, for I would show the lady, your daughter, how she should manage a horse of this blood, which is something of a trick?"

"If you will," answered Castell—"that is, if the weather is fine," for the offer was made so courteously that it could scarcely be refused.

D'Aguilar bowed, and they re-entered the house, talking of other matters. When they were in the hall again, he asked whether their kinsman Peter had reached his destination safely, adding:

"I pray you, do not tell me where it is, for I wish to be able to put my hand upon my heart and swear to all concerned, and especially to certain fellows who are still seeking for him, that I know nothing of his hiding-place."

Castell answered that he had, since but a few minutes before a letter had come from him announcing his safe arrival, tidings at which Margaret looked up, then, remembering her promise, said that she was glad to hear of it, as the roads were none too safe, and spoke indifferently of something else. D'Aguilar added that he also was glad, then, rising, took his leave "till seven on the morrow."

When he had gone, Castell gave Margaret a letter, addressed to her in Peter's stiff, upright hand, which she read eagerly. It began and ended with sweet words, but, like his speech, was brief and to the point, saying only that he had accomplished his journey without adventure, and was very glad to find himself again in the old house where he was born, and amongst familiar fields and faces. On the morrow he was to see the tradesmen as to alterations and repairs which were much needed, even the moat being choked with mud and weeds. His last sentence was: "I much mistrust me of that fine Spaniard, and I am jealous to think that he should be near to you while I am far away. Beware of him, I say—beware of him. May the Mother of God and all the saints have you in their keeping! Your most true affianced lover."

This letter Margaret answered before she slept, for the messenger was to return at dawn, telling Peter, amongst other things, of the gift which d'Aguilar had brought her, and how she and her father were forced to accept it, but bidding him not be jealous, since, although the gift was welcome, she liked the giver little, who did but count the hours till her true lover should come back again and take her to himself.

Next morning she was up early, clothed in her riding-dress, for the day was very fine, and by seven o'clock d'Aguilar appeared, mounted on a great horse. Then the Spanish jennet was brought out, and deftly he lifted her to the saddle, showing her how she must pull but lightly on the reins, and urge or check her steed with her voice alone, using no whip or spur.

A perfect beast it proved to be, indeed, gentle as a lamb, and easy, yet very spirited and swift.

D'Aguilar was a pleasant cavalier also, talking of many things grave and gay, until at length even Castell forgot his thoughts, and grew cheerful as they cantered forward through the fresh spring morning by heath and hill and woodland, listening to the singing of the birds, and watching the husbandmen at their labour. This ride was but the first of several that they took, since d'Aguilar knew their hours of exercise, even when they changed them, and whether they asked him or not, joined or met them in such a natural fashion that they could not refuse his company. Indeed, they were much puzzled to know how he came to be so well acquainted with their movements, and even with the direction in which they proposed to ride, but supposed that he must have it from the grooms, although these were commanded to say nothing, and always denied having spoken with him. That Betty should speak of such matters, or even find opportunity of doing so, never chanced to cross their minds, who did not guess that if they rode with d'Aguilar in the morning, Betty often walked with him in the evening when she was supposed to be at church, or sewing, or visiting her aunt upon the wharf at Westminster. But of these walks the foolish girl said nothing, for her own reasons.

Now, as they rode together, although he remained very courteous and respectful, the manner of d'Aguilar towards Margaret grew ever more close and intimate. Thus he began to tell her stories, true or false, of his past life, which seemed to have been strange and eventful enough; to hint, too, of a certain hidden greatness that pertained to him which he did not dare to show, and of high ambitions which he had. He spoke also of his loneliness, and his desire to lose it in the companionship of a kindred heart, if he could find one to share his wealth, his station, and his hopes; while all the time his dark eyes, fixed on Margaret, seemed to say, "The heart I seek is such a one as yours." At length, at some murmured word or touch, she took affright, and, since she could not avoid him abroad, determined to stay at home, and, much as she loved the sport, to ride no more till Peter should return. So she gave out that she had hurt her knee, which made the saddle painful to her, and the beautiful Spanish mare was left idle in the stable, or mounted only by the groom.

Thus for some days she was rid of d'Aguilar, and employed herself in reading and working, or in writing long letters to Peter, who was busy enough at Dedham, and sent her thence many commissions to fulfil.

One afternoon Castell was seated in his office deciphering letters which had just reached him. The night before his best ship, of over two hundred tons burden, which was named the *Margaret*, after his daughter, had come safely into the mouth of the Thames from Spain. That evening she was to reach her berth at Gravesend with the tide, when Castell proposed to go aboard of her to see to the unloading of her cargo. This was the last of his ships which remained unsold, and it was his plan to re-load and victual her at once with goods that were waiting, and send her back to the port of Seville, where his Spanish partners, in whose name she was already registered, had agreed to take her over at a fixed price. This done, it was only left for him to hand over his business to the merchants who had purchased it in London, after which he would be free to depart, a very wealthy man, and spend the evening of his days at peace in Essex, with his daughter and her husband, as now he so greatly longed to do. So soon as they were within the river banks the captain of this ship, Smith by name, had landed the cargo-master with letters and a manifest of cargo, bidding him hire a horse and bring them to Master Castell's house in Holborn. This the man had done safely, and it was these letters that Castell read.

One of them was from his partner Bernaldez in Seville; not in answer to that which he had written on the night of the opening of this history—for this there had been no time—yet dealing with matters whereof it treated. In it was this passage:

"You will remember what I wrote to you of a certain envoy who has been sent to the Court of London, who is called d'Aguilar, for as our cipher is so secret, and it is important that you should be warned, I take the risk of writing his name. Since that letter I have learned more concerning this grandee, for such he is. Although he calls himself plain Don d'Aguilar, in truth he is the Marquis of Morella, and on one side, it is said, of royal blood, if not on both, since he is reported to be the son born out of wedlock of Prince Carlos of Viana, the half-brother of the king. The tale runs that Carlos, the learned and gentle, fell in love with a Moorish lady of Aguilar of high birth and great wealth, for she had rich estates at Granada and elsewhere, and, as he might not marry her because of the difference of their rank and faiths, lived with her without marriage, of which union one son was born. Before Prince Carlos died, or was poisoned, and while he was still a prisoner at Morella, he gave to, or procured for this boy the title of marquis, choosing from some fancy the name of Morella, that place where he had suffered so much. Also he settled some private lands upon him. After the prince died, the Moorish lady, his lover, who had secretly become a Christian, took her son to live at her palace in Granada, where she died also some ten years ago, leaving all her great wealth to him, for she never married. At this time it is said that his life was in danger, for the reason that, although he was half a Moor, too much of the blood-royal ran in his veins. But the Marquis was clever, and persuaded the king and queen that he had no ambition beyond his pleasures. Also the Church interceded for him, since to it he proved himself a faithful son, persecuting all heretics, especially the Jews, and even Moors, although they are of his own blood. So in the end he was confirmed in his possessions and left alone, although he refused to become a priest.

"Since then he has been made an agent of the Crown at Granada, and employed upon various embassies to London, Rome, and elsewhere, on matters connected with the faith and the establishment of the Holy Inquisition. That is why he is again in England at this moment, being charged to obtain the names and particulars concerning all Maranos settled there, especially if they trade with Spain. I have seen the names of those of whom he must inquire most closely, and that is why I write to you so fully, since yours is first upon the list. I think, therefore, that you do wisely to wind up your business with this country, and especially to sell your ships to us outright and quickly, since otherwise they might be seized—like yourself, if you came here. My counsel to you is—hide your wealth, which will be great when we have paid you all we owe, and go to some place where you will be forgotten for a while, since that bloodhound d'Aguilar, for so he calls himself, after his mother's birthplace, has not tracked you to London for nothing. As yet, thanks be to God, no suspicion has fallen on any of us; perhaps because we have many in our pay."

When Castell had finished transcribing all this passage he read it through carefully. Then he went into the hall, where a fire burned, for the day was cold, and threw the translation on to it, watching until it was consumed, after which he returned to his office, and hid away the letter in a secret cupboard behind the panelling of the wall. This done, he sat himself in his chair to think.

"My good friend Juan Bernaldez is right," he said to himself; "d'Aguilar, or the Marquis Morella, does not nose me and the others out for nothing. Well, I shall not trust myself in Spain, and the money, most of it, except what is still to come from Spain, is put out where it will never be found by him, at good interest too. All seems safe enough—and yet I would to God that Peter and Margaret were fast married, and that we three sat together, out of sight and mind, in the Old Hall at Dedham. I have carried on this game too long. I should have closed my books a year ago; but the trade was so good that I could not. I was wise also, who in this one lucky year have nearly doubled my fortune. And yet it would have been safer, before they guessed that I was so rich. Greed—mere greed—for I do not need this money which may destroy us all! Greed! The ancient pitfall of my race."

As he thought thus there came a knock upon his door. Snatching up a pen he dipped it in the ink-horn and, calling "Enter," began to add a column of figures on a paper before him.

The door opened; but he seemed to take no heed, so diligently did he count his figures. Yet, although his eyes were fixed upon

H. Rider Haggard

the paper, in some way that he could not understand he was well aware that d'Aguilar and no other stood in the room behind him, the truth being, no doubt, that unconsciously he had recognised his footstep. For a moment the knowledge turned him cold—he who had just been reading of the mission of this man—and feared what was to come. Yet he acted well.

"Why do you disturb me, Daughter?" he said testily, and without looking round. "Have not things gone ill enough with half the cargo destroyed by sea-water, and the rest, that you must trouble me while I sum up my losses?" And, casting the pen down, he turned his stool round impatiently.

Yes! there sure enough stood d'Aguilar, very handsomely arrayed, and smiling and bowing as was his custom.

CHAPTER VIII

D'AGUILAR SPEAKS

"Losses?" said d'Aguilar. "Do I hear the wealthy John Castell, who holds half the trade with Spain in the hollow of his hand, talk of losses?"

"Yes, Senor, you do. Things have gone ill with this ship of mine that has barely lived through the spring gales. But be seated."

"Indeed, is that so?" said d'Aguilar as he sat down. "What a lying jade is rumour! For I was told that they had gone very well. Doubtless, however, what is loss to you would be priceless gain to one like me."

Castell made no answer, but waited, feeling that his visitor had not come to speak with him of his trading ventures.

"Senor Castell," said d'Aguilar, with a note of nervousness in his voice, "I am here to ask you for something."

"If it be a loan, Senor, I fear that the time is not opportune." And he nodded towards the sheet of figures.

"It is not a loan; it is a gift."

"Anything in my poor house is yours," answered Castell courteously, and in Oriental form.

H. Rider Haggard

"I rejoice to hear it, Senor, for I seek something from your house."

Castell looked a question at him with his quick black eyes.

"I seek your daughter, the Senora Margaret, in marriage."

Castell stared at him, then a single word broke from his lips.

"Impossible."

"Why impossible?" asked d'Aguilar slowly, yet as one who expected some such answer. "In age we are not unsuited, nor perhaps in fortune, while of rank I have enough, more than you guess perhaps. I vaunt not myself, yet women have thought me not uncomely. I should be a good friend to the house whence I took a wife, where perchance a day may come when friends will be needed; and lastly, I desire her not for what she may bring with her, though wealth is always welcome, but—I pray you to believe it—because I love her."

"I have heard that the Senor d'Aguilar loves many women, yonder in Granada."

"As I have heard that the *Margaret* had a prosperous voyage, Senor Castell. Rumour, as I said but now, is a lying jade. Yet I will not copy her. I have been no saint. Now I would become one, for Margaret's sake. I will be true to your daughter, Senor. What say you now?"

Castell only shook his head.

"Listen," went on d'Aguilar. "I am more than I seem to be; she who weds me will not lack for rank and titles."

"Yes, you are the Marquis de Morella, the reputed son of Prince Carlos of Viana by a Moorish mother, and therefore nephew to his Majesty of Spain."

D'Aguilar looked at him, then bowed and said:

"Your information is good—as good as mine, almost. Doubtless you do not like that bar in the blood. Well, if it were not there, I should be where Ferdinand is, should I not? So I do not like it either, though it is good blood and ancient—that of those high-bred Moors. Now, may not the nephew of a king and the son of a princess of Granada be fit to mate with the daughter of—a Jew, yes, a Marano, and of a Christian English lady, of good family, but no more?"

Castell lifted his hand as though to speak; but d'Aguilar went on:

"Deny it not, friend; it is not worth while here in private. Was there not a certain Isaac of Toledo who, hard on fifty years ago, left Spain, for his own reasons, with a little son, and in London became known as Joseph Castell, having, with his son, been baptized into the Holy Church? Ah! you see you are not the only one who studies genealogies."

"Well, Senor, if so, what of it?"

"What of it? Nothing at all, friend Castell. It is an old story, is it not, and, as that Isaac is long dead and his son has been a good Christian for nearly fifty years and had a Christian wife and child, who will trouble himself about such a matter? If he were openly a Hebrew now, or worse still, if pretending to be a Christian, he in secret practised the rites of the accursed Jews, why then—"

"Then what?"

"Then, of course, he would be expelled this land, where no Jew may live, his wealth would be forfeit to its king, whose ward his daughter would become, to be given in marriage where he willed, while he himself, being Spanish born, might perhaps be handed over to the power of Spain, there to make answer to these charges. But we wander to strange matters. Is that alliance still impossible, Senor?"

Castell looked him straight in the eyes and answered:

"Yes."

There was something so bold and direct in his utterance of the word that for a moment d'Aguilar seemed to be taken aback. He had not expected this sharp denial.

"It would be courteous to give a reason," he said presently.

"The reason is simple, Marquis. My daughter is already betrothed, and will ere long be wedded."

D'Aguilar did not seem surprised at this intelligence.

"To that brawler, your kinsman, Peter Brome, I suppose?" he said interrogatively. "I guessed as much, and by the saints I am sorry for her, for he must be a dull lover to one so fair and bright; while as a husband—" And he shrugged his shoulders. "Friend Castell, for her sake you will break off this match."

"And if I will not, Marquis?"

"Then I must break it off for you in the interest of all of us, including, of course, myself, who love her, and wish to lift her to a great place, and of yourself, whom I desire should pass your old age in peace and wealth, and not be hunted to your death like a mad dog."

"How will you break it, Marquis? by—"

"Oh no, Senor!" answered d'Aguilar, "not by other men's swords—if that is what you mean. The worthy Peter is safe from them so far as I am concerned, though if he should come face to face with mine, then let the best man win. Have no fear, friend, I do not practise murder, who value my own soul too much to soak it in blood, nor would I marry a woman except of her own free will. Still, Peter may die, and the fair Margaret may still place her hand in mine and say, 'I choose you as my husband.'"

"All these things, and many others, may happen, Marquis; but I do not think it likely that they will happen, and for my part, whilst thanking you for it, I decline your honourable offer, believing that my daughter will be more happy in her present humble state with the man she has chosen. Have I your leave to return to my accounts?" And he rose.

"Yes, Senor," answered d'Aguilar, rising also; "but add an item to those losses of which you spoke, that of the friendship of Carlos, Marquis de Morella, and on the other side enter again that of his hate. Man!" he added, and his dark, handsome face turned very evil as he spoke, "are you mad? Think of the little tabernacle behind the altar in your chapel, and what it contains."

Castell stared at him, then said:

"Come, let us see. Nay, fear no trick; like you I remember my soul, and do not stain my hands with blood. Follow me, so you will be safe."

Curiosity, or some other reason, prompted d'Aguilar to obey, and presently they stood behind the altar.

"Now," said Castell, as he drew the tapestry and opened the secret door, "look!" D'Aguilar peered into the place; but where should have been the table, the ark, the candlesticks, and the roll of the law of which Betty had told him, were only old dusty boxes filled with parchments and some broken furniture.

"What do you see?" asked Castell.

"I see, friend, that you are even a cleverer Jew than I thought. But this is a matter that you must explain to others in due season. Believe me, I am no inquisitor." Then without more words he turned and left him.

When Castell, having shut the secret door and drawn the tapestry, hurried from the chapel, it was to find that the marquis had departed.

He went back to his office much disturbed, and sat himself down there to think. Truly Fate, that had so long been his friend, was turning its face against him. Things could not have gone worse. D'Aguilar had discovered the secret of his faith through his spies, and, having by some accursed mischance fallen in love with his daughter's beauty, was become his bitter enemy because he must refuse her to him. Why must he refuse her? The man was of great position and noble blood; she would become the wife of one of the first grandees of Spain, one who stood nearest to the throne. Perhaps—such a thing was possible—she might live herself to be queen, or the mother of kings. Moreover, that marriage meant safety for himself; it meant a quiet age, a peaceable death in his own bed—for, were he fifty times a Marano, who would touch the father-in-law of the Marquis de Morella? Why? Just because he had promised her in marriage to Peter Brome, and through all his life as a merchant he had never yet broken with a bargain because it went against himself. That was the answer. Yet almost he could find it in his heart to wish that he had never made that bargain; that he had kept Peter, who had waited so long, waiting for another month. Well, it was too late now. He had passed his word, and he would keep it, whatever the cost might be.

Rising, he called one of the servants, and bade her summon Margaret. Presently she returned, saying that her mistress had gone out walking with Betty, adding also that his horse was at the door for him to ride to the river, where he was to pass the night on board his ship.

Taking paper, he bethought him that he would write to Margaret, warning her against the Spaniard. Then, remembering that she had nothing to fear from him, at any rate at present, and that it was not wise to set down such matters, he told her only to take good care of herself, and that he would be back in the morning.

That evening, when Margaret was in her own little sitting-chamber which adjoined the great hall, the door opened, and she looked up from the work upon which she was engaged, to see d'Aguilar standing before her.

"Senor!" she said, amazed, "how came you here?"

"Senora," he answered, closing the door and bowing, "my feet brought me. Had I any other means of coming I think that I should not often be absent from our side."

"Spare me your fine words, I pray you, Senor," answered Margaret, frowning. "It is not fitting that I should receive you thus alone at night, my father being absent from the house." And she made as though she would pass him and reach the door.

D'Aguilar, who stood in front of it, did not move, so perforce she stopped half way.

"I found that he was absent," he said courteously, "and that is why I venture to address you upon a matter of some importance. Give me a few minutes of your time, therefore, I beseech you."

Now, at once the thought entered Margaret's mind that he had some news of Peter to communicate to her—bad news perhaps.

"Be seated, and speak on, Senor," she said, sinking into a chair, while he too sat down, but still in front of the door.

"Senora," he said, "my business in this country is finished, and in a few days I sail hence for Spain." And he hesitated a moment.

"I trust that your voyage will be pleasant," said Margaret, not knowing what else to answer.

"I trust so also, Senora, since I have come to ask you if you will share it. Listen, before you refuse. To-day I saw your father, and begged your hand of him. He would give me no answer, neither yea nor nay, saying that you were your own mistress, and that I must seek it from your lips."

"My father said that?" gasped Margaret, astonished, then bethought her that he might have had reasons for speaking so, and went on rapidly, "Well, it is short and simple. I thank you, Senor; but stay in England."

"Even that I would be willing to do for your sake Senora, though, in truth, I find it a cold and barbarous country."

"If so, Senor d'Aguilar, I think that I should go to Spain. I pray you let me pass."

"Not till you have heard me out, Senora, when I trust that your words will be more gentle. See now I am a great man in my own country. Although it suits me to pass here incognito as plain Senor d'Aguilar I am the Marquis of Morella, the nephew of Ferdinand the King, with some wealth and station, official and private. If you disbelieve me, I can prove it to you."

"I do not disbelieve," answered Margaret indifferently, "it may well be so; but what is that to me?"

"Then is it not something, Lady, that I, who have blood-royal in my veins, should seek the daughter of a merchant to be my wife?"

"Nothing at all—to me, who am satisfied with my humble lot."

"Is it nothing to you that I should love as I do, with all my heart and soul? Marry me, and I tell you that I will lift you high, yes, perhaps even to the throne."

She thought a moment, then asked:

"The bribe is great, but how would you do that? Many a maid has been deceived with false jewels, Senor."

"How has it been done before? Not every one loves Ferdinand. I have many friends who remember that my father was poisoned by his father and Ferdinand's, he being the elder son. Also, my mother was a princess of the Moors, and if I, who dwell among them as the envoy of their Majesties, threw in my sword with theirs—or there are other ways. But I am speaking things that have never passed my lips before, which, were they known, would cost me my head—let it serve to show how much I trust you."

"I thank you, Senor, for your trust; but this crown seems to me set upon a peak that it is dangerous to climb, and I had sooner sit in safety on the plain."

"You reject the pomp," went on d'Aguilar in his passionate, pleading voice, "then will not the love move you? Oh! you shall be worshipped as never woman was. I swear to you that in your eyes there is a light which has set my heart on fire, so that it burns night and day, and will not be quenched. Your voice is my sweetest music, your hair is a cord that binds me to you faster than the prisoner's chain, and, when you pass, for me Venus walks the earth. More, your mind is pure and noble as your beauty, and by the aid of it I shall be lifted up through the high places of the earth to some white throne in heaven. I love you, my lady, my fair Margaret; because of you, all other women are become coarse and hateful in my sight. See how much I love you, that I, one of the first grandees of Spain, do this for your sweet sake," and suddenly he cast himself upon his knees before her, and lifting the hem of her dress pressed it to his lips.

H. Rider Haggard

Margaret looked down at him, and the anger that was rising in her breast melted, while with it went her fear. This man was much in earnest; she could not doubt it. The hand that held her robe trembled like shaken water, his face was ashen, and in his dark eyes swam tears. What cause had she to be afraid of one who was so much her slave?

"Senor," she said very gently, "rise, I pray you. Do not waste all this love upon one who chances to have caught your fancy, but who is quite unworthy of it, and far beneath you; one, moreover, by whom it may not be returned. Senor, I am already affianced. Therefore, put me out of your mind and find some other love."

He rose and stood in front of her.

"Affianced," he said, "I knew it. Nay, I will say no ill of the man; to revile one more fortunate is poor argument. But what is it to me if you are affianced? What to me if you were wed? I should seek you all the same, who have no choice. Beneath me? You are as far above me as a star, and it would seem as hard to reach. Seek some other love? I tell you, lady, that I have sought many, for not all are so hard to win, and I hate them every one. You I desire alone, and shall desire till I be dead, aye, and you I will win or die. No, I will not die till you are my own. Have no fear, I will not kill your lover, save perhaps in fair fight; I will not force you to give yourself to me, should I find the chance, but with your own lips I will yet listen to you asking me to be your husband. I swear it by Him Who died for us. I swear that, laying aside all other ends, to that sole purpose I will devote my days. Yes, and should you chance to pass from earth before me, then I will follow you to the very gates of death and clasp you there."

Now again Margaret's fear returned to her. This man's passion was terrible, yet there was a grandeur in it; Peter had never spoken to her in so high a fashion.

"Senor," she said almost pleadingly, "corpses are poor brides;

have done with such sick fancies, which surely must be born of your Eastern blood."

"It is your blood also, who are half a Jew, and, therefore, at least you should understand them."

"Mayhap I do understand, mayhap I think them great in their own fashion, yes, noble even, and admire, if it can be noble to seek to win away another man's betrothed. But, Senor, I am that man's betrothed, and all of me, my body and my soul, is his, nor would I go back upon my word, and so break his heart, to win the empire of the earth. Senor, once more I implore you to leave this poor maid to the humble life that she has chosen, and to forget her."

"Lady," answered d'Aguilar, "your words are wise and gentle, and I thank you for them. But I cannot forget you, and that oath I swore just now I swear again, thus." And before she could prevent him, or even guess what he was about to do, he lifted the gold crucifix that hung by a chain about her neck, kissed it, and let it fall gently back upon her breast, saying, "See, I might have kissed your lips before you could have stayed me, but that I will never do until you give me leave, so in place of them I kiss the cross, which till then we both must carry. Lady, my lady Margaret, within a day or two I sail for Spain, but your image shall sail with me, and I believe that ere long our paths must cross again. How can it be otherwise since the threads of your life and mine were intertwined on that night outside the Palace of Westminster—intertwined never to be separated till one of us has ceased to be, and then only for a little while. Lady, for the present, farewell."

Then swiftly and silently as he had come, d'Aguilar went.

It was Betty who let him out at the side door, as she had let him in. More, glancing round to see that she was not observed—for it chanced now that Peter was away with some of the best men, and the master was out with others, no one was on watch this night—leaving the door ajar that she might re-enter, she followed him a little way, till they came to an old arch, which in some bygone time had led to a house now pulled down. Into this dark place Betty slipped, touching d'Aguilar on the arm as she did so. For a moment he hesitated, then, muttering some Spanish oath between his teeth, followed her.

"Well, most fair Betty," he said, "what word have you for me now?"

"The question is, Senor Carlos," answered Betty with scarcely suppressed indignation, "what word you have for me, who dared so much for you to-night? That you have plenty for my cousin, I know, since standing in the cold garden I could hear you talk, talk, talk, through the shutters, as though for your very life."

"I pray that those shutters had no hole in them," reflected d'Aguilar to himself. "No, there was a curtain also; she can have seen nothing." But aloud he answered: "Mistress Betty, you should not stand about in this bitter wind; you might fall ill, and then what should I suffer?"

"I don't know, nothing perhaps; that would be left to me. What I want to understand is, why you plan to come to see me, and then spend an hour with Margaret?"

"To avert suspicion, most dear Betty. Also I had to talk to her of this Peter, in whom she seems so greatly interested. You are very shrewd, Betty—tell me, is that to be a match?"

"I think so; I have been told nothing, but I have noticed many things, and almost every day she is writing to him, though why she should care for that owl of a man I cannot guess."

"Doubtless because she appreciates solid worth, Betty, as I do in you. Who can account for the impulses of the heart, which come, say some of the learned, from heaven, and others, from hell? At least it is no affair of ours, so let us wish them happiness, and, after they are married, a large and healthy family. Meanwhile, dear Betty, are you making ready for your voyage to Spain?"

"I don't know," answered Betty gloomily. "I am not sure that I trust you and your fine words. If you want to marry me, as you swear, and be sure I look for nothing less, why cannot it be before we start, and how am I to know that you will do so when we get there?"

"You ask many questions, Betty, all of which I have answered before. I have told you that I cannot marry you here because of that permission which is necessary on account of the difference in our ranks. Here, where your place is known, it is not to be had; there, where you will pass as a great English lady—as of course you are by birth—I can obtain it in an hour. But if you have any doubts, although it cuts me to the heart to say it, it would be best that we should part at once. I will take no wife who does not trust me fully and alone. Say then, cruel Betty, do you wish to leave me?"

"You know I don't; you know it would kill me," she answered in a voice that was thick with passion, "you know I worship the ground you tread on, and hate every woman you go near, yes, even my cousin who has been so good to me, and whom I love. I will take the risk and come with you, believing you to be an honest gentleman, who would not deceive a girl who trusts him; and if you do, may God deal with you as I shall, for I am no toy to be broken and thrown away, as you would find out. Yes, I will take the risk because you have made me love you so that I cannot live without you."

"Betty, your words fill me with rapture, showing me that I have not misread your noble mind; but speak a little lower—there are echoes in this hole. Now for the plans, for time is short, and you may be missed. When I am about to sail I will invite Mistress Margaret and yourself to come aboard my ship."

H. Rider Haggard

"Why not invite me without my cousin Margaret?" asked Betty.

"Because it would excite suspicion which we must avoid—do not interrupt me. I will invite you both or get you there upon some other pretext, and then I will arrange that she shall be brought ashore again and you taken on. Leave it all to me, only swear that you will obey any instructions I may send you for if you do not, I tell you that we have enemies in high places who may part us for ever. Betty, I will be frank, there is a great lady who is jealous, and watches you very closely. Do you swear?"

"Yes, yes, I swear. But about the great lady?"

"Not a word about her—on your life—and mine. You shall hear from me shortly. And now, sweetheart—good-night."

"Good-night," said Betty, but still she did not stir.

Then, understanding that she expected something more, d'Aguilar nerved himself to the task, and touched her hair with his lips.

Next moment he regretted it, for even that tempered salute fanned her passion into flame.

Throwing her arms about his neck Betty drew his face to hers and kissed him many times, till at length he broke, half choking, from her embrace, and escaped into the street.

"Mother of Heaven!" he muttered to himself, "the woman is a volcano in eruption. I shall feel her kisses for a week," and he rubbed his face ruefully with his hand. "I wish I had made some other plan; but it is too late to change it now—she would betray everything. Well, I will be rid of her somehow, if I have to drown her. A hard fate to love the mistress and be loved of the maid!"

CHAPTER IX

THE SNARE

On the following morning, when Castell returned, Margaret told him of the visit of d'Aguilar, and of all that had passed between them, told him also that he was acquainted with their secret, since he had spoken of her as half a Jew.

"I know it, I know it," answered her father, who was much disturbed and very angry, "for yesterday he threatened me also. But let that go, I can take my chance; now I would learn who brought this man into my house when I was absent, and without my leave."

"I fear that it was Betty," said Margaret, "who swears that she thought she did no wrong."

"Send for her," said Castell. Presently Betty came, and, being questioned, told a long story.

She said she was standing by the side door, taking the air, when Senor d'Aguilar appeared, and, having greeted her, without more words walked into the house, saying that he had an appointment with the master.

"With me?" broke in Castell. "I was absent."

"I did not know that you were absent, for I was out when you rode away in the afternoon, and no one had spoken of it to

H. Rider Haggard

me, so, thinking that he was your friend, I let him in, and let him out again afterwards. That is all I have to say."

"Then I have to say that you are a hussy and a liar, and that, in one way or the other, this Spaniard has bribed you," answered Castell fiercely. "Now, girl, although you are my wife's cousin, and therefore my daughter's kin, I am minded to turn you out on to the street to starve."

At this Betty first grew angry, then began to weep; while Margaret pleaded with her father, saying that it would mean the girl's ruin, and that he must not take such a sin upon him. So the end of it was, that, being a kind-hearted man, remembering also that Betty Dene was of his wife's blood, and that she had favoured her as her daughter did, he relented, taking measures to see that she went abroad no more save in the company of Margaret, and that the doors were opened only by men-servants.

So this matter ended.

That day Margaret wrote to Peter, telling him of all that had happened, and how the Spaniard had asked her in marriage, though the words that he used she did not tell. At the end of her letter, also, she bade him have no fear of the Senor d'Aguilar or of any other man, as he knew where her heart was.

When Peter received this writing he was much vexed to learn that both Master Castell and Margaret had incurred the enmity of d'Aguilar, for so he guessed it must be, also that Margaret should have been troubled with his love-making; but for the rest he thought little of the matter, who trusted her as he trusted heaven. Still it made him anxious to return to London as soon as might he, even though he must take the risk of the Spaniards' daggers. Within three days, however, he received other letters both from Castell and from Margaret, which set his fears at rest.

These told him that d'Aguilar had sailed for Spain indeed,

Castell said that he had seen him standing on the poop of the Ambassador de Ayala's vessel as it dropped down the Thames towards the sea. Moreover, Margaret had a note of farewell from his hand, which ran:

"Adieu, sweet lady, till that predestined hour when we meet again. I go, as I must, but, as I told you, your image goes with me.

"Your worshipper till death,

"MORELLA."

"He may take her image so long as I keep herself and if he comes back with his worship, I promise him that death and he shall not be far apart," was Peter's grim comment as he laid the paper down. Then he went on with his letters, which told that now, when the Spaniards had gone, and there was nothing more to fear, he was awaited in London. Indeed, Castell fixed a day when he should arrive—May 31st—that was within a week, adding that on its morrow—namely, June 1st, for Margaret would not be wed in May, the Virgin Mary's month, since she held it to be unlucky—their marriage might take place as quietly as they would.

Margaret wrote the same news, and in such sweet words that he kissed her letter, then hastened to answer it, shortly, after his custom, for Peter was no great scribe, saying, that if the saints willed it he would be with them by nightfall on the last day of May, and that in all England there was no happier man than he.

* * * * *

Now all that week Margaret was very busy preparing her marriage robe, and other garments also, for it was settled that on the next day they should ride together down to Dedham, in Essex, whither her father would follow them shortly. The Old Hall was not ready, indeed, nor would it be for some time; but

Peter had furnished certain rooms in it which might serve them for the summer season, and by winter time the house would be finished and open.

Castell was busy also, for now, having worked very hard at the task, his ship the *Margaret* was almost refitted and laden, so that he hoped to get her to sea on this same May 31st, and thus be clear of the last of his business, except the handing over of his warehouses and stock to those who had bought them. These great affairs kept him much at Gravesend, where the ship lay, but, as he had no dread of further trouble now that d'Aguilar and the other Spaniards, among them that band of de Ayala's servants who had vowed to take Peter's life, were gone, this did not disturb him.

Oh! happy, happy was Margaret during those sweet spring days, when her heart was bright and clear as the skies from which all winter storms had passed. So happy was she indeed, and so full of a hundred joyful cares, that she found no time to take note of her cousin Betty, who worked with her at her wedding broideries, and helped to make preparations for the journey which should follow after. Had she done so, she might have seen that Betty was anxious and distressed, like one who waited for some tidings that did not come, and from hour to hour fought against anguish and despair But she took no note, whose heart was too full of her own matters, and who did but count the hours till she should see her lover back and pass to his arms, a wife.

Thus the time went on until the appointed day of Peter's return, the morrow of her marriage, for which all things were now prepared, down to Peter's wedding garments, that were finer than any she had yet seen him wear, and the decking of the neighbouring church with flowers. In the early morning her father rode away to Gravesend with the most of his men-servants for the ship *Margaret* was to sail at the following dawn and there was yet much to be done before she could lift anchor. Still, he had promised to be back by nightfall in time to meet Peter who, leaving Dedham that morning, could not reach them before then.

At length it was past four of the afternoon, and everything being finished, Margaret went to her room to dress herself anew, that she might look fine in Peter's eyes when he should come. Betty she did not take with her, for there were things to which her cousin must attend; moreover, her heart was so full that she wished to be alone a while.

Betty's heart was full also, but not with joy. She had been deceived. The fine Spanish Don, who had made her love him so desperately, had sailed away and left her without a word. She could not doubt it, he had been seen standing on the ship—and not one word. It was cruel, cruel, and now she must help another woman to be made a happy wife, she who was beggared of hope and love. Moodily, full of bitterness, she went about her tasks, biting her lips and wiping her fine eyes with the sleeve of her robe, when suddenly the door opened, and a servant, not one of their own, but a strange man who had been brought in to help at the morrow's feast, called out that a sailor wished to speak with her.

"Then let him enter here; I have no time to go out to listen to his talk," snapped Betty.

Presently the sailor was shown in, the man who brought him leaving the room at once. He was a dark fellow, with sly black eyes, who, had he not spoken English so well, might have been taken for a Spaniard.

"Who are you, and what is your business?" asked Betty sharply.

"I am the carpenter of the ship *Margaret*," he answered, "and I am here to say that our master Castell has met with an accident there, and desires that Mistress Margaret, his daughter, should come to him at once."

"What accident?" asked Betty.

"In seeing to the stowage of cargo he slipped and fell down the hold, hurting his back and breaking his right arm, and that is why he cannot write. He is in great pain; but the physician whom we summoned bade me tell Mistress Margaret that at present he has no fear for his life. Are you Mistress Margaret?"

"No," answered Betty; "but I will go to her at once; do you bide here."

"Then are you her cousin, Mistress Betty Dene, for if so I have something for you?"

"I am. What is it?"

"This," said the man, drawing out a letter which he handed to her.

"Who gave you this?" asked Betty suspiciously. "I do not know his name, but he was a noble-looking Spanish Don, and a liberal one too. He had heard of the accident on the *Margaret*, and, knowing my errand, asked me if I would deliver this letter to you, for the fee of a gold ducat, and promise to say nothing of it to any one else."

"Some rude gallant, doubtless," said Betty, tossing her head; "they are ever writing to me. Bide here; I go to Mistress Margaret."

Once she was outside the door Betty broke the seal of the letter eagerly enough, for she had been taught with Margaret, and could read well. It ran:

"BELOVED,

"*You thought me faithless and gone, but it is not so. I was silent only because I knew you could not come alone who are watched; but now the God of Love gives us our chance. Doubtless your cousin will bring you with her to visit her father, who lies on his ship sadly hurt. While she is with him I have made a plan to rescue you, and then we can be wed and sail at once—yes, to-night or to-morrow, for with much trouble, knowing that you wished it, I have even succeeded in bringing that about, and a priest will be waiting to marry us. Be silent, and show no doubt or fear, whatever happens, lest we should be parted for always. Be sure then that your cousin comes that you may accompany her. Remember that your true love waits you.*

"C. d'A."

When Betty had mastered the contents of this amorous effusion she went pale with joy, and turned so faint that she was like to fall. Then a doubt struck her that it might be some trick. No, she knew the writing—it was d'Aguilar's, and he was true to her, and would marry her as he had promised, and take her to be a great lady in Spain. If she hesitated now she might lose him for ever—him whom she would follow to the end of the world. In an instant her mind was made up, for Betty had plenty of courage. She would go, even though she must desert the cousin whom she loved.

Thrusting the letter into her bosom she ran to Margaret's room, and, bursting into it, told her of the man and his sad message. But of that letter she said nothing. Margaret turned white at the news, then, recovering herself, said:

"I will come and speak with him at once." And together they went down the stairs.

To Margaret the sailor repeated his story, nor could all her questions shake it. He told her how the mischance had happened, for he had seen it, so he said, and where her father's hurts were, adding, that although the physician held that as yet he was in no danger of his life, Master Castell thought otherwise, and did nothing but cry that his daughter should be brought to him at once.

Still Margaret doubted and hesitated, for she feared she knew

H. Rider Haggard

not what.

"Peter should be here within two hours at most," she said to Betty. "Would it not be best to wait for him?"

"Oh! Margaret, and what if your father should die in the meanwhile? Perhaps he knows better how deep his hurts are than does this leech. If so, you would have a sore heart for all your life. Sure you had better go, or at the least I will."

Still Margaret wavered, till the sailor said:

"Lady, if it is your will to come, I can guide you to where a boat waits to take you across the river. If not, I must be gone, for the ship sails with the moonrise, and they only wait your coming to carry the master, your father, to the warehouse on shore thinking it best that you should be present. If you do not come, this will be done as gently as possible, and there you must seek him to-morrow, alive or dead." And the man took up his cap as though to leave.

"I will come with you," said Margaret. "Betty you are right; order the two horses to be saddled mine and the groom's, with a pillion on which you can ride, for I will not send you or go alone, understand that this sailor has his own horse."

The man nodded, and accompanied Betty to the stable. Then Margaret took pen and wrote hastily to Peter, telling him of their evil chance, and bidding him follow her at once to the ship, or, if it had sailed to the warehouse. "I am loth to go," she added "alone with a girl and a strange man, yet I must since my heart is torn with fear for my beloved father. Sweetheart, follow me quickly."

This done, she gave the letter to that servant who had shown in the sailor, bidding him hand it, without fail, to Master Peter Brome when he came, which the man promised to do.

Then she fetched plain dark cloaks for herself and Betty, with hoods to them, that their faces might not be seen, and presently they were mounted.

"Stay!" said Margaret to the sailor as they were about to start. "How comes it that my father did not send one of his own men instead of you, and why did none write to me?"

The man looked surprised; he was a very good actor.

"His people were tending him," he said, "and he bade me to go because I knew the way, and had a good, hired horse ashore which I have used when riding with messages to London about new timbers and other matters. As for writing, the physician began a letter, but he was so slow and long that Master Castell ordered me to be off without it. It seems," the man added, addressing Betty with some irritation, "that Mistress Margaret misdoubts me. If so, let her find some other guide, or bide at home. It is naught to me, who have only done as I was bidden."

Thus did this cunning fellow persuade Margaret that her fears were nothing, though, remembering the letter from d'Aguilar, Betty was somewhat troubled. The thing had a strange look, but, poor, vain fool, she thought to herself that, even if there were some trick, it was certainly arranged only that she might seem to be taken, who could not come alone. In truth she was blind and mad, and cared not what she did, though, let this be said for her, she never dreamed that any harm was meant towards her cousin Margaret, or that a lie had been told as to Master Castell and his hurts.

Soon they were out of London, and riding swiftly by the road that followed the north bank of the river, for their guide did not take them over the bridge, as he said the ship was lying in mid-stream and that the boat would be waiting on the Tilbury shore. But there was more than twenty miles to travel, and, push on as they would, night had fallen ere ever they came there. At length, when they were weary of the dark and the rough road, the sailor pulled up at a spot upon the river's brink—where there was a little wharf, but no houses that they could see—saying that this was the place. Dismounting, he gave his horse to the groom to hold, and, going to the wharf, asked in a loud voice if the boat from the *Margaret* was there, to which a voice answered, "Aye." Then he talked for a minute to those in the boat, though what he said they could not hear, and ran back again, bidding them dismount, and adding that they had done well to come, as Master Castell was much worse, and did nothing but cry for his daughter.

The groom he told to lead the horses a little way along the bank till he found an inn that stood there, where he must await their return or further orders, and to Betty he suggested that she should go with him, as there was but little place left in the boat. This she was willing enough to do, thinking it all part of the plan for her carrying off; but Margaret would have none of it, saying that unless her cousin came with her she would not stir another step. So grumbling a little the sailor gave way, and hurried them both to some wooden steps and down these into a boat, of which they could but dimly see the outline.

So soon as ever they were seated side by side in the stern it was pushed off, and rowed away rapidly into the darkness, while one of the sailors lit a lantern which he fastened to the bow, and far out on the river, as though in answer to the signal, another star of light appeared, towards which they headed. Now Margaret, speaking through the gloom, asked the rowers of her father's state; but the sailor, their guide, prayed her not to trouble them, as the tide ran very swiftly and they must give all their mind to their business lest they should overset. So she was silent, and, racked with doubts and fears, watched that star of light growing ever nearer, till at length it hung above them.

"Is that the ship *Margaret*?" cried their guide, and again a voice answered "Aye."

"Then tell Master Castell that his daughter has come at last," he shouted again, and in another minute a rope had been thrown to them, and they were fast alongside a ladder on to which Betty, who was nearest to it, was pushed the first, except for their guide, who had run up the wooden steps very swiftly.

Betty, who was active and strong, followed him, Margaret coming next. As she reached the deck Betty thought she heard a voice say in Spanish, of which she understood something, "Fool! Why have you brought both?" but the answer she could not catch. Then she turned and gave her hand to Margaret, and together they walked forward to the foot of the mast.

"Lead me to my father," said Margaret.

Whereon the guide answered:

"Yes, this way, Mistress, but come alone, for the sight of two of you at once may disturb him."

"Nay," she answered, "my cousin comes with me." And she took Betty's hand and clung to it.

Shrugging his shoulders the sailor led them forwards, and as they went she noted that men were hauling on a sail, while other men, who sang a strange, wild song, worked on what seemed to be a windlass. Now they reached a cabin, and entered it, the door being shut behind them. In the cabin a man sat at a table with a lamp hanging over his head. He rose and turned towards them, bowing, and Margaret saw that it was—*d'Aguilar!*

Betty stood silent; she had expected to meet him, though not here and thus. Her foolish heart bounded so at the sight of him that she seemed to choke, and could only wonder dimly what mistake had been made, and how he would explain to Margaret and get her away, leaving herself and him together to be married. Indeed, she searched the cabin with her eyes to see where the priest was waiting, then noting a door beyond, thought that doubtless he must be hidden there. As for Margaret, she uttered a little stifled cry, then, being a brave

H. Rider Haggard

woman, one of that high nature which grows strong in the face of trouble, straightened herself to her full height and said in a low, fierce voice:

"What do you here? Where is my father?"

"Senora," he answered humbly, "I am on board my ship, the *San Antonio*, and as for your father, he is either on his ship, the *Margaret*, or more likely, by now, at his house in Holborn."

At these words Margaret reeled back till the wall of the cabin stayed her, and there she rested.

"Spare me your reproaches," went on d'Aguilar hurriedly. "I will tell you all the truth. First, be not anxious as to your father; no accident has happened to him; he is sound and well. Forgive me if you have suffered pain and doubt; but there was no other way. That tale was only one of love's snares and tricks—" He paused, overcome, fascinated by Margaret's face, which of a sudden had grown awful—that of a goddess of vengeance, of a Medusa, which seemed to chill his blood to ice.

"A snare! A trick!" she muttered hoarsely, while her eyes flamed on him like burning stars. "Thus then I pay you for your tricks." And in an instant he became aware that she had snatched a dagger from her bosom and was springing on him.

He could not move; those fearful eyes held him fast. In another moment that steel would have pierced his heart. But Betty had seen also, and, thrusting her strong arms about Margaret, held her back, crying:

"Listen, you do not understand. It is I he wants—not you; I whom he loves, and who love him, and am about to marry him. You he will send back home."

"Loose me," said Margaret, in such a voice that Betty's arms fell from her, and she stood there, the dagger still in her hand.

"Now," she said to d'Aguilar, "the truth, and be swift with it. What means this woman?"

"She knows best," answered d'Aguilar uneasily. "It has pleased her to wrap herself in this web of conceits."

"Which it has pleased you to spin, perchance. Speak, girl!"

"He made love to me," gasped Betty; "and I love him. He promised to marry me. He sent me a letter but to-day—here it is," and she drew it out.

"Read," said Margaret; and Betty read.

"So *you* have betrayed me," said Margaret, "you, my cousin, whom I have sheltered and cherished."

"No," cried Betty. "I never thought to betray you; sooner would I have died. I believed that your father was hurt, and that while you were visiting him that man would take me."

"What have you to say?" asked Margaret of d'Aguilar in the same dreadful voice. "You offered your accursed love to me— and to her, and you have snared us both. Man, what have you to say?"

"Only this", he answered, trying to look brave, "that woman is a fool, whose vanity I played on that I might make use of her to keep near to you."

"Do you hear, Betty? do you hear?" cried Margaret with a terrible little laugh; but Betty only groaned as though she were dying.

"I love you, and you only," went on d'Aguilar "As for your cousin, I will send her ashore. I have committed this sin because I could not help myself. The thought that you were to be married to another man to-morrow drove me mad, and I dared all to take you from his arms, even though you should

H. Rider Haggard

never come to mine. Did I not swear to you," he said with an attempt at his old gallantry, "that your image should accompany me to Spain, whither we are sailing now?" And as he spoke the words the ship lurched a little in the wind.

Margaret made no answer, only toyed with the dagger blade, and watched him with eyes that glittered more coldly than its steel.

"Kill me, if you will, and have done," he went on in a voice that was desperate with love and shame. "So shall I be rid of all this torment."

Then Margaret seemed to awake, for she spoke to him in a new voice—a measured, frozen voice. "No," she answered, "I will not stain my hands even with your blood, for why should I rob God of His own vengeance? If you attempt to touch me, or even to separate me from this poor woman whom you have fooled, then I will kill—not you, but myself, and I swear to you that my ghost shall accompany you to Spain, and from Spain down to the hell that awaits you. Listen, Carlos d'Aguilar, Marquis of Morella, this I know about you, that you believe in God and hear His anger. Well, I call down upon you the vengeance of Almighty God. I see it hang above your head. I say that it shall fall upon you, waking and sleeping, loving and hating, in life and in death to all eternity. Do your worst, for you shall do it all in vain. Whether I die or whether I live, every pang that you cause me to suffer, every misery that you have brought, or shall bring, upon the head of my betrothed, my father, and this woman, shall be repaid to you a millionfold in this world and the next. Now do you still wish that I should accompany you to Spain, or will you let me go?"

"I cannot," he answered hoarsely; "it is too late."

"So be it, I will accompany you to Spain, I and Betty Dene, and the vengeance of Almighty God that hovers over you. Of this at least be sure—I hate you, I despise you, but I fear you not at all. Go." Then d'Aguilar stumbled from that cabin, and the two women heard the door bolted behind him.

H. Rider Haggard

CHAPTER X

THE CHASE

About the time that Margaret and Betty were being rowed aboard the *San Antonio*, Peter Brome and his servants, who had been delayed an hour or more by the muddy state of the roads, pulled rein at the door of the house in Holborn. For over a month he had been dreaming of this moment of return, as a man does who expects such a welcome as he knew awaited him, and who on the morrow was to be wed to a lovely and beloved bride. He had thought how Margaret would be watching at the window, how, spying him advancing down the street, she would speed to the door, how he would leap from his horse and take her to his arms in front of every one if need be—for why should they be ashamed who were to be wed upon the morrow?

But there was no Margaret at the window, or at any rate he could not see her, for it was dark. There was not even a light; indeed the whole face of the old house seemed to frown at him through the gloom. Still, Peter played his part according to the plan; that is, he leapt from his horse, ran to the door and tried to enter, but could not for it was locked, so he hammered on it with the handle of his sword, till at length some one came and unbolted. It was the hired man with whom Margaret had left the letter, and he held a lantern in his hand.

The sight of him frightened Peter, striking a chill to his heart.

"Who are you?" he asked; then, without waiting for an answer, went on, "Where are Master Castell and Mistress Margaret?"

The man answered that the master was not yet back from his ship, and that the Lady Margaret had gone out nearly three hours before with her cousin Betty and a sailor—all of them on horseback.

"She must have ridden to meet me, and missed us in the dark," said Peter aloud, whereon the man asked whether he spoke to Master Brome, since, if so, he had a letter for him.

"Yes," answered Peter, and snatched it from his hand, bidding him close the door and hold up the lantern while he read, for he could see that the writing was that of Margaret.

"A strange story," he muttered, as he finished it. "Well, I must away," and he turned to the door again.

As he stretched out his hand to the key, it opened, and through it came Castell, as sound as ever he had been.

"Welcome, Peter!" he cried in a jolly voice. "I knew you were here, for I saw the horses; but why are you not with Margaret?"

"Because Margaret has gone to be with you, who should be hurt almost to death, or so says this letter."

"To be with me—hurt to the death! Give it me—nay, read it, I cannot see."

So Peter read.

"I scent a plot," said Castell in a strained voice as he finished, "and I think that hound of a Spaniard is at the bottom of it, or Betty, or both. Here, you fellow, tell us what you know, and be swift if you would keep a sound skin."

"That would I, why not?" answered the man, and told all the

tale of the coming of the sailor.

"Go, bid the men bring back the horses, all of them," said Castell almost before he had done; "and, Peter, look not so dazed, but come, drink a cup of wine. We shall need it, both of us, before this night is over. What! is there never a fellow of all my servants in the house?" So he shouted till his folk, who had returned with him from the ship, came running from the kitchen.

He bade them bring food and liquor, and while they gulped down the wine, for they could not eat, Castell told how their Mistress Margaret had been tricked away, and must be followed. Then, hearing the horses being led back from the stables, they ran to the door and mounted, and, followed by their men, a dozen or more of them, in all, galloped off into the darkness, taking another road for Tilbury, that by which Margaret went, not because they were sure of this, but because it was the shortest.

But the horses were tired, and the night was dark and rainy, so it came about that the clock of some church struck three of the morning before ever they drew near to Tilbury. Now they were passing the little quay where Margaret and Betty had entered the boat, Castell and Peter riding side by side ahead of the others in stern silence, for they had nothing to say, when a familiar voice hailed them—that of Thomas the groom.

"I saw your horses' heads against the sky," he explained, "and knew them."

"Where is your mistress?" they asked both in a breath.

"Gone, gone with Betty Dene in a boat, from this quay, to be rowed to the *Margaret*, or so I thought. Having stabled the horses as I was bidden, I came back here to await them. But that was hours ago, and I have seen no soul, and heard nothing except the wind and the water, till I heard the galloping of your horses."

"On to Tilbury, and get boats," said Castell. "We must catch the *Margaret* ere she sails at dawn. Perhaps the women are aboard of her."

"If so, I think Spaniards took them there, for I am sure they were not English in that craft," said Thomas, as he ran by the side of Castell's horse, holding to the stirrup leather.

His master made no answer, only Peter groaned aloud, for he too was sure that they were Spaniards.

An hour later, just as the dawn broke, they with their men climbed to the deck of the *Margaret* while she was hauling up her anchor. A few words with her captain, Jacob Smith, told them the worst. No boat had left the ship, no Margaret had come aboard her. But some six hours before they had watched the Spanish vessel, *San Antonio*, that had been berthed above them, pass down the river. Moreover, two watermen in a skiff, who brought them fresh meat, had told them that while they were delivering three sheep and some fowls to the *San Antonio*, just before she sailed, they had seen two tall women helped up her ladder, and heard one of them say in English, "Lead me to my father."

Now they knew all the awful truth, and stared at each other like dumb men.

It was Peter who found his tongue the first, and said slowly:

"I must away to Spain to find my bride, if she still lives, and to kill that fox. Get you home, Master Castell."

"My home is where my daughter is," answered Castell fiercely. "I go a-sailing also."

"There is danger for you in that land of Spaniards, if ever we get yonder," said Peter meaningly.

"If it were the mouth of hell, still I would go," replied Castell.

"Why should I not who seek a devil?"

"That we do both," said Peter, and stretching out his hand he took that of Castell. It was the pledge of the father and the lover to follow her who was all to them, till death stayed their quest.

Castell thought a little while, then gave orders that all the crew should be called together on deck in the waist of the ship, which was a carack of about two hundred tons burden, round fashioned, and sitting deep in the water, but very strongly built of oak, and a swift sailer. When they were gathered, and with them the officers and their own servants, accompanied by Peter, he went and addressed them just as the sun was rising. In few and earnest words he told them of the great outrage that had been done, and how it was his purpose and that of Peter Brome who had been wickedly robbed of the maid who this day should have become his wife, to follow the thieves across the sea to Spain, in the hope that by the help of God, they might rescue Margaret and Betty. He added that he knew well this was a service of danger, since it might chance that there would be fighting, and he was loth to ask any man to risk life or limb against his will, especially as they came out to trade and not to fight. Still, to those who chose to accompany them, should they win through safely, he promised double wage, and a present charged upon his estate, and would give them writings to that effect. As for those who did not, they could leave the ship now before she sailed.

When he had finished, the sailormen, of whom there were about thirty, with the stout-hearted captain, Jacob Smith, a sturdy-built man of fifty years of age, at the head of them, conferred together, and at last, with one exception—that of a young new-married man, whose heart failed him—they accepted the offer, swearing that they would see the thing through to the end, were it good or ill, for they were all Englishmen, and no lovers of the Spaniards. Moreover, so bitter a wrong stirred their blood. Indeed, although for the most part they were not sailors, six of the twelve men who had ridden with them from London prayed that they might come too, for the love they had to Margaret, their master, and Peter; and they took them. The other six they sent ashore again, bearing letters to Castell's friends, agents, and reeves, as to the transfer of his business and the care of his lands, houses, and other properties during his absence. Also, they took a short will duly signed by Castell and witnessed, wherein he left all his goods of whatever sort that remained unsettled or undevised, to Margaret and Peter, or the survivor of them, or their heirs, or failing these, for the purpose of founding a hospital for the poor. Then these men bade them farewell and departed, very heavy at heart, just as the anchor was hauled home, and the sails began to draw in the stiff morning breeze.

About ten o'clock they rounded the Nore bank safely, and here spoke a fishing-boat, who told them that more than six hours before they had seen the *San Antonio* sail past them down Channel, and noted two women standing on her deck, holding each other's hands and gazing shorewards. Then, knowing that there was no mistake, there being nothing more that they could do, worn out with grief and journeying, they ate some food and went to their cabin to sleep.

As he laid him down Peter remembered that at this very hour he should have been in church taking Margaret as his bride— Margaret, who was now in the power of the Spaniard—and swore a great and bitter oath that d'Aguilar should pay him back for all this shame and agony. Indeed, could his enemy have seen the look on Peter's face he might well have been afraid, for this Peter was an ill man to cross, and had no forgiving heart; also, his wrong was deep.

For four days the wind held, and they ran down Channel before it, hoping to catch sight of the Spaniard; but the *San Antonio* was a swift caravel of 250 tons with much canvas, for she carried four masts, and although the *Margaret* was also a good sailer, she had but two masts, and could not come up with her. Or, for anything they knew, they might have missed her on the seas. On the afternoon of the fourth day, when they were off the Lizard, and creeping along very slowly under a light breeze, the look-out man reported a ship lying becalmed ahead. Peter, who had the eyes of a hawk, climbed up the mast to look at her, and presently called down that he believed from her shape and rig she must be the caravel, though of this he could not be sure as he had never seen her. Then the captain, Smith, went up also, and a few minutes later returned saying that without doubt it was the *San Antonio*.

Now there was a great and joyful stir on board the *Margaret*, every man seeing to his sword and their long or cross bows, of which there were plenty, although they had no bombards or cannon, that as yet were rare on merchant ships. Their plan was to run alongside the *San Antonio* and board her, for thus they hoped to recover Margaret. As for the anger of the king, which might well fall on them for this deed, since he would think little of the stealing of a pair of Englishwomen, of that they must take their chance.

Within half an hour everything was ready, and Peter, pacing to and fro, looked happier than he had done since he rode away to Dedham. The light breeze still held, although, if it reached the *San Antonio*, it did not seem to move her, and, with the help of it, by degrees they came to within half a mile of the caravel. Then the wind dropped altogether, and there the two ships lay. Still the set of the tide, or some current, seemed to be drawing them towards each other, so that when the night closed in they were not more than four hundred paces apart, and the Englishmen had great hopes that before morning they would close, and be able to board by the light of the moon.

But this was not to be, since about nine o'clock thick clouds rose up which covered the heavens, while with the clouds came strong winds blowing off the land, and, when at length the dawn broke, all they could see of the *San Antonio* was her topmasts as she rose upon the seas, flying southwards swiftly. This, indeed, was the last sight they had of her for two long weeks.

From Ushant all across the Bay the airs were very light and variable, but when at length they came off Finisterre a gale sprang up from the north-east which drove them forward very fast. It was on the second night of this gale, as the sun set, that, running out of some mist and rain, suddenly they saw the *San Antonio* not a mile away, and rejoiced, for now they knew that she had not made for any port in the north of Spain, as, although she was bound for Cadiz, they feared she might have done to trick them. Then the rain came on again, and they saw her no more.

All down the coast of Portugal the weather grew more heavy day by day, and when they reached St. Vincent's Cape and bore round for Cadiz, it blew a great gale. Now it was that for the third time they viewed the *San Antonio* labouring ahead of them, nor, except at night, did they lose sight of her any more until the end of that voyage. Indeed, on the next day they nearly came up with her, for she tried to beat in to Cadiz, but, losing one of her masts in a fierce squall, and seeing that the *Margaret*, which sailed better in this tempest, would soon be aboard of her, abandoned her plan, and ran for the Straits of Gibraltar.

Past Tarifa Point they went, having the coast of Africa on their right; past the bay of Algegiras, where the *San Antonio* did not try to harbour; past Gibraltar's grey old rock, where the signal fires were burning, and so at nightfall, with not a mile between them, out into the Mediterranean Sea.

Here the gale was furious, so that they could scarcely carry a rag of canvas, and before morning lost one of their topmasts. It was an anxious night, for they knew not if they would live through it; moreover, the hearts of Castell and of Peter were torn with fear lest the Spaniard should founder and take Margaret with her to the bottom of the sea. When at length the wild, stormy dawn broke, however, they saw her, apparently in an evil case, labouring away upon their starboard bow, and by noon came to within a furlong of her, so that they could see the sailors crawling about on her high poop and

H. Rider Haggard

stern. Yes, and they saw more than this, for presently two women ran from some cabin waving a white cloth to them; then were hustled back, whereby they learned that Margaret and Betty still lived and knew that they followed, and thanked God. Presently, also, there was a flash, and, before ever they heard the report, a great iron bullet fell upon their decks and, rebounding, struck a sailor, who stood by Peter, on the breast, and dashed him away into the sea. The *San Antonio* had fired the bombard which she carried, but as no more shots came they judged that the cannon had broke its lashings or burst.

A while after the *San Antonio*, two of whose masts were gone, tried to put about and run for Malaga, which they could see far away beneath the snow-capped mountains of the Sierra. But this the Spaniard could not do, for while she hung in the wind the *Margaret* came right atop of her, and as her men laboured at the sails, every one of the Englishmen who could be spared, under the command of Peter, let loose on them with their long shafts and crossbows, and, though the heaving deck of the *Margaret* was no good platform, and the wind bent the arrows from their line, they killed and wounded eight or ten of them, causing them to loose the ropes so that the *San Antonio* swung round into the gale again. On the high tower of the caravel, his arm round the sternmost mast, stood d'Aguilar, shouting commands to his crew. Peter fitted an arrow to his string and, waiting until the *Margaret* was poised for a moment on the crest of a great sea, aimed and loosed, making allowance for the wind.

True to line sped that shaft of his, yet, alas! a span too high, for when a moment later d'Aguilar leapt from the mast, the arrow quivered in its wood, and pinned to it was the velvet cap he wore. Peter ground his teeth in rage and disappointment; almost he could have wept, for the vessels swung apart again, and his chance was gone.

"Five times out of seven," he said bitterly, "can I send a shaft through a bull's ring at fifty paces to win a village badge, and now I cannot hit a man to save my love from shame. Surely

God has forsaken me!"

Through all that afternoon they held on, shooting with their bows whenever a Spaniard showed himself, and being shot at in return, though little damage was done to either side. But this they noted—that the *San Antonio* had sprung a leak in the gale, for she was sinking deeper in the water. The Spaniards knew it also, and, being aware that they must either run ashore or founder, for the second time put about, and, under the rain of English arrows, came right across the bows of the *Margaret*, heading for the little bay of Calahonda, that is the port of Motril, for here the shore was not much more than a league away.

"Now," said Jacob Smith, the captain of the *Margaret*, who stood under the shelter of the bulwarks with Castell and Peter, "up that bay lies a Spanish town. I know it, for I have anchored there, and if once the *San Antonio* reaches it, good-bye to our lady, for they will take her to Granada, not thirty miles away across the mountains, where this Marquis of Morella is a mighty man, for there is his palace. Say then, master, what shall we do? In five more minutes the Spaniard will be across our bows again. Shall we run her down, which will be easy, and take our chance of picking up the women, or shall we let them be taken captive to Granada and give up the chase?"

"Never," said Peter. "There is another thing that we can do—follow them into the bay, and attack them there on shore."

"To find ourselves among hundreds of the Spaniards, and have our throats cut," answered Smith, the captain, coolly.

"If we ran them down," asked Castell, who had been thinking deeply all this while, "should we not sink also?"

"It might be so," answered Smith; "but we are built of English oak, and very stout forward, and I think not. But she would sink at once, being near to it already, and the odds are that the

H. Rider Haggard

women are locked in the cabin or between decks out of reach of the arrows, and must go with her."

"There is another plan," said Peter sternly, "and that is to grapple with her and board her, and this I will do."

The captain, a stout man with a flat face that never changed, lifted his eyebrows, which was his only way of showing surprise.

"What!" he said. "In this sea? I have fought in some wars, but never have I known such a thing."

"Then, friend, you shall know it now, if I can but find a dozen men to follow me," answered Peter with a savage laugh. "What? Shall I see my mistress carried off before my eyes and strike no blow to save her? Rather will I trust in God and do it, and if I die, then die I must, as a man should. There is no other way."

Then he turned and called in a loud voice to those who stood around or loosed arrows at the Spaniard:

"Who will come with me aboard yonder ship? Those who live shall spend their days in ease thereafter, that I promise, and those who fall will win great fame and Heaven's glory."

The crew looked at the waves running hill high, and the water-logged Spaniard labouring in the trough of them as she came round slowly in a wide circle, very doubtfully, as well they might, and made no answer. Then Peter spoke again.

"There is no choice," he said. "If we give that ship our stem we can sink her, but then how will the women be saved? If we leave her alone, mayhap she will founder, and then how will the women be saved? Or she may win ashore, and they will be carried away to Granada, and how can we snatch them out of the hand of the Moors or of the power of Spain? But if we can take the ship, we may rescue them before they go down or reach land. Will none back me at this inch?"

"Aye, son," said old Castell, "I will."

Peter stared at him in surprise. "You—at your years!" he said.

"Yes, at my years. Why not? I have the fewer to risk."

Then, as though he were ashamed of his doubts, one brawny sailorman stepped forward and said that he was ready for a cut at the Spanish thieves in foul weather as in fair. Next all Castell's household servants came out in a body for love of him and Peter and their lady, and after them more sailors, till nearly half of those aboard, something over twenty in all, declared that they were ready for the venture, wherein Peter cried, "Enough." Smith would have come also; but Castell said No, he must stop with the ship.

Then, while the carack's head was laid so as to cut the path of the *San Antonio* circling round them slowly like a wounded swan, and the boarders made ready their swords and knives, for here archery would not avail them, Castell gave some orders to the captain. He bade him, if they were cut down or taken, to put about and run for Seville, and there deliver over the ship and her cargo to his partners and correspondents, praying them in his name to do their best by means of gold, for which the sale value of the vessel and her goods should be chargeable, or otherwise, to procure the release of Margaret and Betty, if they still lived, and to bring d'Aguilar, the Marquis of Morella, to account for his crime. This done, he called to one of his servants to buckle on him a light steel breastplate from the ship's stores. But Peter would wear no iron because it was too heavy, only an archer's jerkin of bull-hide, stout enough to turn a sword-cut, such as the other boarders put on also with steel caps, of both of which they had a plenty in the cabin.

Now the *San Antonio*, having come round, was steering for the mouth of the bay in such fashion that she would pass them within fifty yards. Hoisting a small sail to give his ship way, the captain, Smith, took the helm of the *Margaret* and steered straight at her so as to cut her path, while the boarders, headed by Peter and Castell, gathered near the bowsprit, lay down there under shelter of the bulwarks, and waited.

CHAPTER XI

THE MEETING ON THE SEA

For another minute or more the *San Antonio* held on until she divined the desperate purpose of her foe. Then, seeing that soon the carack's prow must crash into her frail side, she shifted her helm and came round several points, so that in the end the *Margaret* ran, not into her, but alongside of her, grinding against her planking, and shearing away a great length of her bulwark. For a few seconds they hung together thus, and, before the seas bore them apart, grapnels were thrown from the *Margaret* whereof one forward got hold and brought them bow to bow. Thus the end of the bowsprit of the *Margaret* projected over the high deck of the *San Antonio*.

"Now for it," said Peter. "Follow me, all." And springing up, he ran to the bowsprit and began to swarm along it.

It was a fearful task. One moment the great seas lifted him high into the air, and the next down he came again till the massive spar crashed on to the deck of the *San Antonio* with such a shock that he nearly flew from it like a stone from a sling. Yet he hung on, and, biding his chance, seized a broken stay-rope that dangled from the end of the bowsprit like a lash from a whip, and began to slide down it. The gale caught him and blew him to and fro; the vessel, pitching wildly, jerked him into the air; the deck of the *San Antonio* rose up and receded like a thing alive. It was near—not a dozen feet beneath him—and loosing his hold he fell upon the forward

H. Rider Haggard

tower without being hurt then, gaining his feet, ran to the broken mast and flinging his left arm about it, with the other drew his sword.

Next instant—how, he never knew—Castell was at his side, and after him came two more men, but one of these rolled from the deck into the sea and was lost. As he vanished, the chain of the grappling iron parted, and the *Margaret* swung away from them, leaving those three alone in the power of their foes, nor, do what she would, could she make fast again. As yet, however, there were no Spaniards to be seen, for the reason that none had dared to stand upon this high tower whereof the bulwarks were all gone, while the bowsprit of the *Margaret* crashed down upon it like a giant's club, and, as she rolled, swept it with its point.

So there they stood, clinging to the mast and waiting for the end, for now their friends were a hundred yards away, and they knew that their case was desperate. A shower of arrows came, loosed from other parts of the ship, and one of these struck the man with them through the throat, so that he fell to the deck clasping at it, and presently rolled into the sea also. Another pierced Castell through his right forearm, causing his sword to drop and slide away from him. Peter seized the arrow, snapped it in two, and drew it out; but Castell's right arm was now helpless, and with his left he could do no more than cling to the broken mast.

"We have done our best, son," he said, "and failed. Margaret will learn that we would have saved her if we could, but we shall not meet her here."

Peter ground his teeth, and looked about him desperately, for he had no words to say. What should he do? Leave Castell and rush for the waist of the ship and so perish, or stay and die there? Nay, he would not be butchered like a bird on a bough, he would fall fighting.

"Farewell," he called through the gale. "God rest our souls!"

Then, waiting till the ship steadied herself, he ran aft, and reaching the ladder that led to her tower, staggered down it to the waist of the vessel, and at its foot halted, holding to the rail.

The scene before him was strange enough, for there, ranged round the bulwarks, were the Spanish men, who watched him curiously, whilst a few paces away, resting against the mast, stood d'Aguilar, who lifted his hand, in which there was no weapon, and addressed him.

"Senor Brome," he shouted, "do not move another step or you are a dead man. Listen to me first, and then do what you will. Am I safe from your sword while I speak?"

Peter nodded his head in assent, and d'Aguilar drew nearer, for even in that more sheltered place it was hard to hear because of the howling of the tempest.

"Senor," he said to Peter, "you are a very brave man, and have done a deed such as none of us have seen before; therefore, I wish to spare you if I may. Also, I have worked you bitter wrong, driven to it by the might of love and jealousy, for which reason also I wish to spare you. To set upon you now would be but murder, and, whatever else I do, I will not murder. First, let me ease your mind. Your lady and mine is aboard here; but fear not, she has come and will come to no harm from me, or from any man while I live. If for no other reason, I do not desire to affront one who, I hope, will be my wife by her own free will, and whom I have brought to Spain that she might not make this impossible by becoming yours. Senor, believe me, I would no more force a woman's will than I would do murder on her lover."

"What did you, then, when you snatched her from her home by some foul trick?" asked Peter fiercely.

"Senor, I did wrong to her and all of you, for which I would make amends."

"What amends? Will you give her back to me?"

"No, that I cannot do, even if she should wish it, of which I am not sure; no—never while I live."

"Bring her forth, and let us hear whether she wishes it or no," shouted Peter, hoping that his words would reach Margaret.

But d'Aguilar only smiled and shook his head, then went on:

"That I cannot either, for it would give her pain. Still, Senor, I will repay the heavy debt that I owe to you, and to you also, Senor." And he bowed towards Castell who, unseen by Peter, had crept down the ladder, and now stood behind him staring at d'Aguilar with cold rage and indignation. "You have wrought us much damage, have you not? hunting us across the seas, and killing sundry of us with your arrows, and now you have striven to board our ship and put us to the sword, a design in which God has frustrated you. Therefore your lives are justly forfeit, and none would blame us if we slew you. Yet I spare you both. If it is possible I will put you back aboard the *Margaret*, and if it is not possible you shall be set free ashore to go unmolested whither you will. Thus I will wipe out my debt and be free of all reproach."

"Do you take me for such a man as yourself?" asked Peter, with a bitter laugh. "I do not leave this ship alive unless my affianced wife, Mistress Margaret, goes with me."

"Then, Senor Brome, I fear that you will leave it dead, as indeed we may all of us, unless we make land soon, for the vessel is filling fast with water. Still, knowing your metal, I looked for some such words from you, and am prepared with another offer which I am sure you will not refuse. Senor, our swords are much of the same length, shall we measure them against each other? I am a grandee of Spain, the Marquis of Morella, and it will, therefore, be no dishonour for you to fight with me."

"I am not so sure," said Peter, "for I am more than that—an honest man of England, who never practised woman-stealing. Still, I will fight you gladly, at sea or on shore, wherever and whenever we meet, till one or both are dead. But what is the stake, and how do I know that some of these," and he pointed to the crew, who were listening intently, "will not stab me from behind?"

"Senor, I have told you that I do not murder, and that would be the foulest murder. As for the stake, it is Margaret to the victor. If you kill me, on behalf of all my company, I swear by our Saviour's Blood that you shall depart with her and her father unharmed, and if I kill you, then you both shall swear that she shall be left with me, and no suit or question raised but to her woman I give liberty, who have seen more than enough of her."

"Nay," broke in Castell, speaking for the first time "I demand the right to fight with you also when my arm is healed."

"I refuse it," answered d'Aguilar haughtily. "I cannot lift my sword against an old man who is the father of the maid who shall be my wife, and, moreover, a merchant and a Jew. Nay, answer me not, lest all these should remember your ill words. I will be generous, and leave you out of the oath. Do your worst against me, Master Castell, and then leave me to do my worst against you. Senor Brome, the light grows bad, and the water gains upon us. Say, are you ready?"

Peter nodded his head, and they stepped forward.

"One more word," said d'Aguilar, dropping his sword-point. "My friends, you have heard our compact. Do you swear to abide by it, and, if I fall, to set these two men and the two ladies free on their own ship or on the land, for the honour of chivalry and of Spain?"

The captain of the *San Antonio* and his lieutenants answered that they swore on behalf of all the crew.

"You hear, Senor Brome. Now these are the conditions—that we fight to the death, but, if both of us should be hurt or wounded, so that we cannot despatch each other, then no further harm shall be done to either of us, who shall be tended till we recover or die by the will of God."

"You mean that we must die on each other's swords or not at all, and if any foul chance should overtake either, other than by his adversary's hand, that adversary shall not dispatch him?"

"Yes, Senor, for in our case such things may happen," and he pointed to the huge seas that towered over them, threatening to engulf the water-logged caravel. "We will take no advantage of each other, who wish to fight this quarrel out with our own right arms."

"So be it," said Peter, "and Master Castell here is the witness to our bargain."

D'Aguilar nodded, kissed the cross-hilt of his sword in confirmation of the pact, bowed courteously, and put himself on his defence.

For a moment they stood facing each other, a well-matched pair—Peter, lean, fierce-faced, long-armed, a terrible man to see in the fiery light that broke upon him from beneath the edge of a black cloud; the Spaniard tall also, and agile, but to all appearance as unconcerned as though this were but a pleasure bout, and not a duel to the death with a woman's fate hanging on the hazard. D'Aguilar wore a breastplate of gold-inlaid black steel and a helmet, while Peter had but his tunic of bull's hide and iron-lined cap, though his straight cut-and-thrust sword was heavier and mayhap half an inch longer than that of his foe.

Thus, then, they stood while Castell and all the ship's company, save the helmsman who steered her to the harbour's mouth, clung to the bulwarks and the cordage of the mainmast, and, forgetful of their own peril, watched in utter silence.

It was Peter who thrust the first, straight at the throat, but d'Aguilar parried deftly, so that the sword point went past his neck, and before it could be drawn back again, struck at Peter. The blow fell upon the side of his steel cap, and glanced thence to his left shoulder, but, being light, did him no harm. Swiftly came the answer, which was not light, for it fell so heavily upon d'Aguilar's breastplate, that he staggered back. After him sprang Peter, thinking that the game was his, but at that moment the ship, which had entered the breakers of the harbour bar, rolled terribly, and sent them both reeling to the bulwarks. Nor did she cease her rolling, so that, smiting and thrusting wildly, they staggered backwards and forwards across the deck, gripping with their left hands at anything they could find to steady them, till at length, bruised and breathless, they fell apart unwounded, and rested awhile.

"An ill field this to fight on, Senor," gasped d'Aguilar.

"I think that it will serve our turn," said Peter grimly, and rushed at him like a bull. It was just then that a great sea came aboard the ship, a mass of green water which struck them both and washed them like straws into the scuppers, where they rolled half drowned. Peter rose the first, coughing out salt water, and rubbing it from his eyes, to see d'Aguilar still upon the deck, his sword lying beside him, and holding his right wrist with his left hand.

"Who gave you the hurt?" he asked, "I or your fall?"

"The fall, Senor," answered d'Aguilar; "I think that it has broken my wrist. But I have still my left hand. Suffer me to arise, and we will finish this fray."

As the words passed his lips a gust of wind, more furious than any that had gone before, concentrated as it was through a gorge in the mountains, struck the caravel at the very mouth of the harbour, and laid her over on her beam ends. For a while it seemed as though she must capsize and sink, till suddenly her mainmast snapped like a stick and went overboard, when, relieved of its weight, by slow degrees she righted herself. Down upon the deck came the cross yard, one end of it crashing through the roof of the cabin in which Margaret and Betty were confined, splitting it in two, while a block attached to the other fell upon the side of Peter's head and, glancing from the steel cap, struck him on the neck and shoulder, hurling him senseless to the deck, where, still grasping his sword, he lay with arms outstretched.

Out of the ruin of the cabin appeared Margaret and Betty, the former very pale and frightened, and the latter muttering prayers, but, as it chanced, both uninjured. Clinging to the tangled ropes they crept forward, seeking refuge in the waist of the ship, for the heavy spar still worked and rolled above them, resting on the wreck of the cabin and the bulwarks, whence presently it slid into the sea. By the stump of the broken mainmast they halted, their long locks streaming in the gale, and here it was that Margaret caught sight of Peter lying upon his back, his face red with blood, and sliding to and fro as the vessel rolled.

She could not speak, but in mute appeal pointed first to him and then to d'Aguilar, who stood near, remembering as she did so her vision in the house at Holborn, which was thus terribly fulfilled. Holding to a rope, d'Aguilar drew near to her and spoke into her ear. "Lady," he said, "this is no deed of mine. We were fighting a fair fight, for he had boarded the ship when the mast fell and killed him. Blame me not for his death, but seek comfort from God."

She heard, and, looking round her wildly, perceived her father struggling towards her; then, with a bitter cry, fell senseless on his breast.

CHAPTER XII

FATHER HENRIQUES

The night came down swiftly, for a great stormcloud, in which jagged lightning played, blotted out the last rays of the sunk sun. Then, with rolling thunder and torrents of rain, the tempest burst over the sinking ship. The mariners could no longer see to steer, they knew not whither they were going, only the lessened seas told them that they had entered the harbour mouth. Presently the *San Antonio* struck upon a rock, and the shock of it threw Castell, who was bending over the senseless shape of Margaret, against the bulwarks and dazed him.

There arose a great cry of "The vessel founders!" and water seemed to be pouring on the deck, though whether this were from the sea or from the deluge of the falling rain he did not know. Then came another cry of "Get out the boat, or we perish!" and a sound of men working in the darkness. The ship swung round and round and settled down. There was a flash of lightning, and by it Castell saw Betty holding the unconscious Margaret in her strong arms. She saw him also, and screamed to him to come to the boat. He started to obey, then remembered Peter. Peter might not be dead; what should he say to Margaret if he left him there to drown? He crept to where he lay upon the deck, and called to a sailor who rushed by to help him. The man answered with a curse, and vanished into the deep gloom. So, unaided, Castell essayed the task of lifting this heavy body, but his right arm being almost useless, could do no more than drag it into a sitting posture, and thus, by slow degrees, across the deck to where he imagined the boat to be.

But here there was no boat, and now the sound of voices came from the other side of the ship, so he must drag it back again. By the time he reached the starboard bulwarks all was silent, and another flash of lightning showed him the boat, crowded with people, upon the crest of a wave, fifty yards or more from him, whilst others, who had not been able to enter, clung to its stern and gunwale. He shouted aloud, but no answer came, either because none were left living on the ship, or because in all that turmoil they could not hear him.

Then Castell, knowing that he had done everything that he could, dragged Peter under the overhanging deck of the forward tower, which gave some little shelter from the rain, and, laying his bleeding head upon his knees so that it might be lifted above the wash of the waters, sat himself down and began to say prayers after the Jewish fashion whilst awaiting his end.

That he was about to die he had no doubt, for the waist of the ship, as he could perceive by the lightning, was almost level with the sea, which, however, here in the harbour was now much calmer than it had been. This he knew, for although the rain still fell steadily and the wind howled above, no spray broke over them. Deeper and deeper sank the caravel as she drifted onwards, till at length the water washed over her deck from side to side, so that Castell was obliged to seat himself on the second step of the ladder down which Peter had charged up on the Spaniards. A while passed, and he became aware that the *San Antonio* had ceased to move, and wondered what this might mean. The storm had rolled away now, and he could see the stars; also with it went the wind. The night grew warmer, too, which was well for him, for otherwise, wet as he was, he must have perished. Still it was a long night, the longest that ever he had spent, nor did any sleep come to relieve his misery or make his end easier, for the pain from the arrow wound in his arm kept him awake.

So there he sat, wondering if Margaret was dead, as Peter seemed to be dead, and if so, whether their spirits were watching him now, watching and waiting till he joined them. He thought, too, of the days of his prosperity until he had seen the accursed face of d'Aguilar, and of all the worthless wealth that was his, and what would become of it. He hoped even that Margaret was gone; better that she should be dead than live on in shame and misery. If there were a God, how came it that He could allow such things to happen in the world? Then he remembered how, when Job sat in just such an evil case, his wife had invited him to curse God and die, and how the patriarch had answered to her, "What! shall we receive good at the hand of God, and shall we not receive evil?" Remembered, too, after all his troubles, what had been the end of that just man, and therefrom took some little comfort. After this a stupor crept over him, and his last thought was that the vessel had sunk and he was departing into the deeps of death.

* * * * *

Listen! A voice called, and Castell awoke to see that it was growing light, and that before him supporting himself on the rail of the ladder, stood the tall form of Peter—Peter with a ghastly, blood-stained countenance, chattering teeth, and glazed, unnatural eyes.

"Do you live, John Castell?" said that hollow voice, "or are we both dead and in hell?"

"Nay," he answered, "I live yet; we are still this side of doom."

"What has chanced?" asked Peter. "I have been lost in a great blackness."

Castell told him briefly.

Peter listened till he had done, then staggered to the bulwark rail and looked about him, making no comment.

"I can see nothing," he said presently—"the mist is too deep; but I think we must lie near the shore. Come, help me. Let us try to find victuals; I am faint."

Castell rose, stretched his cramped limbs, and going to him, placed his uninjured arm round Peter's middle, and thus supported him towards the stern of the ship, where he guessed that the main cabin would be. They found and entered it, a small place, but richly furnished, with a carved crucifix screwed to its sternmost wall. A piece of pickled meat and some of the hard wheaten cakes such as sailors use, lay upon the floor where they had been cast from the table, while in a swinging rack above stood flagons of wine and of water. Castell found a horn mug, and filling it with wine gave it to Peter, who drank greedily, then handed it back to him, who also drank. Afterwards they cut off portions of the meat with their knives, and swallowed them, though Peter did this with great difficulty because of the hurt to his head and neck. Then they drank more wine, and, somewhat refreshed, left the place.

The mist was still so thick that they could see nothing, and therefore they went into the wreck of that cabin which had been occupied by Margaret and Betty, sat themselves down upon the bed wherein they had slept, and waited. Resting thus, Peter noted that this cabin had been fitted sumptuously as though for the occupation of a great lady, for even the vessels were of silver, and in a wardrobe, whereof the doors were open, hung beautiful gowns. Also, there were a few written books, on the outer leaves of one of which Margaret had set down some notes and a prayer of her own making, petitioning that Heaven would protect her; that Peter and her father might be living and learn the truth of what had befallen, and that it would please the saints to deliver her, and to bring them together again. This book Peter thrust away within his jerkin to study at his leisure.

Now the sun rose suddenly above the eastern range of the

mountains wherewith they were surrounded. Leaving the cabin, they climbed to the forecastle tower and gazed about them, to find that they were in a land-locked harbour, and stranded not more than a hundred yards from the shore. By tying a piece of iron to a rope and letting it down into the sea, they discovered that they lay upon a ridge, and that there were but four feet of water beneath their bow, and, having learned this, determined to wade to the beach. First, however, they went back to the cabin and filled a leather bag they found with food and wine. Then, by an afterthought, they searched for the place where d'Aguilar slept, and discovered it between decks; also a strong-box which they made shift to break open with an iron bar.

In it was a great store of gold, placed there, no doubt, for the payment of the crew, and with it some jewels. The jewels they left, but the money they divided and stowed it about them to serve their needs should they come safe ashore. Then they washed each other's wounds and bound them up, and descending the ladder which had been thrown over the ship's side when the Spaniards escaped in the boat, let themselves down into the sea and bade farewell to the *San Antonio*.

By now the wind had fallen and the sun shone brightly, warming their chilled blood; also the water, which was quite calm, did not rise much above their middles, so that they were able—the bottom being smooth and sandy—to wade without trouble to the shore. As they drew near to it they saw people gathering there, and guessed that they came from the little town of Motril, which lay up the river that here ran into the bay. Also they saw other things—namely, the boat of the *San Antonio* upon the shore, and rejoiced to know that it had come safe to land, for it rested upon its keel with but little water in its bottom. Lying here and there also were the corpses of drowned men, five or six of them: no doubt those sailors who had swum after the boat or clung to its gunwale, but among these bodies none were those of women.

When at length they reached the shore, very few people were

　　　　　　　　H. Rider Haggard

left there, for of the rest some had begun to wade out towards the ship to plunder her, whilst others had gone to fetch boats for the same purpose. Therefore, the company who awaited them consisted only of women, children, three old men, and a priest. The last, a hungry-eyed, smooth-faced, sly-looking man, advanced to greet them courteously, bidding them thank God for their escape.

"That we do indeed," said Castell; "but tell us, Father, where are our companions?"

"There are some of them," answered the priest, pointing to the dead bodies; "the rest, with the two senoras, started two hours ago for Granada. The Marquis of Morella, from whom I hold this cure, told us that his ship had sunk, and that no one else was left alive, and, as the mist hid everything, we believed him. That is why we were not here before, for," he added significantly, "we are poor folk, to whom the saints send few wrecks."

"How did they go to Granada, Father?" asked Castell. "On foot?"

"Nay, Senor, they took all the horses and mules in the village by force, though the marquis promised that he would return them and pay for their hire later, and we trusted him because we must. The ladies wept much, and prayed us to take them in and keep them; but this the marquis would not allow, although they seemed so sad and weary. God send that we see our good beasts back again," he added piously.

"Have you any left for us? We have a little money, and can pay for them if they be not too dear."

"Not one, Senor—not one; the place has been cleared even down to the mares in foal. But, indeed you seem scarcely fit to ride at present, who have undergone so much," and he pointed to Peter's wounded head and Castell's bandaged arm. "Why do you not stay and rest awhile?"

"Because I am the father of one of the senoras, and doubtless she thinks me drowned, and this senor is her affianced husband," answered Castell briefly.

"Ah!" said the priest, looking at them with interest, "then what relation to her is the marquis? Well, perhaps I had better not ask, for this is no confessional, is it? I understand that you are anxious, for that great grandee has the reputation of being gay—an excellent son of the Church, but without doubt very gay," and he shook his shaven head and smiled. "But come up to the village, Senors, where you can rest and have your hurts attended to; afterwards we will talk."

"We had best go," said Castell in English to Peter. "There are no horses on this beach, and we cannot walk to Granada in our state."

Peter nodded, and, led by the priest, whose name they discovered to be Henriques, they started.

On the crest of the hill a few hundred paces away they turned and looked back, to see that every able-bodied inhabitant of the village seemed by now to be engaged in plundering the stranded vessel.

"They are paying themselves for the mules and horses," said Fray Henriques with a shrug. "So I see," answered Castell, "but you—" and he stopped.

"Oh, do not be afraid for me," replied the priest with a cunning little smile. "The Church does not loot; but in the end the Church gets her share. These are a pious folk. Only when he learns that the caravel did not sink after all, I fear the marquis will demand an account of us."

Then they limped on over the hill, and presently saw the white-walled and red-roofed village beneath them on the banks of the river.

H. Rider Haggard

Five minutes later their guide stopped at a door in a roughly paved street, which he opened with a key.

"My humble dwelling, when I am in residence here, and not at Granada," he said, "in which I shall be honoured to receive you. Look, near by is the church."

Then they entered a patio, or courtyard, where some orange-trees grew round a fountain of water, and a life-sized crucifix stood against the wall. As he passed this sacred emblem Peter bowed and crossed himself, an example that Castell did not follow. The priest looked at him sharply.

"Surely, Senor," he said, "you should do reverence to the symbol of our Saviour, who, by His mercy, have just been saved from the death which the marquis told me had overtaken both of you."

"My right arm is hurt," answered Castell readily, "so I must do that reverence in my heart."

"I understand, Senor; but if you are a stranger to this country, which you do not seem to be, who speak its tongue so well, with your permission I will warn you that here it is wise not to confine your reverences to the heart. Of late the directors of the Inquisition have become somewhat strict, and expect that the outward forms should be observed as well. Indeed, when I was a familiar of the Holy Office at Seville, I have seen men burned for the neglect of them. You have two arms and a head, Senor, also a knee that can be bent."

"Pardon me," answered Castell to this lecture. "I was thinking of other matters. The carrying off of my daughter at the hands of your patron, the Marquis of Morella, for instance."

Then, making no reply, the priest led them through his sitting-room to a bed-chamber with high barred windows, that, although it was large and lofty, reminded them somehow of a prison cell. Here he left them, saying that he would go to find the local surgeon, who, it seemed, was a barber also, if, indeed, he were not engaged in "lightening the ship," recommending them meanwhile to take off their wet clothes and lie down to rest.

A woman having brought hot water and some loose garments in which to wrap themselves while their own were drying, they undressed and washed and afterwards, utterly worn out, threw themselves down and fell asleep upon the beds, having first hidden away their gold in the food bag, which Peter placed beneath his pillow. Two hours later or more they were awakened by the arrival of Father Henriques and the barber-surgeon, accompanied by the woman-servant, and who brought them back their clothes cleaned and dried.

When the surgeon saw Peter's hurt to the left side of his neck and shoulder, which now were black, swollen, and very stiff, he shook his head, and said that time and rest alone could cure it, and that he must have been born under a fortunate star to have escaped with his life, which, save for his steel cap and leather jerkin, he would never have done. As no bones were broken, however, all that he could do was to dress the parts with some soothing ointment and cover them with clean cloths. This finished, he turned to Castell's wound, that was through the fleshy part of the right forearm, and, having syringed it out with warm water and oil, bound it up, saying that he would be well in a week. He added drily that the gale must have been fiercer even than he thought, since it could blow an arrow through a man's arm—a saying at which the priest pricked up his ears.

To this Castell made no answer, but producing a piece of Morella's gold, offered it to him for his services, asking him at the same time to procure them mules or horses, if he could. The barber promised to try to do so, and being well pleased with his fee, which was a great one for Motril, said that he would see them again in the evening, and if he could hear of any beasts would tell them of it then. Also he promised to bring them some clothes and cloaks of Spanish make, since

H. Rider Haggard

those they had were not fit to travel in through that country, being soiled and blood-stained.

After he had gone, and the priest with him, who was busy seeing to the division of the spoils from the ship and making sure of his own share, the servant, a good soul, brought them soup, which they drank. Then they lay down again upon the beds and talked together as to what they should do.

Castell was downhearted, pointing out that they were still as far from Margaret as ever, who was now once more lost to them, and in the hand of Morella, whence they could scarcely hope to snatch her. It would seem also that she was being taken to the Moorish city of Granada, if she were not already there, where Christian law and justice had no power.

When he had heard him out, Peter, whose heart was always stout, answered:

"God has as much power in Granada as in London, or on the seas whence He has saved us. I think, Sir, that we have great reason to be thankful to God, seeing that we are both alive to-day, who might so well have been dead, and that Margaret is alive also, and, as we believe, unharmed. Further, this Spanish thief of women is, it would seem, a strange man, that is, if there be any truth in his words, for although he could steal her, it appears that he cannot find it in his heart to do her violence, but is determined to win her only with her own consent, which I think will not be had readily. Also, he shrinks from murder, who, when he could have butchered us, did not do so."

"I have known such men before," said Castell, "who hold some sins venial, but others deadly to their souls. It is a fruit of superstition."

"Then, Sir, let us pray that Morella's superstitions may remain strong, and get us to Granada as quickly as we can, for there, remember, you have friends, both among the Jews and Moors, who have traded with the place for many years, and these may give us shelter. Therefore, though things are bad, still they might be worse."

"That is so," answered Castell more cheerfully, "if, indeed, she has been taken to Granada; and as to this, we will try to learn something from the barber or the Father Henriques."

"I put no faith in that priest, a sly fellow who is in the pay of Morella," answered Peter.

Then they were silent, being still very weary, and having nothing more to say, but much to think about.

About sundown the doctor came back and dressed their wounds. He brought with him a stock of clothes of Spanish make, hats and two heavy cloaks fit to travel in, which they bought from him at a good price. Also, he said that he had two fine mules in the courtyard, and Castell went out to look at them. They were sorry beasts enough, being poor and wayworn, but as no others were to be had they returned to the room to talk as to the price of them and their saddles. The chaffering was long, for he asked twice their value, which Castell said poor shipwrecked men could not pay; but in the end they struck a bargain, under which the barber was to keep and feed the mules for the night, and bring them round next morning with a guide who would show them the road to Granada. Meanwhile, they paid him for the clothes, but not for the beasts.

Also they tried to learn something from him about the Marquis of Morella, but, like the Fray Henriques, the man was cunning, and kept his mouth shut, saying that it was ill for poor men like himself to chatter of the great, and that at Granada they could hear everything. So he went away, leaving some medicine for them to drink, and shortly afterwards the priest appeared.

He was in high good-humour, having secured those jewels

H. Rider Haggard

which they had left behind in the iron coffer as his share of the spoil of the ship. Taking note of him as he showed and fondled them, Castell added up the man, and concluded that he was very avaricious; one who hated the poverty in which he had been reared, and would do much for money. Indeed, when he spoke bitterly of the thieves who had been at the ship's strong-box and taken nearly all the gold, Castell determined that he must never know who those thieves were, lest they should meet with some accident on their journey.

At length the trinkets were put away, and the priest said that they must sup with him, but lamented that he had no wine to give them, who was forced to drink water; whereon Castell prayed him to procure a few flasks of the best at their charges, which, nothing loth, he sent his servant out to do.

So, dressed in their new Spanish clothes, and having all the gold hidden about them in two money-belts that they had bought from the barber at the same time, they went in to supper, which consisted of a Spanish dish called *olla podrida*— a kind of rich stew—bread, cheese, and fruit. Also the wine that they had bought was there, very good and strong, and, whilst taking but little of it themselves for fear they should fever their wounds, they persuaded Father Henriques to drink heartily, so that in the end he forgot his cunning, and spoke with freedom. Then, seeing that he was in a ripe humour, Castell asked him about the Marquis of Morella, and how it happened that he had a house in the Moorish capital of Granada.

"Because he is half a Moor," answered the priest. "His father, it is said, was the Prince of Viana, and his mother a lady of royal Moorish blood, from whom he inherited great wealth, and his lands and palace in Granada. There, too, he loves to dwell, who, although he is so good a Christian by faith, has many heathen tastes, and, like the Moors, surrounds himself with a seraglio of beautiful women, as I know, for often I act as his chaplain, as in Granada there are no priests. Moreover, there is a purpose in all this, for, being partly of their blood, he is accredited to the court of their sultan, Boabdil, by Ferdinand and Isabella in whose interests he works in secret. For, strangers, you should know, if you do not know it already, that their Majesties have for long been at war against the Moor, and purpose to take what remains of his kingdom from him, and make it Christian, as they have already taken Malaga, and purified it by blood and fire from the accursed stain of infidelity."

"Yes," said Castell, "we heard that in England, for I am a merchant who have dealings with Granada, whither I am going on my affairs."

"On what affairs then goes the senora, who you say is your daughter, and what is that story that the sailors told of, about a fight between the *San Antonio* and an English ship, which indeed we saw in the offing yesterday? And why did the wind blow an arrow through your arm, friend Merchant? And how came it that you two were left aboard the caravel when the marquis and his people escaped?"

"You ask many questions, holy Father. Peter, fill the glass of his reverence; he drinks nothing who thinks that it is always Lent. Your health, Father. Ah! well emptied. Fill it again, Peter, and pass me the flask. Now I will begin to answer you with the story of the shipwreck." And he commenced an endless tale of the winds and sails and rocks and masts carried away, and of the English ship that tried to help the Spanish ship, and so forth, till at length the priest, whose glass Peter filled whenever his head was turned, fell back in his chair asleep.

"Now," whispered Peter in English across the table to Castell—"now I think that we had best go to bed, for we have learned much from this holy spy—as I take him to be—and told little."

So they crept away quietly to their chamber, and, having swallowed the draught that the doctor had given them, said their prayers each in his own fashion, locked the door, and lay down to rest as well as their wounds and sore anxieties would allow them.

CHAPTER XIII

THE ADVENTURE OF THE INN

Peter did not sleep well, for, notwithstanding all the barber's dressing, his hurt pained him much. Moreover, he was troubled by the thought that Margaret must be sure that both he and her father were dead, and of the sufferings of her sore heart. Whenever he dozed off he seemed to see her awake and weeping, yes, and to hear her sobs and murmurings of his name. When the first light of dawn crept through the high-barred windows, he arose and called Castell, for they could not dress without each other's help. Then they waited until they heard the sound of men talking and of beasts stamping in the courtyard without. Guessing that this was the barber with the mules, they unlocked their door and, finding the servant yawning in the passage, persuaded her to let them out of the house.

The barber it was, sure enough, and with him a one-eyed youth mounted on a pony, who, he said, would guide them to Granada. So they returned with him into the house, where he looked at their wounds, shaking his head over that of Peter, who, he said, ought not to travel so soon. After this came more haggling as to the price of the mules, saddlery, saddle-bags in which they packed their few spare clothes, hire of the guide and his horse, and so forth, since, anxious as they were to get away, they did not dare to seem to have money to spare.

At length everything was settled, and as their host, Father

Henriques, had not yet appeared, they determined to depart without bidding him farewell, leaving some money in acknowledgment of his hospitality and as a gift to his church. Whilst they were handing it over to the servant, however, together with a fee for herself, the priest joined them, unshaven, and holding his hand to his tonsured head whilst he explained, what was not true, that he had been celebrating some early Mass in the church; then asked whither they were going.

They told him, and pressed their gift upon him, which he accepted, nothing loth, though its liberality seemed to make him more urgent to delay their departure. They were not fit to travel; the roads were most unsafe; they would be taken captive by the Moors, and thrown into a dungeon with the Christian prisoners; no one could enter Granada without a passport, he declared, and so forth, to all of which they answered that they must go.

Now he appeared to be much disturbed, and said finally that they would bring him into trouble with the Marquis of Morella—how or why, he would not explain, though Peter guessed that it might be lest the marquis should learn from them that this priest, his chaplain, had been plundering the ship which he thought sunk, and possessing himself of his jewels. At length, seeing that the man meant mischief and would stop them in some fashion if they delayed, they bade him farewell hastily, and, pushing past him, mounted the mules that stood outside and rode away with their guide.

As they went they heard the priest, who now was in a rage, abusing the barber who had sold them the beasts, and caught the words "Spies," "English senoras," and "Commands of the Marquis," so that they were glad when at length they found themselves outside the town, where as yet few were stirring, and riding unmolested on the road to Granada.

This road proved to be no good one, and very hilly; moreover, the mules were even worse than they had thought, that which

Peter rode stumbling continually. Now they asked the youth, their guide, how long it would take them to reach Granada; but all he answered them was:

"*Quien sabe*?" (Who knows?) "It depends upon the will of God."

An hour later they asked him again, whereon he replied:

Perhaps to-night, perhaps to-morrow, perhaps never, as there were many thieves about, and if they escaped the thieves they would probably be captured by the Moors.

"I think there is one thief very near to us," said Peter in English, looking at this ill-favoured young man, then added in his broken Spanish, "Friend, if we fall in with robbers or Moors, the first one who dies will be yourself," and he tapped the hilt of his sword.

The lad uttered a Spanish curse, and turned the head of his pony round as though he would ride back to Motril, then changed his mind and pushed on a long way in front of them, nor could they come near him again for hours. So hard was the road and so feeble were the mules that, notwithstanding a midday halt to rest them, it was nightfall before they reached the top of the Sierra, and in the last sunset glow, separated from them by the rich *vega* or plain, saw the minarets and palaces of Granada. Now they wished to push on, but their guide swore that it was impossible, as in the dark they would fall over precipices while descending to the plain. There was a *venta* or inn near by, he said, where they could sleep, starting again at dawn.

When Castell said that they did not wish to go to an inn, he answered that they must, since they had eaten what food they had, and here on the road there was no fodder for the beasts. So, reluctantly enough, they consented, knowing that unless they were fed the mules would never carry them to Granada, whereon the guide, pointing out the house to them, a lonely

H. Rider Haggard

place in a valley about a hundred yards from the road, said that he would go on to make arrangements, and galloped off.

As they approached this hostelry, which was surrounded by a rough wall for purposes of defence, they saw the one-eyed youth engaged in earnest conversation with a fat, ill-favoured man who had a great knife stuck in his girdle. Advancing to them, bowing, this man said that he was the host, and, in reply to their request for food and a room, told them that they could have both.

They rode into the courtyard, whereon the inn-keeper locked the door in the wall behind them, explaining that it was to keep out robbers, and adding that they were fortunate to be where they could sleep quite safely. Then a Moor came and led away their mule to the stable, and they accompanied the landlord into the sitting-room, a long, low apartment furnished with tables and benches, on which sat several rough-looking fellows, drinking wine. Here the host suddenly demanded payment in advance, saying that he did not trust strangers. Peter would have argued with him; but Castell, thinking it best to comply, unbuttoned his garments to get at his money, for he had no loose coin in his pocket, having paid away the last at Motril.

His right hand being still helpless, this he did with his left, and so awkwardly that the small doubloon he took hold of slipped from his fingers and fell on to the floor. Forgetting that he had not re-fastened the belt, he bent down to pick it up, whereon a number of gold pieces of various sorts, perhaps twenty of them, fell out and rolled hither and thither on the ground. Peter, watching, saw the landlord and the other men in the room exchange a quick and significant glance. They rose, however, and assisted to find the money, which the host returned to Castell, remarking with an unpleasant smile, that if he had known that his guests were so rich he would have charged them more for their accommodation.

"Of your good heart I pray you not," answered Castell, "for

that is all our worldly goods," and even as he spoke another gold piece, this time a large doubloon, which had remained in his clothing, slipped to the floor.

"Of course, Senor," the host replied as he picked this up also and handed it back politely, "but shake yourself, there may still be a coin or two in your doublet." Castell did so, whereon the gold in his belt, loosened by what had fallen out, rattled audibly, and the audience smiled again, while the host congratulated him on the fact that he was in an honest house, and not wandering on the mountains, which were the home of so many bad men.

Having pocketed his money with the best grace he could, and buckled his belt beneath his robe, Castell and Peter sat down at a table a little apart, and asked if they could have some supper. The host assented, and called to the Moorish servant to bring food, then sat down also, and began to put questions to them, of a sort which showed that their guide had already told all their story.

"How did you learn of our shipwreck?" asked Castell by way of answer.

"How? Why, from the people of the marquis, who stopped here to drink a cup of wine when he passed to Granada yesterday with his company and two senoras. He said that the *San Antonio* had sunk, but told us nothing of your being left aboard of her."

"Then forgive us, friend, if we, whose business is of no interest to you, copy his discretion, as we are weary and would rest."

"Certainly, Senors—certainly," replied the man; "I go to hasten your supper, and to fetch you a flask of the wine of Granada worthy of your degree," and he left them.

A while later their food came—good meat enough of its sort—and with it the wine in an earthenware jug, which, as he filled their horn mugs, the host said he had poured out of the flask himself that the crust of it might not slip. Castell thanked him, and asked him to drink a cup to their good journey; but he declined, answering that it was a fast day with him, on which he was sworn to touch only water. Now Peter, who had said nothing all this time, but noted much, just touched the wine with his lips, and smacked them as though in approbation while he whispered in English to Castell:

"Drink it not; it is drugged!"

"What says your son?" asked the host.

"He says that it is delicious, but suddenly he has remembered what I too forgot, that the doctor at Motril forbade us to touch wine for fear lest we should worsen the hurts that we had in the shipwreck. Well, let it not be wasted. Give it to your friends. We must be content with thinner stuff." And taking up a jug of water that stood upon the table, he filled an empty cup with it and drank, then passed it to Peter, while the host looked at them sourly.

Then, as though by an afterthought, Castell rose and politely presented the jug of wine and the two filled mugs to the men who were sitting at a table close by, saying that it was a pity that they should not have the benefit of such fine liquor. One of these fellows, as it chanced, was their own guide, who had come in from tending the mules. They took the mugs readily enough, and two of them tossed off their contents, whereon, with a smothered oath, the landlord snatched away the jug and vanished with it.

Castell and Peter went on with their meal, for they saw their neighbours eating of the same dish, as did the landlord also, who had returned, and, it seemed to Peter, was watching the two men who had drunk the wine with an anxious eye. Presently one of these rose from the table and, going to a bench on the other side of the room, flung himself down upon it and became quite silent, while their one-eyed guide stretched out his arms and fell face forward so that his head rested on an empty plate, where he remained apparently insensible. The host sprang up and stood irresolute, and Castell, rising, said that evidently the poor lad was sleepy after his long ride, and as they were the same, would he be so courteous as to show them to their room?

He assented readily, indeed it was clear that he wished to be rid of them, for the other men were staring at the guide and their companion, and muttering amongst themselves.

"This way, Senors," he said, and led them to the end of the place where a broad step-ladder stood. Going up it, a lamp in his hand, he opened a trap-door and called to them to follow him, which Castell did. Peter, however, first turned and said good-night to the company who were watching them; at the same moment, as though by accident or thoughtlessly, half drawing his sword from its scabbard. Then he too went up the ladder, and found himself with the others in an attic.

It was a bare place, the only furniture in it being two chairs and two rough wooden bedsteads without heads to them, mere trestles indeed, that stood about three feet apart against a boarded partition which appeared to divide this room from some other attic beyond. Also, there was a hole in the wall immediately beneath the eaves of the house that served the purpose of a window, over which a sack was nailed. "We are poor folk," said the landlord as they glanced round this comfortless garret, "but many great people have slept well here, as doubtless you will also," and he turned to descend the ladder.

"It will serve," answered Castell; "but, friend, tell your men to leave the stable open, as we start at dawn, and be so good as to give me that lamp."

"I cannot spare the lamp," he grunted sulkily, with his foot already on the first step.

H. Rider Haggard

Peter strode to him and grasped his arm with one hand, while with the other he seized the lamp. The man cursed, and began to fumble at his belt, as though for a knife, whereon Peter, putting out his strength, twisted his arm so fiercely that in his pain he loosed the lamp, which remained in Peter's hand. The inn-keeper made a grab at it, missed his footing and rolled down the ladder, falling heavily on the floor below.

Watching from above, to their relief they saw him pick himself up, and heard him begin to revile them, shaking his fist and vowing vengeance. Then Peter shut down the trap-door. It was ill fitted, so that the edge of it stood up above the flooring, also the bolt that fastened it had been removed, although the staples in which it used to work remained. Peter looked round for some stick or piece of wood to pass through these staples, but could find nothing. Then he bethought him of a short length of cord that he had in his pocket, which served to tie one of the saddle-bags in its place on his mule. This he fastened from one staple to the other, so that the trap-door could not be lifted more than an inch or two.

Reflecting that this might be done, and the cord cut with a knife passed through the opening, he took one of the chairs and stood it so that two of its legs rested on the edge of the trap-door and the other two upon the boarding of the floor. Then he said to Castell:

"We are snared birds; but they must get into the cage before they wring our necks. That wine was poisoned, and, if they can, they will murder us for our money—or because they have been told to do so by the guide. We had best keep awake to-night."

"I think so," answered Castell anxiously. "Listen, they are talking down below."

Talking they were, as though they debated something, but after a while the sound of voices died away. When all was silent they hunted round the attic, but could find nothing that was unusual to such places. Peter looked at the window-hole, and, as it was large enough for a man to pass through, tried to drag one of the beds beneath it, thinking that if any such attempt were made, he who lay thereon would have the thief at his mercy, only to find, however, that these were screwed to the floor and immovable. As there was nothing more that they could do, they went and sat upon these beds, their bare swords in their hands, and waited a long while, but nothing happened.

At length the lamp, which had been flickering feebly for some time, went out, lacking oil, and except for the light which crept through the window-place, for now they had torn away the sacking that hung over it, they were in darkness.

A little while later they heard the sound of a horse's hoofs, and the door of the house open and shut, after which there was more talking below, and mingling with it a new voice which Peter seemed to remember.

"I have it," he whispered to Castell. "Here is our late host, Father Henriques, come to see how his guests are faring."

Another half-hour and the waning moon rose, throwing a beam of light into their chamber; also they heard horse's hoofs again. Going to the window, Peter looked out of it and saw the horse, a fine beast, being held by the landlord, then a man came and mounted it and, at some remark of his, turned his face upwards towards their window. It was that of Father Henriques.

The two whispered together for a while till the priest blessed the landlord in Latin words and rode away, and again they heard the door of the house close.

"He is off to Granada, to warn Morella his master of our coming," said Castell, as they reseated themselves upon the beds.

"To warn Morella that we shall never come, perhaps; but we

will beat him yet," replied Peter.

The night wore on, and Castell, who was very weary, sank back upon the bolster and began to doze, when suddenly the chair that was set upon the trap-door fell over with a great clatter, and he sprang up, asking what that noise might be.

"Only a rat," answered Peter, who saw no good in telling him the truth—namely, that thieves or murderers had tried to open the trap-door.

Then he crept down the room, felt the cord, to find that it was still uncut, and replaced the chair where it had been. This done, Peter came back to the bed and threw himself down upon it as though he would slumber, though never was he more wide awake. The weariness of Castell had overcome him again, however, for he snored at his side.

For a long while nothing further happened, although once the ray of moonlight was cut off, and for an instant Peter thought that he saw a face at the window. If so, it vanished and returned no more. Now from behind their heads came faint sounds, like those of stifled breathing, like those of naked feet; then a slight creaking and scratching in the wall—a mouse's tooth might have caused it—and suddenly, right in that ray of moonlight, a cruel-looking knife and a naked arm projected through the panelling.

The knife flickered for a second over the breast of the sleeping Castell as though it were a living thing that chose the spot where it would strike. One second—only one—for the next Peter had drawn himself up, and with a sweep of the sword which lay unscabbarded at his side, had shorn that arm off above the elbow, just where it projected from the panelling.

"What was that?" asked Castell again, as something fell upon him.

"A snake," answered Peter, "a poisonous snake. Wake up now,

and look."

Castell obeyed, staring in silence at the horrible arm which still clasped the great knife, while from beyond the panelling there came a stifled groan, then a sound as of a heavy body stumbling away.

"Come," said Peter, "let us be going, unless we would stop here for ever. That fellow will soon be back to seek his arm."

"Going! How?" asked Castell.

"There seems to be but one road, and that a rough one, through the window and over the wall," answered Peter. "Ah! there they come; I thought so." And as he spoke they heard the sound of men scrambling up the ladder.

They ran to the window-place and looked out, but there seemed to be no one below, and it was not more than twelve feet from the ground. Peter helped Castell through it, then, holding his sound arm with both his own, lowered him as far as he could, and let go. He dropped on to his feet, fell to the ground, then rose again, unhurt. Peter was about to follow him when he heard the chair tumble over again, and, looking round, saw the trap-door open, to fall back with a crash. They had cut the cord!

The figure of a man holding a knife appeared in the faint light, followed by the head of another man. Now it was too late for him to get through the window-place safely; if he attempted it he would be stabbed in the back. So, grasping his sword with both hands, Peter leapt at that man, aiming a great stroke at his shadowy mass. It fell upon him somewhere, for down he went and lay quite still. By now the second man had his knee upon the edge of flooring. Peter thrust him through, and he sank backwards on to the heads of others who were following him, sweeping the ladder with his weight, so that all of them tumbled in a heap at its foot, save one who hung to the edge of the trap frame by his hands. Peter slammed its door to, crushing them so that he loosed his grip, with a howl. Then, as he had nothing else, he dragged the body of the dead man on to it and left him there.

Next he rushed to the window, sheathing his sword as he ran, scrambled through it, and, hanging by his arms, let himself drop, coming to the ground safely, for he was very agile, and in the excitement of the fray forgot the hurt to his head and shoulder.

"Where now?" asked Castell, as he stood by him panting.

"To the stable for the mules. No, it is useless; we have no time to saddle them, and the outer gate is locked. The wall—the wall—we must climb it! They will be after us in a minute."

They ran thither and found that, though ten feet high, fortunately this wall was built of rough stone, which gave an easy foothold. Peter scrambled up first, then, lying across its top, stretched down his hand to Castell, and with difficulty— for the man was heavy and crippled—dragged him to his side. Just then they heard a voice from their garret shout:

"The English devils have gone! Get to the door and cut them off."

"Come on," said Peter. So together they climbed, or rather fell, down the wall on to a mass of prickly-pear bush, which broke the shock but tore them so sorely in a score of places that they could have shrieked with the pain. Somehow they freed themselves, and, bleeding all over, broke from that accursed bush, struggling up the bank of the ditch in which it grew, ran for the road, and along it towards Granada.

Before they had gone a hundred yards they heard shoutings, and guessed that they were being followed. Just here the road crossed a ravine full of boulders and rough scrubby growth, whereas beyond it was bare and open. Peter seized Castell and dragged him up this ravine till they came to a place where, behind a great stone, there was a kind of hole, filled with bushes and tall, dead grass, into which they plunged and hid themselves.

"Draw your sword," he said to Castell. "If they find us, we will die as well as we can."

He obeyed, holding it in his left hand.

They heard the robbers run along the road; then, seeing that they had missed their victims, these returned again, five or six of them, and fell to searching the ravine. But the light was very bad, for here the rays of the moon did not penetrate, and they could find nothing. Presently two of them halted within five paces of them and began to talk, saying that the swine must still be hidden in the yard, or perhaps had doubled back for Motril.

"I don't know where they are hidden," answered the other man; "but this is a poor business. Fat Pedro's arm is cut clean off, and I expect he will bleed to death, while two of the other fellows are dead or dying, for that long-legged Englishman hits hard, to say nothing of those who drank the drugged wine, and look as though they would never wake. Yes, a poor business to get a few doubloons and please a priest, but oh! if I had the hogs here I—" And he hissed out a horrible threat. "Meanwhile we had best lie up at the mouth of this place in case they should still be hidden here."

Peter heard him and listened. All the other men had gone, running back along the road. His blood was up, and the thorn pricks stung him sorely. Saying no word, out of his lair he came with that terrible sword of his aloft.

The men caught sight of him, and gave a gasp of fear. It was the last sound that one of them ever made. Then the other turned and ran like a hare. This was he who had uttered the threat.

"Stop!" whispered Peter, as he overtook him—"stop, and do what you promised."

The brute turned, and asked for mercy, but got none.

"It was needful," said Peter to Castell presently; "you heard—they were going to wait for us."

"I do not think that they will try to murder any more Englishmen at that inn," panted Castell, as he ran along beside him.

CHAPTER XIV

INEZ AND HER GARDEN

For two hours or more John Castell and Peter travelled on the Granada road, running when it was smooth, walking when it was rough, and stopping from time to time to get their breath and listen. But the night was quite silent, no one seemed to be pursuing them. Evidently the remaining cut-throats had either taken another way or, having their fill of this adventure, wanted to see no more of Peter and his sword.

At length the dawn broke over the great misty plain, for now they were crossing the *vega*. Then the sun rose and dispelled the vapours, and a dozen miles or more away they saw Granada on its hill. They saw each other also, and a sorry sight they were, torn by the sharp thorns, and stained with blood from their scratches. Peter was bare-headed too, for he had lost his cap, and almost beside himself now that the excitement had left him, from lack of sleep, pain, and weariness. Moreover, as the sun rose, it grew fearfully hot upon that plain, and its fierce rays, striking full upon his head, seemed to stupefy him, so that at last they were obliged to halt and weave a kind of hat out of corn and grasses, which gave him so strange an appearance that some Moors, whom they met going to their toil, thought that he must be a madman, and ran away.

Still they crawled forward, refreshing themselves with water whenever they could find any in the irrigation ditches that these people used for their crops, but covering little more than a mile an hour. Towards noon the heat grew so dreadful that they were obliged to lie down to rest under the shade of some palm-like trees, and here, absolutely outworn, they sank into a kind of sleep.

They were awakened by a sound of voices, and staggered to their feet, drawing their swords, for they thought that the thieves from the inn had overtaken them. Instead of these ruffianly murderers, however, they saw before them a body of eight Moors, beautifully mounted upon white horses, and clad in turbans and flowing robes, the like of which Peter had never yet beheld, who sat there regarding them gravely with their quiet eyes, and, as it seemed, not without pity.

"Put up your swords, Senors," said the leader of these Moors in excellent Spanish—indeed, he seemed to be a Spaniard dressed in Eastern garments—"for we are many and fresh; and you are but two and wounded."

They obeyed, who could do nothing else.

"Now tell us, though there is little need to ask," went on the captain, "you are those men of England who boarded the *San Antonio* and escaped when she was sinking, are you not?"

Castell nodded, then answered:

"We boarded her to seek—"

"Never mind what you sought," the captain answered; "the names of exalted ladies should not be mentioned before strange men. But you have been in trouble again since then, at the inn yonder, where this tall senor bore himself very bravely. Oh! we have heard all the story, and give him honour who can wield a sword so well in the dark."

"We thank you," said Castell, "but what is your business with us?"

"Senor, we are sent by our master, his Excellency, the high Lord and Marquis of Morella, to find you and bring you to be his guests at Granada."

"So the priest has told. I thought as much," muttered Peter.

"We pray you to come without trouble, as we do not wish to do any violence to such gallant men," went on the captain. "Be pleased to mount two of these horses, and ride with us."

"I am a merchant, with friends of my own at Granada," answered Castell. "Cannot we go to them, who do not seek the hospitality of the marquis?"

"Senor, our orders are otherwise, and here the word of our master, the marquis, is a law that may not be broken."

"I thought that Boabdil was king of Granada," said Castell.

"Without doubt he is king, Senor, and by the grace of Allah will remain so, but the marquis is allied to him in blood; also, while the truce lasts, he is a representative of their Majesties of Spain in our city," and, at a sign, two of the Moors dismounted and led forward their horses, holding the stirrups, and offering to help them to the saddle.

"There is nothing for it," said Peter; "we must go." So, awkwardly enough, for they were very stiff, they climbed on to the beasts and rode away with their captors.

The sun was sinking now, for they had slept long, and by the time they reached the gates of Granada the muezzins were calling to the sunset prayer from the minarets of the mosques.

It was but a very dim and confused idea that Peter gathered of the great city of the Moors, as, surrounded by their white-robed escort, he rode he knew not whither. Narrow winding streets, white houses, shuttered windows, crowds of courteous, somewhat silent people, all men, and all clad in those same

H. Rider Haggard

strange, flowing dresses, who looked at them curiously, and murmured words which afterwards he came to learn meant "Christian prisoners," or sometimes "Christian dogs"; fretted and pointed arches, and a vast fairy-like building set upon a hill. He was dazed with pain and fatigue as, a long-legged, blood-stained figure, crowned with his quaint hat of grasses, he rode through that wondrous and imperial place.

Yet no man laughed at him, absurd as he must have seemed; but perhaps this was because under the grotesqueness of his appearance they recognised something of his quality. Or they might have heard rumours of his sword-play at the inn and on the ship. At any rate, their attitude was that of courteous dislike of the Christian, mingled with respect for the brave man in misfortune.

At length, after mounting a long rise, they came to a palace on a mount, facing the vast, red-walled fortress which seemed to dominate the place, which he afterwards knew as the Alhambra, but separated from it by a valley. This palace was a very great building, set on three sides of a square, and surrounded by gardens, wherein tall cypress-trees pointed to the tender sky. They rode through the gardens and sundry gateways till they came to a courtyard where servants, with torches in their hands, ran out to meet them. Somebody helped him off his horse, somebody supported him up a flight of marble steps, beneath which a fountain splashed, into a great, cool room with an ornamented roof. Then Peter remembered no more.

*   *   *   *   *

A time went by, a long, long time—in fact it was nearly a month—before Peter really opened his eyes to the world again. Not that he had been insensible for all this while—that is, quite—for at intervals he had become aware of that large, cool room, and of people talking about him—especially of a dark-eyed, light-footed, and pretty woman with a white wimple round her face, who appeared to be in charge of him.

Occasionally he thought that this must be Margaret, and yet knew that it could not, for she was different. Also, he remembered that once or twice he had seemed to see the haughty, handsome face of Morella bending over him, as though he watched curiously to learn whether he would live or not, and then had striven to rise to fight him, and been pressed back by the soft, white hands of the woman that yet were so terribly strong.

Now, when he awoke at last, it was to see her sitting there with a ray of sunlight from some upper window falling on her face, sitting with her chin resting on her hand and her elbow on her knee, and contemplating him with a pretty, puzzled look. She made a sweet picture thus, he thought. Then he spoke to her in his slow Spanish, for somehow he knew that she would not understand his own tongue.

"You are not Margaret," he said.

At once the dream went out of the woman's soft eyes; she became intensely interested, and, rising, advanced towards him, a very gracious figure, who seemed to sway as she walked.

"No, no," she said, bending over him and touching his forehead with her taper fingers; "my name is Inez. You wander still, Senor."

"Inez what?" he asked.

"Inez only," she answered, "Inez, a woman of Granada, the rest is lost. Inez, the nurse of sick men, Senor."

"Where then is Margaret—the English Margaret?"

A veil of secrecy seemed to fall over the woman's face, and her voice changed as she answered, no longer ringing true, or so it struck his senses made quick and subtle by the fires of fever:

"I know no English Margaret. Do you then love her—this

English Margaret?"

"Aye," he answered, "she was stolen from me; I have followed her from far, and suffered much. Is she dead or living?"

"I have told you, Senor, I know nothing, although"—and again the voice became natural—"it is true that I thought you loved somebody from your talk in your illness."

Peter pondered a while, then he began to remember, and asked again:

"Where is Castell?"

"Castell? Was he your companion, the man with a hurt arm who looked like a Jew? I do not know where he is. In another part of the city, perhaps. I think that he was sent to his friends. Question me not of such matters, who am but your sick-nurse. You have been very ill, Senor. Look!" And she handed him a little mirror made of polished silver, then, seeing that he was too weak to take it, held it before him.

Peter saw his face, and groaned, for, except the red scar upon his cheek, it was ivory white and wasted to nothing.

"I am glad Margaret did not see me like this," he said, with an attempt at a smile, "bearded too, and what a beard! Lady, how could you have nursed one so hideous?"

"I have not found you hideous," she answered softly; "besides, that is my trade. But you must not talk, you must rest. Drink this, and rest," and she gave him soup in a silver bowl, which he swallowed readily enough, and went to sleep again.

Some days afterwards, when Peter was well on the road to convalescence, his beautiful nurse came and sat by him, a look of pity in her tender, Eastern eyes.

"What is it now, Inez?" he asked, noting her changed face.

"Senor Pedro, you spoke to me a while ago, when you woke up from your long sleep, of a certain Margaret, did you not? Well, I have been inquiring of this Dona Margaret, and have no good news to tell of her."

Peter set his teeth, and said:

"Go on, tell me the worst."

"This Margaret was travelling with the Marquis of Morella, was she not?"

"She had been stolen by him," answered Peter.

"Alas! it may be so; but here in Spain, and especially here in Granada, that will scarcely screen the name of one who has been known to travel with the Marquis of Morella."

"So much the worse for the Marquis of Morella when I meet him again," answered Peter sternly. "What is your story, Nurse Inez?"

She looked with interest at his grim, thin face, but, as it seemed to him, with no displeasure.

"A sad one. As I have told you, a sad one. It seems that the other day this senora was found dead at the foot of the tallest tower of the marquis's palace, though whether she fell from it, or was thrown from it, none know."

Peter gasped, and was silent for a while; then asked:

"Did you see her dead?"

"No, Senor; others saw her."

"And told you to tell me? Nurse Inez, I do not believe your tale. If the Dona Margaret, my betrothed, were dead I should know it; but my heart tells me that she is alive."

H. Rider Haggard

"You have great faith, Senor," said the woman, with a note of admiration in her voice which she could not suppress, but, as he observed, without contradicting him.

"I have faith," he answered. "Nothing else is left; but so far it has been a good crutch."

Peter made no further allusion to the subject, only presently he asked:

"Tell me, where am I?"

"In a prison, Senor."

"Oh! a prison, with a beautiful woman for jailer, and other beautiful women"—and he pointed to a fair creature who had brought something into the room—"as servants. A very fine prison also," and he looked about him at the marbles and arches and lovely carving.

"There are men without the gate, not women," she replied, smiling.

"I daresay; captives can be tied with ropes of silk, can they not? Well, whose is this prison?"

She shook her head.

"I do not know, Senor. The Moorish king's perhaps—you yourself have said that I am only the jailer."

"Then who pays you?"

"Perhaps I am not paid, Senor; perhaps I work for love," and she glanced at him swiftly, "or hate," and her face changed.

"Not hate of me, I think," said Peter.

"No, Senor, not hate of you. Why should I hate you who have

been so helpless and so courteous to me?" and she bent the knee to him a little.

"Why indeed? especially as I am also grateful to you who have nursed me back to life. But then, why hide the truth from a helpless man?"

Inez glanced about her; the room was empty now. She bent over him and whispered:

"Have you never been forced to hide the truth? No, I read it in your face, and you are not a woman—an erring woman."

They looked into each other's eyes a while, then Peter asked: "Is the Dona Margaret really dead?"

"I do not know," she answered; "I was told so." And as though she feared lest she should betray herself, Inez turned and left him quickly.

The days went by, and through the slow degrees of convalescence Peter grew strong again. But they brought him no added knowledge. He did not know where he dwelt or why he was there. All he knew was that he lived a prisoner in a sumptuous palace, or as he suspected, for of this he could not be sure, since the arched windows of one side of the building were walled up, in the wing of a palace. Nobody came near to him except the fair Inez, and a Moor who either was deaf or could understand nothing that he said to him in Spanish. There were other women about, it is true, very pretty women all of them, who acted as servants, but none of these were allowed to approach him; he only saw them at a distance.

Therefore Inez was his sole companion, and with her he grew very intimate, to a certain extent, but no further. On the occasion that has been described she had lifted a corner of her veil which hid her true self, but a long while passed before she enlarged her confidence. The veil was kept down very close indeed. Day by day he questioned her, and day by day, without the slightest show of irritation, or even annoyance, she parried his questions. They knew perfectly well that they were matching their wits against each other; but as yet Inez had the best of the game, which, indeed, she seemed to enjoy. He would talk to her also of all sorts of things—the state of Spain, the Moorish court, the danger that threatened Granada, whereof the great siege now drew near, and so forth—and of these matters she would discourse most intelligently, with the result that he learned much of the state of politics in Castile and Granada, and greatly improved his knowledge of the Spanish tongue.

But when of a sudden, as he did again and again, he sprang some question on her about Morella, or Margaret, or John Castell, that same subtle change would come over her face, and the same silence would seal her lips.

"Senor," she said to him one day with a laugh, "you ask me of secrets which I might reveal to you—perhaps—if you were my husband or my love, but which you cannot expect a nurse, whose life hangs on it, to answer. Not that I wish you to become my husband or my lover," she added, with a little nervous laugh.

Peter looked at her with his grave eyes.

"I know that you do not wish that," he said, "for how could I attract one so gay and beautiful as you are?"

"You seem to attract the English Margaret," she replied quickly in a nettled voice.

"To have attracted, you mean, as you tell me that she is dead," he answered; and, seeing her mistake, Inez bit her lip. "But," he went on, "I was going to add, though it may have no value for you, that you have attracted me as your true friend."

"Friend!" she said, opening her large eyes, "what talk is this? Can the woman Inez find a friend in a man who is under sixty?"

"It would appear so," he answered. And again with that graceful little curtsey of hers she went away, leaving him very puzzled. Two days later she appeared in his room, evidently much disturbed.

"I thought that you had left me altogether, and I am glad to see you, for I tire of that deaf Moor and of this fine room. I want fresh air."

"I know it," she answered; "so I have come to take you to walk in a garden."

He leapt for joy at her words, and snatching at his sword, which had been left to him, buckled it on.

"You will not need that," she said.

"I thought that I should not need it in yonder inn, but I did," he answered. Whereat she laughed, then turned, put her hand upon his shoulder and spoke to him earnestly.

"See, friend," she whispered, "you want to walk in the fresh air—do you not?—and to learn certain things—and I wish to tell you them. But I dare not do it here, where we may at any moment be surrounded by spies, for these walls have ears indeed. Well, when we walk in that garden, would it be too great a penance for you to put your arm about my waist—you who still need support?"

"No penance at all, I assure you," answered Peter with something like a smile. For after all he was a man, and young; while the waist of Inez was as pretty as all the rest of her. "But," he added, "it might be misunderstood."

"Quite so, I wish it to be misunderstood: not by me, who know that you care nothing for me and would as soon place your arm round that marble column."

Peter opened his lips to speak, but she stopped him at once.

"Oh! do not waste falsehoods on me, in which of a truth you have no art," she said with evident irritation. "Why, if you had the money, you would offer to pay me for my nursing, and who knows, I might take it! Understand, you must either do this, seeming to play the lover to me, or we cannot walk together in that garden."

Peter hesitated a little, guessing a plot, while she bent forward till her lips almost touched his ear and said in a still lower voice:

"And I cannot tell you how, perhaps—I say perhaps—you may come to see the remains of the Dona Margaret, and certain other matters. Ah!" she added after a pause, with a little bitter laugh, "now you will kiss me from one end of the garden to the other, will you not? Foolish man! Doubt no more; take your chance, it may be the last."

"Of what? Kissing you? Or the other things?"

"That you will find out," she said, with a shrug of her shoulders. "Come!"

Then, while he followed dubiously, she led him down the length of the great room to a door with a spy-hole in the top of it, that was set in a Moorish archway at the corner.

This door she opened, and there beyond it, a drawn scimitar in his hand, stood a tall Moor on guard. Inez spoke a word to him, whereon he saluted with his scimitar and let them pass across the landing to a turret stair that lay beyond, which they descended. At its foot was another door, whereon she knocked four times. Bolts shot back, keys turned, and it was opened by a black porter, beyond whom stood a second Moor, also with drawn sword. They passed him as they had passed the first, turned down a little passage to the right, ending in some steps, and came to a third door, in front of which she halted.

"Now," she said, "nerve yourself for the trial."

"What trial?" he asked, supporting himself against the wall, for he found his legs still weak.

"This," she answered, pointing to her waist, "and these," and she touched her rich, red lips with her taper finger-points. "Would you like to practise a little, my innocent English knight, before we go out? You look as though you might seem awkward and unconvincing."

"I think," answered Peter drily, for the humour of the situation moved him, "that such practice is somewhat dangerous for me. It might annoy you before I had done. I will postpone my happiness until we are in the garden."

"I thought so," she answered; "but look now, you must play the part, or I shall suffer, who am bearing much for you."

"I think that I may suffer also," he murmured, but not so low that she did not catch his words.

"No, friend Pedro," she said, turning on him, "it is the woman who suffers in this kind of farce. She pays; the man rides away to play another," and without more ado she opened the door, which proved to be unlocked and unguarded.

Beyond the foot of some steps lay a most lovely garden. Great, tapering cypresses grew about it, with many orange-trees and flowering shrubs that filled the soft, southern air with odours. Also there were marble fountains into which water splashed from the mouths of carven lions, and here and there arbours with stone seats, whereon were laid soft cushions of many colours. It was a veritable place of Eastern delight and dreams, such as Peter had never known before he looked upon it on that languorous eve—he who had not seen the sky or flowers for so many weary weeks of sickness. It was secluded also, being surrounded by a high wall, but at one place the tall, windowless tower of some other building of red stone soared

H. Rider Haggard

up between and beyond two lofty cypress-trees.

"This is the harem garden," Inez whispered, "where many a painted favourite has flitted for a few happy, summer hours, till winter came and the butterfly was broken," and, as she spoke, she dropped her veil over her face and began to descend the stairs.

CHAPTER XV

PETER PLAYS A PART

"Stop," said Peter from the shadow of the doorway, "I fear this business, Inez, and I do not understand why it is needful. Why cannot you say what you have to say here?"

"Are you mad?" she answered almost fiercely through her veil. "Do you think that it can be any pleasure for me to seem to make love to a stone shaped like a man, for whom I care nothing at all—except as a friend?" she added quickly. "I tell you, Senor Peter, that if you do not do as I tell you, you will never hear what I have to say, for I shall be held to have failed in my business, and within a few minutes shall vanish from you for ever—to my death perhaps; but what does that matter to you? Choose now, and quickly, for I cannot stand thus for long."

"I obey you, God forgive me!" said the distraught Peter from the darkness of the doorway; "but must I really—?"

"Yes, you must," she answered with energy, "and some would not think that so great a penance."

Then she lifted the corner of her veil coyly and, peeping out beneath it, called in a soft, clear voice, "Oh! forgive me, dear friend, if I have run too fast for you, forgetting that you are still so very weak. Here, lean upon me; I am frail, but it may serve." And she passed up the steps again, to reappear in

H. Rider Haggard

another moment with Peter's hand resting on her shoulder.

"Be careful of these steps," she said, "they are so slippery"—a statement to which Peter, whose pale face had grown suddenly red, murmured a hearty assent. "Do not be afraid," she went on in her flute-like voice; "this is the secret garden, where none can hear words, however sweet, and none can see even a caress, no, not the most jealous woman. That is why in old days it was called the Sultana's Chamber, for there at the end of it was where she bathed in the summer season. What say you of spies? Oh! yes, in the palace there are many, but to look towards this place, even for the Guardian of the Women, was always death. Here there are no witnesses, save the flowers and the birds."

As she spoke thus they reached the central path, and passed up it slowly, Peter's hand still upon the shoulder of Inez, and her white arm about him, while she looked up into his eyes.

"Bend closer over me," she whispered, "for truly your face is like that of a wooden saint," and he bent. "Now," she went on, "listen. Your lady lives, and is well—kiss me on the lips, please, that news is worth it. If you shut your eyes you can imagine that I am she."

Again Peter obeyed, and with a better grace than might have been expected.

"She is a prisoner in this same palace," she went on, "and the marquis, who is mad for love of her, seeks by all means, fair or foul, to make her his wife!"

"Curse him!" exclaimed Peter with another embrace.

"Till a few days ago she thought you dead; but now she knows that you are alive and recovering. Her father, Castell, escaped from the place where he was put, and is in hiding among his friends, the Jews, where even Morella cannot find him; indeed, he believes him fled from the city. But he is not fled, and, having much gold, has opened a door between himself and his daughter."

Here she stopped to return the embrace with much warmth. Then they passed under some trees, and came to the marble baths where the sultanas were supposed to have bathed in summer, for this place had been one of the palaces of the Kings of Granada before they lived in the Alhambra. Here Inez sat down upon a seat and loosened some garment about her throat, for the evening was very hot.

"What are you doing?" Peter asked doubtfully, for he was filled with many fears.

"Cooling myself," she answered; "your arm was warm, and we may sit here for a few minutes."

"Well, go on with your tale," he said.

"I have little more to say, friend, except that if you wish to send any message, I might perhaps be able to take it."

"You are an angel," he exclaimed.

"That is another word for messenger, is it not? Continue."

"Tell her—that if she hears anything of all this business, it isn't true."

"On that point she may form her own opinion," replied Inez demurely. "If I were in her place I know what mine would be. Don't waste time; we must soon begin to walk again."

Peter stared at her, for he could understand nothing of all this play. Apparently she read his look, for she answered it in a quiet, serious voice:

"You are wondering what everything means, and why I am doing what I do. I will tell you, Senor, and you can believe me

H. Rider Haggard

or not as you like. Perhaps you think that I am in love with you. It would not be wonderful, would it? Besides, in the old tales, that always happens—the lady who nurses the Christian knight and worships him and so forth."

"I don't think anything of the sort; I am not so vain."

"I know it, Senor, you are too good a man to be vain. Well, I do all these things, not for love of you, or any one, but for hate—for hate. Yes, for hate of Morella," and she clenched her little hand, hissing the words out between her teeth.

"I understand the feeling," said Peter. "But—but what has he done to *you*?"

"Do not ask me, Senor. Enough that once I loved him—that accursed priest Henriques sold me into his power—oh! a long while ago, and he ruined me, making me what I am, and—I bore his child, and—and it is dead. Oh! Mother of God, my boy is dead, and since then I have been an outcast and his slave—they have slaves here in Granada, Senor—dependent on him for my bread, forced to do his bidding, forced to wait upon his other loves; I, who once was the sultana; I, of whom he has wearied. Only to-day—but why should I tell you of it? Well, he has driven me even to this, that I must kiss an unwilling stranger in a garden," and she sobbed aloud.

"Poor girl!—poor girl!" said Peter, patting her hand kindly with his thin fingers. "Henceforth I have another score against Morella, and I will pay it too."

"Will you?" she asked quickly. "Ah! if so, I would die for you, who now live only to be revenged upon him. And it shall be my first vengeance to rob him of that noble-looking mistress of yours, whom he has stolen away and has set his heart upon wholly, because she is the first woman who ever resisted him—him, who thinks that he is invincible."

"Have you any plan?" asked Peter.

"As yet, none. The thing is very difficult. I go in danger of my life, for if he thought that I betrayed him he would kill me like a rat, and think no harm of it. Such things can be done in Granada without sin, Senor, and no questions asked—at least if the victim be a woman of the murderer's household. I have told you already that if I had refused to do what I have done this evening I should certainly have been got rid of in this way or that, and another set on at the work. No, I have no plan yet, only it is I through whom the Senor Castell communicates with his daughter, and I will see him again, and see her, and we will make some plan. No, do not thank me. He pays me for my services, and I am glad to take his money, who hope to escape from this hell and live on it elsewhere. Yet, not for all the money in the world would I risk what I am risking, though in truth it matters not to me whether I live or die. Senor, I will not disguise it from you, all this scene will come to the Dona Margaret's ears, but I will explain it to her."

"I pray you, do," said Peter earnestly—"explain it fully."

"I will—I will. I will work for you and her and her father, and if I cease to work, know that I am dead or in a dungeon, and fend for yourselves as best you may. One thing I can tell you for your comfort—no harm has been done to this lady of yours. Morella loves her too well for that. He wishes to make her his wife. Or perhaps he has sworn some oath, as I know that he has sworn that he will not murder you—which he might have done a score of times while you have lain a prisoner in his power. Why, once when you were senseless he came and stood over you, a dagger in his hand, and reasoned out the case with me. I said, 'Why do you not kill him?' knowing that thus I could best help to save your life. He answered, 'Because I will not take my wife with her lover's blood upon my hands, unless I slay him in fair fight. I swore it yonder in London. It was the offering which I made to God and to my patron saint that so I might win her fairly, and if I break that oath, God will be avenged upon me here and hereafter. Do my bidding, Inez. Nurse him well, so that if he dies, he dies without sin of mine,' No, he will not murder you or harm her. Friend Pedro, he

H. Rider Haggard

dare not."

"Can you think of nothing?" asked Peter.

"Nothing—as yet nothing. These walls are high, guards watch them day and night, and outside is the great city of Granada where Morella has much power, and whence no Christian may escape. But he would marry her. And there is that handsome fool-woman, her servant, who is in love with him—oh! she told me all about it in the worst Spanish I ever heard, but the story is too long to repeat; and the priest, Father Henriques—he who wished that you might be killed at the inn, and who loves money so much. Ah! now I think I see some light. But we have no more time to talk, and I must have time to think. Friend Pedro, make ready your kisses, we must go on with our game, and, in truth, you play but badly. Come now, your arm. There is a seat prepared for us yonder. Smile and look loving. I have not art enough for both. Come!—come!" And together they walked out of the dense shadow of the trees and past the marble bath of the sultanas to a certain seat beneath a bower on which were cushions, and lying among them a lute.

"Seat yourself at my feet," she said, as she sank on to the bench. "Can you sing?"

"No more than a crow," he answered.

"Then I must sing to you. Well, it will be better than the love-making." Then in a very sweet voice she began to warble amorous Moorish ditties that she accompanied upon the lute, whilst Peter, who was weary in body and disturbed in mind, played a lover's part to the best of his ability, and by degrees the darkness gathered.

At length, when they could no longer see across the garden, Inez ceased singing and rose with a sigh.

"The play is finished and the curtain down," she said; "also it is time that you went in out of this damp. Senor Pedro, you are a very bad actor; but let us pray that the audience was compassionate, and took the will for the deed."

"I did not see any audience," answered Peter.

"But it saw you, as I dare say you will find out by-and-by. Follow me now back to your room, for I must be going about your business—and my own. Have you any message for the Senor Castell?"

"None, save my love and duty. Tell him that, thanks to you, although still somewhat feeble, I am recovered of my hurt upon the ship and the fever which I took from the sun, and that if he can make any plan to get us all out of this accursed city and the grip of Morella I will bless his name and yours."

"Good, I will not forget. Now be silent. Tomorrow we will walk here again; but be not afraid, then there will be no more need for love-making."

Margaret sat by the open window-place of her beautiful chamber in Morella's palace. She was splendidly arrayed in a rich, Spanish dress, whereof the collar was stiff with pearls, she who must wear what it pleased her captor to give her. Her long tresses, fastened with a jewelled band, flowed down about her shoulders, and, her hand resting on her knee, from her high tower prison she gazed out across the valley at the dim and mighty mass of the Alhambra and the ten thousand lights of Granada which sparkled far below. Near to her, seated beneath a silver hanging-lamp, and also clad in rich array, was Betty.

"What is it, Cousin?" asked the girl, looking at her anxiously. "At least you should be happier than you were, for now you know that Peter is not dead, but almost recovered from his sickness and in this very palace; also, that your father is well and hidden away, plotting for our escape. Why, then, are you so sad, who should be more joyful than you were?"

"Would you learn, Betty? Then I will tell you. I am betrayed.

Peter Brome, the man whom I looked upon almost as my husband, is false to me."

"Master Peter false!" exclaimed Betty, staring at her open-mouthed. "No, it is not possible. I know him; he could not be, who will not even look at another woman, if that is what you mean."

"You say so. Then, Betty, listen and judge. You remember this afternoon, when the marquis took us to see the wonders of this palace, and I went thinking that perhaps I might find some path by which afterwards we could escape?"

"Of course I remember, Margaret. We do not leave this cage so often that I am likely to forget."

"Then you will remember also that high-walled garden in which we walked, where the great tower is, and how the marquis and that hateful priest Father Henriques and I went up the tower to study the prospect from its roof, I thinking that you were following me."

"The waiting-women would not let me," said Betty. "So soon as you had passed in they shut the door and told me to bide where I was till you returned. I went near to pulling the hair out of the head of one of them over it, since I was afraid for you alone with those two men. But she drew her knife, the cat, and I had none."

"You must be careful, Betty," said Margaret, "lest some of these heathen folk should do you a mischief."

"Not they," she answered; "they are afraid of me. Why, the other day I bundled one of them, whom I found listening at the door, head first down the stairs. She complained to the marquis, but he only laughed at her, and now she lies abed with a plaster on her nose. But tell me your tale."

"We climbed the tower," said Margaret, "and from its topmost room looked out through the windows that face south at all the mountains and the plain over which they dragged us from Motril. Presently the priest, who had gone to the north wall, in which there are no windows, and entered some recess there, came out with an evil smile upon his face, and whispered something to the marquis, who turned to me and said:

"The father tells me of an even prettier scene which we can view yonder. Come, Senora, and look."

"So I went, who wished to learn all that I could of the building. They led me into a little chamber cut in the thickness of the stone-work, in the wall of which are slits like loop-holes for the shooting of arrows, wide within, but very narrow without, so that I think they cannot be seen from below, hidden as they are between the rough stones of the tower.

"This is the place," said the marquis, "where in the old days the kings of Granada, who were always jealous, used to sit to watch their women in the secret garden. It is told that thus one of them discovered his sultana making love to an astrologer, and drowned them both in the marble bath at the end of the garden. Look now, beneath us walk a couple who do not guess that we are the witnesses of their vows."

"So I looked idly enough to pass the time, and there I saw a tall man in a Moorish dress, and with him, for their arms were about each other, a woman. As I was turning my head away who did not wish to spy upon them thus, the woman lifted her face to kiss the man, and I knew her for that beautiful Inez who has visited us here at times, as a spy I think. Presently, too, the man, after paying her back her embrace, glanced about him guiltily, and I saw his face also, and knew it."

"Who was it?" asked Betty, for this gossip of lovers interested her.

"Peter Brome, no other," Margaret answered calmly, but with a note of despair in her voice. "Peter Brome, pale with recent sickness, but no other man."

"The saints save us! I did not think he had it in him!" gasped Betty with astonishment.

"They would not let me go," went on Margaret; "they forced me to see it all. The pair tarried for a while beneath some trees by the bath and were hidden there. Then they came out again and sat them down upon a marble seat, while the woman sang songs and the man leaned against her lovingly. So it went on until the darkness fell, and we went, leaving them there. Now," she added, with a little sob, "what say you?"

"I say," answered Betty, "that it was not Master Peter, who has no liking for strange ladies and secret gardens."

"It was he, and no other man, Betty."

"Then, Cousin, he was drugged or drunk or bewitched, not the Peter whom we know."

"Bewitched, perchance, by that bad woman, which is no excuse for him."

Betty thought a while. She could not doubt the evidence, but from her face it was clear that she took no severe view of the offence.

"Well, at the worst," she said, "men, as I have known them, are men. He has been shut up for a long while with that minx, who is very fair and witching, and it was scarcely right to watch him through a slit in a tower. If he were my lover, I should say nothing about it."

"I will say nothing to him about that or any other matter," replied Margaret sternly. "I have done with Peter Brome."

Again Betty thought, and spoke.

"I seem to see a trick. Cousin Margaret, they told you he was dead, did they not? And then that news came to us that he was not dead, only sick, and here. So the lie failed. Now they tell you, and seem to show you, that he is faithless. May not all this have been some part played for a purpose by the woman?"

"It takes two to play such parts, Betty. If you had seen—"

"If I had seen, *I* should have known whether it was but a part or love made in good earnest; but you are too innocent to judge. What said the marquis all this while, and the priest?"

"Little or nothing, only smiled at each other, and at length, when it grew dark and we could see no more, asked me if I did not think that it was time to go—me! whom they had kept there all that while to be the witness of my own shame."

"Yes, they kept you there—did they not?—and brought you there just at the right time—did they not?—and shut me out of the tower so that I might not be with you—oh! and all the rest. Now, if you have any justice in you, Cousin, you will hear Peter's side of this story before you judge him."

"I have judged him," answered Margaret coldly, "and, oh! I wish that I were dead."

Margaret rose from her seat and, stepping to the window-place in the tower which was built upon the edge of a hill, searched the giddy depth beneath with her eyes, where, two hundred feet below, the white line of a roadway showed faintly in the moonlight.

"It would be easy, would it not," she said, with a strained laugh, "just to lean out a little too far upon this stone, and then one swift rush and darkness—or light—for ever—which, I wonder?"

"Light, I think," said Betty, jerking her back from the window—"the light of hell fire, and plenty of it, for that

H. Rider Haggard

would be self-murder, nothing else, and besides, what would one look like on that road? Cousin, don't be a fool. If you are right, it isn't you who ought to go out of that window; and if you are wrong, then you would only make a bad business worse. Time enough to die when one must, say I—which, perhaps, will be soon enough. Meanwhile, if I were you, I would try to speak to Master Peter first, if only to let him know what I thought of him."

"Mayhap," answered Margaret, sinking back into a chair, "but I suffer—how can you know what I suffer?"

"Why should I not know?" asked Betty. "Are you the only woman in the world who has been fool enough to fall in love? Can I not be as much in love as you are? You smile, and think to yourself that the poor relation, Betty, cannot feel like her rich cousin. But I do—I do. I know that he is a villain, but I love this marquis as much as you hate him, or as much as you love Peter, because I can't help myself; it is my luck, that's all. But I am not going to throw myself out of a window; I would rather throw him out and square our reckoning, and that I swear I'll do, in this way or the other, even if it should cost me what I don't want to lose—my life," And Betty drew herself up beneath the silver lamp with a look upon her handsome, determined face, which was so like Margaret's and yet so different, that, could he have seen it, might well have made Morella regret that he had chosen this woman for a tool.

While Margaret studied her wonderingly she heard a sound, and glanced up to see, standing before them, none other than the beautiful Spaniard, or Moor, for she knew not which she was, Inez, that same woman whom, from her hiding-place in the tower, she had watched with Peter in the garden.

"How did you come here?" she asked coldly.

"Through the door, Senora, that was left unlocked, which is not wise of those who wish to talk privately in such a place as this," she answered with a humble curtsey.

"The door is still unlocked," said Margaret, pointing towards it.

"Nay, Senora, you are mistaken; here is its key in my hand. I pray you do not tell your lady to put me out, which, being so strong, she well can do, for I have words to say to you, and if you are wise you will listen to them."

Margaret thought a moment, then answered:

"Say on, and be brief."

H. Rider Haggard

CHAPTER XVI

BETTY SHOWS HER TEETH

"Senora," said Inez, "you think that you have something against me."

"No," answered Margaret, "you are—what you are; why should I blame you?"

"Well, against the Senor Brome then?"

"Perhaps, but that is between me and him. I will not discuss it with you."

"Senora," went on Inez, with a slow smile, "we are both innocent of what you thought you saw."

"Indeed; then who is guilty?"

"The Marquis of Morella."

Margaret made no answer, but her eyes said much.

"Senora, you do not believe me, nor is it wonderful. Yet I speak the truth. What you saw from the tower was a play in which the Senor Brome took his part badly enough, as you may have noticed, because I told him that my life hung on it. I have nursed him through a sore sickness, Senora, and he is not ungrateful."

"So I judged; but I do not understand you."

"Senora, I am a slave in this house, a discarded slave. Perhaps you can guess the rest, it is a common story here. I was offered my freedom at a price, that I should weave myself into this man's heart, I who am held fair, and make him my lover. If I failed, then perhaps I should be sold as a slave—perhaps worse. I accepted—why should I not? It was a small thing to me. On the one hand, life, freedom, and wealth, an hidalgo of good blood and a gallant friend for a little while, and, on the other, the last shame or blackness which doubtless await me now—if I am found out. Senora, I failed, who in truth did not try hard to succeed. The man looked on me as his nurse, no more, and to me he was one very sick, no more. Also, we grew to be true friends, and in this way or in that I learned all his story, learned also why the trap was baited thus—that you might be deceived and fall into a deeper trap. Senora, I could not explain it all to him, indeed, in that chamber where we were spied on, I had but little chance. Still, it was necessary that he should seem to be what he is not, so I took him into the garden and, knowing well who watched us, made him act his part, well enough to deceive you it would seem."

"Still I do not understand," said Margaret more softly. "You say that your life or welfare hung on this shameful business. Then why do you reveal it to me now?"

"To save you from yourself, Senora, to save my friend the Senor Brome, and to pay back Morella in his own coin."

"How will you do these things?"

"The first two are done, I think, but the third is difficult. It is of that I come to speak with you, at great risk. Indeed, had not my master been summoned to the court of the Moorish king I could not have come, and he may return at any time."

"Have you some plan?" asked Margaret, leaning towards her eagerly.

"No plan as yet, only an idea." She turned and looked at Betty, adding,

"This lady is your cousin, is she not, though of a different station, and somewhat far away?"

Margaret nodded.

"You are not unlike," went on Inez, "of much the same height and shape, although the Senora Betty is stronger built, and her eyes are blue and her hair golden, whereas your eyes are black and your hair chestnut. Beneath a veil, or at night, it would not be easy to tell you apart if your hands were gloved and neither of you spoke above a whisper."

"Yes," said Margaret, "what then?"

"Now the Senora Betty comes into the play," replied Inez. "Senora Betty, have you understood our talk?"

"Something, not quite all," answered Betty.

"Then what you do not understand your lady must interpret, and be not angry with me, I pray you, if I seem to know more of you and your affairs than you have ever told me. Render my words now, Dona Margaret."

Then, after this was done, and she had thought awhile, Inez continued slowly, Margaret translating from Spanish into English whenever Betty could not understand:

"Morella made love to you in England, Senora Betty—did he not?—and won your heart as he has won that of many another woman, so that you came to believe that he was carrying you off to marry you, and not your cousin?"

"What affair is that of yours, woman?" asked Betty, flushing angrily.

"None at all, save that I could tell much such another story, if you cared to listen. But hear me out, and then answer me a question, or rather, answer the question first. Would you like to be avenged upon this high-born knave?"

"Avenged?" answered Betty, clenching her hands and hissing the words through her firm, white teeth. "I would risk my life for it."

"As I do. It seems that we are of one mind there. Then I think that perhaps I can show you a way. Look now, your cousin has seen certain things which women placed as she is do not like to see. She is jealous, she is angry—or was until I told her the truth. Well, to-night or to-morrow, Morella will come to her and say, 'Are you satisfied? Do you still refuse me in favour of a man who yields his heart to the first light-of-love who tempts him? Will you not be my wife?' What if she answer, 'Yes, I will.' Nay, be silent both of you, and hear me out. What if then there should be a secret marriage, *and the Senora Betty should chance to wear the bride's veil*, while the Dona Margaret, in the robe of Betty, was let go with the Senor Brome and her father?"

Inez paused, watching them both, and playing with the fan she held, while, the rendering of her words finished, Margaret and Betty stared at her and at each other, for the audacity and fearfulness of this plot took their breath away. It was Margaret who spoke the first.

"You must not do it, Betty," she said. "Why, when the man found you out, he would kill you." But Betty took no heed of her, and thought on. At length she looked up and answered:

"Cousin, it was my vain folly that brought you all into this trouble, therefore I owe something to you, do I not? I am not afraid of the man—he is afraid of me; and if it came to killing—why, let Inez lend me that knife of hers, and I think that perhaps I should give the first blow. And—well, I think I love him, rascal though he is, and, afterwards, perhaps we might make it up, who can say?—while, if not—But tell me, you, Inez, should I be his legal wife according to the law of this land?"

"Assuredly," answered Inez, "if a priest married you and he placed the ring upon your hand and named you wife. Then, when once the words of blessing have been said, the Pope alone can loose that knot, which may be risked, for there would be much to explain, and is this a tale that Morella, a good servant of the Church, would care to take to Rome?"

"It would be a trick," broke in Margaret—"a very ugly trick."

"And what was it he played on me and you?" asked Betty. "Nay, I'll chance it, and his rage, if only I can be sure that you and Peter will go free, and your father with you."

"But what of this Inez?" asked Margaret, bewildered.

"She will look after herself," answered Inez. "Perchance, if all goes well, you will let me ride with you. And now I dare stop no longer, I go to see your father, the Senor Castell, and if anything can be arranged, we will talk again. Meanwhile, Dona Margaret, your affianced is nearly well again at last and sends his heart's love to you, and, I counsel you, when Morella speaks turn a gentle ear to him."

Then with another deep curtsey she glided to the door, unlocked it, and left the room.

* * * * *

An hour later Inez was being led by an old Jew, dressed in a Moslem robe and turban, through one of the most tortuous and crowded parts of Granada. It would seem that this Jew was known there, for his appearance, accompanied by a veiled woman, apparently caused no surprise to those followers of the Prophet that he met, some of whom, indeed, saluted him with humility.

"These children of Mahomet seem to love you, Father Israel," said Inez.

"Yes, yes, my dear," answered the old fellow with a chuckle; "they owe me money, that is why, and I am getting it in before the great war comes with the Spaniards, so they would sweep the streets for me with their beards—all of which is very good for the plans of our friend yonder. Ah! he who has crowns in his pocket can put a crown upon his head; there is nothing that money will not do in Granada. Give me enough of it, and I will buy his sultana from the king."

"This Castell has plenty?" asked Inez shortly.

"Plenty, and more credit. He is one of the richest men in England. But why do you ask? He would not think of you, who is too troubled about other things."

Inez only laughed bitterly, but did not resent the words. Why should she? It was not worth while.

"I know," she answered, "but I mean to earn some of it all the same, and I want to be sure that there is enough for all of us."

"There is enough, I have told you there is enough and to spare," answered the Hebrew Israel as he tapped on a door in a dirty-looking wall.

It opened as though by magic, and they crossed a paved patio, or courtyard, to a house beyond, a tumble-down place of Moorish architecture.

"Our friend Castell, being in seclusion just now, has hired the cellar floor," said Israel with a chuckle to Inez, "so be pleased to follow me, and take care of the rats and beetles."

Then he led her down a rickety stair which opened out of the courtyard into vaults filled with vats of wine, and, having lit a taper, through these, shutting and locking sundry doors behind him, to what appeared to be a very damp wall covered with cobwebs, and situated in a dark corner of a wine-cave. Here he stopped and tapped again in his peculiar fashion, whereon a portion of the wall turned outwards on a pivot, leaving an opening through which they could pass.

"Well managed, isn't it?" chuckled Israel. "Who would think of looking for an entrance here, especially if he owed the old Jew money? Come in, my pretty, come in."

Inez followed him into this darksome hole, and the wall closed behind them. Then, taking her by the arm, he turned first to the right, next to the left, opened a door with a key which he carried, and, behold, they stood in a beautifully furnished room well lighted with lamps, for it seemed to have no windows. "Wait here," he said to Inez, pointing to a couch on which she sat herself down, "while I fetch my lodger," and he vanished through some curtains at the end of the room.

Presently these opened again, and Israel reappeared through them with Castell, dressed now in Moorish robes, and looking somewhat pale from his confinement underground, but otherwise well enough. Inez rose and stood before him, throwing back her veil that he might see her face. Castell searched her for a while with his keen eyes that noted everything, then said:

"You are the lady with whom I have been in communication through our friend here, are you not? Prove it to me now by repeating my messages."

Inez obeyed, telling him everything.

"That is right," he said, "but how do I know that I can trust you? I understand you are, or have been, the lover of this man Morella, and such an one he might well employ as a spy to bring us all to ruin."

"Is it not too late to ask such questions, Senor? If I am not to be trusted, already you and your people are in the hollow of my hand?"

"Not at all, not at all, my dear," said Israel. "If we see the slightest cause to doubt you, why, there are many great vats in this place, one of which, at a pinch, would serve you as a coffin, though it would be a pity to spoil the good wine."

Inez laughed as she answered:

"Save your wine, and your time too. Morella has cast me off, and I hate him, and wish to escape from him and rob him of his prize. Also, I desire money to live on afterwards, and this you must give to me or I do not stir, or rather the promise of it, for you Jews keep your word, and I do not ask a maravedi from you until I have played my part."

"And then how many maravedis do you ask, young woman?"

Inez named a sum, at the mention of which both of them opened their eyes, and old Israel exclaimed drily:

"Surely—surely you must be one of us."

"No," she answered, "but I try to follow your example, and, if I am to live at all, it shall be in comfort."

"Quite so," said Castell, "we understand. But now tell us, what do you propose to do for this money?"

"I propose to set you, your daughter, the Dona Margaret, and her lover, the Senor Brome, safe and free outside the walls of Granada, and to leave the Marquis of Morella married to another woman."

"What other woman? Yourself?" asked Castell, fixing on this last point in the programme.

"No, Senor, not for all the wealth of both of you. To your

dependent and your daughter's relative, the handsome Betty."

"How will you manage that?" exclaimed Castell, amazed.

"These cousins are not unlike, Senor, although the link of blood between them is so thin. Listen now, I will tell you." And she explained the outlines of her plan.

"A bold scheme enough," said Castell, when she had finished, "but even if it can be done, would that marriage hold?"

"I think so," answered Inez, "if the priest knew—and he could be bribed—and the bride knows. But if not, what would it matter, since Rome alone can decide the question, and long before that is done the fates of all of us will be settled."

"Rome—or death," said Castell; and Inez read what he was afraid of in his eyes.

"Your Betty takes her chance," she replied slowly, "as many a one has done before her with less cause. She is a woman with a mind as strong as her body. Morella made her love him and promised to marry her. Then he used her to steal your daughter, and she learned that she had been no more than a stalking-heifer, from behind which he would net the white swan. Do you not think, therefore, that she has something to pay him back, she through whom her beloved mistress and cousin has been brought into all this trouble? If she wins, she becomes the wife of a grandee of Spain, a marchioness; and if she loses, well, she has had her fling for a high stake, and perhaps her revenge. At least she is willing to take her chance, and, meanwhile, all of you can be gone."

Castell looked doubtfully at the Jew Israel, who stroked his white beard and said:

"Let the woman set out her scheme. At any rate she is no fool, and it is worth our hearing, though I fear that at the best it must be costly."

"I can pay," said Castell, and motioned to Inez to proceed.

As yet, however, she had not much more to say, save that they must have good horses at hand, and send a messenger to Seville, whither the *Margaret* had been ordered to proceed, bidding her captain hold his ship ready to sail at any hour, should they succeed in reaching him.

These things, then, they arranged, and a while later Inez and Israel departed, the former carrying with her a bag of gold.

That same night Inez sought the priest, Henriques of Motril, in that hall of Morella's palace which was used as a private chapel, saying that she desired to speak with him under pretence of making confession, for they were old friends—or rather enemies.

As it chanced she found the holy father in a very ill humour. It appeared that Morella also was in a bad humour with Henriques, having heard that it was he who had possessed himself of the jewels in his strong-box on the *San Antonio*. Now he insisted upon his surrendering everything, and swore, moreover, that he would hold him responsible for all that his people had stolen from the ship, and this because he said that it was his fault that Peter Brome had escaped the sea and come on to Granada.

"So, Father," said Inez, "you, who thought yourself rich, are poor again."

"Yes, my daughter, and that is what chances to those who put their faith in princes. I have served this marquis well for many years—to my soul's hurt, I fear me—hoping that he who stands so high in the favour of the Church would advance me to some great preferment. But instead, what does he do? He robs me of a few trinkets that, had I not found them, the sea would have swallowed or some thief would have taken, and declares me his debtor for the rest, of which I know nothing."

"What preferment did you want, Father? I see that you have one in your mind."

"Daughter, a friend had written to me from Seville that if I have a hundred gold doubloons to pay for it, he can secure me the place of a secretary in the Holy Office where I served before as a familiar until the marquis made me his chaplain, and gave the benefice of Motril, which proved worth nothing, and many promises that are worth less. Now those trinkets would fetch thirty, and I have saved twenty, and came here to borrow the other fifty from the marquis, to whom I have done so many good turns—as *you* know well, Inez. You see the end of that quest," and he groaned angrily.

"It is a pity," said Inez thoughtfully, "since those who serve the Inquisition save many souls, do they not, including their own? For instance," she added, and the priest winced at the words, "I remember that they saved the soul of my own sister and would have saved mine, had I been—what shall I say?— more—more prejudiced. Also, they get a percentage of the goods of wicked heretics, and so become rich and able to advance themselves."

"That is so, Inez. It was the chance of a lifetime, especially to one who, like myself, hates heretics. But why speak of it now when that cursed, dissolute marquis—" and he checked himself.

Inez looked at him.

"Father," she asked, "if I happen to be able to find you those hundred gold doubloons, would you do something for me?"

The priest's foxy face lit up.

"I wonder what there is that I would not do, my daughter!"

"Even if it brought you into a quarrel with the marquis?

"Once I was a secretary to the Inquisition of Seville, he would have more reason to fear me than I him. Aye, and fear me he should, who bear him no love," answered the priest with a snarl.

"Then listen, Father. I have not made my confession yet; I have not told you, for instance, that I also hate this marquis, and with good cause—though perhaps you know that already. But remember that if you betray me, you will never see those hundred gold doubloons, and some other holy priest will be appointed secretary at Seville. Also worse things may happen to you."

"Proceed, my daughter," he said unctuously; "are we not in the confessional—or near it?"

So she told him all the plot, trusting to the man's avarice and other matters to protect her, for Inez hated Fray Henriques bitterly, and knew him from the crown of his shaven head to the soles of his erring feet, as she had good cause to do. Only she did not tell him whence the money was to come.

"That does not seem a very difficult matter," he said, when she had finished. "If a man and a woman, unwed and outside the prohibited degrees, appear before me to be married, I marry them, and once the ring has passed and the office is said, married they are till death or the Pope part them."

"And suppose that the man thinks he is marrying another woman, Father?"

The priest shrugged his shoulders.

"He should know whom he is marrying; that is his affair, not the Church's or mine. The names need not be spoken too loudly, my daughter."

"But you would give me a writing of the marriage with them set out plain?"

"Certainly. To you or to anybody else; why should I not?—that is, if I were sure of this wedding fee."

Inez lifted her hand, and showed beneath it a little pile of ten doubloons.

"Take them, Father," she said; "they will not be counted in the contract. There are others where they came from, whereof twenty will be paid before the marriage, and eighty when I have that writing at Seville."

He swept up the coins and pocketed them, saying:

"I will trust you, Inez."

"Yes," she answered as she left him, "we must trust each other now—must we not?—seeing that you have the money, and both our necks are in the same noose. Be here, Father, to-morrow at the same time, in case I have more confessions to make, for, alas! this is a sinful world, as you should know very well."

CHAPTER XVII

THE PLOT

On the morning following these conversations, just after Margaret and Betty had breakfasted, Inez appeared, and, as before, locked the door behind her.

"Senoras," she said calmly, "I have arranged that little business of which I spoke to you yesterday, or at least the first act of the play, since it remains for you to write the rest. Now I am sent to say that the noble Marquis of Morella craves leave to see you, Dona Margaret, and within an hour. So there is no time to lose."

"Tell us what you have done, Inez?" said Margaret.

"I have seen your worshipful father, Dona Margaret; here is the token of it, which you will do well to destroy when you have read." And she handed her a slip of paper, whereon was written in her father's writing, and in English:

"BELOVED DAUGHTER,

"This messenger, who I think may be trusted by you, has made arrangements with me which she will explain. I approve, though the risk is great. Your cousin is a brave girl, but, understand, I do not force her to this dangerous enterprise. She must choose her own road, only I promise that if she escapes and we live I will not forget her deed.

The messenger will bring me your answer. God be with us all, and farewell.

"J.C."

Margaret read this letter first to herself and then aloud to Betty, and, having read, tore it into tiny fragments and threw them from the turret window.

"Speak now," she said; and Inez told her everything.

"Can you trust the priest?" asked Margaret, when she had finished.

"He is a great villain, as I have reason to know; still, I think I can," she answered, "while the cabbage is in front of the donkey's nose—I mean until he has got all the money. Also, he has committed himself by taking some on account. But before we go further, the question is—does this lady play?" and she pointed to Betty.

"Yes, I play," said Betty, when she understood everything. "I won't go back upon my word; there is too much at stake. It is an ugly business for me, I know well enough, but," she added slowly, setting her firm mouth, "I have debts to pay all round, and I am no Spanish putty to be squeezed flat—like some people," and she glanced at the humble-looking Inez. "So, before all is done, it may be uglier for him."

When she had mastered the meaning of this speech the soft-voiced Inez lifted her gentle eyes in admiration, and murmured a Spanish proverb as to what is supposed to occur when Satan encounters Beelzebub in a high-walled lane. Then, being a lady of resource and experience, the plot having been finally decided upon, not altogether with Margaret's approval, who feared for Betty's fate when it should be discovered, Inez began to instruct them both in various practical expedients, by means of which the undoubted general resemblance of these cousins might be heightened and their differences toned down. To this end she promised to furnish them with certain hair-washes, pigments, and articles of apparel.

"It is of small use," said Betty, glancing first at herself and then at the lovely Margaret, "for even if they change skins, who can make the calf look like the fawn, though they chance to feed in the same meadow? Still, bring your stuffs and I will do my best; but I think that a thick veil and a shut mouth will help me more than any of them, also a long gown to hide my feet."

"Surely they are charming feet," said Inez politely, adding to herself, "to carry you whither you wish to go." Then she turned to Margaret and reminded her that the marquis desired to see her, and waited for her answer.

"I will not meet him alone," said Margaret decidedly.

"That is awkward," answered Inez, "as I think he has words to say to you which he does not wish others to hear, especially the senora yonder," and she nodded towards Betty.

"I will not meet him alone," repeated Margaret.

"Yet, if things are to go forward as we have arranged, you must meet him, Dona Margaret, and give him that answer which he desires. Well, I think it can be arranged. The court below is large. Now, while you and the marquis talk at one end of it, the Senora Betty and I might walk out of earshot at the other. She needs more instruction in our Spanish tongue; it would be a good opportunity to begin our lessons."

"But what am I to say to him?" asked Margaret nervously.

"I think," answered Inez, "that you must copy the example of that wonderful actor, the Senor Peter, and play a part as well as you saw him do, or even better, if possible."

"It must be a very different part then," replied Margaret, stiffening visibly at certain recollections.

The gentle Inez smiled as she said:

"Yes, but surely you can seem jealous, for that is natural to us all, and you can yield by degrees, and you can make a bargain as the price of yourself in marriage."

"What exact bargain should I make?"

"I think that you shall be securely wed by a priest of your own Church, and that letters, signed by that priest and announcing the marriage, shall be delivered to the Archbishop of Seville, and to their Majesties King Ferdinand and Queen Isabella. Also, of course, you must arrange that the Senor Brome and your father, the Senor Castell, and your cousin Betty here shall be escorted safe out of Granada before your marriage, and that you shall see them pass through the gate beneath your turret window, swearing that thereafter, at nightfall of the same day, you will suffer the priest to do his office and make you Morella's wife. By that time they should be well upon their road, and, after the rite is celebrated, I will receive the signed papers from the priest and follow them, leaving the false bride to play her part as best she can."

Again Margaret hesitated; the thing seemed too complicated and full of danger. But while she thought, a knock came on the door.

"That is to tell me that Morella awaits your answer in the court," said Inez. "Now, which is it to be? Remember that there is no other chance of escape for you, or the others, from this guarded town—at least I can see none."

"I accept," said Margaret hurriedly, "and God help us all, for we shall need Him."

"And you, Senora Betty?"

"Oh! I made up my mind long ago," answered Betty coolly. "We can only fail, when we shall be no worse off than before."

"Good. Then play your parts well, both of you. After all, they should not be so difficult, for the priest is safe, and the marquis will never scent such a trick as this. Fix the marriage for this day week, as I have much to think of and make ready," and she went.

*   *   *   *   *

Half an hour later Margaret sat under the cool arcade of the marble court, and with her, Morella, while upon the further side of its splashing fountain and out of earshot, Betty and Inez walked to and fro in the shadow.

"You sent for me, Marquis," said Margaret presently, "and, being your prisoner, I have come because I must. What is your pleasure with me?"

"Dona Margaret," he answered gravely, "can you not guess? Well, I will tell you, lest you should guess wrong. First, it is to ask your forgiveness as I have done before, for the many crimes to which my love, my true love, for you has driven me. This time yesterday I knew well that I could expect none. To-day I dare to hope that it may be otherwise."

"Why so, Marquis?"

"Last evening you looked into a certain garden and saw two people walking there—yonder is one of them," and he nodded towards Inez. "Shall I go on?"

"No," she answered in a low voice, and passing her hands before her face. "Only tell me who and what is that woman?" and in her turn she looked towards Inez.

"Is it necessary?" he asked. "Well, if you wish to know, she is a Spaniard of good blood who with her sister was taken captive by the Moors. A certain priest, who took an interest in the sister, brought her to my notice and I bought her from them; so, as her parents were dead and she had nowhere else to go, she elected to stay in my house. You must not judge such things too harshly; they are common here. Also, she has been very useful to me, being clever, for through her I have intelligence of many things. Of late, however, she has grown tired of this life, and wishes to earn her freedom, which I have promised her in return for certain services, and to leave Granada."

"Was the nursing of my betrothed one of those services, Marquis?"

He shrugged his shoulders.

"As you will, Senora. Certainly I forgive her this indiscretion, if at last she has shown you the truth about that man for whose sake you have endured so much. Margaret, now that you know him for what he is, say, do you still cling to him?"

She rose and walked a few steps down the arcade, then came back and asked:

"Are you any better than this fallen man?"

"I think so, Margaret, for since I knew you I am a risen man; all my old self is left behind me, I am a new creature, and my sins have been for you, not against you. Hear me, I beseech you. I stole you away, it is true, but I have done you no harm, and will do you none. For your sake also I have spared your father when I had but to make a sign to remove him from my path. I suffered him to escape from the prison where he was confined, and I know the place where he thinks himself hidden to-day among the Jews of Granada. Also, I nursed Peter Brome back to life, when at any hour I could have let him die, lest afterwards I might have it on my conscience that, but for my love for you, he might perhaps still be living. Well, you have seen him as he is, and what say you now? Will you still reject me? Look on me," and he drew up his tall and stately shape, "and tell me, am I such a man as a woman should be ashamed to own as husband? Remember, too, that I have much to give you in this land of Spain, whereof you shall become one of the greatest ladies, or perhaps in the future," he added significantly, "even more. War draws near, Margaret; this city and all its rich territories will fall into the hands of Spain, and afterwards I shall be their governor, almost their king."

"And if I refuse?" asked Margaret.

"Then," he answered sternly, "you bide here, and that false lover of yours bides here, and your father bides here to take the chance of war as Christian captives with a thousand others who languish in the dungeons of the Alhambra, while, my mission ended, I go hence to play my part in battle amongst my peers, as one of the first captains of their Most Catholic Majesties. Yet it is not to your fears that I would appeal, but to your heart, for I seek your love and your dear companionship through life, and, if I can help it, desire to work you and yours no harm."

"You desire to work them no harm. Then, if I were to fall in with your humour, would you let them go in safety?—I mean my father and the Senor Brome and my cousin Betty, whom, if you were as honest as you pretend to be, you should ask to bide with you as your wife, and not myself."

"The last I cannot do," he answered, flushing. "God knows I meant her no hurt, and only used her to keep near to and win news of you, thinking her, to tell truth, somewhat other than she is."

"Are no women honest here in Spain, then, my lord Marquis?"

"A few, a very few, Dona Margaret. But I erred about Betty, whom I took for a simple serving-girl, and to whom, if need be, I am ready to make all amends."

"Except that which is due to a woman you have asked to be your wife, and who in our country could claim the fulfilment of your promise, or declare you shamed. But you have not answered. Would they go free?"

"As free as air—especially the Senora Betty," he added with a little smile, "for to speak truth, there is something in that woman's eyes which frightens me at times. I think that she has a long memory. Within an hour of our marriage you shall look down from your window and see them depart under escort, every one, to go whither they will."

"Nay," answered Margaret, "it is not enough. I should need to see them go before, and then, if I consented, not till the sun had set would I pay the price of their ransom."

"Then do you consent? he asked eagerly.

"My lord Marquis, it would seem that I must. My betrothed has played me false. For a month or more I have been prisoner in your palace, which I understand has no good name, and, if I refuse, you tell me that all of us will be cast into yonder dungeons to be sold as slaves or die prisoners of the Moors. My lord Marquis, fate and you leave me but little choice. On this day week I will marry you, but blame me not if you find me other than you think, as you have found my cousin whom you befooled. Till then, also, I pray you that you will leave me quite untroubled. If you have arrangements to make or commands to send, the woman Inez yonder will serve as messenger, for of her I know the worst."

"I will obey you in all things, Dona Margaret," he answered humbly. "Do you desire to see your father or—" and he paused.

"Neither of them," she answered. "I will write to them and send my letters by this Inez. Why should I see them," she added passionately, "who have done with the old days when I was free and happy, and am about to become the wife of the most noble Marquis of Morella, that honourable grandee of Spain, who tricked a poor girl by a false promise of marriage, and used her blind and loving folly to trap and steal me from my home? My lord, till this day week I bid you farewell," and, walking from the arcade to the fountain, she called aloud to Betty to accompany her to their rooms.

The week for which Margaret had bargained had gone by. All was prepared. Inez had shown to Morella the letters that his bride to be wrote to her father and to Peter Brome; also the answers, imploring and passionate, to the same. But there were other letters and other answers which she had not shown. It was afternoon, swift horses were ready in the courtyard, and with them an escort, while, disguised as Moors, Castell and Peter waited under guard in a chamber close at hand. Betty, dressed in the robes of a Moorish woman, and thickly veiled, stood before Morella, to whom Inez had led her.

"I come to tell you," she said, "that at sundown, three hours after we have passed beneath her window, my cousin and mistress will wait to be made your wife, but if you try to disturb her before then she will be no wife of yours, or any man's."

"I obey," answered Morella; "and, Senora Betty, I pray your pardon, and that you will accept this gift from me in token of your forgiveness." And with a low bow he handed to her a beautiful necklace of pearls.

"I take them," said Betty, with a bitter laugh, "as they may serve to buy me a passage back to England. But forgive you I do not, Marquis of Morella, and I warn you that there is a score between us which I may yet live to settle. You seem to have won, but God in Heaven takes note of the wickedness of men, and in this way or in that He always pays His debts. Now I go to bid farewell to my cousin Margaret, but to you I do not bid farewell, for I think that we shall meet again," and with a sob she let fall the veil which she had lifted above her lips to speak and departed with Inez, to whom she whispered as they went, "He will not linger for any more good-byes with Betty Dene."

H. Rider Haggard

They entered Margaret's room and locked the door behind them. She was seated on a low divan wrapped in a loose robe, and by her side, glittering with silver and with gems, lay her bridal veil and garments.

"Be swift," said Inez to Betty, who stripped off her Moorish dress and the long, flowing veil that was wrapped about her head, whereon it was seen that her hair had changed greatly in colour, from yellow to dark chestnut indeed, while her eyes, ringed about with pigments, and made lustrous by drugs dropped into them, looked no longer blue, but black like Margaret's. Yes, and wonder of wonders, on the right side of the chin and on the back of the neck were moles, or beauty-spots, just such as Margaret had borne there from her birth! In short, their stature being much the same, though Betty was more thickly built, except in the strongest light it would not have been easy to distinguish them apart, even unveiled, for at all such arts of the altering of the looks of women, Inez was an adept, and she had done her best.

Now Margaret clothed herself in the white robes and the thick head-dress that hid her face, all except a little crack left for the eyes to peep through, whilst Betty, with the help of Inez, arrayed herself in the wondrous wedding robe beset with jewels that was Morella's bridal gift, and hid her dyed tresses beneath the pearl-sewn veil. Within ten minutes all was finished, even to the dagger that Betty had tied about her beneath her robe, and the two transformed women stood staring at each other.

"It is time to go," said Inez.

Then Margaret broke out:

"I do not like this business; I never did. When he discovers all, that man's rage will be terrible, and he will kill her. I repent that I have consented to the plot."

"It is too late to repent now, Senora," said Inez.

"Cannot Betty be got away also?" asked Margaret desperately.

"It is just possible," answered Inez; "thus, before the marriage, according to the old custom here, I hand the cups of wine to the bridegroom and the bride. That for the marquis will be drugged, since he must not see too clear to-night. Well, I might brew it stronger so that within half an hour he would not know whether he were married or single, and then, perhaps, she might escape with me and come to join you. But it is very risky, and, of course, if we were discovered—the stitch would be out of the wineskin, and the cellar floor might be stained!"

Now Betty interrupted:

"Keep your stitches whole, Cousin; if any skins are to be pricked it can't be helped, and at least you won't have to wipe up the mess. I am not going to run away from the man, more likely he will run away from me. I look well in this fine dress of yours, and I mean to wear it out. Now begone—begone, before some of them come to seek me. Don't you grieve for me; I'll lie in the bed that I have made, and if the worst comes to the worst, I have money in my pocket—or its worth—and we will meet again in England. Come, give my love and duty to Master Peter and your father, and if I should see them no more, bid them think kindly of Betty Dene, who was such a plague to them."

Then, taking Margaret in her strong arms, she kissed her again and again, and fairly thrust her from the room.

But when they were gone, poor Betty sat down and cried a little, till she remembered that hot tears might melt the paint upon her face, and, drying them, went to the window and watched.

A while later, from her lofty niche, she saw six Moorish horsemen riding along the white road to the embattled gate. After them came two men and a woman, all splendidly mounted, also dressed as Moors, and then six other horsemen. They passed the gate which was opened for them and began to mount the slope beyond. At the crest of it the woman halted and, turning, waved a handkerchief. Betty answered the signal, and in another minute they had vanished, and she was alone.

Never did she spend a more weary afternoon. Two hours later, still watching at her window, she saw the Moorish escort return, and knew that all was well, and that by now, Margaret, her lover, and her father were safely started on their journey. So she had not risked her life in vain.

CHAPTER XVIII

THE HOLY HERMANDAD

Down the long passages, through the great, fretted halls, across the cool marble courts, flitted Inez and Margaret. It was like a dream. They went through a room where women, idling or working at tapestries, looked at them curiously. Margaret heard one of them say to another:

"Why does the Dona Margaret's cousin leave her?" And the answer, "Because she is in love with the marquis herself, and cannot bear to stay."

"What a fool!" said the first woman. "She is good looking, and would only have had to wait a few weeks."

They passed an open door, that of Morella's own chambers. Within it he stood and watched them go by. When they were opposite to him some doubt or idea seemed to strike his mind, for he looked at them keenly, stepped forward, then, thinking better of it, or perhaps remembering Betty's bitter tongue, halted and turned aside. That danger had gone by!

At length, none hindering them, they reached the yard where the escort and the horses waited. Here, standing under an archway, were Castell and Peter. Castell greeted Margaret in English and kissed her through her veil, while Peter, who had not seen her close since months before he rode away to Dedham, stared at her with all his eyes, and began to draw near to her, designing to find out, as he was sure he could do if once he touched her, whether indeed this were Margaret, or only Betty after all. Guessing what was in his mind, and that he might reveal everything, Inez, who held a long pin in her hand with which she was fastening her veil that had come loose, pretended to knock against him, and ran the point deep into his arm, muttering, "Fool!" as she did so. He sprang back with an oath, the guard smiled, and she began to pray his pardon.

Castell helped Margaret on to her horse, then mounted his own, as did Peter, still rubbing his arm, but not daring to look towards Margaret, whose hand Inez shook familiarly in farewell as though she were her equal, addressing her the while in terms of endearment such as Spanish women use to each other. An officer of Morella's household came and counted them, saying:

"Two men and a woman. That is right, though I cannot see the woman's face."

For a moment he seemed to be about to order her to unveil, but Inez called to him that it was not decent before all these Moors, whereon he nodded and ordered the captain to proceed.

They rode through the arch of the castle along the roadway, through the great gate of the wall also, where the guard questioned their escort, stared at them, and, after receiving a present from Castell, let them go, telling them they were lucky Christians to get alive out of Granada, as indeed they were.

At the brow of the rise Margaret turned and waved her handkerchief towards that high window which she knew so well. Another handkerchief was waved in answer, and, thinking of the lonely Betty watching them there while she awaited the issue of her desperate venture, Margaret went on, weeping beneath her veil. For an hour they rode forward, speaking few words to each other, till at length they came to the cross-roads, one of which ran to Malaga, and the other towards Seville.

Here the escort halted, saying that their orders were to leave them at this point, and asking which road they intended to take. Castell answered that to Malaga, whereon the captain replied that they were wise, as they were less likely to meet bands of marauding thieves who called themselves Christian soldiers, and murdered or robbed all travellers who fell into their hands. Then Castell offered him a present, which he accepted gravely, as though he did him a great favour, and, after bows and salutations, they departed.

As soon as the Moors were gone the three rode a little way towards Malaga. Then, when there was nobody in sight, they turned across country and gained the Seville road. At last they were alone and, halting beneath the walls of a house that had been burnt in some Christian raid, they spoke together freely for the first time, and oh! what a moment was that for all of them!

Peter pushed his horse alongside that of Margaret, crying:

"Speak, beloved. Is it truly you?"

But Margaret, taking no heed of him, leant over and, throwing her arm around her father's neck, kissed him again and again through her veil, blessing God that they had lived to meet in safety. Peter tried to kiss her also; but she caused her horse to move so that he nearly fell from his saddle.

"Have a care, Peter," she said to him, "or your love of kissing will lead you into more trouble." Whereon, guessing of what she spoke, he coloured furiously, and began to explain at length.

"Cease," she said—"cease. I know all that story, for I saw you," then, relenting, with some brief, sweet words of greeting and gratitude, gave him her hand, which he kissed often enough.

H. Rider Haggard

"Come," said Castell, "we must push on, who have twenty miles to cover before we reach that inn where Israel has arranged that we should sleep to-night. We will talk as we go." And talk they did, as well as the roughness of the road and the speed at which they must travel would allow.

Riding as hard as they were able, at length they came to the *venta*, or rough hostelry, just as the darkness closed in. At the sight of it they thanked God aloud, for this place was across the Moorish border, and now they had little to fear from Granada. The host, a half-bred Spaniard and a Christian, expected them, having received a message from Israel, with whom he had had dealings, and gave them two rooms, rude enough, but sufficient, and good food and wine, also stabling and barley for their horses, bidding them sleep well and have no fear, as he and his people would watch and warn them of any danger.

Yet it was late before they slept, who had so much to say to each other—especially Peter and Margaret—and were so happy at their escape, if only for a little while. Yet across their joy, like the sound of a funeral bell at a merry feast, came the thought of Betty and that fateful marriage in which ere now she must have played her part. Indeed, at last Margaret knelt down and offered up prayers to Heaven that the saints might protect her cousin in the great peril which she had incurred for them, nor was Peter ashamed to join her in that prayer. Then they embraced—especially Peter and Margaret—and laid them down, Castell and his daughter in one room, and Peter in the other, and slept as best they could.

Half an hour before dawn Peter was up seeing to the horses while the others breakfasted and packed the food that the landlord had made ready for their journey. Then he also swallowed some meat and wine, and at the first break of day, having discharged their reckoning and taken a letter from their host to those of other inns upon the road, they pressed on towards Seville, very thankful to find that as yet there were no signs of their being pursued.

All that day, with short pauses to rest themselves and their horses, they rode on without accident, for the most part over a fertile plain watered by several rivers which they crossed at fords or over bridges. As night fell they reached the old town of Oxuna, which for many hours they had seen set upon its hill before them, and, notwithstanding their Moorish dress, made their way almost unobserved in the darkness to that inn to which they had been recommended. Here, although he stared at their garments, on finding that they had plenty of money, the landlord received them well enough, and again they were fortunate in securing rooms to themselves. It had been their purpose to buy Spanish clothes in this town, but, as it happened, it was a feast day, and at night every shop in the place was closed, so they could get none. Now, as they greatly desired to reach Seville by the following nightfall, hoping under cover of the darkness to find and come aboard of their ship, the *Margaret*, which they knew lay safely in the river, and had been advised by messenger of their intended journey, it was necessary for them to leave Oxuna before the dawn. So, unfortunately enough as it proved, it was impossible for them to put off their Moorish robes and clothe themselves as Christians.

They had hoped, too, that here at Oxuna Inez might overtake them, as she had promised to do if she could, and give them tidings of what had happened since they left Granada. But no Inez came. So, comforting themselves with the thought that however hard she rode it would be difficult for her to reach them, who had some hours' start, they left Oxuna in the darkness before any one was astir.

Having crossed some miles of plain, they passed up through olive groves into hills where cork-trees grew, and here stopped to eat and let the horses feed. Just as they were starting on again, Peter, looking round, saw mounted men—a dozen or more of them of very wild aspect—cantering through the trees evidently with the object of cutting them off.

"Thieves!" he said shortly. "Ride for it."

H. Rider Haggard

So they began to gallop, and their horses, although somewhat jaded, being very swift, passed in front of these men before they could regain the road. The band shouted to them to surrender, and, as they did not stop, loosed a few arrows and pursued them, while they galloped down the hillside on to a plain which separated them from more hills also clothed with cork-trees. This plain was about three miles wide and boggy in places. Still they kept well ahead of the brigands, as they took them to be, hoping that they would give up the pursuit or lose sight of them amongst the trees. As they entered these, however, to their dismay they saw, drawn up in front of them and right across the road, another band of rough-looking men, perhaps twelve in all.

"Trap!" said Peter. "We must ride through them—it is our only chance," at the same time spurring his horse to the front and drawing his sword.

Choosing the spot where their line was weakest he dashed through it easily enough but next second heard a cry from Margaret, and pulled his horse round to see that her mare had fallen, and that she and Castell were in the hands of the thieves. Indeed, already rough men had hold of her, and one of them was trying to tear the veil from her face. With a shout of rage Peter charged them, and struck so fierce a blow that his sword cut through the fellow's helmet into his skull, so that he fell down, dying or dead, Margaret's veil still in his hand.

Then they rushed at him, five or six of them, and, although he wounded another man, dragged him from his horse, and, as he lay upon his back, sprang at him to finish him before he could rise. Already their knives and swords were over him, and he was making his farewells to life, when he heard a voice command them to desist and bind his arms. This was quickly done, and he was suffered to rise from the ground to see before him, not Morella, as he half expected, but a man clad in fine armour beneath his rough cloak, evidently an officer of rank. "What kind of a Moor are you," he asked, "who dare to kill the soldiers of the Holy Hermandad in the heart of the King's country?" and he pointed to the dead man.

"I am not a Moor," answered Peter in his rough Spanish. "I am a Christian escaped from Granada, and I cut down that man because he was trying to insult my betrothed, as you would have done, Senor. I did not know that he was a soldier of the Hermandad; I thought him a common thief of the hills."

This speech, or as much as he could understand of it, seemed to please the officer, but before he could answer, Castell said:

"Sir Officer, the senor is an Englishman, and does not speak your language well—"

"He uses his sword well, anyhow," interrupted the captain, glancing at the dead soldier's cloven helm and head.

"Yes, Sir, he is of your trade and, as the scar upon his face shows, has fought in many wars. Sir, what he tells you is true. We are Christian captives escaped from Granada and flying to Seville with my daughter, to whom I pray you to do no harm, to ask for the protection of their gracious Majesties, and to find a passage back to England."

"You do not look like an Englishman," answered the captain; "you look like a Marano."

"Sir, I cannot help my looks. I am a merchant of London, Castell by name. It is one well known in Seville and throughout this land, where I have large dealings, as, if I can but see him, your king himself will acknowledge. Be not deceived by our dress, which we had to put on in order to escape from Granada, but, I beseech you, let us go on to Seville."

"Senor Castell," answered the officer, "I am the Captain Arrano of Puebla, and, since you would not stop when we called to you, and have killed one of my best soldiers, to Seville you must certainly go, but with me, not by yourselves. You are my prisoners, but have no fear. No violence shall be done to you or the lady, who must take your trials for your deeds before the King's court, and there tell your story, true or false."

So, having been disarmed of their swords, they were allowed to remount their horses and taken on towards Seville as prisoners.

"At least," said Margaret to Peter, "we have nothing more to fear from highwaymen, and have escaped these soldiers' swords unhurt."

"Yes," answered Peter with a groan, "but I hoped that to-night we should have slept upon the *Margaret* while she slipped down the river towards the open sea, and not in a Spanish jail. Now, as fate will have it, for the second time I have killed a man on your behalf, and all the business will begin again. Truly our luck is bad!"

"I think it might be worse, and I cannot blame you for that deed," answered Margaret, remembering the rough hands of the dead soldier, whom some of his comrades had stopped behind to bury.

During all the remainder of that long day they rode on through the burning heat, across the rich, cultivated plain, towards the great city of Seville, whereof the Giralda, which once had been the minaret of a Moorish mosque, towered hundreds of feet into the air before them. At length, towards evening, they entered the eastern suburbs of the vast city and, passing through them and a great gate beyond, began to thread its tortuous streets.

"Whither go we, Captain Arrano?" asked Castell presently.

"To the prison of the Holy Hermandad to await your trial for the slaying of one of its soldiers," answered the officer.

"I pray that we may get there soon then," said Peter, looking at

Margaret, who, overcome with fatigue, swayed upon her saddle like a flower in the wind.

"So do I," muttered Castell, glancing round at the dark faces of the people, who, having discovered that they had killed a Spanish soldier, and taking them to be Moors, were marching alongside of them in great numbers, staring sullenly, or cursing them for infidels. Indeed, once when they passed a square, a priest in the mob cried out, "Kill them!" whereon a number of rough fellows made a rush to pull them off their horses, and were with difficulty beaten back by the soldiers.

Foiled in this attempt they began to pelt them with garbage, so that soon their white robes were stained and filthy. One fellow, too, threw a stone which struck Margaret on the wrist, causing her to cry out and drop her rein. This was too much for the hot-blooded Peter, who, spurring his horse alongside of him, before the soldiers could interfere, hit him such a buffet in the face that the man rolled upon the ground. Now Castell thought that they would certainly be killed, but to his surprise the mob only laughed and shouted such things as "Well hit, Moor!" "That infidel has a strong arm," and so forth.

Nor was the officer angry, for when the man rose, a knife in his hand, he drew his sword and struck him down again with the flat of it, saying to Peter:

"Do not sully your hand with such street swine, Senor."

Then he turned and commanded his men to charge the crowd ahead of them.

So they got through these people and, after many twists and turns down side streets to avoid the main avenues, came to a great and gloomy building and into a courtyard through barred gates that were opened at their approach and shut after them. Here they were ordered to dismount and their horses led away, while the officer, Arrano, entered into conversation with the governor of the prison, a man with a stern but not unkindly face, who surveyed them with much curiosity. Presently he approached and asked them if they could pay for good rooms, as if not he must put them in the common cells.

Castell answered, "Yes," and, by way of earnest of it, produced five pieces of gold, and giving them to the Captain Arrano, begged him to distribute them among his soldiers as a thankoffering for their protection of them through the streets. Also, he said loudly enough for every one to hear, that he would be willing to compensate the relatives of the man whom Peter had killed by accident—an announcement that evidently impressed his comrades very favourably. Indeed one of them said he would bear the message to his widow, and, on behalf of the rest, thanked him for his gift. Then having bade farewell to the officer, who told them that they would meet again before the judges, they were led through the various passages of the prison to two rooms, one small and one of a fair size with heavily barred windows, given water to wash in, and told that food would be brought to them.

In due course it came, carried by jailers—meat, eggs, and wine, and glad enough were they to see it. While they ate, also the governor appeared with a notary, and, having waited till their meal was finished, began to question them.

"Our story is long," said Castell, "but with your leave I will tell it you, only, I pray you, suffer my daughter, the Dona Margaret, to go to rest, for she is quite outworn, and if you will you can question her to-morrow."

The governor assenting, Margaret threw off her veil to embrace her father, thus showing her beauty for the first time, whereat the governor and the notary stared amazed. Then having given Peter her hand to kiss, and curtseyed to the governor and the notary, she went to her bed in the next room, which opened out of that in which they were.

When she had gone, Castell told his story of how his daughter had been kidnapped by the Marquis of Morella, a name that caused the governor to open his eyes very wide, and brought from London to Granada, whither they, her father and her betrothed, had followed her and escaped. But of Betty and all the business of the changed bride he said nothing. Also, knowing that these must come out in any case, he told them his name and business, and those of his partners and correspondents in Seville, the firm of Bernaldez, which was one that the governor knew well enough, and prayed that the head of that firm, the Senor Juan Bernaldez, might be communicated with and allowed to visit them on the next morning. Lastly, he explained that they were no thieves or adventurers, but English subjects in misfortune, and again hinted that they were both able and willing to pay for any kindness or consideration that was shown to them, of all of which sayings the governor took note.

Also this officer said that he would communicate with his superiors, and, if no objection were made, send a messenger to ask the Senor Bernaldez to attend at the prison on the following day. Then at length he and the notary departed, and, the jailers having cleared away the food and locked the door, Castell and Peter lay down on the beds that they had made ready for them, thankful enough to find themselves at Seville, even though in a prison, where indeed they slept very well that night.

On the following morning they woke much refreshed, and, after they had breakfasted, the governor appeared, and with him none other than the Senor Juan Bernaldez, Castell's secret correspondent and Spanish partner, whom he had last seen some years before in England, a stout man with a quiet, clever face, not over given to words.

Greeting them with a deference that was not lost upon the governor, he asked whether he had leave to speak with them alone. The governor assented and went, saying he would return within an hour. As soon as the door was closed behind him, Bernaldez said:

H. Rider Haggard

"This is a strange place to meet you in, John Castell, yet I am not altogether surprised, since some of your messages reached me through our friends the Jews; also your ship, the *Margaret*, lies refitted in the river, and to avoid suspicion I have been lading her slowly with a cargo for England, though how you will come aboard that ship is more than I can say. But we have no time to waste. Tell me all your story, keeping nothing back."

So they told him everything as quickly as they could, while he listened silently. When they had done, he said, addressing Peter:

"It is a thousand pities, young sir, that you could not keep your hands off that soldier, for now the trouble that was nearly done with has begun anew, and in a worse shape. The Marquis of Morella is a very powerful man in this kingdom, as you may know from the fact that he was sent to London by their Majesties to negotiate a treaty with your English King Henry as to the Jews and their treatment, should any of them escape thither after they have been expelled from Spain. For nothing less is in the wind, and I would have you know that their Majesties hate the Jews, and especially the Maranos, whom already they burn by dozens here in Seville," and he glanced meaningly at Castell.

"I am very sorry," said Peter, "but the fellow handled her roughly, and I was maddened at the sight and could not help myself. This is the second time that I have come into trouble from the same cause. Also, I thought that he was but a bandit."

"Love is a bad diplomatist," replied Bernaldez, with a little smile, "and who can count last year's clouds? What is done, is done. Now I will try to arrange that the three of you shall be brought straight before their Majesties when they sit to hear cases on the day after to-morrow. With the Queen you will have a better chance than at the hands of any alcalde. She has a heart, if only one can get at it—that is, except where Jews and Maranos are concerned," and again he glanced at Castell.

"Meanwhile, there is money in plenty, and in Spain we ride to heaven on gold angels," he added, alluding to that coin and the national corruption.

Before they could say more the governor returned, saying that the Senor Bernaldez' time was up, and asking if they had finished their talk.

"Not altogether," said Margaret. "Noble Governor, is it permitted that the Senor Bernaldez should send me some Christian clothes to wear, for I would not appear before your judges in this soiled heathen garb, nor, I think, would my father or the Senor Brome?"

The governor laughed, and said he thought that might be arranged, and even allowed them another five minutes, while they talked of what these clothes should be. Then he departed with Bernaldez, leaving them alone.

It was not until the latter had gone, however, that they remembered that they had forgotten to ask him whether he had heard anything of the woman Inez, who had been furnished with his address, but, as he had said nothing of her, they felt sure that she could not have arrived in Seville, and once more were much afraid as to what might have happened after they had left Granada.

That night, to their grief and alarm, a new trouble fell on them. Just as they finished their supper the governor appeared and said that, by order of the Court before which they must be tried, the Senor Brome, who was accused of murder, must be separated from them. So, in spite of all they could say or do, Peter was led away to a separate cell, leaving Margaret weeping.

CHAPTER XIX

BETTY PAYS HER DEBTS

Betty Dene was not a woman afflicted with fears or apprehensions. Born of good parents, but in poverty, for six-and-twenty years she had fought her own way in a rough world and made the best of circumstances. Healthy, full-blooded, tough, affectionate, romantic, but honest in her way, she was well fitted to meet the ups and downs of life, to keep her head above the waters of a turbulent age, and to pay back as much as she received from man or woman.

Yet those long hours which she passed alone in the high turret chamber, waiting till they summoned her to play the part of a false bride, were the worst that she had ever spent. She knew that her position was, in a sense, shameful, and like to end in tragedy, and, now that she faced it in cold blood, began to wonder why she had chosen so to do. She had fallen in love with the Spaniard almost at first sight, though it is true that something like this had happened to her before with other men. Then he had played his part with her, till, quite deceived, she gave all her heart to him in good earnest, believing in her infatuation that, notwithstanding the difference of their place and rank, he desired to make her his wife for her own sake.

Afterwards came that bitter day of disillusion when she learned, as Inez had said to Castell, that she was but a stalking heifer used for the taking of the white swan, her cousin and mistress—that day when she had been beguiled by the letter which was still hid in her garments, and for her pains heard herself called a fool to her face. In her heart she had sworn to be avenged upon Morella then, and now the hour had come in which to fulfil her oath and play him back trick for cruel trick.

Did she still love the man? She could not say. He was pleasing to her as he had always been, and when that is so women forgive much. This was certain, however—love was not her guide to-night. Was it vengeance then that led her on? Perhaps; at least she longed to be able to say to him, "See what craft lies hid even in the bosom of an outwitted fool."

Yet she would not have done it for vengeance' sake alone, or rather she would have paid herself in some other fashion. No, her real reason was that she must discharge the debt due to Margaret and Peter, and to Castell who had sheltered her for years. She it was who had brought them into all this woe, and it seemed but just that she should bring them out again, even at the cost of her own life and womanly dignity. Or, perchance, all three of these powers drove her on,—love for the man if it still lingered, the desire to be avenged upon him, and the desire to snatch his prey from out his maw. At least she had set the game, and she would play it out to its end, however awful that might be.

The sun sank, the darkness closed about her, and she wondered whether ever again she would see the dawn. Her brave heart quailed a little, and she gripped the dagger hilt beneath her splendid, borrowed robe, thinking to herself that perhaps it might be wisest to drive it into her own breast, and not wait until a balked madman did that office for her. Yet not so, for it is always time to die when one must.

A knock came at the door, and her courage, which had sunk so low, burned up again within her. Oh! she would teach this Spaniard that the Englishwoman, whom he had made believe was his desired mistress, could be his master. At any rate, he should hear the truth before the end.

H. Rider Haggard

She unlocked the door, and Inez entered bearing a lamp, by the light of which she scanned her with her quiet eyes.

"The bridegroom is ready," she said slowly that Betty might understand, "and sends me to lead you to him. Are you afraid?"

"Not I," answered Betty. "But tell me, how will the thing be done?"

"The marquis meets us in the ante-room to that hall which is used as a chapel, and there on behalf of the household I, as the first of the women, give you both the cups of wine. Be sure that you drink of that which I hold in my left hand, passing the cup up beneath your veil so as not to show your face, and speak no word, lest he should recognise your voice. Then we shall go into the chapel, where the priest Henriques waits, also all the household. But that hall is great, and the lamps are feeble, so none will know you there. By this time also the drugged wine will have begun to work upon Morella's brain, wherefore, provided that you use a low voice, you may safely say, 'I, Betty, wed thee, Carlos,' not 'I, Margaret, wed thee.' Then, when it is over, he will lead you away to the chambers prepared for you, where, if there is any virtue in my wine, he will sleep sound to-night, that is, as soon as the priest has given me the marriage-lines, whereof I will hand you one copy and keep the others. Afterwards—" and she shrugged her shoulders.

"What becomes of you?" asked Betty, when she had fully mastered these instructions.

"Oh! I and the priest start to-night for a ride together to Seville, where his money awaits him; ill company for a woman who means henceforth to be honest and rich, but better than none. Perhaps we shall meet again there, or perhaps we shall not; at least, you know where to seek me and the others, at the house of the Senor Bernaldez. Now it is time. Are you ready to be made a marchioness of Spain?"

"Of course," answered Betty coolly, and they started.

Through the empty halls and corridors they went, and oh! surely no Eastern plot that had been conceived in them was quite so bold and desperate as theirs. They reached the ante-chamber to the chapel, and took their stand outside of the circle of light that fell from its hanging lamps. Presently a door opened, and through it came Morella, attended by two of his secretaries. He was splendidly arrayed in his usual garb of black velvet, and about his neck hung chains of gold and jewels, and to his breast were fastened the glittering stars and orders pertaining to his rank. Never, or so thought Betty, had Morella seemed more magnificent and handsome. He was happy also, who was about to drink of that cup of joy which he so earnestly desired. Yes, his face showed that he was happy, and Betty, noting it, felt remorse stirring in her breast. Low he bowed before her, while she curtseyed to him, bending her tall and graceful form till her knee almost touched the ground. Then he came to her and whispered in her ear:

"Most sweet, most beloved," he said, "I thank heaven that has led me to this joyous hour by many a rough and dangerous path. Most dear, again I beseech you to forgive all the sorrow and the ill that I have brought upon you, remembering that it was done for your adored sake, that I love you as woman has been seldom loved, you and you only, and that to you, and you only, will I cling until my death's day. Oh! do not tremble and shrink, for I swear that no woman in Spain shall have a better or a more loyal lord. You I will cherish alone, for you I will strive by night and day to lift you to great honour and satisfy your every wish. Many and pleasant may the years be that we shall spend side by side, and peaceful our ends when at last we lay us down side by side to sleep awhile and wake again in heaven, whereof the shadow lies on me to-night. Remembering the past, I do not ask much of you—as yet; still, if you are minded to give me a bridal gift that I shall prize above crowns or empires, say that you forgive me all that I have done amiss, and in token, lift that veil of yours and kiss me on the lips."

Betty heard this speech, whereof she only fully understood the end, and trembled. This was a trial that she had not foreseen. Yet it must be faced, for speak she dared not. Therefore, gathering up her courage, and remembering that the light was at her back, after a little pause, as though of modesty and reluctance, she raised the pearl-embroidered veil, and, bending forward beneath its shadow, suffered Morella to kiss her on the lips.

It was over, the veil had fallen again, and the man suspected nothing.

"I am a good artist," thought Inez to herself, "and that woman acts better than the wooden Peter. Scarcely could I have done it so well myself."

Then, the jealousy and hate that she could not control glittering in her soft eyes, for she too had loved this man, and well, Inez lifted the golden cups that had been prepared, and, gliding forward, beautiful in her broidered, Eastern robe, fell upon her knee and held them to the bridegroom and the bride. Morella took that from her right hand, and Betty that from her left, nor, intoxicated as he was already with that first kiss of love, did he pause to note the evil purpose which was written on the face of his discarded slave. Betty, passing the cup beneath her veil, touched it with her lips and returned it to Inez; but Morella, exclaiming, "I drink to you, sweet bride, most fair and adored of women," drained his to the dregs, and cast it back to Inez as a gift in such fashion that the red wine which clung to its rim stained her white robes like a splash of blood.

Humbly she bowed, humbly she gathered the precious vessel from the floor; but when she rose again there was triumph in her eyes—not hate.

Now Morella took his bride's hand and, followed by his gentlemen and Inez, walked to the curtains that were drawn as they came into the great hall beyond, where had mustered all his household, perhaps a hundred of them. Between their bowing ranks they passed, a stately pair, and, whilst sweet voices sang behind some hidden screen, walked onward to the altar, where stood the waiting priest. They kneeled down upon the gold-embroidered cushions while the office of the Church was read over them. The ring was set upon Betty's hand—scarce, it would seem, could he find her finger—the man took the woman to wife, the woman took the man for husband. His voice was thick, and hers was very low; of all that listening crowd none could hear the names they spoke.

It was over. The priest bowed and blessed them. They signed some papers, there by the light of the altar candles. Father Henriques filled in certain names and signed them also, then, casting sand upon them, placed them in the outstretched hand of Inez, who, although Morella never seemed to notice, gave one to the bride, and thrust the other two into the bosom of her robe. Then both she and the priest kissed the hands of the marquis and his wife, and asked his leave to be gone. He bowed his head vaguely, and—if any had been there to listen—within ten short minutes they might have heard two horses galloping hard towards the Seville gate.

Now, escorted by pages and torch-bearers, the new-wed pair repassed those dim and stately halls, the bride, veiled, mysterious, fateful; the bridegroom, empty-eyed, like one who wanders in his sleep. Thus they reached their chamber, and its carved doors shut behind them.

*   *   *   *   *

It was early morning, and the serving-women who waited without that room were summoned to it by the sound of a silver gong. Two of them entered and were met by Betty, no longer veiled, but wrapped in a loose robe, who said to them:

"My lord the marquis still sleeps. Come, help me dress and make ready his bath and food."

H. Rider Haggard

The women stared at her, for now that she had washed the paint from her face they knew well that this was the Senora Betty and not the Dona Margaret, whom, they had understood, the marquis was to marry. But she chid them sharply in her bad Spanish, bidding them be swift, as she would be robed before her husband should awake. So they obeyed her, and when she was ready she went with them into the great hall where many of the household were gathered, waiting to do homage to the new-wed pair, and greeted them all, blushing and smiling, saying that doubtless the marquis would be among them soon, and commanding them meanwhile to go about their several tasks.

So well did Betty play her part indeed, that, although they also were bewildered, none questioned her place or authority, who remembered that after all they had not been told by their lord himself which of these two English ladies he meant to marry. Also, she distributed among the meaner of them a present of money on her husband's behalf and her own, and then ate food and drank some wine before them all, pledging them, and receiving their salutations and good wishes.

When all this was done, still smiling, Betty returned to the marriage-chamber, closing its door behind her, sat her down on a chair near the bed, and waited for the worst struggle of all—that struggle on which hung her life. See! Morella stirred. He sat up, gazing about him and rubbing his brow. Presently his eyes lit upon Betty, seated stern and upright in her high chair. She rose and, coming to him, kissed him and called him "Husband," and, still half-asleep, he kissed her back. Then she sat down again in her chair and watched his face.

It changed, and changed again. Wonder, fear, amaze, bewilderment, flitted over it, till at last he said in English:

"Betty, where is my wife?"

"Here," answered Betty.

He stared at her. "Nay, I mean the Dona Margaret, your cousin and my lady, whom I wed last night. And how come you here? I thought that you had left Granada."

Betty looked astonished.

"I do not understand you," she answered. "It was my cousin Margaret who left Granada. I stayed here to be married to you, as you arranged with me through Inez."

His jaw dropped.

"Arranged with you through Inez! Mother of Heaven! what do you mean?"

"Mean?" she answered—"I mean what I say. Surely"—and she rose in indignation—"you have never dared to try to play some new trick upon me?"

"Trick!" muttered Morella. "What says the woman? Is all this a dream, or am I mad?"

"A dream, I think. Yes, it must be a dream, since certainly it was to no madman that I was wed last night. Look," and she held before him that writing of marriage signed by the priest, by him, and by herself, which stated that Carlos, Marquis of Morella, was on such a date, at Granada, duly married to the Senora Elizabeth Dene of London in England.

He read it twice, then sank back gasping; while Betty hid away the parchment in her bosom.

Then presently he seemed to go mad indeed. He raved, he cursed, he ground his teeth, he looked round for a sword to kill her or himself, but could find none. And all the while Betty sat still and gazed at him like some living fate.

At length he was weary, and her turn came.

H. Rider Haggard

"Listen," she said. "Yonder in London you promised to marry me; I have it hidden away, and in your own writing. By agreement I fled with you to Spain. By the mouth of your messenger and former love this marriage was arranged between us, I receiving your messages to me, and sending back mine to you, since you explained that for reasons of your own you did not wish to speak of these matters before my cousin Margaret, and could not wed me until she and her father and her lover were gone from Granada. So I bade them farewell, and stayed here alone for love of you, as I fled from London for love of you, and last night we were united, as all your household know, for but now I have eaten with them and received their good wishes. And now you dare—you dare to tell me, that I, your wife—I, who have sacrificed everything for you, I, the Marchioness of Morella, am *not* your wife. Well, go, say it outside this chamber, and hear your very slaves cry 'Shame' upon you. Go, say it to your king and your bishops, aye, and to his Holiness the Pope himself, and listen to their answer. Why, great as you are, and rich as you are, they will hale you to a mad-house or a prison."

Morella listened, rocking himself to and fro upon the bed, then with an oath sprang towards her, to be met by a dagger-point glinting in his eyes.

"Hear me again," she said as he shrank back from that cold steel. "I am no slave and no weakling; you shall not murder me or thrust me away. I am your wife and your equal, aye, and stronger than you in body and in mind, and I will have my rights in the face of God and man."

"Certainly," he said with a kind of unwilling admiration— "certainly you are no weakling. Certainly, also, you have paid back all you owe me with a Jew's interest. Or, mayhap, you are not so clever as I think, but just a strong-minded fool, and it is that accursed Inez who has settled her debts. Oh! to think of it," and he shook his fist in the air, "to think that I believed myself married to the Dona Margaret, and find you in her place—*you*!"

"Be silent," she said, "you man without shame, who first fly at the throat of your new-wedded wife and then insult her by saying that you wish you were wedded to another woman. Be silent, or I will unlock the door and call your own people and repeat your monstrous talk to them." And she drew herself to her full height and stood over him on the bed.

Morella, his first rage spent, looked at her reflectively, and not without a certain measure of homage.

"I think," he remarked, "that if he did not happen to be in love with another woman and to believe that he had married her, you, my good Betty, would make a useful wife to any man who wished to get on in the world. I understood you to say that the door is locked, and if I might hazard a guess, you have the key, as also you happen to have a dagger. Well, I find the air in this place close, and I want to go *out*."

"Where to?" asked Betty.

"Let us say, to join Inez."

"What," she asked, "would you already be running after that woman again? Do you already forget that you are married?"

"It seems that I am not to be allowed to forget it. Now, let us bargain. I wish to leave Granada for a while, and without scandal. What are your terms? Remember that there are two to which I will not consent. I will not stop here with you, and you shall not accompany me. Remember also, that, although you hold the dagger at present, it is not wise of you to try to push this jest too far."

"As you did when you decoyed me on board the *San Antonio*," said Betty. "Well, our honeymoon has not begun too sweetly, and I do not mind if you go away for a while—to look for Inez. Swear now that you mean me no harm, and that you will not plot my death or disgrace, or in any way interfere with my liberty or position here in Granada. Swear it on the Rood."

H. Rider Haggard

And she took down a silver crucifix that hung upon the wall over the bed and handed it to him. For she knew Morella's superstitions, and that if once he swore upon this symbol he dare not break his oath.

"And if I will not swear?" he asked sullenly.

"Then," she answered, "you stop here until you do, you who are anxious to be gone. I have eaten food this morning, you have not; I have a dagger, you have none; and, being as we are, I am sure that no one will venture to disturb us until Inez and your friend the priest have gone further than you can follow."

"Very well, I will swear," he said, and he kissed the crucifix and threw it down, "You can stop here and rule my house in Granada, and I will do you no mischief, nor trouble you in any way. But if you come out of Granada, then we cross swords."

"You mean that you intend to leave this city? Then, here is paper and ink. Be so good as to sign an order to the stewards of your estates, within the territories of the Moorish king, to pay all their revenue to me during your absence, and to your servants to obey me in everything."

"It is easy to see that you were brought up in the house of a Jew merchant," said Morella, biting the pen and considering this woman who, whether she were hawk or pigeon, knew so well how to feather her nest. "Well, if I grant you this position and these revenues, will you leave me alone and cease to press other claims upon me?"

Now Betty, bethinking her of those papers that Inez had carried away with her, and that Castell and Margaret would know well how to use them if there were need, bethinking her also that if she pushed him too far at the beginning she might die suddenly as folk sometimes did in Granada, answered:

"It is much to ask of a deluded woman, but I still have some pride, and will not thrust myself in where it seems I am not wanted. Therefore, so be it. Till you seek me or send for me, I will not seek you so long as you keep your bargain. Now write the paper, sign it, and call in your secretaries to witness the signature."

"In whose favour must I word it?" he asked.

"In that of the Marquessa of Morella," she answered, and he, seeing a loophole in the words, obeyed her, since if she were not his wife this writing would have no value.

Somehow he must be rid of this woman. Of course he might cause her to be killed; but even in Granada people could not kill one to whom they had seemed to be just married without questions being asked. Moreover, Betty had friends, and he had enemies who would certainly ask them if she vanished away. No, he would sign the paper and fight the case afterwards, for he had no time to lose. Margaret had slipped away from him, and if once she escaped from Spain he knew that he would never see her more. For aught he knew, she might already have escaped or be married to Peter Brome. The very thought of it filled him with madness. There had been a conspiracy against him; he was outwitted, robbed, befooled. Well, hope still remained—and vengeance. He could still fight Peter, and perhaps kill him. He could hand over Castell, the Jew, to the Inquisition. He could find a way to deal with the priest Henriques and the woman Inez, and, perhaps, if fortune favoured him he could get Margaret back into his power.

Oh! yes, he would sign anything if only thereby he was set at liberty and freed for a while from this servant who called herself his wife, this strong-minded, strong-bodied, clever Englishwoman, of whom he had thought to make a tool, and who had made a tool of him.

So Betty dictated and he wrote: yes, it had come to this—she dictated and he wrote, and signed too. The order was comprehensive. It gave power to the most honourable Marquessa of Morella to act for him, her husband, in all things during his absence from Granada. It commanded that all rents and profits due to him should be paid to her, and that all his servants and dependants should obey her as though she were himself, and that her receipt should be as good as his receipt.

When the paper was written, and Betty had spelt it over carefully to see that there was no omission or mistake, she unlocked the door, struck upon the gong, and summoned the secretaries to witness their lord's signature to a settlement. Presently they came, bowing, and offering many felicitations, which to himself Morella vowed he would remember against them.

"I have to go a journey," he said. "Witness my signature to this document, which provides for the carrying on of my household and the disposal of my property during my absence."

They stared and bowed.

"Read it aloud first," said Betty, "so that my lord and husband may be sure that there is no mistake."

One of them obeyed, but before ever he had finished the furious Morella shouted to them from the bed:

"Have done and witness, then go, order me horses and an escort, for I ride at once."

So they witnessed in a great hurry, and left the room. Betty left with them, holding the paper in her hand, and when she reached the large hall where the household were gathered waiting to greet their lord, she commanded one of the secretaries to read it out to all of them, also to translate it into the Moorish tongue that every one might understand. Then she hid it away with the marriage lines, and, seating herself in the midst of the household, ordered them to prepare to receive the most noble marquis.

They had not long to wait, for presently he came out of the room like a bull into the arena, whereon Betty rose and curtseyed to him, and at her word all his servants bowed themselves down in the Eastern fashion. For a moment he paused, again like the bull when he sees the picadors and is about to charge. Then he thought better of it, and, with a muttered curse, strode past them.

Ten minutes later, for the third time within twenty-four hours, horses galloped from the palace and through the Seville gate.

"Friends," said Betty in her awkward Spanish, when she knew that he had gone, "a sad thing has happened to my husband, the marquis. The woman Inez, whom it seems he trusted very much, has departed, stealing a treasure that he valued above everything on earth, and so I, his new-made wife, am left desolate while he tries to find her."

H. Rider Haggard

CHAPTER XX

ISABELLA OF SPAIN

On the afternoon following his first visit, Castell's agent, Bernaldez, arrived again at the prison of the Hermandad at Seville accompanied by a tailor, a woman, and a chest full of clothes. The governor ordered these two persons to wait while the garments were searched under his own eye, but Bernaldez he permitted to be led at once to the prisoners. As soon as he was with them he said:

"Your marquis has been married fast enough."

"How do you know that?" asked Castell.

"From the woman Inez, who arrived with the priest last night, and gave me the certificates of his union with Betty Dene signed by himself. I have not brought them with me lest I should be searched, when they might have been taken away; but Inez has come disguised as a sempstress, so show no surprise when you see her, if she is admitted. Perhaps she will be able to tell the Dona Margaret something of what passed if she is allowed to fit her robes alone. After that she must lie hidden for fear of the vengeance of Morella; but I shall know where to put my hand upon her if she is wanted. You will all of you be brought before the queen to-morrow, and then I, who shall be there, will produce the writings." Scarcely were the words out of his mouth when the governor appeared, and with him the tailor and Inez, who curtseyed and glanced at

Margaret out of the corners of her soft eyes, looking at them all as though with curiosity, like one who had never seen or heard of them before.

When the dresses had been produced, Margaret asked whether she might be allowed to try them on with the woman in her own chamber, as she had not been measured for them.

The governor answered that as both the sempstress and the robes had been searched, there was no objection, so the two of them retired—Inez, with her arms full of garments.

"Tell me all about it," whispered Margaret as soon as the door was closed. "I die to hear your story."

So, while she fitted the clothes, since in that place they could never be sure but that they were watched through some secret loophole, Inez, with her mouth full of aloe thorns, which those of the trade used as pins, told her everything down to the time of her escape from Granada. When she came to that part of the tale where the false bride had lifted her veil and kissed the bridegroom, Margaret gasped in her amaze.

"Oh! how could she do it?" she said, "I should have fainted first."

"She has a good courage, that Betty—turn to the light, please, Senora—I could not have acted better myself—I think it is a little high on the left shoulder. He never guessed a thing, the besotted fool, and that was before I gave him the wine, for he wasn't likely to guess much afterwards. Did the senora say it was tight under the arm? Well, perhaps a little, but this stuff stretches. What I want to know is, what happened afterwards? Your cousin is the bull that I put my money on: I believe she will clear the ring. A woman with a nerve of steel; had I as much I should have been the Marchioness of Morella long ago, or there would be another marquis by now. There, the sit of the skirt is perfect; the senora's beautiful figure looks more beautiful in it than ever. Well, whoever lives will learn all about it, and it is no use worrying. Meanwhile, Bernaldez has paid me the money—and a handsome sum too—so you needn't thank me. I only worked for hire—and hate. Now I am going to lie low, as I don't want to get my throat cut, but he can find me if I am really needed.

"The priest? Oh, he is safe enough. We made him sign a receipt for his cash. Also, I believe that he has got his post as a secretary to the Inquisition, and began his duties at once as they were short-handed, torturing Jews and heretics, you know, and stealing their goods, both of which occupations will exactly suit him. I rode with him all the way to Seville, and he tried to make love to me, the slimy knave, but I paid him out," and Inez smiled at some pleasant recollection. "Still, I did not quarrel with him outright, as he may come in useful. Who knows? There's the governor calling me. One moment, Excellency, only one moment!

"Yes, Senora, with those few alterations the dress will be perfect. You shall have it back tonight without fail, and I can cut the others that you have been pleased to order from the same pattern. Oh! I thank you, Senora, you are too good to a poor girl, and," in a whisper, "the Mother of God have you in her guard, and send that Peter has improved in his love making!" and, half hidden in garments, Inez bowed herself out of the room through the door which the governor had already opened.

About nine o'clock on the following morning one of the jailers came to summon Margaret and her father to be led before the court. Margaret asked anxiously if the Senor Brome was coming too, but the man replied that he knew nothing of the Senor Brome, as he was in one of the cells for dangerous criminals, which he did not serve.

So forth they went, dressed in their new clothes, which were as fine as money could buy, and in the latest Seville fashion, and were conducted to the courtyard. Here, to her joy, Margaret saw Peter waiting for them under guard, and dressed also in the Christian garments which they had begged might be supplied to him at their cost. She sprang to his side, none hindering her, and, forgetting her bashfulness, suffered him to embrace her before them all, asking him how he had fared since they were parted.

"None too well," answered Peter gloomily, "who did not know if we should ever meet again; also, my prison is underground, where but little light comes through a grating, and there are rats in it which will not let a man sleep, so I must lie awake the most of the night thinking of you. But where go we now?"

"To be put upon our trial before the queen, I think. Hold my hand and walk close beside me, but do not stare at me so hard. Is aught wrong with my dress?"

"Nothing," answered Peter. "I stare because you look so beautiful in it. Could you not have worn a veil? Doubtless there are more marquises about this court."

"Only the Moors wear veils, Peter, and now we are Christians again. Listen—I think that none of them understand English. I have seen Inez, who asked after you very tenderly—nay, do not blush, it is unseemly in a man. Have you seen her also? No—well, she escaped from Granada as she planned, and Betty is married to the marquis."

"It will never hold good," answered Peter shaking his head, "being but a trick, and I fear that she will pay for it, poor woman! Still, she gave us a start, though, so far as prisons go, I was better off in Granada than in that rat-trap."

"Yes," answered Margaret innocently, "you had a garden to walk in there, had you not? No, don't be angry with me. Do you know what Betty did?" And she told him of how she had lifted her veil and kissed Morella without being discovered.

"That isn't so wonderful," said Peter, "since if they are painted up young women look very much alike in a half-lit room—"

"Or garden?" suggested Margaret.

"What is wonderful," went on Peter, scorning to take note of this interruption, "is that she could consent to kiss the man at all. The double-dealing scoundrel! Has Inez told you how he treated her? The very thought of it makes me ill."

"Well, Peter, he didn't ask you to kiss him, did he? And as for the wrongs of Inez, though doubtless you know more about them than I do, I think she has given him an orange for his pomegranate. But look, there is the Alcazar in front of us. Is it not a splendid castle? You know, it was built by the Moors."

"I don't care who it was built by," said Peter, "and it looks to me like any other castle, only larger. All I know about it is that I am to be tried there for knocking that ruffian on the head— and that perhaps this is the last we shall see of each other, as probably they will send me to the galleys, if they don't do worse."

"Oh! say no such thing. I never thought of it; it is not possible!" answered Margaret, her dark eyes filling with tears.

"Wait till your marquis appears, pleading the case against us, and you will see what is or is not possible," replied Peter with conviction. "Still, we have come through some storms, so let us hope for the best."

At that moment they reached the gate of the Alcazar, which they had approached from their prison through gardens of orange-trees, and soldiers came up and separated them. Next they were led across a court, where many people hurried to and fro, into a great marble-columned room glittering with gold, which was called the Hall of Justice. At the far end of this place, seated on a throne set upon a richly carpeted dais and surrounded by lords and counsellors, sat a magnificently attired lady of middle age. She was blue-eyed and red-haired, with a fair-skinned, open countenance, but very reserved and quiet in her demeanour.

"The Queen," muttered the guard, saluting, as did Castell and Peter, while Margaret curtseyed.

A case had just been tried, and the queen Isabella, after consultation with her assessors, was delivering judgment in few words and a gentle voice. As she spoke, her mild blue eyes fell upon Margaret, and, held it would seem by her beauty, rested on her till they wandered off to the tall form of Peter and the dark, Jewish-looking Castell by him, at the sight of whom she frowned a little.

That case was finished, and other suitors stood up in their turn, but the queen, waving her hand and still looking at Margaret, bent down and asked a question of one of the officers of the court, then gave an order, whereon the officer rising, summoned "John Castell, Margaret Castell, and Peter Brome, all of England," to appear at the bar and answer to the charge of murder of one Luiz of Basa, a soldier of the Holy Hermandad.

At once they were brought forward, and stood in a line in front of the dais, while the officer began to read the charge against them.

"Stay, friend," interposed the queen, "these accused are the subjects of our good brother, Henry of England, and may not understand our language, though one of them, I think"—and she glanced at Castell—"was not born in England, or at any rate of English blood. Ask them if they need an interpreter."

The question was put, and all of them answered that they could speak Spanish, though Peter added that he did so but indifferently.

"You are the knight, I think, who is charged with the commission of this crime," said Isabella, looking at him.

"Your Majesty, I am not a knight, only a plain esquire, Peter Brome of Dedham in England. My father was a knight, Sir

Peter Brome, but he fell at my side, fighting for Richard, on Bosworth Field, where I had this wound," and he pointed to the scar upon his face, "but was not knighted for my pains."

Isabella smiled a little, then asked:

"And how came you to Spain, Senor Peter Brome?"

"Your Majesty," answered Peter, Margaret helping from time to time when he did not know the Spanish words, "this lady at my side, the daughter of the merchant John Castell who stands by her, is my affianced—"

"Then you have won the love of a very beautiful maiden, Senor," interrupted the queen; "but proceed."

"She and her cousin, the Senora Dene, were kidnapped in London by one who I understand is the nephew of the King Ferdinand, and an envoy to the English court, who passed there as the Senor d'Aguilar, but who in Spain is the Marquis of Morella."

"Kidnapped! and by Morella!" exclaimed the queen.

"Yes, your Majesty, cozened on board his ship and kidnapped. The Senor Castell and I followed them, and, boarding their vessel, tried to rescue them, but were shipwrecked at Motril. The marquis carried them away to Granada, whither we followed also, I being sorely hurt in the shipwreck. There, in the palace of the marquis, we have lain prisoners many weeks, but at length escaped, purposing to come to Seville and seek the protection of your Majesties. On the road, while we were dressed as Moors, in which garb we compassed our escape, we were attacked by men that we thought were bandits, for we had been warned against such evil people. One of them rudely molested the Dona Margaret, and I cut him down, and by misfortune killed him, for which manslaughter I am here before you to-day. Your Majesty, I did not know that he was a soldier of the Holy Hermandad, and I pray you pardon my offence, which was done in ignorance, fear, and anger, for we are willing to pay compensation for this unhappy death."

Now some in the court exclaimed:

"Well spoken, Englishman!"

Then the queen said:

"If all this tale be true, I am not sure that we should blame you over much, Senor Brome; but how know we that it is true? For instance, you said that the noble marquis stole two ladies, a deed of which I can scarcely think him capable. Where then is the other?"

"I believe," answered Peter, "that she is now the wife of the Marquis of Morella."

"The wife! Who bears witness that she is the wife? He has not advised us that he was about to marry, as is usual."

Then Bernaldez stood forward, stating his name and occupation, and that he was a correspondent of the English merchant, John Castell, and producing the certificate of marriage signed by Morella, Betty, and the priest Henriques, handed it up to the queen saying that he had received them in duplicate by a messenger from Granada, and had delivered the other to the Archbishop of Seville.

The queen, having looked at the paper, passed it to her assessors, who examined it very carefully, one of them saying that the form was not usual, and that it might be forged.

The queen thought a little while, then said:

"That is so, and in one way only can we know the truth. Let our warrant issue summoning before us our cousin, the noble Marquis of Morella, the Senora Dene, who is said to be his wife, and the priest Henriques of Motril, who is said to have married them. When they have arrived, all of them, the king my husband and I will examine into the matter, and, until then, we will not suffer our minds to be prejudiced by hearing any more of this cause."

Now the governor of the prison stood forward, and asked what was to be done with the captives until the witnesses could be brought from Granada. The queen answered that they must remain in his charge, and be well treated, whereon Peter prayed that he might be given a better cell with fewer rats and more light. The queen smiled, and said that it should be so, but added that it would be proper that he should still be kept apart from the lady to whom he was affianced, who could dwell with her father. Then, noting the sadness on their faces, she added:

"Yet I think they may meet daily in the garden of the prison."

Margaret curtseyed and thanked her, whereon she said very graciously:

"Come here, Senora, and sit by me a little," and she pointed to a footstool at her side. "When I have done this business I desire a few words with you."

So Margaret was brought up upon the dais, and sat down at her Majesty's left hand upon the broidered footstool, and very fair indeed she looked placed thus above the crowd, she whose beauty and whose bearing were so royal; but Castell and Peter were led away back to the prison, though, seeing so many gay lords about, the latter went unwillingly enough. A while later, when the cases were finished, the queen dismissed the court save for certain officers, who stood at a distance, and, turning to Margaret, said:

"Now, fair maiden, tell me your story, as one woman to another, and do not fear that anything you say will be made use of at the trial of your lover, since against you, at any rate at present, no charge is laid. Say, first, are you really the affianced of that tall gentleman, and has he really your heart?"

"All of it, your Majesty," answered Margaret, "and we have suffered much for each other's sake." Then in as few words as she could she told their tale, while the queen listened earnestly.

"A strange story indeed, and if it be all true, a shameful," she said when Margaret had finished. "But how comes it that if Morella desired to force you into marriage, he is now wed to your companion and cousin? What are you keeping back from me?" and she glanced at her shrewdly.

"Your Majesty," answered Margaret, "I was ashamed to speak the rest, yet I will trust you and do so, praying your royal forgiveness if you hold that we, who were in desperate straits, have done what is wrong. My cousin, Betty Dene, has paid back Morella in his own false gold. He won her heart and promised to marry her, and at the risk of her own life she took my place at the altar, thereby securing our escape."

"A brave deed, if a doubtful," said the queen, "though I question whether such a marriage will be upheld. But that is a matter for the Church to judge of, and I must speak of it no more. Certainly it is hard to be angry with any of you. What did you say that Morella promised you when he asked you to marry him in London?"

"Your Majesty, he promised that he would lift me high, perhaps even"—and she hesitated—"to that seat in which you sit."

Isabella frowned, then laughed, and said, as she looked her up and down:

"You would fit it well, better than I do in truth. But what else did he say?"

"Your Majesty, he said that not every one loves the king, his uncle; that he had many friends who remembered that his father was poisoned by the father of the king, who was Morella's grandfather; also, that his mother was a princess of the Moors, and that he might throw in his lot with theirs, or that there were other ways in which he could gain his end."

"So, so," said the queen. "Well, though he is such a good son of the Church, and my lord is so fond of him, I never loved Morella, and I thank you for your warning. But I must not speak to you of such high matters, though it seems that some have thought otherwise. Fair Margaret, have you aught to ask of me?"

"Yes, your Majesty—that you will deal gently with my true love when he comes before you for trial, remembering that he is hot of head and strong of arm, and that such knights as he—for knightly is his blood—cannot brook to see their ladies mishandled by rough men, and the wrappings that shield them torn from off their bosoms. Also, I pray that I may be protected from Morella, that he may not be allowed to touch or even to speak to me, who, for all his rank and splendour, hate him as though he were some poisoned snake."

"I have said that I must not prejudge your case, you beautiful English Margaret," the queen answered with a smile, "yet I think that neither of those things you ask will cause justice to slip the bandage that is about her eyes. Go, and be at peace. If you have spoken truth to me, as I am sure you have, and Isabella of Spain can prevent it, the Senor Brome's punishment shall not be heavy, nor shall the shadow of the Marquis of Morella, the base-born son of a prince and of some royal infidel"—these words she spoke with much bitterness—"so much as fall upon you, though I warn you that my lord the king loves the man, as is but natural, and will not condemn him lightly. Tell me one thing. This lover of yours is brave, is he not?"

"Very brave," answered Margaret, smiling.

"And he can ride a horse and hold a lance, can he not, at any rate in your quarrel?"

"Aye, your Majesty, and wield a sword too, as well as most knights, though he has been but lately sick. Some learned that on Bosworth Field."

"Good. Now farewell," and she gave Margaret her hand to kiss. Then, calling two of her officers, she bade them conduct her back to the prison, and say that she should have liberty to send messages or to write to her, the queen, if she should so desire.

On the night of that same day Morella galloped into Seville. Indeed he should have been there long before, but misled by the story of the Moors who had escorted Peter, Margaret, and her father out of Granada and seen them take the Malaga road, he travelled thither first, only to find no trace of them in that city. Then he returned and tracked them to Seville, where he was soon made acquainted with all that had happened. Amongst other things, he discovered that ten hours before swift messengers had been despatched to Granada, commanding his attendance and that of Betty, with whom he had gone through the form of marriage.

On the following morning he asked an audience with the queen, but it was refused to him, and the king, his uncle, was away. Next he tried to win admission into the prison and see Margaret, only to find that neither his high rank and authority nor any bribe would suffice to unlock its doors. The queen had commanded otherwise, he was informed, and knew therefrom that in this matter he must reckon with Isabella as an enemy. Then he bethought him of revenge, and began a search for Inez and the priest Henriques of Motril, only to find that the former had vanished, none knew whither, and the holy father was safe within the walls of the Inquisition, whence he was careful not to emerge, and where no layman, however highly placed, could enter to lay a hand upon one of its officers. So, full of rage and disappointment, he took counsel of lawyers and friends, and prepared to defend the suit which he saw would be brought against him, hoping that chance might yet deliver Margaret into his hands. One good card he held, which now he determined to play. Castell, as he knew, was a Jew who for years had posed as a Christian, and for such there was no mercy in Seville. Perhaps for her father's sake he might yet be able to work upon Margaret, whom now he desired to win more fiercely than ever before.

At least it was certain that he would try this, or any other means, however base, rather than see her married to his rival, Peter Brome. Also there was the chance that this Peter might be condemned to imprisonment, or even to death, for the killing of a soldier of the Hermandad.

So Morella made him ready for the great struggle as best he could, and, since he could not stop her coming, awaited the arrival of Betty in Seville.

CHAPTER XXI

BETTY STATES HER CASE

Seven days had passed, during which time Margaret and her father had rested quietly in the prison, where, indeed, they dwelt more as guests than as captives. Thus they were allowed to receive what visitors they would, and among them Juan Bernaldez, Castell's connection and agent, who told them of all that passed without. Through him they sent messengers to meet Betty on her road and apprise her of how things stood, and of the trial in which her cause would be judged.

Soon the messengers returned, stating that the "Marchioness of Morella" was travelling in state, accompanied by a great retinue, that she thanked them for their tidings, and hoped to be able to defend herself at all points.

At this news Castell stared and Margaret laughed, for, although she did not know all the story, she was sure that in some way Betty had the mastery of Morella, and would not be easily defeated, though how she came to be travelling with a great retinue she could not imagine. Still, fearing lest she should be attacked or otherwise injured, she wrote a humble letter to the queen, praying that her cousin might be defended from all danger at the hands of any one whomsoever until she had an opportunity of giving evidence before their Majesties.

Within an hour came the answer that the lady was under the royal protection, and that a guard had been sent to escort her

H. Rider Haggard

and her party and to keep her safe from interference of any sort; also, that for her greater comfort, quarters had been prepared for her in a fortress outside of Seville, which would be watched night and day, and whence she would be brought to the court.

Peter was still kept apart from them, but each day at noon they were allowed to meet him in the walled garden of the prison, where they talked together to their heart's content. Here, too, he exercised himself daily at all manly games, and especially at sword-play with some of the other prisoners, using sticks for swords. Further, he was allowed the use of his horse that he had ridden from Granada, on which he jousted in the yard of the castle with the governor and certain other gentlemen, proving himself better at that play than any of them. These things he did vigorously and with ardour, for Margaret had told him of the hint which the queen gave her, and he desired to get back his full strength, and to perfect himself in the handling of every arm which was used in Spain.

So the time went by, until one afternoon the governor informed them that Peter's trial was fixed for the morrow, and that they must accompany him to the court to be examined also upon all these matters. A little later came Bernaldez, who said that the king had returned and would sit with the queen, and that already this affair had made much stir in Seville, where there was much curiosity as to the story of Morella's marriage, of which many different tales were told. That Margaret and her father would be discharged he had little doubt, in which case their ship was ready for them; but of Peter's chances he could say nothing, for they depended upon what view the king took of his offence, and, though unacknowledged, Morella was the king's nephew and had his ear.

Afterwards they went down into the garden, and there found Peter, who had just returned from his jousting, flushed with exercise, and looking very manly and handsome. Margaret took his hand and, walking aside, told him the news.

"I am glad," he answered, "for the sooner this business is begun the sooner it will be done. But, Sweet," and here his face grew very earnest, "Morella has much power in this land, and I have broken its law, so none know what the end will be. I may be condemned to death or imprisoned, or perhaps, if I am given the chance, with better luck I may fall fighting, in any of which cases we shall be separated for a while, or altogether. Should this be so, I pray that you will not stay here, either in the hope of rescuing me, or for other reasons; since, while you are in Spain, Morella will not cease from his attempts to get hold of you, whereas in England you will be safe from him."

When Margaret heard these words she sobbed aloud, for the thought that harm might come to Peter seemed to choke her.

"In all things I will do your bidding," she said, "yet how can I leave you, dear, while you are alive, and if, perchance, you should die, which may God prevent, how can I live on without you? Rather shall I seek to follow you very swiftly."

"I do not desire that," said Peter. "I desire that you should endure your days till the end, and come to meet me where I am in due season, and not before. I will add this, that if in after-years you should meet any worthy man, and have a mind to marry him, you should do so, for I know well that you will never forget me, your first love, and that beyond this world lie others where there are no marryings or giving in marriage. Let not my dead hand lie heavy upon you, Margaret."

"Yet," she replied in gentle indignation, "heavy must it always lie, since it is about my heart. Be sure of this, Peter, that if such dreadful ill should fall upon us, as you left me so shall you find me, here or hereafter."

"So be it," he said with a sigh of relief, for he could not bear to think of Margaret as the wife of some other man, even after he was gone, although his honest, simple nature, and fear lest her life might be made empty of all joy, caused him to say what he

H. Rider Haggard

had said.

Then behind the shelter of a flowering bush they embraced each other as do those who know not whether they will ever kiss again, and, the hour of sunset having come, parted as they must.

On the following morning once more Castell and Margaret were led to the Hall of Justice in the Alcazar; but this time Peter did not go with them. The great court was already full of counsellors, officers, gentlemen, and ladies who had come from curiosity, and other folk connected with or interested in the case. As yet, however, Margaret could not see Morella or Betty, nor had the king and queen taken their seats upon the throne. Peter was already there, standing before the bar with guards on either side of him, and greeted them with a smile and a nod as they were ushered to their chairs near by. Just as they reached them also trumpets were blown, and from the back of the hall, walking hand in hand, appeared their Majesties of Spain, Ferdinand and Isabella, whereat all the audience rose and bowed, remaining standing till they were seated on the thrones.

The king, whom they now saw for the first time, was a thickset, active man with pleasant eyes, a fair skin, and a broad forehead, but, as Margaret thought, somewhat sly-faced—the face of a man who never forgot his own interests in those of another. Like the queen, he was magnificently attired in garments broidered with gold and the arms of Aragon, while in his hand he held a golden sceptre surmounted by a jewel, and about his waist, to show that he was a warlike king, he wore his long, cross-handled sword. Smilingly he acknowledged the homage of his subjects by lifting his hand to his cap and bowing. Then his eye fell upon the beautiful Margaret, and, turning, he put a question to the queen in a light, sharp voice, asking if that were the lady whom Morella had married, and, if so, why in the name of heaven he wished to be rid of her.

Isabella answered that she understood that this was the senora whom he had desired to marry when he married some one else, as he alleged by mistake, but who was in fact affianced to the prisoner before them; a reply at which all who heard it laughed.

At this moment the Marquis of Morella, accompanied by his gentlemen and some long-gowned lawyers, appeared walking up the court, dressed in the black velvet that he always wore, and glittering with orders. Upon his head was a cap, also of black velvet, from which hung a great pearl, and this cap he did not remove even when he bowed to the king and queen, for he was one of the few grandees of Spain who had the right to remain covered before their Majesties. They acknowledged his salutation, Ferdinand with a friendly nod and Isabella with a cold bow, and he, too, took the seat that had been prepared for him. Just then there was a disturbance at the far end of the court, where one of its officers could be heard calling:

"Way! Make way for the Marchioness of Morella!" At the sound of this name the marquis, whose eyes were fixed on Margaret, frowned fiercely, rising from his seat as though to protest, then, at some whispered word from a lawyer behind him, sat down again.

Now the crowd of spectators separated, and Margaret, turning to look down the long hall, saw a procession advancing up the lane between them, some clad in armour and some in white Moorish robes blazoned with the scarlet eagle, the cognisance of Morella. In the midst of them, her train supported by two Moorish women, walked a tall and beautiful lady, a coronet upon her brow, her fair hair outspread, a purple cloak hanging from her shoulders, half hiding that same splendid robe sewn with pearls which had been Morella's gift to Margaret, and about her white bosom the chain of pearls which he had presented to Betty in compensation for her injuries.

Margaret stared and stared again, and her father at her side murmured:

"It is our Betty! Truly fine feathers make fine birds." Yes, Betty it was without a doubt, though, remembering her in her humble woollen dress at the old house in Holborn, it was hard to recognise the poor companion in this proud and magnificent lady, who looked as though all her life she had trodden the marble floors of courts, and consorted with nobles and with queens. Up the great hall she came, stately, imperturbable, looking neither to the right nor to the left, taking no note of the whisperings about her, no, nor even of Morella or of Margaret, till she reached the open space in front of the bar where Peter and his guards, gazing with all their eyes, hastened to make place for her. There she curtseyed thrice, twice to the queen, and once to the king, her consort; then, turning, bowed to the marquis, who fixed his eyes upon the ground and took no note, bowed to Castell and Peter, and lastly, advancing to Margaret, gave her her cheek to kiss. This Margaret did with becoming humility, whispering in her ear:

"How fares your Grace?"

"Better than you would in my shoes," whispered Betty back with ever so slight a trembling of her left eyelid; while Margaret heard the king mutter to the queen:

"A fine peacock of a woman. Look at her figure and those big eyes. Morella must be hard to please."

"Perhaps he prefers swans to peacocks," answered the queen in the same voice with a glance at Margaret, whose quieter and more refined beauty seemed to gain by contrast with that of her nobly built and dazzling-skinned cousin. Then she motioned to Betty to take the seat prepared for her, which she did, with her suite standing behind her and an interpreter at her side.

"I am somewhat bewildered," said the king, glancing from Morella to Betty and from Margaret to Peter, for evidently the humour of the situation did not escape him. "What is the exact case that we have to try?"

Then one of the legal assessors, or alcaldes, rose and said that the matter before their Majesties was a charge against the Englishman at the bar of killing a certain soldier of the Holy Hermandad, but that there seemed to be other matters mixed up with it.

"So I gather," answered the king; "for instance, an accusation of the carrying off of subjects of a friendly Power out of the territory of that Power; a suit for nullity of a marriage, and a cross-suit for the declaration of the validity of the said marriage—and the holy saints know what besides. Well, one thing at a time. Let us try this tall Englishman."

So the case was opened against Peter by a public prosecutor, who restated it as it had been laid before the queen. The Captain Arrano gave his evidence as to the killing of the soldier, but, in cross-examination by Peter's advocate, admitted, for evidently he bore no malice against the prisoner, that the said soldier had roughly handled the Dona Margaret, and that the said Peter, being a stranger to the country, might very well have taken them for a troop of bandits or even Moors. Also, he added, that he could not say that the Englishman had intended to kill the soldier.

Then Castell and Margaret gave their evidence, the latter with much modest sweetness. Indeed, when she explained that Peter was her affianced husband, to whom she was to have been wed on the day after she had been stolen away from England, and that she had cried out to him for help when the dead soldier caught hold of her and rent away her veil, there was a murmur of sympathy, and the king and queen began to talk with each other without paying much heed to her further words.

Next they spoke to two of the judges who sat with them, after which the king held up his hand and announced that they had come to a decision on the case. It was, that, under the circumstances, the Englishman was justified in cutting down the soldier, especially as there was nothing to show that he meant to kill him, or that he knew that he belonged to the

Holy Hermandad. He would, therefore, be discharged on the condition that he paid a sum of money, which, indeed, it appeared had already been paid to the man's widow, in compensation for the man's death, and a further small sum for Masses to be said for the welfare of his soul.

Peter began to give thanks for this judgment; but while he was still speaking the king asked if any of those present wished to proceed in further suits. Instantly Betty rose and said that she did. Then, through her interpreter, she stated that she had received the royal commands to attend before their Majesties, and was now prepared to answer any questions or charges that might be laid against her.

"What is your name, Senora?" asked the king.

"Elizabeth, Marchioness of Morella, born Elizabeth Dene, of the ancient and gentle family of Dene, a native of England," answered Betty in a clear and decided voice.

The king bowed, then asked:

"Does any one dispute this title and description?"

"I do," answered the Marquis of Morella, speaking for the first time.

"On what grounds, Marquis?"

"On every ground," he answered. "She is not the Marchioness of Morella, inasmuch as I went through the ceremony of marriage with her believing her to be another woman. She is not of ancient and gentle family, since she was a servant in the house of the merchant Castell yonder, in London."

"That proves nothing, Marquis," interrupted the king. "My family may, I think, be called ancient and gentle, which you will be the last to deny, yet I have played the part of a servant on an occasion which I think the queen here will remember"—

an allusion at which the audience, who knew well enough to what it referred, laughed audibly, as did her Majesty[1]. "The marriage and rank are matters for proof," went on the king, "if they are questioned; but is it alleged that this lady has committed any crime which prevents her from pleading?"

"None," answered Betty quickly, "except that of being poor, and the crime, if it is one, as it may be, of having married that man, the Marquis of Morella," whereat the audience laughed again.

"Well, Madam, you do not seem to be poor now," remarked the king, looking at her gorgeous and bejewelled apparel; "and here we are more apt to think marriage a folly than a crime," a light saying at which the queen frowned a little. "But," he added quickly, "set out your case, Madam, and forgive me if, until you have done so, I do not call you Marchioness."

[Footnote 1: When travelling from Saragossa to Valladolid to be married to Isabella, Ferdinand was obliged to pass himself off as a valet. Prescott says: "The greatest circumspection, therefore, was necessary. The party journeyed chiefly in the night; Ferdinand assumed the disguise of a servant and, when they halted on the road, took care of the mules and served his companions at table."]

"Here is my case, Sire," said Betty, producing the certificate of marriage and handing it up for inspection.

The judges and their Majesties inspected it, the queen remarking that a duplicate of this document had already been submitted to her and passed on to the proper authorities.

"Is the priest who solemnised the marriage present?" asked the king; whereon Bernaldez, Castell's agent, rose and said that he was, though he neglected to add that his presence had been secured for no mean sum.

One of the judges ordered that he should be called, and

presently the foxy-faced Father Henriques, at whom the marquis glared angrily, appeared bowing, and was sworn in the usual form, and, on being questioned, stated that he had been priest at Motril, and chaplain to the Marquis of Morella, but was now a secretary of the Holy Office at Seville. In answer to further questions he said that, apparently by the bridegroom's own wish, and with his full consent, on a certain date at Granada, he had married the marquis to the lady who stood before them, and whom he knew to be named Betty Dene; also, that at her request, since she was anxious that proper record should be kept of her marriage, he had written the certificates which the court had seen, which certificates the marquis and others had signed immediately after the ceremony in his private chapel at Granada. Subsequently he had left Granada to take up his appointment as a secretary to the Inquisition at Seville, which had been conferred on him by the ecclesiastical authorities in reward of a treatise which he had written upon heresy. That was all he knew about the affair.

Now Morella's advocate rose to cross-examine, asking him who had made the arrangements for the marriage. He answered that the marquis had never spoken to him directly on the subject—at least he had never mentioned to him the name of the lady; the Senora Inez arranged everything.

Now the queen broke in, asking where was the Senora Inez, and who she was. The priest replied that the Senora Inez was a Spanish woman, one of the marquis's household at Granada, whom he made use of in all confidential affairs. She was young and beautiful, but he could say no more about her. As to where she was now he did not know, although they had ridden together to Seville. Perhaps the marquis knew.

Now the priest was ordered to stand down, and Betty tendered herself as a witness, and through her interpreter told the court the story of her connection with Morella. She said that she had met him in London when she was a member of the household of the Senor Castell, and that at once he began to make love to her and won her heart. Subsequently he suggested that she should elope with him to Spain, promising to marry her at once, in proof of which she produced the letter he had written, which was translated and handed up for the inspection of the court—a very awkward letter, as they evidently thought, although it was not signed with the writer's real name. Next Betty explained the trick by which she and her cousin Margaret were brought on board his ship, and that when they arrived there the marquis refused to marry her, alleging that he was in love with her cousin and not with her—a statement which she took to be an excuse to avoid the fulfilment of his promise. She could not say why he had carried off her cousin Margaret also, but supposed that it was because, having once brought her upon the ship, he did not know how to be rid of her.

Then she described the voyage to Spain, saying that during that voyage she kept the marquis at a distance, since there was no priest to marry them; also, she was sick and much ashamed, who had involved her cousin and mistress in this trouble. She told how the Senors Castell and Brome had followed in another vessel, and boarded the caravel in a storm; also of the shipwreck and their journey to Granada as prisoners, and of their subsequent life there. Finally she described how Inez came to her with proposals of marriage, and how she bargained that if she consented, her cousin, the Senor Castell, and the Senor Brome should go free. They went accordingly, and the marriage took place as arranged, the marquis first embracing her publicly in the presence of various people—namely, Inez and his two secretaries, who, except Inez, were present, and could bear witness to the truth of what she said.

After the marriage and the signing of the certificates she had accompanied him to his own apartments, which she had never entered before, and there, to her astonishment, in the morning, he announced that he must go a journey upon their Majesties' business. Before he went, however, he gave her a written authority, which she produced, to receive his rents and manage his matters in Granada during his absence, which authority she read to the gathered household before he left.

H. Rider Haggard

She had obeyed him accordingly until she had received the royal command, receiving moneys, giving her receipt for the same, and generally occupying the unquestioned position of mistress of his house.

"We can well believe it," said the king drily. "And now, Marquis, what have you to answer to all this?"

"I will answer presently," replied Morella, who trembled with rage. "First suffer that my advocate cross-examine this woman."

So the advocate cross-examined, though it cannot be said that he had the better of Betty. First he questioned her as to her statement that she was of ancient and gentle family, whereon Betty overwhelmed the court with a list of her ancestors, the first of whom, a certain Sieur Dene de Dene, had come to England with the Norman Duke, William the Conqueror. After him, so she still swore, the said Denes de Dene had risen to great rank and power, having been the favourites of the kings of England, and fought for them generation after generation.

By slow degrees she came down to the Wars of the Roses, in which she said her grandfather had been attainted for his loyalty, and lost his land and titles, so that her father, whose only child she was—being now the representative of the noble family, Dene de Dene—fell into poverty and a humble place in life. However, he married a lady of even more distinguished race than his own, a direct descendant of a noble Saxon family, far more ancient in blood than the upstart Normans. At this point, while Peter and Margaret listened amazed, at a hint from the queen, the bewildered court interfered through the head alcalde, praying her to cease from the history of her descent, which they took for granted was as noble as any in England.

Next she was examined as to her relations with Morella in London, and told the tale of his wooing with so much detail and imaginative power that in the end that also was left unfinished. So it was with everything. Clever as Morella's advocate might be, sometimes in English and sometimes in the Spanish tongue, Betty overwhelmed him with words and apt answers, until, able to make nothing of her, the poor man sat down wiping his brow and cursing her beneath his breath.

Then the secretaries were sworn, and after them various members of Morella's household, who, although somewhat unwillingly, confirmed all that Betty had said as to his embracing her with lifted veil and the rest. So at length Betty closed her case, reserving the right to address the court after she had heard that of the marquis.

Now the king, queen, and their assessors consulted for a little while, for evidently there was a division of opinion among them, some thinking that the case should be stopped at once and referred to another tribunal, and others that it should go on. At length the queen was heard to say that at least the Marquis of Morella should be allowed to make his statement, as he might be able to prove that all this story was a fabrication, and that he was not even at Granada at the time when the marriage was alleged to have taken place.

The king and the alcaldes assenting, the marquis was sworn and told his story, admitting that it was not one which he was proud to repeat in public. He narrated how he had first met Margaret, Betty, and Peter at a public ceremony in London, and had then and there fallen in love with Margaret, and accompanied her home to the house of her father, the merchant John Castell.

Subsequently he discovered that this Castell, who had fled from Spain with his father in childhood, was that lowest of mankind, an unconverted Jew who posed as a Christian (at this statement there was a great sensation in court, and the queen's face hardened), although it is true that he had married a Christian lady, and that his daughter had been baptized and brought up as a Christian, of which faith she was a loyal member. Nor did she know—as he believed—that her father remained a Jew, since, otherwise, he would not have continued to seek her as his wife. Their Majesties would be aware, he went on, that, owing to reasons with which they were acquainted, he had means of getting at the truth of these matters concerning the Jews in England, as to which, indeed, he had already written to them, although, owing to his shipwreck and to the pressure of his private affairs, he had not yet made his report on his embassy in person.

Continuing, he said that he admitted that he had made love to the serving-woman, Betty, in order to gain access to Margaret, whose father mistrusted him, knowing something of his mission. She was a person of no character.

Here Betty rose and said in a clear voice:

"I declare the Marquis of Morella to be a knave and a liar. There is more good character in my little finger than in his whole body, and," she added, "than in that of his mother before him"—an allusion at which the marquis flushed, while, satisfied for the present with this home-thrust, Betty sat down.

He had proposed to Margaret, but she was not willing to marry him, as he found that she was affianced to a distant cousin of hers, the Senor Peter Brome, a swashbuckler who was in trouble for the killing of a man in London, as he had killed the soldier of the Holy Hermandad in Spain. Therefore, in his despair, being deeply enamoured of her, and knowing that he could offer her great place and fortune, he conceived the idea of carrying her off, and to do so was obliged, much against his will, to abduct Betty also.

So after many adventures they came to Granada, where he was able to show the Dona Margaret that the Senor Peter Brome was employing his imprisonment in making love to that member of his household, Inez, who had been spoken of, but now could not be found.

Here Peter, who could bear this no longer, also rose and called him a liar to his face, saying that if he had the opportunity he would prove it on his body, but was ordered by the king to sit down and be silent.

Having been convinced of her lover's unfaithfulness, the marquis went on, the Dona Margaret had at length consented to become his wife on condition that her father, the Senor Brome, and her servant, Betty Dene, were allowed to escape from Granada—

"Where," remarked the queen, "you had no right to detain them, Marquis. Except, perhaps, the father, John Castell," she added significantly.

Where, he admitted with sorrow, he had no right to detain them.

"Therefore," went on the queen acutely, "there was no legal or moral consideration for this alleged promise of marriage,"—a point at which the lawyers nodded approvingly.

The marquis submitted that there was a consideration; that at any rate the Dona Margaret wished it. On the day arranged for the wedding the prisoners were let go, disguised as Moors, but he now knew that through the trickery of the woman Inez, whom he believed had been bribed by Castell and his fellow-Jews, the Dona Margaret escaped in place of her servant, Betty, with whom he subsequently went through the form of marriage, believing her to be Margaret.

As regards the embrace before the ceremony, it took place in a shadowed room, and he thought that Betty's face and hair must have been painted and dyed to resemble those of Margaret. For the rest, he was certain that the ceremonial cup of wine that he drank before he led the woman to the altar was drugged, since he only remembered the marriage itself very dimly, and after that nothing at all until he woke upon the following morning with an aching brow to see Betty sitting by him. As for the power of administration which she produced, being perfectly mad at the time with rage and disappointment, and sure that if he stopped there any longer he should commit the crime of killing this woman who had deceived him so cruelly, he gave it that he might escape from her. Their Majesties would notice also that it was in favour of the Marchioness of Morella. As this marriage was null and void, there was no Marchioness of Morella. Therefore, the document was null and void also. That was the truth, and all he had to say.

CHAPTER XXII

THE DOOM OF JOHN CASTELL

His evidence finished, the Marquis of Morella sat down, whereon, the king and queen having whispered together, the head alcalde asked Betty if she had any questions to put to him. She rose with much dignity, and through her interpreter said in a quiet voice:

"Yes, a great many. Yet she would not debase herself by asking a single one until the stain which he had cast upon her was washed away, which she thought could only be done in blood. He had alleged that she was a woman of no character, and he had further alleged that their marriage was null and void. Being of the sex she was, she could not ask him to make good his assertions at the sword's point, therefore, as she believed she had the right to do according to all the laws of honour, she asked leave to seek a champion—if an unfriended woman could find one in a strange land—to uphold her fair name against this base and cruel slander."

Now, in the silence that followed her speech, Peter rose and said:

"I ask the permission of your Majesties to be that champion. Your Majesties will note that according to his own story I have suffered from this marquis the bitterest wrong that one man can receive at the hands of another. Also, he has lied in saying that I am not true to my affianced lady, the Dona Margaret, and surely I have a right to avenge the lie upon him. Lastly, I declare that I believe the Senora Betty to be a good and upright woman, upon whom no shadow of shame has ever fallen, and, as her countryman and relative, I desire to uphold her good name before all the world. I am a foreigner here with few friends, or none, yet I cannot believe that your Majesties will withhold from me the right of battle which all over the world in such a case one gentleman may demand of another. I challenge the Marquis of Morella to mortal combat without mercy to the fallen, and here is the proof of it."

Then, stepping across the open space before the bar, he drew the leathern gauntlet off his hand and threw it straight into Morella's face, thinking that after such an insult he could not choose but fight.

With an oath Morella snatched at his sword; but, before he could draw it, officers of the court threw themselves on him, and the king's stern voice was heard commanding them to cease their brawling in the royal presences.

"I ask your pardon, Sire," gasped Morella, "but you have seen what this Englishman did to me, a grandee of Spain."

"Yes," broke in the queen, "but we have also heard what you, a grandee of Spain, did to this gentleman of England, and the charge you brought against him, which, it seems, the Dona Margaret does not believe."

"In truth, no, your Majesty," said Margaret. "Let me be sworn also, and I can explain much of what the marquis has told to you. I never wished to marry him or any man, save this one," and she touched Peter on the arm, "and anything that he or I may have done, we did to escape the evil net in which we were snared."

"We believe it," answered the queen with a smile, then fell to consulting with the king and the alcaldes.

For a long time they debated in voices so low that none could hear what they said, looking now at one and now at another of the parties to this strange suit. Also, some priest was called into their council, which Margaret thought a bad omen. At length they made up their minds, and in a low, quiet voice and measured words her Majesty, as Queen of Castile, gave the judgment of them all. Addressing herself first to Morella, she said:

"My lord Marquis, you have brought very grave charges against the lady who claims to be your wife, and the Englishman whose affianced bride you admit you snatched away by fraud and force. This gentleman, on his own behalf and on behalf of these ladies, has challenged you to a combat to the death in a fashion that none can mistake. Do you accept his challenge?"

"I would accept it readily enough, your Majesty," answered Morella in sullen tones, "since heretofore none have doubted my courage; but I must remember that I am"—and he paused, then added—"what your Majesties know me to be, a grandee of Spain, and something more, wherefore it is scarcely lawful for me to cross swords with a Jew-merchant's clerk, for that was this man's high rank and office in England."

"You could cross them with me on your ship, the *San Antonio*," exclaimed Peter bitterly, "why then are you ashamed to finish what you were not ashamed to begin? Moreover, I tell you that in love or war I hold myself the equal of any woman-thief and bastard in this kingdom, who am one of a name that has been honoured in my own."

Now again the king and queen spoke together of this question of rank—no small one in that age and country. Then Isabella said:

"It is true that a grandee of Spain cannot be asked to meet a simple foreign gentleman in single combat. Therefore, since he has thought fit to raise it, we uphold the objection of the

Marquis of Morella, and declare that this challenge is not binding on his honour. Yet we note his willingness to accept the same, and are prepared to do what we can to make the matter easy, so that it may not be said that a Spaniard, who has wrought wrong to an Englishman, and been asked openly to make the amend of arms in the presence of his sovereigns, was debarred from so doing by the accident of his rank. Senor Peter Brome, if you will receive it at our hands, as others of your nation have been proud to do, we propose, believing you to be a brave and loyal man of gentle birth, to confer upon you the knighthood of the Order of St. James, and thereby and therein the right to consort with as equal, or to fight as equal, any noble of Spain, unless he should be of the right blood-royal, to which place we think the most puissant and excellent Marquis of Morella lays no claim."

"I thank your Majesties," said Peter, astonished, "for the honour that you would do to me, which, had it not been for the fact that my father chose the wrong side on Bosworth Field, being of a race somewhat obstinate in the matter of loyalty, I should not have needed to accept from your Majesties. As it is I am very grateful, since now the noble marquis need not feel debased in settling our long quarrel as he would desire to do."

"Come hither and kneel down, Senor Peter Brome," said the queen when he had finished speaking.

He obeyed, and Isabella, borrowing his sword from the king, gave him the accolade by striking him thrice upon the right shoulder and saying:

"Rise, Sir Peter Brome, Knight of the most noble Order of Saint Iago, and by creation a Don of Spain."

He rose, he bowed, retreating backwards as was the custom, and thereby nearly falling off the dais, which some people thought a good omen for Morella. As he went the king said:

"Our Marshal, Sir Peter, will arrange the time and manner of your combat with the marquis as shall be most convenient to you both. Meanwhile, we command you both that no unseemly word or deed should pass between you, who must soon meet face to face to abide the judgment of God in battle *a l'outrance*. Rather, since one of you must die so shortly, do we entreat you to prepare your souls to appear before His judgment-seat. We have spoken."

Now the audience appeared to think that the court was ended, for many of them began to rise; but the queen held up her hand and said:

"There remain other matters on which we must give judgment. The senora here," and she pointed to Betty, "asks that her marriage should be declared valid, or so we understand, and the Marquis of Morella asks that his marriage with the said senora should be declared void, or so we understand. Now this is a question over which we claim no power, it having to do with a sacrament of the Church. Therefore we leave it to his Holiness the Pope in person, or by his legate, to decide according to his wisdom in such manner as may seem best to him, if the parties concerned should choose to lay their suit before him. Meanwhile, we declare and decree that the senora, born Elizabeth Dene, shall everywhere throughout our dominions, until or unless his Holiness the Pope shall decide to the contrary, be received and acknowledged as the Marchioness of Morella, and that during his lifetime her reputed husband shall make due provision for her maintenance, and that after his death, should no decision have been come to by the court of Rome upon her suit, she shall inherit and enjoy that proportion of his lands and property which belongs to a wife under the laws of this realm."

Now, while Betty bowed her thanks to their Majesties till the jewels on her bodice rattled, and Morella scowled till his face looked as black as a thunder-cloud above the mountains, the audience, whispering to each other, once more rose to disperse. Again the queen held up her hand, for the judgment was not

H. Rider Haggard

yet finished.

"We have a question to ask of the gallant Sir Peter Brome and the Dona Margaret, his affianced. Is it still their desire to take each other in marriage?"

Now Peter looked at Margaret, and Margaret looked at Peter, and there was that in their eyes which both of them understood, for he answered in a clear voice:

"Your Majesty, that is the dearest wish of both of us."

The queen smiled a little, then asked: "And do you, Senor John Castell, consent and allow your daughter's marriage to this knight?"

"I do, indeed," he answered gravely. "Had it not been for this man here," and he glanced with bitter hatred at Morella, "they would have been united long ago, and to that end," he added with meaning, "such little property as I possessed has been made over to trustees in England for their benefit and that of their children. Therefore I am henceforward dependent upon their charity."

"Good," said the queen. "Then one question remains to be put, and only one. Is it your wish, both of you, that you should be wed before the single combat between the Marquis of Morella and Sir Peter Brome? Remember, Dona Margaret, before you answer, that in this event you may soon be made a widow, and that if you postpone the ceremony you may never be a wife."

Now Margaret and Peter spoke a few words together, then the former answered for them both.

"Should my lord fall," she said in her sweet voice that trembled as she uttered the words, "in either case my heart will be widowed and broken. Let me live out my days, therefore, bearing his name, that, knowing my deathless grief, none may thenceforth trouble me with their love, who desire to remain his bride in heaven."

"Well spoken," said the queen. "We decree that here in our cathedral of Seville you twain shall be wed on the same day, but before the Marquis of Morella and you, Sir Peter Brome, meet in single combat. Further, lest harm should be attempted against either of you," and she looked sideways at Morella, "you, Senora Margaret, shall be my guest until you leave my care to become a bride, and you, Sir Peter, shall return to lodge in the prison whence you came, but with liberty to see whom you will, and to go when and where you will, but under our protection, lest some attempt should be made on you."

She ceased, whereon suddenly the king began speaking in his sharp, thin voice.

"Having settled these matters of chivalry and marriage," he said, "there remains another, which I will not leave to the gentle lips of our sovereign Lady, that has to do with something higher than either of them—namely, the eternal welfare of men's souls, and of the Church of Christ on earth. It has been declared to us that the man yonder, John Castell, merchant of London, is that accursed thing, a Jew, who for the sake of gain has all his life feigned to be a Christian, and, as such, deceived a Christian woman into marriage; that he is, moreover, of our subjects, having been born in Spain, and therefore amenable to the civil and spiritual jurisdiction of this realm."

He paused, while Margaret and Peter stared at each other affrighted. Only Castell stood silent and unmoved, though he guessed what must follow better than either of them.

"We judge him not," went on the king, "who claim no authority in such high matters, but we do what we must do—we commit him to the Holy Inquisition, there to take his trial!"

Now Margaret cried aloud. Peter stared about him as though for help, which he knew could never come, feeling more afraid than ever he had been in all his life, and for the first time that day Morella smiled. At least he would be rid of one enemy. But Castell went to Margaret and kissed her tenderly. Then he shook Peter by the hand, saying:

"Kill that thief," and he looked at Morella, "as I know you will, and would if there were ten as bad at his back. And be a good husband to my girl, as I know you will also, for I shall ask an account of you of these matters when we meet where there is neither Jew nor Christian, priest nor king. Now be silent, and bear what must be borne as I do, for I have a word to say before I leave you and the world.

"Your Majesties, I make no plea for myself, and when I am questioned before your Inquisition the task will be easy, for I desire to hide nothing, and will tell the truth, though not from fear or because I shrink from pain. Your Majesties, you have told us that these two, who, at least, are good enough Christians from their birth, shall be wed. I would ask you if any spiritual crime, or supposed crime, of mine will be allowed to work their separation, or to their detriment in any way whatsoever."

"On that point," answered the queen quickly, as though she wished to get in her words before the king or any one else could speak, "you have our royal word, John Castell. Your case is apart from their case, and nothing of which you may be convicted shall affect them in person or," she added slowly, "in property."

"A large promise," muttered the king.

"It is my promise," she answered decidedly, "and it shall be kept at any cost. These two shall marry, and if Sir Peter lives through the fray they shall depart from Spain unharmed, nor shall any fresh charge be brought against them in any court of the realm, nor shall they be persecuted or proceeded against in any other realm or on the high seas at our instance or that of our officers. Let my words be written down, and one copy of them signed and filed and another copy given to the Dona Margaret."

"Your Majesty," said Castell, "I thank you, and now, if die I must, I shall die happy. Yet I make bold to tell you that had you not spoken them it was my purpose to kill myself, here before your eyes, since that is a sin for which none can be asked to suffer save the sinner. Also, I say that this Inquisition which you have set up shall eat out the heart of Spain and bring her greatness to the dust of death. The torture and the misery of those Jews, than whom you have no better or more faithful subjects, shall be avenged on the heads of your children's children for so long as their blood endures."

He finished speaking, and, while something that sounded like a gasp of fear rose from that crowded court as the meaning of Castell's bold words came home to his auditors, the crowd behind him separated, and there appeared, walking two by two, a file of masked and hooded monks and a guard of soldiers, all of whom doubtless were in waiting. They came to John Castell, they touched him on the shoulder, they closed around him, hiding him as it were from the world, and in the midst of them he vanished away.

Peter's memories of that strange day in the Alcazar at Seville always remained somewhat dim and blurred. It was not wonderful. Within the space of a few hours he had been tried for his life and acquitted. He had seen Betty, transformed from a humble companion into a magnificent and glittering marchioness, as a chrysalis is transformed into a butterfly, urge her strange suit against the husband who had tricked her, and whom she had tricked, and, for the while at any rate, more than hold her own, thanks to her ready wit and native strength of character.

As her champion, and that of Margaret, he had challenged Morella to a single combat, and when his defiance was refused on the ground of his lack of rank, by the favour of the great Isabella, who wished to use him as her instrument, doubtless because of those secret ambitions of Morella's which Margaret had revealed to her, he had been suddenly advanced to the high station of a Knight of the Order of St. James of Spain, to which, although he cared little for it, otherwise he might vainly have striven to come.

More, and better far, the desire of his heart would at length be attained, for now it was granted to him to meet his enemy, the man whom he hated with just cause, upon a fair field, without favour shown to one or the other, and to fight him to the death. He had been promised, further, that within some few days Margaret should be given to him as wife, although it well might be that she would keep that name but for a single hour, and that until then they both should dwell safe from Morella's violence and treachery; also that, whatever chanced, no suit should lie against them in any land for aught that they did or had done in Spain.

Lastly, when all seemed safe save for that chance of war, whereof, having been bred to such things, he took but little count; when his cup, emptied at length of mire and sand, was brimming full with the good red wine of battle and of love, when it was at his very lips indeed, Fate had turned it to poison and to gall. Castell, his bride's father, and the man he loved, had been haled to the vaults of the Inquisition, whence he knew well he would come forth but once more, dressed in a yellow robe "relaxed to the civil arm," to perish slowly in the fires of the Quemadero, the place of burning of heretics.

What would his conquest over Morella avail if Heaven should give him power to conquer? What kind of a bridal would that be which was sealed and consecrated by the death of the bride's father in the torturing fires of the Inquisition? How would they ever get the smell of the smoke of that sacrifice out of their nostrils? Castell was a brave man; no torments would make him recant. It was doubtful even if he would be at the pains to deny his faith, he who had only been baptized a

Christian by his father for the sake of policy, and suffered the fraud to continue for the purposes of his business, and that he might win and keep a Christian wife. No, Castell was doomed, and he could no more protect him from priest and king than a dove can protect its nest from a pair of hungry peregrines.

Oh that last scene! Never could Peter forget it while he lived— the vast, fretted hall with its painted arches and marble columns; the rays of the afternoon sun piercing the window-places, and streaming like blood on to the black robes of the monks as, with their prey, they vanished back into the arcade where they had lurked; Margaret's wild cry and ashen face as her father was torn away from her, and she sank fainting on to Betty's bejewelled bosom; the cruel sneer on Morella's lips; the king's hard smile; the pity in the queen's eye; the excited murmurings of the crowd; the quick, brief comments of the lawyers; the scratching of the clerk's quill as, careless of everything save his work, he recorded the various decrees; and above it all as it were, upright, defiant, unmoved, Castell, surrounded by the ministers of death, vanishing into the blackness of the arcade, vanishing into the jaws of the tomb.

CHAPTER XXIII

FATHER HENRIQUES AND THE BAKER'S OVEN

A week had gone by. Margaret was in the palace, where Peter had been to see her twice, and found her broken-hearted. Even the fact that they were to be wed upon the following Saturday, the day fixed also for the combat between Peter and Morella, brought her no joy or consolation. For on the next day, the Sunday, there was to be an "Act of Faith," an *auto-da-fe* in Seville, when wicked heretics, such as Jews, Moors, and persons who had spoken blasphemy, were to suffer for their crimes—some by fire on the Quemadero, or place of burning, outside the city; some by making public confession of their grievous sin before they were carried off to perpetual and solitary imprisonment; some by being garotted before their bodies were given to the flames, and so forth. In this ceremony it was known that John Castell had been doomed to play a leading part.

On her knees, with tears and beseechings, Margaret had prayed the queen for mercy. But in this matter those tears produced no more effect upon the heart of Isabella than does water dripping on a diamond. Gentle enough in other ways, where questions of the Faith were concerned she had the craft of a fox and the cruelty of a tiger. She was even indignant with Margaret. Had not enough been done for her? she asked. Had she not even passed her royal word that no steps should be taken to deprive the accused of such property as he might own in Spain if he were found guilty, and that none of those penalties which, according to law and custom fell upon the children of such infamous persons, should attach to her, Margaret? Was she not to be publicly married to her lover, and, should he survive the combat, allowed to depart with him in honour without even being asked to see her father expiate his iniquity? Surely, as a good Christian she should rejoice that he was given this opportunity of reconciling his soul with God and be made an example to others of his accursed faith. Was she then a heretic also?

So she stormed on, till Margaret crept from her presence wondering whether this creed could be right that would force the child to inform against and bring the parent to torment. Where were such things written in the sayings of the Saviour and His Apostles? And if they were not written, who had invented them?

"Save him!—save him!" Margaret had gasped to Peter in despair. "Save him, or I swear to you, however much I may love you, however much we may seem to be married, never shall you be a husband to me."

"That seems hard," replied Peter, shaking his head mournfully, "since it was not I who gave him over to these devils, and probably the end of it would be that I should share his fate. Still, I will do what a man can."

"No, no," she cried in despair; "do nothing that will bring you into danger." But he had gone without waiting for her answer.

It was night, and Peter sat in a secret room in a certain baker's shop in Seville. There were present there besides himself the Fray Henriques—now a secretary to the Holy Inquisition, but disguised as a layman—the woman Inez, the agent Bernaldez, and the old Jew, Israel of Granada.

"I have brought him here, never mind how," Inez was saying, pointing to Henriques. "A risky and disagreeable business enough. And now what is the use of it?"

"No use at all," answered the Fray coolly, "except to me who pocket my ten gold pieces."

"A thousand doubloons if our friend escapes safe and sound," put in the old Jew Israel. "God in Heaven! think of it, a thousand doubloons."

The secretary's eyes gleamed hungrily.

"I could do with them well enough," he answered, "and hell could spare one filthy Jew for ten years or so, but I see no way. What I do see, is that probably all of you will join him. It is a great crime to try to tamper with a servant of the Holy Office."

Bernaldez turned white, and the old Jew bit his nails; but Inez tapped the priest upon the shoulder.

"Are you thinking of betraying us?" she asked in her gentle voice. "Look here, friend, I have some knowledge of poisons, and I swear to you that if you attempt it, you shall die within a week, tied in a double knot, and never know whence the dose came. Or I can bewitch you, I, who have not lived a dozen years among the Moors for nothing, so that your head swells and your body wastes, and you utter blasphemies, not knowing what you say, until for very shame's sake they toast you among the faggots also."

"Bewitch me!" answered Henriques with a shiver. "You have done that already, or I should not be here."

"Then, if you do not wish to be in another place before your time," went on Inez, still tapping his shoulder gently, "think, think! and find a way, worthy servant of the Holy Office."

"A thousand doubloons!—a thousand gold doubloons!" croaked old Israel, "or if you fail, sooner or later, this month or next, this year or next, death—death as slow and cruel as we can make it. There are two Inquisitions in Spain, holy Father; but one of them does its business in the dark, and your name is on its ledger."

Now Henriques was very frightened, as well he might be with all those eyes glaring at him.

"You need fear nothing," he said, "I know the devilish power of your league too well, and that, if I kill you all, a hundred others I have never seen or heard of would dog me to my death, who have taken your accursed money."

"I am glad that you understand at last, dear friend," said the soft, mocking voice of Inez, who stood behind the monk like an evil genius, and again tapped him affectionately on the shoulder, this time with the bare blade of a poniard. "Now be quick with that plan of yours. It grows late, and all holy people should be abed."

"I have none. I defy you," he answered furiously.

"Very well, friend—very well; then I will say good night, or rather farewell, since I am not likely to meet you again in this world." "Where are you going?" he asked anxiously.

"Oh! to the palace to meet the Marquis of Morella and a friend of his, a relation indeed. Look you here. I have had an offer of pardon for my part in that marriage if I can prove that a certain base priest knew that he was perpetrating a fraud. Well, I *can* prove it—you may remember that you wrote me a note—and, if I do, what happens to such a priest who chances to have incurred the hatred of a grandee of Spain and of his noble relation?"

"I am an officer of the Holy Inquisition; no one dare touch me," he gasped.

"Oh! I think that there are some who would take the risk. For instance—the king."

Fray Henriques sank back in his chair. Now he understood

whom Inez meant by the noble relative of Morella, understood also that he had been trapped. "On Sunday morning," he began in a hollow whisper, "the procession will be formed, and wind through the streets of the city to the theatre, where the sermon will be preached before those who are relaxed proceed to the Quemadero. About eight o'clock it turns on to the quay for a little way only, and here will be but few spectators, since the view of the pageant is bad, nor is the road guarded there. Now, if a dozen determined men were waiting disguised as peasants with a boat at hand, perhaps they might—" and he paused.

Then Peter, who had been watching and listening to all this play, spoke for the first time, asking:

"In such an event, reverend Sir, how would those determined men know which was the victim that they sought?"

"The heretic John Castell," he answered, "will be seated on an ass, clad in a *zamarra* of sheepskin painted with fiends and a likeness of his own head burning—very well done, for I, who can draw, had a hand in it. Also, he alone will have a rope round his neck, by which he may be known."

"Why will he be seated on an ass?" asked Peter savagely. "Because you have tortured him so that he cannot walk?"

"Not so—not so," said the Dominican, shrinking from those fierce eyes. "He has never been questioned at all, not a single turn of the *mancuerda*, I swear to you, Sir Knight. What was the use, since he openly avows himself an accursed Jew?"

"Be more gentle in your talk, friend," broke in Inez, with her familiar tap upon the shoulder. "There are those here who do not think so ill of Jews as you do in your Holy House, but who understand how to apply the *mancuerda*, and can make a very serviceable rack out of a plank and a pulley or two such as lie in the next room. Cultivate courtesy, most learned priest, lest before you leave this place you should add a cubit to your stature."

"Go on," growled Peter.

"Moreover," added Fray Henriques shakily, "orders came that it was not to be done. The Inquisitors thought otherwise, as they believed—doubtless in error—that he might have accomplices whose names he would give up; but the orders said that as he had lived so long in England, and only recently travelled to Spain, he could have none. Therefore he is sound—sound as a bell; never before, I am told, has an impenitent Jew gone to the stake in such good case, however worthy and worshipful he might be."

"So much the better for you, if you do not lie," answered Peter. "Continue!"

"There is nothing more to say, except that I shall be walking near to him with the two guards, and, of course, if he were snatched away from us, and there were no boats handy in which to pursue, we could not help it, could we? Indeed, we priests, who are men of peace, might even fly at the sight of cruel violence."

"I should advise you to fly fast and far," said Peter. "But, Inez, what hold have you on this friend of yours? He will trick everybody."

"A thousand doubloons—a thousand doubloons!" muttered old Israel like a sleepy parrot.

"He may think to screw more than that out of the carcases of some of us, old man. Come, Inez, you are quick at this game. How can we best hold him to his word?"

"Dead, I think," broke in Bernaldez, who knew his danger as the partner and relative of Castell, and the nominal owner of the ship *Margaret* in which it was purposed that he should escape. "We know all that he can tell, and if we let him go he will betray us soon or late. Kill him out of the way, I say, and burn his body in the oven."

Now Henriques fell upon his knees, and with groans and tears began to implore mercy.

"Why do you complain so?" asked Inez, watching him with reflective eyes. "The end would be much gentler than that which you righteous folk mete out to many more honest men, yes, and women too. For my part, I think that the Senor Bernaldez gives good counsel. Better that you should die, who are but one, than all of us and others, for you will understand that we cannot trust you. Has any one got a rope?"

Now Henriques grovelled on the ground before her, kissing the hem of her robe, and praying her in the name of all the saints to show pity on one who had been betrayed into this danger by love of her.

"Of money you mean, Toad," she answered, kicking him with her slippered foot. "I had to listen to your talk of love while we journeyed together, and before, but here I need not, and if you speak of it again you shall go living into that baker's oven. Oh! you have forgotten it, but I have a long score to settle with you. You were a familiar of the Holy Office here at Seville— were you not?—before Morella promoted you to Motril for your zeal, and made you one of his chaplains? Well, I had a sister," And she knelt down and whispered a name into his ear.

He uttered a sound—it was more of a scream than a gasp.

"I had nothing to do with her death," he protested. "She was brought within the walls of the Holy House by some one who had a grudge against her and bore false witness."

"Yes, I know. It was you who had the grudge, you snake-souled rogue, and it was you who gave the false witness. It was you, also, who but the other day volunteered the corroborative evidence that was necessary against Castell, saying that he had passed the Rood at your house in Motril without doing it reverence, and other things. It was you, too, who urged your superiors to put him to the question, because you said he was rich and had rich friends, and much money could be wrung out of him and them, whereof you were to get your share. Oh! yes, my information is good, is it not? Even what passes in the dungeons of the Holy House comes to the ears of the woman Inez. Well, do you still think that baker's oven too hot for you?"

By this time Henriques was speechless with terror. There he knelt upon the floor, glaring at this soft-voiced, remorseless woman who had made a tool and a fool of him; who had beguiled him there that night, and who hated him so bitterly and with so just a cause. Peter was speaking now.

"It would be better not to stain our hands with the creature's blood," he said. "Caged rats give little sport, and he might be tracked. For my part, I would leave his judgment to God. Have you no other way, Inez?"

She thought a while, then prodded the Fray Henriques with her foot, saying:

Get up, sainted secretary to the Holy Office, and do a little writing, which will be easy to you. See, here are pens and paper. Now I'll dictate:

Most Adorable Inez,

"Your dear message has reached me safely here in this accursed Holy House, where we lighten heretics of their sins to the benefit of their souls, and of their goods to the benefit of our own bodies—"

"I cannot write it," groaned Henriques; "it is rank heresy."

"No, only the truth," answered Inez.

"Heresy and the truth—well, they are often the same thing. They would burn me for it."

"That is just what many heretics have urged. They have died gloriously for what they hold to be the truth, why should not you? Listen," she went on more sternly. "Will you take your chance of burning on the Quemadero, which you will not do unless you betray us, or will you certainly burn more privately, but better, in a baker's oven, and within half an hour? Ah! I thought you would not hesitate. Continue your letter, most learned scribe. Are those words down? Yes. Now add these:

I note all you tell me about the trial at the Alcazar before their Majesties. I believe that the Englishwoman will win her case. That was a very pretty trick that I played on the most noble marquis at Granada. Nothing neater was ever done, even in this place. Well, I owed him a long score, and I have paid him off in full. I should like to have seen his exalted countenance when he surveyed the features of his bride, the waiting-woman, and knew that the mistress was safe away with another man. The nephew of the king, who would like himself to be king some day, married to an English waiting-woman! Good, very good, dear Inez.

"Now, as regards the Jew, John Castell. I think that the matter may possibly be managed, provided that the money is all right, for, as you know, I do not work for nothing. Thus—" And Inez dictated with admirable lucidity those suggestions as to the rescue of Castell, with which the reader is already acquainted, ending the letter as follows:

These Inquisitors here are cruel beasts, though fonder of money than of blood; for all their talk about zeal for the Faith is so much wind behind the mountains. They care as much for the Faith as the mountain cares for the wind, or, let us say, as I do. They wanted to torture the poor devil, thinking that he would rain maravedis; but I gave a hint in the right quarter, and their fun was stopped. Carissima, I must stop also; it is my hour for duty, but I hope to meet you as arranged, and we will have a merry evening. Love to the newly married marquis, if you meet him, and to yourself you know how much.

Your

HENRIQUES.

"POSTSCRIPTUM.—This position will scarcely be as remunerative as I hoped, so I am glad to be able to earn a little outside, enough to buy you a present that will make your pretty eyes shine."

"There!" said Inez mildly, "I think that covers everything, and would burn you three or four times over. Let me read it to see that it is plainly written and properly signed, for in such matters a good deal turns on handwriting. Yes, that will do. Now you understand, don't you, if anything goes wrong about the matter we have been talking of—that is, if the worthy John Castell is not rescued, or a smell of our little plot should get into the wind—this letter goes at once to the right quarter, and a certain secretary will wish that he had never been born. Man!" she added in a hissing whisper, "you shall die by inches as my sister did."

"A thousand doubloons if the thing succeeds, and you live to claim them," croaked old Israel. "I do not go back upon my word. Death and shame and torture or a thousand doubloons. Now he knows our terms, blindfold him again, Senor Bernaldez, and away with him, for he poisons the air. But first you, Inez, be gone and lodge that letter where you know."

*   *   *   *   *

That same night two cloaked figures, Peter and Bernaldez, were rowed in a little boat out to where the *Margaret* lay in the river, and, making her fast, slipped up the ship's side into the cabin. Here the stout English captain, Smith, was waiting for them, and so glad was the honest fellow to see Peter that he cast his arms about him and hugged him, for they had not met since that desperate adventure of the boarding of the *San Antonio*.

"Is your ship fit for sea, Captain?" asked Peter.

"She will never be fitter," he answered. "When shall I get sailing orders?"

"When the owner comes aboard," answered Peter.

"Then we shall stop here until we rot; they have trapped him in their Inquisition. What is in your mind, Peter Brome?— what is in your mind? Is there a chance?"

"Aye, Captain, I think so, if you have a dozen fellows of the right English stuff between decks."

"We have got that number, and one or two more. But what's the plan?"

Peter told him.

"Not so bad," said Smith, slapping his heavy hand upon his knee; "but risky—very risky. That Inez must be a good girl. I should like to marry her, notwithstanding her bygones."

Peter laughed, thinking what an odd couple they would make. "Hear the rest, then talk," he said. "See now! On Saturday next Mistress Margaret and I are to be married in the cathedral; then, towards sunset, the Marquis of Morella and I run our course in the great bull-ring yonder, and you and half a dozen of your men will be present. Now, I may conquer or I may fail—"

"Never!—never!" said the captain. "I wouldn't give a pair of old boots for that fine Spaniard's chance when you get at him. Why, you will crimp him like a cod-fish!"

"God knows!" answered Peter. "If I win, my wife and I make our adieux to their Majesties, and ride away to the quay, where the boat will be waiting, and you will row us on board the *Margaret*. If I fail, you will take up my body, and, accompanied by my widow, bring it in the same fashion on board the *Margaret*, for I shall give it out that in this case I wish to be embalmed in wine and taken back to England for burial. In either event, you will drop your ship a little way down the river round the bend, so that folk may think that you have sailed. In the darkness you must work her back with the tide and lay her behind those old hulks, and if any ask you why, say that three of your men have not yet come aboard, and that you have dropped back for them, and whatever else you like. Then, in case I should not be alive to guide you, you and ten or twelve of the best sailors will land at the spot that this gentleman will show you to-morrow, wearing Spanish cloaks so as not to attract attention, but being well armed underneath them, like idlers from some ship who had come ashore to see the show. I have told you how you may know Master Castell. When you see him make a rush for him, cut down any that try to stop you, tumble him into the boat, and row for your lives to the ship, which will slip her moorings and get up her canvas as soon as she sees you coming, and begin to drop down the river with the tide and wind, if there is one. That is the plot, but God alone knows the end of it! which depends upon Him and the sailors. Will you play this game for the love of a good man and the rest of us? If you succeed, you shall be rich for life, all of you."

"Aye," answered the captain, "and there's my hand on it. So sure as my name is Smith, we will hook him out of that hell if men can do it, and not for the money either. Why, Peter, we have sat here idle so long, waiting for you and our lady, that we shall be glad of the fun. At any rate, there will be some dead Spaniards before they have done with us, and, if we are worsted, I'll leave the mate and enough hands upon the ship to bring her safe to Tilbury. But we won't be—we won't be. By this day week we will all be rolling homewards across the Bay with never a Spaniard within three hundred miles, you and your lady and Master Castell, too. I know it! I tell you, lad, I know it!"

"How do you know it?" asked Peter curiously.

"Because I dreamed it last night. I saw you and Mistress Margaret sitting sweet as sugar, with your arms around each other's middles, while I talked to the master, and the sun went down with the wind blowing stiff from sou-sou-west, and a gale threatening. I tell you that I dreamed it—I who am not given to dreams."

CHAPTER XXIV

THE FALCON STOOPS

It was the marriage day of Margaret and Peter. Clad in white armour that had been sent to him as a present from the queen, a sign and a token of her good wishes for his success in his combat with Morella, wearing the insignia of a Knight of St. James hanging by a ribbon from his neck, his shield emblazoned with his coat of the stooping falcon, which appeared also upon the white cloak that hung from his shoulders, behind him a squire of high degree, who carried his plumed casque and lance, and accompanied by an escort of the royal guards, Peter rode from his quarters in the prison to the palace gates, and waited there as he had been bidden. Presently they opened, and through them, seated on a palfrey, appeared Margaret, wonderfully attired in white and silver, but with her veil lifted so that her face could be seen. She was companioned by a troop of maidens mounted, all of them, on white horses, and at her side, almost outshining her in glory of apparel, and attended by all her household, rode Betty, Marchioness of Morella—at any rate for that present time.

Although she could never be less than beautiful, it was a worn and pale Margaret who bowed her greetings to the bridegroom without those palace gates. What wonder, since she knew that within a few hours his life must be set upon the hazard of a desperate fray. What wonder, since she knew that to-morrow her father was doomed to be burnt living upon the Quemadero.

H. Rider Haggard

They met, they greeted; then, with silver trumpets blowing before them, the glittering procession wound its way through the narrow streets of Seville. But few words passed between them, whose hearts were too full for words, who had said all they had to say, and now abided the issue of events. Betty, however, whom many of the populace took for the bride, because her air was so much the happier of the two, would not be silent. Indeed she chid Margaret for her lack of gaiety upon such an occasion.

"Oh, Betty!—Betty!" answered Margaret, "how can I be gay, upon whose heart lies the burden of to-morrow?"

"A pest upon the burden of to-morrow!" exclaimed Betty. "The burden of to-day is enough for me, and that is not so bad to bear. Never shall we have another such ride as this, with all the world staring at us, and every woman in Seville envying us and our good looks and the favour of the queen."

"I think it is you they stare at and envy," said Margaret, glancing at the splendid woman at her side, whose beauty she knew well over-shadowed her own rarer loveliness, at any rate in a street pageant, as in the sunshine the rose overshadows the lily.

"Well," answered Betty, "if so, it is because I put the better face on things, and smile even if my heart bleeds. At least, your lot is more hopeful than mine. If your husband has to fight to the death presently, so has mine, and between ourselves I favour Peter's chances. He is a very stubborn fighter, Peter, and wonderfully strong—too stubborn and strong for any Spaniard."

"Well, that is as it should be," said Margaret, smiling faintly, "seeing that Peter is your champion, and if he loses, you are stamped as a serving-girl, and a woman of no character."

"A serving-girl I was, or something not far different," replied Betty in a reflective voice, "and my character is a matter between me and Heaven, though, after all, it might scrape through where others fail to pass. So these things do not trouble me over much. What troubles me is that if my champion wins he kills my husband."

"You don't want him to be killed then?" asked Margaret, glancing at her.

"No, I think not," answered Betty with a little shake in her voice, and turning her head aside for a moment. "I know he is a scoundrel, but, you see, I always liked this scoundrel, just as you always hated him, so I cannot help wishing that he was going to meet some one who hits a little less hard than Peter. Also, if he dies, without doubt his heirs will raise suits against me."

"At any rate your father is not going to be burnt to-morrow," said Margaret to change the subject, which, to tell the truth, was an awkward one.

"No, Cousin, if my father had his deserts, according to all accounts, although the lineage that I gave of him is true enough, doubtless he was burnt long ago, and still goes on burning—in Purgatory, I mean—though God knows I would never bring a faggot to his fire. But Master Castell will not be burnt, so why fret about it."

"What makes you say that?" asked Margaret, who had not confided the details of a certain plot to Betty.

"I don't know, but I am sure that Peter will get him out somehow. He is a very good stick to lean on, Peter, although he seems so hard and stupid and silent, which, after all, is in the nature of sticks. But look, there is the cathedral—is it not a fine place?—and a great crowd of people waiting round the gate. Now smile, Cousin. Bow and smile as I do."

They rode up to the great doors, where Peter, springing to the ground, assisted his bride from her palfrey. Then the procession formed, and they entered the wonderful place, preceded by vergers with staves, and by acolytes. Margaret had never visited it before, and never saw it again, but all her life the memory of it remained clear and vivid in her mind. The cold chill of the air within, the semi-darkness after the glare of the sunshine, the seven great naves, or aisles, stretching endlessly to right and left, the dim and towering roof, the pillars that sprang to it everywhere like huge forest trees aspiring to the skies, the solemn shadows pierced by lines of light from the high-cut windows, the golden glory of the altars, the sounds of chanting, the sepulchres of the dead—a sense of all these things rushed in upon her, overpowering her and stamping the picture of them for ever on her memory.

Slowly they passed onward to the choir, and round it to the steps of the great altar of the chief chapel. Here, between the choir and the chapel, was gathered the congregation—no small one—and here, side by side to the right and without the rails, in chairs of state, sat their Majesties of Spain, who had chosen to grace this ceremony with their presence. More, as the bride came, the queen Isabella, as a special act of grace, rose from her seat and, bending forward, kissed her on the cheek, while the choir sang and the noble music rolled. It was a splendid spectacle, this marriage of hers, celebrated in perhaps the most glorious fane in Europe. But even as Margaret noted it and watched the bishops and priests decked with glittering embroideries, summoned there to do her honour, as they moved to and fro in the mysterious ceremonial of the Mass, she bethought her of other rites equally glorious that would take place on the morrow in the greatest square of Seville, where these same dignitaries would condemn fellow human beings—perhaps among them her own father—to be married to the cruel flame.

Side by side they knelt before the wondrous altar, while the incense-clouds from the censers floated up one by one till they were lost in the gloom above, as the smoke of to-morrow's sacrifice would lose itself in the heavens, she and her husband, won at last, won after so many perils, perhaps to be lost again for ever before night fell upon the world. The priests chanted, the gorgeous bishop bowed over them and muttered the marriage service of their faith, the ring was set upon her hand, the troths were plighted, the benediction spoken, and they were man and wife till death should them part, that death which stood so near to them in this hour of life fulfilled. Then they two, who already that morning had made confession of their sins, kneeling alone before the altar, ate of the holy Bread, sealing a mystery with a mystery.

All was done and over, and rising, they turned and stayed a moment hand in hand while the sweet-voiced choir sang some wondrous chant. Margaret's eyes wandered over the congregation till presently they lighted upon the dark face of Morella, who stood apart a little way, surrounded by his squires and gentlemen, and watched her. More, he came to her, and bowing low, whispered to her:

"We are players in a strange game, my lady Margaret, and what will be its end, I wonder? Shall I be dead to-night, or you a widow? Aye, and where was its beginning? Not here, I think. And where, oh where shall this seed we sow bear fruit? Well, think as kindly of me as you can, since I loved you who love me not."

And again bowing, first to her, then to Peter, he passed on, taking no note of Betty, who stood near, considering him with her large eyes, as though she also wondered what would be the end of all this play.

Surrounded by their courtiers, the king and queen left the cathedral, and after them came the bridegroom and the bride. They mounted their horses and in the glory of the southern sunlight rode through the cheering crowd back to the palace and to the marriage feast, where their table was set but just below that of their Majesties. It was long and magnificent; but little could they eat, and, save to pledge each other in the ceremonial cup, no wine passed their lips. At length some trumpets blew, and their Majesties rose, the king saying in his thin, clear voice that he would not bid his guests farewell, since very shortly they would all meet again in another place, where the gallant bridegroom, a gentleman of England, would champion the cause of his relative and countrywoman against one of the first grandees of Spain whom she alleged had done her wrong. That fray, alas! would be no pleasure joust, but to the death, for the feud between these knights was deep and bitter, and such were the conditions of their combat. He could not wish success to the one or to the other; but of this he was sure, that in all Seville there was no heart that would not give equal honour to the conqueror and the conquered, sure also that both would bear themselves as became brave knights of Spain and England.

Then the trumpets blew again, and the squires and gentlemen who were chosen to attend him came bowing to Peter, and saying that it was time for him to arm. Bride and bridegroom rose and, while all the spectators fell back out of hearing, but watching them with curious eyes, spoke some few words together.

"We part," said Peter, "and I know not what to say."

"Say nothing, husband," she answered him, "lest your words should weaken me. Go now, and bear you bravely, as you will for your own honour and that of England, and for mine. Dead or living you are my darling, and dead or living we shall meet once more and be at rest for aye. My prayers be with you, Sir Peter, my prayers and my eternal love, and may they bring strength to your arm and comfort to your heart."

Then she, who would not embrace him before all those folk, curtseyed till her knee almost touched the ground, while low he bent before her, a strange and stately parting, or so thought that company; and taking the hand of Betty, Margaret left him.

*　*　*　*　*

Two hours had gone by. The Plaza de Toros, for the great square where tournaments were wont to be held was in the hands of those who prepared it for the *auto-da-fe* of the morrow, was crowded as it had seldom been before. This place was a huge amphitheatre—perchance the Romans built it— where all sorts of games were celebrated, among them the baiting of bulls as it was practised in those days, and other semi-savage sports. Twelve thousand people could sit upon the benches that rose tier upon tier around the vast theatre, and scarce a seat was empty. The arena itself, that was long enough for horses starting at either end of it to come to their full speed, was strewn with white sand, as it may have been in the days when gladiators fought there. Over the main entrance and opposite to the centre of the ring were placed the king and queen with their lords and ladies, and between them, but a little behind, her face hid by her bridal veil, sat Margaret, upright and silent as a statue. Exactly in front of them, on the further side of the ring in a pavilion, and attended by her household, appeared Betty, glittering with gold and jewels, since she was the lady in whose cause, at least in name, this combat was to be fought *a l'outrance*. Quite unmoved she sat, and her presence seemed to draw every eye in that vast assembly which talked of her while it waited, with a sound like the sound of the sea as it murmurs on a beach at night.

Now the trumpets blew, and silence fell, and then, preceded by heralds in golden tabards, Carlos, Marquis of Morella, followed by his squires, rode into the ring through the great entrance. He bestrode a splendid black horse, and was arrayed in coal-black armour, while from his casque rose black ostrich plumes. On his shield, however, painted in scarlet, appeared the eagle crowned with the coronet of his rank, and beneath, the proud motto—"What I seize I tear." A splendid figure, he pressed his horse into the centre of the arena, then causing it to wheel round, pawing the air with its forelegs, saluted their Majesties by raising his long, steel-tipped lance, while the multitude greeted him with a shout. This done, he and his company rode away to their station at the north end of the ring.

Again the trumpets sounded, and a herald appeared, while after him, mounted on a white horse, and clad in his white armour that glistened in the sun, with white plumes rising from his casque, and on his shield the stooping falcon blazoned in gold with the motto of "For love and honour" beneath it, appeared the tall, grim shape of Sir Peter Brome. He, too, rode out into the centre of the arena, and, turning his horse quite soberly, as though it were on a road, lifted his lance in salute. Now there was no cheering, for this knight was a foreigner, yet soldiers who were there said to each other that he looked like one who would not easily be overthrown.

A third time the trumpets sounded, and the two champions, advancing from their respective stations, drew rein side by side in front of their Majesties, where the conditions of the combat were read aloud to them by the chief herald. They were short. That the fray should be to the death unless the king and queen willed otherwise and the victor consented; that it should be on horse or on foot, with lance or sword or dagger, but that no broken weapon might be replaced and no horse or armour changed; that the victor should be escorted from the place of combat with all honour, and allowed to depart whither he would, in the kingdom or out of it, and no suit or blood-feud raised against him; and that the body of the fallen be handed over to his friends for burial, also with all honour. That the issue of this fray should in no way affect any cause pleaded in Courts ecclesiastical or civil, by the lady who asserted herself to be the Marchioness of Morella, or by the most noble Marquis of Morella, whom she claimed as her husband.

These conditions having been read, the champions were asked if they assented to them, whereon each of them answered, "Aye!" in a clear voice. Then the herald, speaking on behalf of Sir Peter Brome, by creation a knight of St. Iago and a Don of Spain, solemnly challenged the noble Marquis of Morella to single combat to the death, in that he, the said marquis, had aspersed the name of his relative, the English lady, Elizabeth Dene, who claimed to be his wife, duly united to him in holy wedlock, and for sundry other causes and injuries worked towards him, the said Sir Peter Brome, and his wife, Dame Margaret Brome, and in token thereof, threw down a gauntlet, which gauntlet the Marquis of Morella lifted upon the point of his lance and cast over his shoulder, thus accepting the challenge.

Now the combatants dropped their visors, which heretofore had been raised, and their squires, coming forward, examined the fastenings of their armour, their weapons, and the girths and bridles of their horses. These being pronounced sound and good, pursuivants took the steeds by the bridles and led them to the far ends of the lists. At a signal from the king a single clarion blew, whereon the pursuivants loosed their hold of the bridles and sprang back. Another clarion blew, and the knights gathered up their reins, settled their shields, and set their lances in rest, bending forward over their horses' necks.

An intense silence fell upon all the watching multitude as that of night upon the sea, and in the midst of it the third clarion blew—to Margaret it sounded like the trump of doom. From twelve thousand throats one great sigh went up, like the sigh of wind upon the sea, and ere it died away, from either end of the arena, like arrows from the bow, like levens from a cloud, the champions started forth, their stallions gathering speed at every stride. Look, they met! Fair on each shield struck a lance, and backward reeled their holders. The keen points glanced aside or up, and the knights, recovering themselves, rushed past each other, shaken but unhurt. At the ends of the lists the squires caught the horses by the bridles and turned them. The first course was run.

Again the clarions blew, and again they started forward, and presently again they met in mid career. As before, the lances struck upon the shields; but so fearful was the impact, that Peter's shivered, while that of Morella, sliding from the topmost rim of his foe's buckler, got hold in his visor bars. Back went Peter beneath the blow, back and still back, till almost he lay upon his horse's crupper. Then, when it seemed that he must fall, the lacings of his helm burst. It was torn from his head, and Morella passed on bearing it transfixed upon his spear point.

"The Falcon falls," screamed the spectators; "he is unhorsed."

But Peter was not unhorsed. Freed from that awful pressure, he let drop the shattered shaft and, grasping at his saddle strap, dragged himself back into the selle. Morella tried to stay his charger, that he might come about and fall upon the Englishman before he could recover himself; but the brute was heady, and would not be turned till he saw the wall of faces in front of him. Now they were round, both of them, but Peter had no spear and no helm, while the lance of Morella was cumbered with his adversary's casque that he strove to shake free from it, but in vain.

"Draw your sword," shouted voices to Peter—the English voices of Smith and his sailors—and he put his hand down to do so, then bethought him of some other counsel, for he let it lie within its scabbard, and, spurring the white horse, came at Morella like a storm.

"The Falcon will be spiked," they screamed. "The Eagle wins!—the Eagle wins!" And indeed it seemed that it must be so. Straight at Peter's undefended face drove Morella's lance, but lo! as it came he let fall his reins and with his shield he struck at the white plumes about its point, the plumes torn from his own head. He had judged well, for up flew those plumes, a little, a very little, yet far enough to give him space, crouching on his saddle-bow, to pass beneath the deadly spear. Then, as they swept past each other, out shot that long, right arm of his and, gripping Morella like a hook of steel, tore him from his saddle, so that the black horse rushed forward riderless, and the white sped on bearing a double burden.

Grasping desperately, Morella threw his arms about his neck, and intertwined, black armour mixed with white, they swayed to and fro, while the frightened horse beneath rushed this way and that till, swerving suddenly, together they fell upon the sand, and for a moment lay there stunned.

"Who conquers?" gasped the crowd; while others answered, "Both are sped!" And, leaning forward in her chair, Margaret tore off her veil and watched with a face like the face of death.

See! As they had fallen together, so together they stirred and rose—rose unharmed. Now they sprang back, out flashed the long swords, and, while the squires caught the horses and, running in, seized the broken spears, they faced each other. Having no helm, Peter held his buckler above his head to shelter it, and, ever calm, awaited the onslaught.

At him came Morella, and with a light, grating sound his sword fell upon the steel. Before he could recover himself Peter struck back; but Morella bent his knees, and the stroke only shore the black plumes from his casque. Quick as light he drove at Peter's face with his point; but the Englishman leapt to one side, and the thrust went past him. Again Morella came at him, and struck so mighty a blow that, although Peter caught it on his buckler, it sliced through the edge of it and fell upon his unprotected neck and shoulder, wounding him, for now red blood showed on the white armour, and Peter reeled back beneath the stroke.

"The Eagle wins!—the Eagle wins! Spain and the Eagle" shouted ten thousand throats. In the momentary silence that followed, a single voice, a clear woman's voice, which even then Margaret knew for that of Inez, cried from among the crowd:

"Nay, the Falcon stoops!"

Before the sound of her words died away, maddened it would seem, by the pain of his wound, or the fear of defeat, Peter shouted out his war-cry of *"A Brome! A Brome"*! and, gathering himself together, sprang straight at Morella as springs a starving wolf. The blue steel flickered in the sunlight, then down it fell, and lo! half the Spaniard's helm lay on the sand, while it was Morella's turn to reel backward—and more, as he did so, he let fall his shield.

"A stroke!—a good stroke!" roared the crowd. "The Falcon!—the Falcon!"

Peter saw that fallen shield, and whether for chivalry's sake, as thought the cheering multitude, or to free his left arm, he cast away his own, and grasping the sword with both hands rushed on the Spaniard. From that moment, helmless though he was, the issue lay in doubt no longer. Betty had spoken of Peter as a stubborn swordsman and a hard hitter, and both of these he now showed himself to be. As fresh to all appearance as when he ran the first course, he rained blow after blow upon the hapless Spaniard, till the sound of his sword smiting on the good Toledo steel was like the sound of a hammer falling continually on the smith's red iron. They were fearful blows, yet still the tough steel held, and still Morella, doing what he might, staggered back beneath them, till at length he came in front of the tribune, in which sat their Majesties and Margaret. Out of the corner of his eye Peter saw the place, and determined in his stout heart that then and there he would end the thing. Parrying a cut which the desperate Spaniard made at his head, he thrust at him so heavily that his blade bent like a bow, and, although he could not pierce the black mail, almost lifted Morella from his feet. Then, as he reeled backwards, Peter whirled his sword on high, and, shouting "*Margaret!*" struck downwards with all his strength. It fell as lightning falls, swift, keen, dazzling the eyes of all who watched. Morella raised his arm to break the blow. In vain! The weapon that he held was shattered, the casque beneath was cloven, and, throwing his arms wide, he fell heavily to the ground and lay there moving feebly.

For an instant there was silence, and in it a shrill woman's voice that cried:

"The Falcon has stooped. The English hawk *has stooped!*"

Then there arose a tumult of shouting. "He is dead!" "Nay, he stirs." "Kill him!" "Spare him; he fought well!"

Peter leaned upon his sword, looking at the fallen foe. Then he glanced upwards at their Majesties, but these sat silent, making no sign, only he saw Margaret try to rise from her seat and speak, to be pulled back to it again by the hands of women. A deep hush fell upon the watching thousands who waited for the end. Peter looked at Morella. Alas! He still lived, his sword and the stout helmet had broken the weight of that stroke, mighty though it had been. The man was but wounded in three places and stunned. "What must I do?" asked Peter in a hollow voice to the royal pair above him.

Now the king, who seemed moved, was about to speak; but the queen bent forward and whispered something to him, and he remained silent. They both were silent. All the intent multitude was silent. Knowing what this dreadful silence meant, Peter cast down his sword and drew his dagger, wherewith to cut the lashings of Morella's gorget and give the *coup de grace*.

Just then it was that for the first time he heard a sound, far away upon the other side of the arena, and, looking thither, saw the strangest sight that ever his eyes beheld. Over the railing of the pavilion opposite to him a woman climbed nimbly as a cat, and from it, like a cat, dropped to the ground full ten feet below, then, gathering up her dress about her knees, ran swiftly towards him. It was Betty! Betty without a doubt! Betty in her gorgeous garb, with pearls and braided hair flying loose behind her. He stared amazed. All stared amazed, and in half a minute she was on them, and, standing over the fallen Morella, gasped out:

"Let him be! I bid you let him be."

Peter knew not what to do or say, so advanced to speak with her, whereon with a swoop like that of a swallow she pounced upon his sword that lay in the sand and, leaping back to

H. Rider Haggard

Morella, shook it on high, shouting:

"You will have to fight me first, Peter."

Indeed, she did more, striking at him so shrewdly with his own sword that he was forced to spring sideways to avoid the stroke. Now a great roar of laughter went up to heaven. Yes, even Peter laughed, for no such thing as this had ever before been seen in Spain. It died away, and again Betty, who had no low voice, shouted in her villainous Spanish:

"He shall kill me before he kills my husband. Give me my husband!"

"Take him, for my part," answered Peter, whereon, letting fall the sword, Betty, filled with the strength of despair, lifted the senseless Spaniard in her strong white arms as though he were a child, and his bleeding head lying on her shoulder, strove to carry him away, but could not.

Then, while all that audience cheered frantically, Peter with a gesture of despair threw down his dagger and once more appealed to their Majesties. The king rose and held up his hand, at the same time motioning to Morella's squires to take him from the woman, which, seeing their cognizance, Betty allowed them to do.

"Marchioness of Morella," said the king, for the first time giving her that title, "your honour is cleared, your champion has conquered, and this fierce fray was to the death. What have you to say?"

"Nothing," answered Betty, "except that I love the man, though he has treated me and others ill, and, as I knew he would if he crossed swords with Peter, has got his deserts for his deeds. I say I love him, and if Peter wishes to kill him, he must kill me first."

"Sir Peter Brome," said the king, "the judgment lies in your hand. We give you the man's life, to grant or to take."

Peter thought a while, then answered:

"I grant him his life if he will acknowledge this lady to be his true and lawful wife, and live with her as such, now and for ever, staying all suits against her."

"How can he do that, you fool," asked Betty, "when you have knocked all his senses out of him with that great sword of yours?"

"Perhaps," suggested Peter humbly, "some one will do it for him."

"Yes," said Isabella, speaking for the first time, "I will. On behalf of the Marquis of Morella I promise these things, Don Peter Brome, before all these people here gathered. I add this: that if he should live, and it pleases him to break this promise made on his behalf to save him from death, then let his name be shamed, yes, let it become a byword and a scorn. Proclaim it, heralds."

So the heralds blew their trumpets and one of them called out the queen's decree, whereat the spectators cheered again, shouting that it was good, and they bore witness to that promise.

Then Morella, still senseless, was borne away by his squires, Betty in her blood-stained robe marching at his side, and his horse having been brought to him again, Peter, wounded though he was, mounted and galloped round the arena amidst plaudits such as that place had never heard, till, lifting his sword in salutation, suddenly he and his gentlemen vanished by the gate through which he had appeared.

Thus strangely enough ended that combat which thereafter was always known as the Fray of the Eagle and the English Hawk.

H. Rider Haggard

CHAPTER XXV

HOW THE *MARGARET* WON OUT TO SEA

It was night. Peter, faint with loss of blood and stiff with bruises, had bade his farewell to their Majesties of Spain, who spoke many soft words to him, calling him the Flower of Knighthood, and offering him high place and rank if he would abide in their service. But he thanked them and said No, for in Spain he had suffered too much to dwell there. So they kissed his bride, the fair Margaret, who clung to her wounded husband like ivy to an oak, and would not be separated from him, even for a moment, that husband whom living she had scarcely hoped to clasp again. Yes, they kissed her, and the queen threw about her a chain from her own neck as a parting gift, and wished her joy of so gallant a lord.

"Alas! your Majesty," said Margaret, her dark eyes filling with tears, "how can I be joyous, who must think of to-morrow?"

Thereon Isabella set her face and answered:

"Dona Margaret Brome, be thankful for what to-day has brought you, and forget to-morrow and that which it must justly take away. Go now, and God be with you both!"

So they went, the little knot of English sailormen, who, wrapped in Spanish cloaks, had sat together in the amphitheatre and groaned when the Eagle struck, and cheered when the Falcon swooped, leading, or rather carrying Peter under cover of the falling night to a boat not far from this Place of Bulls. In this they embarked unobserved, for the multitude, and even Peter's own squires believed that he had returned with his wife to the palace, as he had given out that he would do. So they were rowed to the *Margaret*, which straightway made as though she were about to sail, and indeed dropped a little way down stream. Here she anchored again, just round a bend of the river, and lay there for the night.

It was a heavy night, and in it there was no place for love or lovers' tenderness. How could there be between these two, who for so long had been tormented by doubts and fears, and on this day had endured such extremity of terror and such agony of joy? Peter's wound also was deep and wide, though his shield had broken the weight of Morella's sword, and its edge had caught upon his shoulder-piece, so that by good chance it had not reached down to the arteries, or shorn into the bone; yet he had lost much blood, and Smith, the captain, who was a better surgeon than might have been guessed from his thick hands, found it needful to wash out the cut with spirit that gave much pain, and to stitch it up with silk. Also Peter had great bruises on his arms and thighs, and his back was hurt by that fall from the white charger with Morella in his arms.

So it came about that most of that night he lay outworn, half-sleeping and half-waking, and when at sunrise he struggled from his berth, it was but to kneel by the side of Margaret and join her in her prayers that her father might be rescued from the hands of these cruel priests of Spain.

Now during the night Smith had brought his ship back with the tide, and laid her under the shelter of those hulks whereof Peter had spoken, having first painted out her name of *Margaret*, and in its place set that of the *Santa Maria*, a vessel of about the same build and tonnage, which, as they had heard, was expected in port. For this reason, or because there were at that time many ships in the river, it happened that none in authority noted her return, or if they did, neglected to report the matter as one of no moment. Therefore, so far all went well.

According to the tale of Henriques, confirmed by what they had learned otherwise, the great procession of the Act of Faith would turn on to the quay at about eight o'clock, and pass along it for a hundred yards or so only, before it wound away down a street leading to the *plaza* where the theatre was prepared, the sermon would be preached, the Mass celebrated, and the "relaxed" placed in cages to be carried to the Quemadero.

At six in the morning Smith mustered those twelve men whom he had chosen to help him in the enterprise, and Peter, with Margaret at his side, addressed them in the cabin, telling them all the plan, and praying them for the sake of their master and of the Lady Margaret, his daughter, to do what men might to save one whom they loved and honoured from so horrible a death.

They swore that they would, every one of them, for their English blood was up, nor did they so much as speak of the great rewards that had been promised to those who lived through this adventure, and to the families of those who fell. Then they breakfasted, girded their swords and knives about them, and put on their Spanish cloaks, though, to speak truth, these lads of Essex and of London made but poor Spaniards. Now, at length the boat was ready, and Peter, although he could scarcely stand, desired to be carried into it that he might accompany them. But the captain, Smith, to whom perhaps Margaret had been speaking, set down his flat foot on the deck and said that he, who commanded there, would suffer no such thing. A wounded man, he declared, would but cumber them who had little room to spare in that small boat, and could be of no service, either on land or water. Moreover, Master Peter's face was known to thousands who had watched it yesterday, and would certainly be recognised, whereas none would take note at such a time of a dozen common sailors landed from some ship to see the show. Lastly, he would do best to stop on board the vessel, where, if anything went wrong, they must be short-handed enough, who, if they could, ought to get her away to sea and across it with all speed.

Still Peter would have gone, till Margaret, throwing her arms about him, asked him if he thought that she would be the better if she lost both her father and her husband, as, if things miscarried, well might happen. Then, being in pain and very weak, he yielded, and Smith, having given his last directions to the mate, and shaken Peter and Margaret by the hand, asking their prayers for all of them, descended with his twelve men into the boat, and dropping down under shelter of the hulks, rowed to the shore as though they came from some other vessel. Now the quay was not more than a bowshot from them, and from a certain spot upon the *Margaret* there was a good view of it between the stern of one hulk and the bow of another. Here, then, Peter and Margaret sat themselves down behind the bulwark, and watched with fears such as cannot be told, while a sharp-eyed seaman climbed to the crow's-nest on the mast, whence he could see over much of the city, and even the old Moorish castle that was then the Holy House of the Inquisition. Presently this man reported that the procession had started, for he saw its banners and the people crowding to the windows and to the roof-tops; also the cathedral bell began to toll slowly. Then came a long, long wait, during which their little knot of sailors, wearing the Spanish cloaks, appeared upon the quay and mingled with the few folk that were gathered there, since the most of the people were collected by thousands on the great *plaza* or in the adjacent streets.

At length, just as the cathedral clock struck eight, the "triumphant" march, as it was called, began to appear upon the quay. First came a body of soldiers with lances; then a crucifix, borne by a priest and veiled in black crape; then a number of other priests, clad in snow-white robes to symbolise their perfect purity. Next followed men carrying wood or leather images of some man or woman who, by flight to a foreign land or into the realms of Death, had escaped the clutches of the Inquisition. After these marched other men in fours, each four of them bearing a coffin that contained the

H. Rider Haggard

body or bones of some dead heretic, which, in the absence of his living person, like the effigies, were to be committed to the flames as a token of what the Inquisition would have done to him if it could—to enable it also to seize his property.

Then came many penitents, their heads shaven, their feet bare, and clad, some in dark-coloured cloaks, some in yellow robes, called the *sanbenito*, which were adorned with a red cross. These were followed by a melancholy band of "relaxed" heretics, doomed to the fire or strangulation at the stake, and clothed in *zamarras* of sheepskin, painted all over with devils and the portraits of their own faces surrounded by flames. These poor creatures wore also flame-adorned caps called *corozas*, shaped like bishops' mitres, and were gagged with blocks of wood, lest they should contaminate the populace by some declaration of their heresy, while in their hands they bore tapers, which the monks who accompanied them relighted from time to time if they became extinguished.

Now the hearts of Peter and Margaret leaped within them, for at the end of this hideous troop rode a man mounted on an ass, clothed in a *zamarra* and *coroza*, but with a noose about his neck. So the Fray Henriques had told the truth, for without doubt this was John Castell. Like people in a dream, they saw him advance in his garb of shame, and after him, gorgeously attired, civil officers, inquisitors, and familiars of noble rank, members of the Council of Inquisition, behind whom was borne a flaunting banner, called the Holy Standard of the Faith.

Now Castell was opposite to the little group of seamen, and, or so it seemed, something went wrong with the harness of the ass on which he sat, for it stopped, and a man in the garb of a secretary stepped to it, apparently to attend to a strap, thus bringing all the procession behind to a halt, while that in front proceeded off the quay and round the corner of a street. Whatever it might be that had happened, it necessitated the dismounting of the heretic, who was pulled roughly off the brute's back, which, as though in joy at this riddance of its burden, lifted its head and brayed loudly.

Men from the thin line of crowd that edged the quay came forward as though to help, and among them were several in capes, such as were worn by the sailors of the *Margaret*. The officers and grandees behind shouted, "Forward!—forward!" whereon those attending to the ass hustled it and its rider a little nearer to the water's edge, while the guards ran back to explain what had happened. Then suddenly a confusion arose, of which it was impossible to distinguish the cause, and next instant Margaret and Peter, still gripping each other, saw the man who had been seated on the ass being dragged rapidly down the steps of the quay, at the foot of which lay the boat of the *Margaret*.

The mate at the helm saw also, for he blew his whistle, a sign at which the anchor was slipped—there was no time to lift it— and men who were waiting on the yards loosed the lashings of certain sails, so that almost immediately the ship began to move.

Now they were fighting on the quay. The heretic was in the boat, and most of the sailors; but others held back the crowd of priests and armed familiars who strove to get at him. One, a priest with a sword in his hand, slipped past them and tumbled into the boat also. At last all were in save a single man, who was attacked by three adversaries—John Smith, the captain. The oars were out, but his mates waited for him. He struck with his sword, and some one fell. Then he turned to run. Two masked familiars sprang at him, one landing on his back, one clinging to his neck. With a desperate effort he cast himself into the water, dragging them with him. One they saw no more, for Smith had stabbed him, the other floated up near the boat, which already was some yards from the quay, and a sailor battered him on the head with an oar, so that he sank.

Smith had vanished also, and they thought he must be drowned. The sailors thought it too, for they began to give way, when suddenly a great brown hand appeared and clasped the stern-sheets, while a bull-voice roared:

"Row on, lads, I'm right enough."

Row they did indeed, till the ashen oars bent like bows, only two of them seized the officer who had sprung into the boat and flung him screaming into the river, where he struggled a while, for he could not swim, gripping at the air with his hands, then disappeared. The boat was in mid-stream now, and shaping her course round the bow of the first hulk beyond which the prow of the *Margaret* began to appear, for the wind was fresh, and she gathered way every moment.

"Let down the ladder, and make ready ropes," shouted Peter.

It was done, but not too soon, for next instant the boat was bumping on their side. The sailors in her caught the ropes and hung on, while the captain, Smith, half-drowned, clung to the stern-sheets, for the water washed over his head.

"Save him first," cried Peter. A man, running down the ladder, threw a noose to him, which Smith seized with one hand and by degrees worked beneath his arms. Then they tackled on to it, and dragged him bodily from the river to the deck, where he lay gasping and spitting out foam and water. By now the ship was travelling swiftly, so swiftly that Margaret was in an agony of fear lest the boat should be towed under and sink.

But these sailor men knew their trade. By degrees they let the boat drop back till her bow was abreast of the ladder. Then they helped Castell forward. He gripped its rungs, and eager hands gripped him. Up he staggered, step by step, till at length his hideous, fiend-painted cap, his white face, whence the beard had been shaved, and his open mouth, in which still was fixed the wooden gag, appeared above the bulwarks, as the mate said afterwards, like that of a devil escaped from hell. They lifted him over, and he sank fainting in his daughter's arms. Then one by one the sailors came up after him—none were missing, though two had been wounded, and were covered with blood. No, none were missing—God had brought them, every one, safe back to the deck of the *Margaret*.

Smith, the captain, spat up the last of his river water and called for a cup of wine, which he drank; while Peter and Margaret drew the accursed gag from her father's mouth, and poured spirit down his throat. Shaking the water from him like a great dog, but saying never a word, Smith rolled to the helm and took it from the mate, for the navigation of the river was difficult, and none knew it so well as he. Now they were abreast the famous Golden Tower, and a big gun was fired at them; but the shot went wide. "Look!" said Margaret, pointing to horsemen galloping southwards along the river's bank.

"Yes," said Peter, "they go to warn the ports. God send that the wind holds, for we must fight our way to sea."

The wind did hold, indeed it blew ever more strongly from the north; but oh! that was a long, evil day. Hour after hour they sped forward down the widening river; now past villages, where knots of people waved weapons at them as they went; now by desolate marshes, plains, and banks clothed with pine.

When they reached Bonanza the sun was low, and when they were off San Lucar it had begun to sink. Out into the wide river mouth, where the white waters tumbled on the narrow bar, rowed two great galleys to cut them off, very swift galleys, which it seemed impossible to escape.

Margaret and Castell were sent below, the crew went to quarters, and Peter crept stiffly aft to where the sturdy Smith stood at the helm, which he would suffer no other man to touch. Smith looked at the sky, he looked at the shore, and the safe, open sea beyond. Then he bade them hoist more sail, all that she could carry, and looked grimly at the two galleys lurking like deerhounds in a pass, that hung on their oars in the strait channel, with the tumbling breakers on either side, through which no ship could sail. "What will you do?" asked

Peter. "Master Peter," he answered between his teeth, "when you fought the Spaniard yesterday I did not ask you what *you* were going to do. Hold your tongue, and leave me to my own trade."

The *Margaret* was a swift ship, but never yet had she moved so swiftly. Behind her shrilled the gale, for now it was no less. Her stout masts bent like fishing poles, her rigging creaked and groaned beneath the weight of the bellying canvas, her port bulwarks slipped along almost level with the water, so that Peter must lie down on the deck, for stand he could not, and watch it running by within three feet of him.

The galleys drew up right across her path. Half a mile away they lay bow by bow, knowing well that no ship could pass the foaming shallows; lay bow by bow, waiting to board and cut down this little English crew when the *Margaret* shortened sail, as shorten sail she must. Smith yelled an order to the mate, and presently, red in the setting sun, out burst the flag of England upon the mainmast top, a sight at which the sailors cheered. He shouted another order, and up ran the last jib, so that now from time to time the port bulwarks dipped beneath the sea, and Peter felt salt water stinging his sore back.

Thus did the *Margaret* shorten sail, and thus did she yield her to the great galleys of Spain.

The captains of the galleys hung on. Was this foreigner mad, or ignorant of the river channel, they wondered, that he would sink with every soul there upon the bar? They hung on, waiting for that leopard flag and those bursting sails to come down; but they never stirred; only straight at them rushed the *Margaret* like a bull. She was not two furlongs away, and she held dead upon her course, till at last those galleys saw *that she would not sink alone.* Like a bull with shut eyes she held dead upon her furious course!

Confusion arose upon the Spanish ships, whistles were blown, men shouted, overseers ran down the planks flogging the slaves, lifted oars shone red in the light of the dying sun as they beat the water wildly. The prows began to back and separate, five feet, ten feet, a dozen feet perhaps; then straight into that tiny streak of open water, like a stone from the hand of the slinger, like an arrow from a bow, rushed the wind-flung *Margaret*.

What happened? Go ask it of the fishers of San Lucar and the pirates of Bonanza, where the tale has been told for generations. The great oars snapped like reeds, the slaves were thrown in crushed and mangled heaps, the tall deck of the port galley was ripped out of her like rent paper by the stout yards of the stooping *Margaret*, the side of the starboard galley rolled up like a shaving before a plane, and the *Margaret* rushed through.

Smith, the captain, looked aft to where, ere they sank, the two great ships, like wounded swans, rolled and fluttered on the foaming bar. Then he put his helm about, called the carpenter, and asked what water she made.

"None, Sir," he answered; "but she will want new tarring. It was oak against eggshells, and we had the speed."

"Good!" said Smith, "shallows on either side; life or death, and I thought I could make room. Send the mate to the helm. I'll have a sleep."

Then the sun vanished beneath the roaring open sea, and, escaped from all the power of Spain, the *Margaret* turned her scarred and splintered bow for Ushant and for England.

ENVOI

Ten years had gone by since Captain Smith took the good ship *Margaret* across the bar of the Guadalquiver in a very notable fashion. It was late May in Essex, and all the woods were green, and all the birds sang, and all the meadows were bright with flowers. Down in the lovely vale of Dedham there was a long, low house with many gables—a charming old house of red brick and timbers already black with age. It stood upon a little hill, backed with woods, and from it a long avenue of ancient oaks ran across the park to the road which led to Colchester and London. Down that avenue on this May afternoon an aged, white-haired man, with quick black eyes, was walking, and with him three children—very beautiful children—a boy of about nine and two little girls, who clung to his hand and garments and pestered him with questions.

"Where are we going, Grandfather?" asked one little girl.

"To see Captain Smith, my dear," he answered.

"I don't like Captain Smith," said the other little girl; "he is so fat, and says nothing."

"I do," broke in the boy, "he gave me a fine knife to use when I am a sailor, and Mother does, and Father, yes, and Grandad too, because he saved him when the cruel Spaniards wanted to put him in the fire. Don't you, Grandad?"

"Yes, my dear," answered the old man. "Look! there is a

squirrel running over the grass; see if you can catch it before it reaches that tree."

Off went the children at full pelt, and the tree being a low one, began to climb it after the squirrel. Meanwhile John Castell, for it was he, turned through the park gate and walked to a little house by the roadside, where a stout man sat upon a bench contemplating nothing in particular. Evidently he expected his visitor, for he pointed to the place beside him, and, as Castell sat down, said:

"Why didn't you come yesterday, Master?"

"Because of my rheumatism, friend," he answered. "I got it first in the vaults of that accursed Holy House at Seville, and it grows on me year by year. They were very damp and cold, those vaults," he added reflectively.

"Many people found them hot enough," grunted Smith, "also, there was generally a good fire at the end of them. Strange thing that we should never have heard any more of that business. I suppose it was because our Margaret was such a favourite with Queen Isabella who didn't want to raise questions with England, or stir up dirty water."

"Perhaps," answered Castell. "The water *was* dirty, wasn't it?"

"Dirty as a Thames mud-bank at low tide. Clever woman, Isabella. No one else would have thought of making a man ridiculous as she did by Morella when she gave his life to Betty, and promised and vowed on his behalf that he would acknowledge her as his lady. No fear of any trouble from him after that, in the way of plots for the Crown, or things of that sort. Why, he must have been the laughing-stock of the whole land—and a laughing-stock never does anything. You remember the Spanish saying, 'King's swords cut and priests' fires burn, but street-songs kill quickest!' I should like to learn more of what has become of them all, though, wouldn't you, Master? Except Bernaldez, of course, for he's been safe in Paris these many years, and doing well there, they say."

"Yes," answered Castell, with a little smile—"that is, unless I had to go to Spain to find out."

Just then the three children came running up, bursting through the gate all together.

"Mind my flower-bed, you little rogues," shouted Captain Smith, shaking his stick at them, whereat they got behind him and made faces.

"Where's the squirrel, Peter?" asked Castell.

"We hunted it out of the tree, Grandad, and right across the grass, and got round it by the edge of the brook, and then—"

"Then what? Did you catch it?"

"No, Grandad, for when we thought we had it sure, it jumped into the water and swam away."

"Other people in a fix have done that before," said Castell, laughing, and bethinking him of a certain river quay.

"It wasn't fair," cried the boy indignantly. "Squirrels shouldn't swim, and if I can catch it I will put it in a cage."

"I think that squirrel will stop in the woods for the rest of its life, Peter."

"Grandad!—Grandad!" called out the youngest child from the gate, whither she had wandered, being weary of the tale of the squirrel, "there are a lot of people coming down the road on horses, such fine people. Come and see."

This news excited the curiosity of the old gentlemen, for not many fine people came to Dedham. At any rate both of them rose, somewhat stiffly, and walked to the gate to look. Yes, the child was right, for there, sure enough, about two hundred yards away, advanced an imposing cavalcade. In front of it, mounted on a fine horse, sat a still finer lady, a very large and handsome lady, dressed in black silks, and wearing a black lace veil that hung from her head. At her side was another lady, much muffled up as though she found the climate cold, and riding between them, on a pony, a gallant looking little boy. After these came servants, male and female, six or eight of them, and last of all a great wain, laden with baggage, drawn by four big Flemish horses.

"Now, whom have we here?" ejaculated Castell, staring at them.

Captain Smith stared too, and sniffed at the wind as he had often done upon his deck on a foggy morning.

"I seem to smell Spaniards," he said, "which is a smell I don't like. Look at their rigging. Now, Master Castell, of whom does that barque with all her sails set remind you?"

Castell shook his head doubtfully.

"I seem to remember," went on Smith, "a great girl decked out like a maypole running across white sand in that Place of Bulls at Seville—but I forgot, you weren't there, were you?"

Now a loud, ringing voice was heard speaking in Spanish, and commanding some one to go to yonder house and inquire where was the gate to the Old Hall. Then Castell knew at once.

"It is Betty," he said. "By the beard of Abraham, it is Betty."

"I think so too; but don't talk of Abraham, Master. He is a dangerous man, Abraham, in these very Christian lands; say, 'By the Keys of St. Peter,' or, 'By St. Paul's infirmities.'"

"Child," broke in Castell, turning to one of the little girls, "run

H. Rider Haggard

up to the Hall and tell your father and mother that Betty has come, and brought half Spain with her. Quickly now, and remember the name, *Betty!*"

The child departed, wondering, by the back way; while Castell and Smith walked towards the strangers.

"Can we assist you, Senora?" asked the former in Spanish.

"Marchioness of Morella, *if* you please—" she began in the same language, then suddenly added in English, "Why, bless my eyes! If it isn't my old master, John Castell, with white wool instead of black!"

"It came white after my shaving by a sainted barber in the Holy House," said Castell. "But come off that tall horse of yours, Betty, my dear—I beg your pardon—most noble and highly born Marchioness of Morella, and give me a kiss."

"That I will, twenty, if you like," she answered, arriving in his arms so suddenly from on high, that had it not been for the sturdy support of Smith behind, they would both of them have rolled upon the ground.

"Whose are those children?" she asked, when she had kissed Castell and shaken Smith by the hand. "But no need to ask, they have got my cousin Margaret's eyes and Peter's long nose. How are they?" she added anxiously.

"You will see for yourself in a minute or two. Come, send on your people and baggage to the Hall, though where they will stow them all I don't know, and walk with us."

Betty hesitated, for she had been calculating upon the effect of a triumphal entry in full state. But at that moment there appeared Margaret and Peter themselves—Margaret, a beautiful matron with a child in her arms, running, and Peter, looking much as he had always been, spare, long of limb, stern but for the kindly eyes, striding away behind, and after him sundry servants and the little girl Margaret.

Then there arose a veritable babel of tongues, punctuated by embracings; but in the end the retinue and the baggage were got off up the drive, followed by the children and the little Spanish-looking boy, with whom they had already made friends, leaving only Betty and her closely muffled-up attendant. This attendant Peter contemplated for a while, as though there were something familiar to him in her general air.

Apparently she observed his interest, for as though by accident she moved some of the wrappings that hid her face, revealing a single soft and lustrous eye and a few square inches of olive-coloured cheek. Then Peter knew her at once.
"How are you, Inez?" he said, stretching out his hand with a smile, for really he was delighted to see her.

"As well as a poor wanderer in a strange and very damp country can be, Don Peter," she answered in her languorous voice, "and certainly somewhat the better for seeing an old friend whom last she met in a certain baker's shop. Do you remember?"

"Remember!" answered Peter. "It is not a thing I am likely to forget. Inez, what became of Fray Henriques? I have heard several different stories."

"One never can be sure," she answered as she uncovered her smiling red lips; "there are so many dungeons in that old Moorish Holy House, and elsewhere, that it is impossible to keep count of their occupants, however good your information. All I know is that he got into trouble over that business, poor man. Suspicions arose about his conduct in the procession which the captain here will recall," and she pointed to Smith. "Also, it is very dangerous for men in such positions to visit Jewish quarters and to write incautious letters—no, not the one you think of; I kept faith—but others, afterwards, begging for it back again, some of which miscarried."

H. Rider Haggard

"Is he dead then?" asked Peter.

"Worse, I think," she answered—"a living death, the 'Punishment of the Wall.'"

"Poor wretch!" said Peter, with a shudder.

"Yes," remarked Inez reflectively, "few doctors like their own medicine."

"I say, Inez," said Peter, nodding his head towards Betty, "that marquis isn't coming here, is he?"

"In the spirit, perhaps, Don Peter, not otherwise."

"So he is really dead? What killed him?"

"Laughter, I think, or, rather, being laughed at. He got quite well of the hurts you gave him, and then, of course, he had to keep the queen's gage, and take the most noble lady yonder, late Betty, as his marchioness. He couldn't do less, after she beat you off him with your own sword and nursed him back to life. But he never heard the last of it. They made songs about him in the streets, and would ask him how his godmother, Isabella, was, because she had promised and vowed on his behalf; also, whether the marchioness had broken any lances for his sake lately, and so forth."

"Poor man!" said Peter again, in tones of the deepest sympathy. "A cruel fate; I should have done better to kill him."

"Much; but don't say so to the noble Betty, who thinks that he had a very happy married life under her protecting care. Really, he ate his heart out till even I, who hated him, was sorry. Think of it! One of the proudest men in Spain, and the most gallant, a nephew of the king, a pillar of the Church, his sovereigns' plenipotentiary to the Moors, and on secret matters—the common mock of the vulgar, yes, and of the great too!"

"The great! Which of them?"

"Nearly all, for the queen set the fashion—I wonder why she hated him so?" Inez added, looking shrewdly at Peter; then without waiting for an answer, went on: "She did it very cleverly, by always making the most of the most honourable Betty in public, calling her near to her, talking with her, admiring her English beauty, and so forth, and what her Majesty did, everybody else did, until my exalted mistress nearly went off her head, so full was she of pride and glory. As for the marquis, he fell ill, and after the taking of Granada went to live there quietly. Betty went with him, for she was a good wife, and saved lots of money. She buried him a year ago, for he died slow, and gave him one of the finest tombs in Spain—it isn't finished yet. That is all the story. Now she has brought her boy, the young marquis, to England for a year or two, for she has a very warm heart, and longed to see you all. Also, she thought she had better go away a while, for her son's sake. As for me, now that Morella is dead, I am head of the household—secretary, general purveyor of intelligence, and anything else you like at a good salary."

"You are not married, I suppose?" asked Peter.

"No," Inez answered; "I saw so much of men when I was younger that I seem to have had enough of them. Or perhaps," she went on, fixing that mild and lustrous eye upon him, "there was one of them whom I liked too well to wish—"

She paused, for they had crossed the drawbridge and arrived opposite to the Old Hall. The gorgeous Betty and the fair Margaret, accompanied by the others, and talking rapidly, had passed through the wide doorway into its spacious vestibule. Inez looked after them, and perceived, standing like a guard at the foot of the open stair, that scarred suit of white armour and riven shield blazoned with the golden falcon, Isabella's gift, in which Peter had fought and conquered the Marquis of Morella. Then she stepped back and contemplated the house critically.

At each end of it rose a stone tower, built for the purposes of defence, and all around ran a deep moat. Within the circle of this moat, and surrounded by poplars and ancient yews, on the south side of the Hall lay a walled pleasaunce, or garden, of turf pierced by paths and planted with flowering hawthorns and other shrubs, and at the end of it, almost hidden in drooping willows, a stone basin of water. Looking at it, Inez saw at once that so far as the circumstances of climate and situation would allow, Peter, in the laying out of this place, had copied another in the far-off, southern city of Granada, even down to the details of the steps and seats. She turned to him and said innocently:

"Sir Peter, are you minded to walk with me in that garden this pleasant evening? I do not see any window in yonder tower."

Peter turned red as the scar across his face, and laughed as he answered:

"There may be one for all that. Get you into the house, dear Inez, for none can be more welcome there; but I walk no more alone with you in gardens."

ABOUT THE AUTHOR

Sir Henry Rider Haggard (June 22, 1856 – May 14, 1925), born in Norfolk, England, was a Victorian writer of adventure novels set in locations considered exotic by readers in his native England.

Haggard had some firsthand experience of these locations, thanks to his extensive travels. He first travelled to Natal Colony in 1875, as secretary to the colonial Governor Bulwer. It was in this role that Haggard was present in Pretoria for the official announcement of the British annexation of the Boer Republic of the Transvaal. In fact, Haggard was forced to read out much of the proclamation following the loss of voice of the official originally entrusted with the duty.

In 1878 he became Registrar of the High Court in the Transvaal, in the region that was to become part of South Africa. He was eventually to return to England to find a wife, bringing Mariana Louisa Margitson back to Africa with him as a bride. Later they had a son named Jock (who died of measles at the age of 10) and three daughters.

Returning again to England in 1882, the couple settled in Ditchingham, Norfolk. Later he lived in Kessingland and had connections with the church in Bungay, Suffolk. He turned to the study of law and was called to the bar in 1884. His practice of law was somewhat desultory, and much of his time was taken up by the writing of novels.

While his novels contain many of the strong preconceptions common to the culture of British colonialism, they are unusual for the degree of sympathy with which he often treats the native populations. Africans often serve heroic roles in his novels, though the protagonists are typically, though not invariably, European. A notable example is Ignosi, the rightful king of Kukuanaland in King Solomon's Mines. Having developed an intense mutual friendship with the three Englishmen who help him reclaim his throne, he wisely accepts their advice to abolish witch hunts and arbitrary capital punishment.

Choose from Thousands of 1stWorldLibrary Classics By

A. M. Barnard
Ada Leverson
Adolphus William Ward
Aesop
Agatha Christie
Alexander Aaronsohn
Alexander Kielland
Alexandre Dumas
Alfred Gatty
Alfred Ollivant
Alice Duer Miller
Alice Turner Curtis
Alice Dunbar
Allen Chapman
Alleyne Ireland
Ambrose Bierce
Amelia E. Barr
Amory H. Bradford
Andrew Lang
Andrew McFarland Davis
Andy Adams
Angela Brazil
Anna Alice Chapin
Anna Sewell
Annie Besant
Annie Hamilton Donnell
Annie Payson Call
Annie Roe Carr
Annonaymous
Anton Chekhov
Archibald Lee Fletcher
Arnold Bennett
Arthur C. Benson
Arthur Conan Doyle
Arthur M. Winfield
Arthur Ransome
Arthur Schnitzler
Arthur Train
Atticus
B.H. Baden-Powell
B. M. Bower
B. C. Chatterjee
Baroness Emmuska Orczy
Baroness Orczy
Basil King
Bayard Taylor
Ben Macomber
Bertha Muzzy Bower
Bjornstjerne Bjornson

Booth Tarkington
Boyd Cable
Bram Stoker
C. Collodi
C. E. Orr
C. M. Ingleby
Carolyn Wells
Catherine Parr Traill
Charles A. Eastman
Charles Amory Beach
Charles Dickens
Charles Dudley Warner
Charles Farrar Browne
Charles Ives
Charles Kingsley
Charles Klein
Charles Hanson Towne
Charles Lathrop Pack
Charles Romyn Dake
Charles Whibley
Charles Willing Beale
Charlotte M. Braeme
Charlotte M. Yonge
Charlotte Perkins Stetson
Clair W. Hayes
Clarence Day Jr.
Clarence E. Mulford
Clemence Housman
Confucius
Coningsby Dawson
Cornelis DeWitt Wilcox
Cyril Burleigh
D. H. Lawrence
Daniel Defoe
David Garnett
Dinah Craik
Don Carlos Janes
Donald Keyhoe
Dorothy Kilner
Dougan Clark
Douglas Fairbanks
E. Nesbit
E. P. Roe
E. Phillips Oppenheim
E. S. Brooks
Earl Barnes
Edgar Rice Burroughs
Edith Van Dyne
Edith Wharton

Edward Everett Hale
Edward J. O'Biren
Edward S. Ellis
Edwin L. Arnold
Eleanor Atkins
Eleanor Hallowell Abbott
Eliot Gregory
Elizabeth Gaskell
Elizabeth McCracken
Elizabeth Von Arnim
Ellem Key
Emerson Hough
Emilie F. Carlen
Emily Bronte
Emily Dickinson
Enid Bagnold
Enilor Macartney Lane
Erasmus W. Jones
Ernie Howard Pie
Ethel May Dell
Ethel Turner
Ethel Watts Mumford
Eugene Sue
Eugenie Foa
Eugene Wood
Eustace Hale Ball
Evelyn Everett-green
Everard Cotes
F. H. Cheley
F. J. Cross
F. Marion Crawford
Fannie E. Newberry
Federick Austin Ogg
Ferdinand Ossendowski
Fergus Hume
Florence A. Kilpatrick
Fremont B. Deering
Francis Bacon
Francis Darwin
Frances Hodgson Burnett
Frances Parkinson Keyes
Frank Gee Patchin
Frank Harris
Frank Jewett Mather
Frank L. Packard
Frank V. Webster
Frederic Stewart Isham
Frederick Trevor Hill
Frederick Winslow Taylor

Friedrich Kerst
Friedrich Nietzsche
Fyodor Dostoyevsky
G.A. Henty
G.K. Chesterton
Gabrielle E. Jackson
Garrett P. Serviss
Gaston Leroux
George A. Warren
George Ade
Geroge Bernard Shaw
George Cary Eggleston
George Durston
George Ebers
George Eliot
George Gissing
George MacDonald
George Meredith
George Orwell
George Sylvester Viereck
George Tucker
George W. Cable
George Wharton James
Gertrude Atherton
Gordon Casserly
Grace E. King
Grace Gallatin
Grace Greenwood
Grant Allen
Guillermo A. Sherwell
Gulielma Zollinger
Gustav Flaubert
H. A. Cody
H. B. Irving
H.C. Bailey
H. G. Wells
H. H. Munro
H. Irving Hancock
H. R. Naylor
H. Rider Haggard
H. W. C. Davis
Haldeman Julius
Hall Caine
Hamilton Wright Mabie
Hans Christian Andersen
Harold Avery
Harold McGrath
Harriet Beecher Stowe
Harry Castlemon
Harry Coghill
Harry Houidini

Hayden Carruth
Helent Hunt Jackson
Helen Nicolay
Hendrik Conscience
Hendy David Thoreau
Henri Barbusse
Henrik Ibsen
Henry Adams
Henry Ford
Henry Frost
Henry James
Henry Jones Ford
Henry Seton Merriman
Henry W Longfellow
Herbert A. Giles
Herbert Carter
Herbert N. Casson
Herman Hesse
Hildegard G. Frey
Homer
Honore De Balzac
Horace B. Day
Horace Walpole
Horatio Alger Jr.
Howard Pyle
Howard R. Garis
Hugh Lofting
Hugh Walpole
Humphry Ward
Ian Maclaren
Inez Haynes Gillmore
Irving Bacheller
Isabel Cecilia Williams
Isabel Hornibrook
Israel Abrahams
Ivan Turgenev
J.G.Austin
J. Henri Fabre
J. M. Barrie
J. M. Walsh
J. Macdonald Oxley
J. R. Miller
J. S. Fletcher
J. S. Knowles
J. Storer Clouston
J. W. Duffield
Jack London
Jacob Abbott
James Allen
James Andrews
James Baldwin

James Branch Cabell
James DeMille
James Joyce
James Lane Allen
James Lane Allen
James Oliver Curwood
James Oppenheim
James Otis
James R. Driscoll
Jane Abbott
Jane Austen
Jane L. Stewart
Janet Aldridge
Jens Peter Jacobsen
Jerome K. Jerome
Jessie Graham Flower
John Buchan
John Burroughs
John Cournos
John F. Kennedy
John Gay
John Glasworthy
John Habberton
John Joy Bell
John Kendrick Bangs
John Milton
John Philip Sousa
John Taintor Foote
Jonas Lauritz Idemil Lie
Jonathan Swift
Joseph A. Altsheler
Joseph Carey
Joseph Conrad
Joseph E. Badger Jr
Joseph Hergesheimer
Joseph Jacobs
Jules Vernes
Julian Hawthrone
Julie A Lippmann
Justin Huntly McCarthy
Kakuzo Okakura
Karle Wilson Baker
Kate Chopin
Kenneth Grahame
Kenneth McGaffey
Kate Langley Bosher
Kate Langley Bosher
Katherine Cecil Thurston
Katherine Stokes
L. A. Abbot
L. T. Meade

L. Frank Baum
Latta Griswold
Laura Dent Crane
Laura Lee Hope
Laurence Housman
Lawrence Beasley
Leo Tolstoy
Leonid Andreyev
Lewis Carroll
Lewis Sperry Chafer
Lilian Bell
Lloyd Osbourne
Louis Hughes
Louis Joseph Vance
Louis Tracy
Louisa May Alcott
Lucy Fitch Perkins
Lucy Maud Montgomery
Luther Benson
Lydia Miller Middleton
Lyndon Orr
M. Corvus
M. H. Adams
Margaret E. Sangster
Margret Howth
Margaret Vandercook
Margaret W. Hungerford
Margret Penrose
Maria Edgeworth
Maria Thompson Daviess
Mariano Azuela
Marion Polk Angellotti
Mark Overton
Mark Twain
Mary Austin
Mary Catherine Crowley
Mary Cole
Mary Hastings Bradley
Mary Roberts Rinehart
Mary Rowlandson
M. Wollstonecraft Shelley
Maud Lindsay
Max Beerbohm
Myra Kelly
Nathaniel Hawthrone
Nicolo Machiavelli
O. F. Walton
Oscar Wilde

Owen Johnson
P.G. Wodehouse
Paul and Mabel Thorne
Paul G. Tomlinson
Paul Severing
Percy Brebner
Percy Keese Fitzhugh
Peter B. Kyne
Plato
Quincy Allen
R. Derby Holmes
R. L. Stevenson
R. S. Ball
Rabindranath Tagore
Rahul Alvares
Ralph Bonehill
Ralph Henry Barbour
Ralph Victor
Ralph Waldo Emmerson
Rene Descartes
Ray Cummings
Rex Beach
Rex E. Beach
Richard Harding Davis
Richard Jefferies
Richard Le Gallienne
Robert Barr
Robert Frost
Robert Gordon Anderson
Robert L. Drake
Robert Lansing
Robert Lynd
Robert Michael Ballantyne
Robert W. Chambers
Rosa Nouchette Carey
Rudyard Kipling
Saint Augustine
Samuel B. Allison
Samuel Hopkins Adams
Sarah Bernhardt
Sarah C. Hallowell
Selma Lagerlof
Sherwood Anderson
Sigmund Freud
Standish O'Grady
Stanley Weyman
Stella Benson
Stella M. Francis

Stephen Crane
Stewart Edward White
Stijn Streuvels
Swami Abhedananda
Swami Parmananda
T. S. Ackland
T. S. Arthur
The Princess Der Ling
Thomas A. Janvier
Thomas A Kempis
Thomas Anderton
Thomas Bailey Aldrich
Thomas Bulfinch
Thomas De Quincey
Thomas Dixon
Thomas H. Huxley
Thomas Hardy
Thomas More
Thornton W. Burgess
U. S. Grant
Upton Sinclair
Valentine Williams
Various Authors
Vaughan Kester
Victor Appleton
Victor G. Durham
Victoria Cross
Virginia Woolf
Wadsworth Camp
Walter Camp
Walter Scott
Washington Irving
Wilbur Lawton
Wilkie Collins
Willa Cather
Willard F. Baker
William Dean Howells
William le Queux
W. Makepeace Thackeray
William W. Walter
William Shakespeare
Winston Churchill
Yei Theodora Ozaki
Yogi Ramacharaka
Young E. Allison
Zane Grey